SEICHŌ MATSUMOTO

Inspector Imanishi Investigates

Translated by Beth Cary

PENGUIN BOOKS

PENGUIN CLASSICS

UK | USA | Canada | Ireland | Australia
India | New Zealand | South Africa

Penguin Classics is part of the Penguin Random House group of companies
whose addresses can be found at global.penguinrandomhouse.com.

Penguin Random House UK
One Embassy Gardens, 8 Viaduct Gardens, London SW11 7BW

penguin.co.uk

Penguin
Random House
UK

First published in Tokyo under the Japanese title *Vessel of Sand (Suna no Utsuwa)*
Published in the United States of America by Soho Press
First published in Penguin Classics 2024
This edition published in Penguin Classics 2025
001

Translator's note: Names in the text are in Japanese order with family name first

Set in 11.25/14pt Dante MT Std
Typeset by Jouve (UK), Milton Keynes
Printed and bound in Great Britain by Clays Ltd, Elcograf S.p.A.

The authorized representative in the EEA is Penguin Random House Ireland,
Morrison Chambers, 32 Nassau Street, Dublin D02 YH68

A CIP catalogue record for this book is available from the British Library

ISBN: 978-0-241-72443-9

PENGUIN MODERN CLASSICS

Inspector Imanishi Investigates

Seichō Matsumoto was born in 1909 in Fukuoka, Japan. Self-educated, Matsumoto published his first book when he was forty years old and he quickly established himself as a master of crime fiction. His exploration of human psychology and Japanese post-war malaise, coupled with the creation of twisting, dark mysteries, made him one of the most acclaimed and best-selling writers in Japan. He received the prestigious Akutagawa Literary Prize in 1950 and the Kikuchi Kan Prize in 1970. He died in 1992.

Inspector Imanishi Investigates

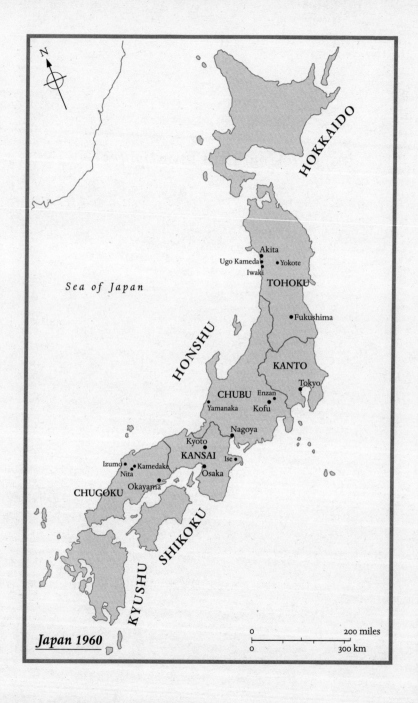

N

HOKKAIDO

Sea of Japan

Akita
Ugo Kameda • • Yokote
Iwaki
TOHOKU

HONSHU

Fukushima

KANTO

CHUBU
Enzan
Yamanaka • Kofu

Tokyo

Nagoya
Kyoto
KANSAI
Izumo • Ise •
Nita • Kamedake
Okayama
CHUGOKU
Osaka

SHIKOKU

KYUSHU

Japan 1960

| 0 | | 200 miles |
| 0 | | 300 km |

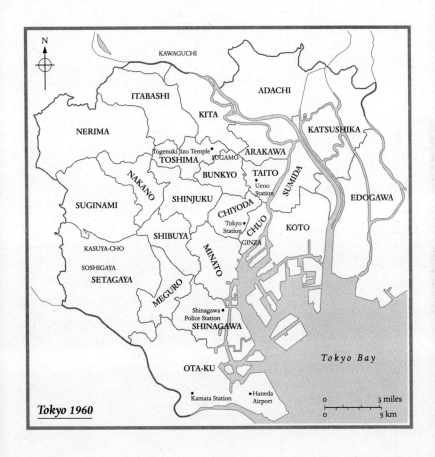

N

KAWAGUCHI

ITABASHI

KITA

ADACHI

NERIMA

KATSUSHIKA

Togenuki Jizo Temple
SUGAMO
TOSHIMA

ARAKAWA

BUNKYO

TAITO

SUMIDA

NAKANO

SHINJUKU

Ueno
Station

SUGINAMI

CHIYODA

EDOGAWA

Tokyo
Station

SHIBUYA

CHUO

KOTO

GINZA

KASUYA-CHO

MINATO

SOSHIGAYA

SETAGAYA

MEGURO

Shinagawa
Police Station
SHINAGAWA

OTA-KU

Tokyo Bay

Kamata Station

Haneda
Airport

0   3 miles

0   5 km

Tokyo 1960

1. Kamata Railroad Yard

The first train on the Keihin-Tohoku Line was scheduled to leave Kamata Station at 4:08 A.M. The engineer, the brakeman, and the conductor left the night duty room shortly after 3:00 A.M. to go to the rail yard. It was dark and cold.

When the young brakeman shone his flashlight under the seventh car, he stiffened, stood still swallowing for a moment, and then began to run, his arms flailing. He flung himself into the engineer's cab, shouting, 'Hey, there's a *tuna.*'

'A dead body?' the engineer laughed. 'We haven't even moved the train yet. How could there be a tuna? Rub your eyes and wake up.'

'No, I'm not mistaken.' The brakeman looked pale. 'I really saw a tuna under the train.'

The engineer and the conductor decided to go see for themselves. When the brakeman shone his flashlight under the seventh car, they saw a human form lying on the rails just in front of the wheels. It glistened in the beam of light. The engineer bent over to look closer. 'Ugh, it's horrible!' he screamed.

The three men stood for a while staring at the body. Then the conductor said, 'Call the police immediately. We don't have much time.' It was only twenty minutes before the 4:08 departure time. The engineer ran back to the office.

'This is an unpleasant business, first thing in the morning,' the conductor said to the brakeman. 'I wonder what happened. The wheels haven't moved at all, but his face is covered with blood.'

The corpse's face looked like a red devil's mask. The head lay pillowed on one rail, the thighs across the other. If the train had started, the face would have been crushed and the hip joint severed by the wheels.

The sky became lighter. By the time the police investigators arrived, the lamps in the railroad yard had been turned off. Chief Inspector Kurozaki Hajime of the Homicide Division was accompanied by eight members of the Homicide and Criminal Investigation divisions.

The rail car involved was left on the tracks, while the others were detached and towed out of the yard. Criminal investigators scurried around this car. They took photographs, sketched diagrams, and drew in red lines on a borrowed map of the railroad yard. When the scene had been recorded, the body was dragged out from under the car. It was that of a man whose face had been battered to an unrecognizable pulp. The eyeballs had nearly popped out, the nose was smashed, and the mouth was split open. The gray hair was matted with blood.

The autopsy revealed the following:

Age: About 54 or 55; slim build.

Cause of death: Strangulation. Numerous bruises and fractures on almost the entire face; on the arms and legs injuries and fractures accompanied by abrasions and welts.

Contents of the stomach: Light yellowish brown, slightly thick liquid (including alcoholic content) mixed with partially digested peanuts. Chemical analysis indicates the presence of a sleeping powder.

Conclusion: From the above evidence, it is presumed that the victim drank some sleeping medicine dissolved in whiskey, and then was strangled; afterward, he was beaten with great force by a blunt-edged instrument (such as a rock or a hammer).

Time elapsed since death: Three to four hours.

The victim had been wearing a cheap suit, shirt, and under-wear, none of which had laundry markings. He seemed to have been a poor laborer, but the police found nothing to indicate his identity. It was assumed that he had been murdered between midnight and one o'clock in the morning.

The murderer had viciously battered the victim's face after death, indicating that the criminal was someone who hated the victim a great deal, or that the murderer had intended to destroy the face totally in order to prevent identification of the body. The investigation team concluded the crime had not been motivated by robbery but was a murder committed by an acquaintance of the victim acting out of hatred, perhaps a crime of passion.

The first step was to identify the victim. Investigators started their questioning in the area around Kamata Station.

The previous night, two people, who might have been the victim and his companion, had been seen at a Torys bar (one of a chain of cheap bars) located near the station. The employees of the bar and the customers who had been there were called in for questioning. According to the bartender and hostesses, the two men had never been in before. They had entered the bar at about 11:30 P.M. The time was fixed by a woman customer, an office clerk, who had been concerned about missing the last Mekama Line train. Memories were vague about the faces of the two customers. Everyone agreed that one definitely had hair that was quite gray. As to the other, some of the witnesses said he was thirty, others that he was about forty years old, and still others that he seemed much younger.

After statements had been taken from the bar staff, bar cus-tomers, and a pair of guitar players who passed by the two men outside the bar, the only fact they all had agreed on was that the victim's accent was of the Tohoku region in northeastern Japan, a dialect with thick *zu-zu* sounds. The younger man seemed to be speaking in standard Japanese.

3

None of the witnesses questioned knew what the subject of the men's conversation had been. They had sat in a booth near the door leading to the rest room. The staff and customers, going back and forth, had overheard only fragments, a few words, a phrase. But Sumiko, a bar hostess, recalled that the younger man had said to the victim, 'Kameda must be the same even now.' A second bar hostess had also overheard the word 'Kameda.'

What had been meant by 'Kameda'? The investigation team concluded that the victim and his assailant were old acquaintances who hadn't seen each other for a long time, that they had accidentally run into each other, and then stopped off at a nearby bar. In their conversation, the topic of their mutual friend, Kameda, had come up. It could be inferred that the gray-haired man had either recently seen or had kept up his friendship with Kameda, while the younger man had not seen Kameda for a while.

Other bits of the conversation included phrases such as 'nostalgic,' 'since that time things haven't gone as I had hoped,' and 'I've finally gotten used to this kind of life.' These were spoken mainly by the victim, the man with the heavy accent. Hardly any of the younger man's words had been heard because he spoke in a low, muffled voice and, whenever someone walked by to go to the rest room, averted his face. The only words attributed to this man were 'Kameda must be the same even now.'

The young man who had appeared in the Torys bar with the victim was considered to be the prime suspect. It was decided that inquiries would be made for him and the victim at cheap apartments and inns in the Ota-ku area of Tokyo, where the Torys bar and Kamata Station were situated.

The evening papers carried large articles on the crime. If the victim had a family, relatives would surely contact the police. But two days later no missing persons report had been filed, and the investigation team that had searched Ota-ku had found no leads.

A meeting of the investigation team was called. Someone suggested, 'Just because he was drinking in a bar near Kamata Station doesn't necessarily mean that he lived in the area. Kamata Station is the junction of the National Railway Line, the Mekama Line, and the Ikegami Line. The victim could have lived near the Mekama or Ikegami lines.' That would expand the area of investigation but general opinion favored this hypothesis.

'The statements of the witnesses confirm that the victim spoke in a Tohoku dialect, but what about the accent of the assailant?' the chief asked. 'The man with the victim, the one we are assuming is the murderer, is the person who asked the victim about Kameda. Though he spoke in standard Japanese, the bar hostess said there might have been a slight northeastern tone to his words. From the content of their conversation, it would seem likely that they knew each other from their hometown in the northeast, rather than having met in Tokyo.'

The investigation team reached a consensus on these two points and agreed to proceed on these assumptions.

One week passed and the identity of the victim was still unknown.

The name Kameda was no doubt quite common in the northeast. Finding every person with this name would be tedious, but it was decided to undertake the search. Headquarters asked the Northeastern District of the National Police Agency to locate every person named Kameda within the jurisdictions of the prefectures of Aomori, Akita, Iwate, Yamagata, Miyagi, and Fukushima.

Residents along the Mekama and Ikegami lines were questioned. Since the victim appeared to be a day laborer, investigators reviewed all records of the daily job placement officers in the vicinity. The inexpensive apartments and inns that might have housed the victim were also checked thoroughly. No one fitting the victim's description turned up. From the violent nature of the murder, headquarters had suspected that the murderer would have been splattered with quite a lot of blood. Every taxi company in Tokyo was notified to see if someone fitting such a description had been picked up as a passenger, without result. The murderer might have hidden somewhere, washed his clothes, and then escaped on an early-morning train. Inquiries made of the train conductors were fruitless. The area surrounding the scene of the crime was combed. There were many vacant lots full of weeds, in which, it was thought, the murderer might have hidden. But no objects related to the murder were found.

Responses to headquarters' request to the Northeast District bureau of the National Police Agency for lists of persons named Kameda started trickling in:

'Kameda Shuichi, Kameda Umekichi, Kameda Katsuzo, Kameda Kameo . . .' Kamedas living in villages all over the six prefectures were listed. There were thirty-two men named Kameda living in northeastern Japan. Headquarters requested that local police forces check out each of these men. Five days later the last responses were received. All thirty-two Kamedas said that none of their family, relatives, friends, or acquaintances was the victim.

'I don't have any idea what to do now,' said the perplexed chief of investigations. 'The problem may be that we have limited the search to the northeast Tohoku region. The mutual friend named Kameda may not be from that region. He could live in Tokyo or in western Japan.'

The team decided to ask the newspapers to stress the name Kameda in articles and to refer replies to the police. But there were none.

The movements of the victim and the murderer before their arrival at the Torys bar were still under investigation. Day after day weary detectives trudged from place to place making inquiries, and came back to headquarters tired out. When detectives were close to capturing a criminal, their expressions were bright no matter how fatigued they were. But when there was no clue, they just looked exhausted.

Imanishi Eitaro was one of these worn-out policemen. The forty-five-year-old detective was hesitant even to return to head-quarters for a cup of tea. He was in charge of making inquiries at the cheap apartments and inns along the Ikegami Line. For the last ten days he had walked that area. Again, today, he returned to headquarters without any leads.

At the daily meeting the investigation team reviewed information brought back by the detectives, but there were no developments. The mood in the meeting room was one of intense frustration, of futility.

It was nearly midnight before Imanishi reached his home that night. Through the slats of the front door he could see that the lights had been turned off. The door was locked from the inside because he hadn't been expected. He rang the buzzer. The light went on inside, and his wife's shadow was cast across the glass door.

'Who is it?' his wife asked.

'It's me.'

The door slid open and Yoshiko appeared in the shadows.

'Welcome home,' she said.

Imanishi entered and slipped off his shoes. Over the past few days, his heels had become worn and scuffed, so his shoes tilted awkwardly on the stone stand. From the two-tatami-mat entry, he entered directly into the four-and-a-half-tatami-mat room. There were three futon mattresses laid out on the tatami. The face of his sleeping son peeked out of one. Imanishi knelt down and tapped his son's cheek.

'Don't wake him up,' his wife scolded gently, standing behind him.

'I haven't seen my son awake for ten days.'

'Will you be late again tomorrow, too?' Yoshiko asked.

'I don't know yet.'

Imanishi walked into the next room and sat down.

'I guess you'd like something to eat?' Yoshiko asked.

'Just some tea over rice would be fine,' Imanishi answered.

'I'll warm up some sake.' Yoshiko smiled and stepped down into the kitchen.

Imanishi rolled over on his stomach and unfolded the newspaper. He closed his eyes. He could hear sounds in the kitchen, then he dozed off for a while.

'It's ready.' Yoshiko shook him to wake him.

When he looked up, the table was set with a warmed carafe of sake. His wife had covered him with a blanket while he was asleep. He threw it off and sat up.

'You must be very tired,' Yoshiko said as she lifted the sake to pour it.

'I'm exhausted.' Imanishi rubbed his eyes.

He drained the cup and picked at the salted fish set out for him. 'It tastes good. Why don't you have some, too?' He handed his sake cup to his wife.

She drank just enough to make him feel comfortable and returned the cup to him.

'It still isn't solved?' she asked.

'Not yet.' Imanishi shook his head as he drank another cup of sake.

Since he had been assigned to the Kamata case, he had come home late every night. Yoshiko was more concerned about her husband's accumulated fatigue than about the solution to the case. She looked up at him and said, 'The newspapers say that you're searching for a person named Kameda. You still haven't come up with anyone?'

Yoshiko almost never asked him about the cases he worked on. He made it a point to try not to talk about work at home.

'Mmm,' Imanishi responded noncommittally.

'I wonder why nothing comes up when there is so much written about the case in the newspapers?'

Imanishi did not respond to this either. He had no desire to talk over his work with his family. Yoshiko had once pressed him about a case he was working on. Imanishi had scolded her, saying she shouldn't pry into cases under investigation. Since then, she had been more reserved. But her curiosity about this case made her forget. Yoshiko asked, 'Are there many people named Kameda?'

'I guess it's not that common a name.' Imanishi felt that he couldn't scold his wife tonight, but he continued to give vague answers.

'I went to the fish store to run an errand today and checked their telephone book. There were a hundred and two Kamedas listed in the Tokyo telephone book,' she said. 'A hundred and two isn't that large a number, but it's not that small either.'

'I wonder,' Imanishi mumbled, as he reached for the second carafe of sake.

He was tired of hearing the name Kameda. No one could appreciate the effort headquarters was making to find this man. Tonight, he wanted to forget about the case and go to sleep.

'I wonder if I've gotten a bit drunk.' His body felt warm.

'You're so tired that the alcohol has hit you very quickly.'

'Maybe I should eat after this one.'

'There isn't much to eat. I didn't know whether you'd even be home tonight.'

'That's all right.'

Yoshiko went to the kitchen again.

Imanishi felt a little light-headed. 'Kameda, eh?' he said, without realizing that he was saying the name aloud. It was on his mind after all. He didn't think he was really drunk, yet he repeated the name several times.

*

The next morning Imanishi slept late. It was almost nine o'clock when he got up. His son had already left for school.

Imanishi washed his face and sat at the dining table. He had slept soundly for a change and felt rested.

'What time do you have to be at work today?' Yoshiko asked as she scooped some rice into his bowl.

'I have to show up by eleven.'

'So you can take your time.'

The morning sun shone on their small garden. The sunshine had become quite strong. Droplets of water glistened on the leaves of the miniature bonsai plants. Yoshiko must have watered them.

'Will you be early tonight?'

'I'm not sure when I'll be home.'

'I hope you'll be able to come home early. Too many late nights in a row can't be good for your health.'

'But that can't be helped in my line of work. Until the case is solved I can't tell whether I'll be early or late.'

'And when this case is solved, there'll be the next one. There's never an end to them.' Yoshiko seemed mildly displeased. But this was just her way of showing that she cared for her husband.

Imanishi pretended not to hear and ate his breakfast of rice and miso soup, pouring the soup over the rice. Having been raised in the countryside, he had never abandoned this custom. His wife criticized his bad manners, but to Imanishi this was the way it tasted best.

His stomach full, Imanishi lay back on the tatami. Perhaps his sleepiness still lingered, for when he lay down, he felt drowsy.

'Why don't you rest a bit before you leave?' Yoshiko brought him a pillow and covered him with a light blanket.

He couldn't fall asleep right away. A women's magazine happened to be lying near the pillow. To take his mind off the case, he opened up the thick glossy magazine. He intended to skim it at random, but another smaller volume fell out of it. It was a supplement, a folded color map entitled 'A Guide to Japan's Famous Hot Spring Areas.' Imanishi lay down and held the map above his head, his attention drawn to the northeastern region of Japan. He was still mulling over the name Kameda. The map highlighted such famous resort areas as Matsushima, Hanamaki Hot Springs, Lake Tazawa, and Lake Towada. The names of the stations were crowded in along the train lines. Reading the unfamiliar station names seemed to conjure up images of the scenery of that area. On the left there was Hachirogata, beyond that, the Oga Peninsula. Noshiro, Koigawa, Oiwake, Akita, Shimohama – these place names drifted before his eyes. Then he saw the name Ugo Kameda.

He jumped up and started getting ready for work.

'What happened?' Yoshiko hurried into the room from the kitchen and contemplated her husband hastily changing into his work clothes. 'Can't you sleep?'

'This is no time to be sleeping,' Imanishi said. 'Hurry up and shine my shoes, will you?'

'But you don't have to be there until eleven. It's still early,' said Yoshiko, looking at the wall clock.

'Never mind, just hurry. I have to leave right away,' he said loudly. He could feel his own excitement mounting.

Imanishi walked quickly along the street. He waited for the bus impatiently.

Investigation headquarters had been set up in a room in the Shinagawa precinct office. It was shortly after ten when Imanishi reached it.

'Hey, you're here early,' a colleague said, patting him on the back.

'Is the chief in?'

'Yeah, he just came in.'

Imanishi entered the room with the sign 'Kamata Railroad Yard Murder Case Investigation Headquarters' on the door. Behind a desk in the center of the room sat Police Inspector Kurozaki. Imanishi went directly to him.

'Good morning, sir,' Imanishi said.

'Morning.' Kurozaki nodded.

'Chief, it's about the Kameda matter,' Imanishi started off.

Kurozaki's hair was slightly frizzy, his eyes were narrow, and he had a double chin. He was a big man with a thick neck that was tucked into his shoulders. He looked up quickly and asked, 'Have you found out anything?'

'I don't know if this is right, but about the name Kameda,' Imanishi began. 'Could it be that it isn't a person's name but a place name?'

'Is there such a place in the Tohoku region?'

'Yes, there is. Actually, I found it on a map this morning.'

'I didn't think of that. That's . . . of course . . . so that's it,' Kurozaki answered, thinking it over. 'Where is this Kameda?' he asked.

'It's in Akita Prefecture.'

The chief yelled, 'Hey, someone bring me a prefectural map.'

A young detective rushed out of the room to borrow a map.

'Boy, am I glad you noticed this,' the chief said.

The detective returned with a folded map flapping in his hand. The chief opened it up at once. 'Imanishi, where is it?'

Imanishi went around the desk to stand beside the chief and peer at the small print. The map that Imanishi had seen that morning had been an inexact drawing. After a moment Imanishi found Akita City. Then, pointing with his little finger, he traced the Uetsu Line.

'Let's see.' The chief peered at the spot. 'I see, Ugo Kameda. It's there.' Just next to Ugo Kameda was a town called Iwaki.

Chief Kurozaki gathered all the detectives together and

announced Imanishi's discovery. The majority opinion was now in favor of Kameda as a place name rather than a person's name. All eyes in the room drifted toward Imanishi.

'We'll send the victim's photo to the area and have the local police inquire as to whether anyone in that area knows the victim,' the chief said.

The response came four days later. Chief Kurozaki took the call.

'This is the investigation chief at the Iwaki station in Akita Prefecture,' the caller began.

'This is Chief Inspector Kurozaki. Thank you very much for all the trouble you went to.'

'About your inquiry . . .'

'Yes?' Kurozaki, grasping the telephone receiver, became tense. 'Were you able to find anything?'

'We made inquiries in the Kameda area, but unfortunately were unable to come up with anyone fitting your description.'

'Is that right?' Kurozaki said in disappointment.

'We took the photograph you sent us and asked various people, but the residents of the Kameda area say they don't know him.'

'What is Kameda like?' Kurozaki asked.

'The population of the Kameda area is at most three to four thousand. It is now part of Iwaki town. There is very little farmland, and most of the industry in this area centers on the production of dried noodles and weaving. The population seems to be declining year by year. If the man in the picture was from Kameda, people would have known immediately, but they all said they had never seen him.'

'Is that so?' But the next words gave hope to the discouraged Kurozaki.

'Though no one fits the description, something strange did happen here.'

'Yes, what do you mean when you say "something strange"?'

'Two days before we received your inquiry, that is, just a week ago, a stranger was seen wandering around the Kameda area. This man also stayed in the one inn in Kameda. Since it's an area where it is unusual to see strangers, he attracted some attention, and one of our men heard about it.'

'What kind of man was he?' the chief asked.

'He was thirty-two or -three years old. At first impression he seemed to be a factory worker. We couldn't figure out why he had come to Kameda. I wanted to inform you in case it might be of interest.'

'Did anything happen while this man was there?'

'No, nothing happened. He didn't cause any trouble. But, as I told you, since he was a total stranger who appeared in the area, I thought it might have some bearing on your inquiry, so I just wanted to mention it.'

'Thank you very much. Was there anything that the man did to attract the attention of the villagers?'

'It's a very small matter, but we can't deny that something like that did occur,' the chief inspector of the Iwaki station continued. 'This may be perfectly normal, but in a country area without any excitement, this man's behavior did attract the attention of the villagers. It's hard to explain in detail over the telephone . . .'

It seemed that the chief inspector was suggesting that someone be sent to that area to continue the investigation.

'Thank you so much. We may be sending someone from here to investigate. If we do, please cooperate with him.'

'Yes, certainly.'

That was the end of the telephone conversation. Chief Kurozaki lit a cigarette and stared at the ceiling as he exhaled. Then he put his elbows on his desk and thought for a while.

An investigation meeting was called.

'Is everyone here?' the chief asked the men assembled in the room. 'Contrary to our initial expectation, this case is causing us enormous trouble. At this point, we have no knowledge of the movements of the victim. The man he was talking to at the Torys bar is the prime suspect, but we have nothing on him either. The only hope we have is the name Kameda.' The chief wearily drank some tea. Taking a breath, he continued, 'According to the phone report I just received from Iwaki station, there was a man wandering around the Kameda area about two days before our inquiry reached them, meaning a week ago. We couldn't get details over the telephone, but I think this Kameda is a very important lead at this point. The telephone call indicated that it would be beneficial if we sent one of our men to that area. What do you think?'

All of those in attendance agreed. The investigation was currently at a standstill. They were willing to grasp at straws. It was decided that someone should be sent to Kameda.

'Imanishi,' the chief said, 'you were the one who found the place name. It'll mean more work, but will you go?'

The meeting room tables were arranged in a U shape. From about the center of one side, Imanishi nodded his head.

'Good. And I'd like someone else to go along. Yoshimura?' the chief said, looking in the other direction.

At the back, a young man stood up.

'I'll do as you ask,' replied the young detective, Yoshimura Hiroshi.

2. Kamata

Imanishi Eitaro returned home at about six o'clock that evening.

'You're home awfully early,' his wife greeted him with surprise.

'I'm not early. I have to go on a business trip. I'm leaving tonight, right away.'

Imanishi flipped off his shoes and walked into the sitting room.

'Where are you going?'

'To the northeast, near Akita,' was all he said. Yoshiko was close-mouthed, but there was no guarantee that she might not let something slip out about her husband's whereabouts. Imanishi was very cautious.

'What time is your train?'

'It leaves Ueno Station at nine P.M.'

'Does this mean that you've discovered who the murderer is?' she asked.

'Nothing like that. We haven't even found a suspect.'

'Then is it a stakeout?'

'No, it's not.' Imanishi became slightly irritated.

'I'm glad, then,' Yoshiko said.

'What are you glad about?'

'I'd be worried if you were going on a stakeout or if you were picking up a suspect. If it's just an investigation, it's not dangerous, so I feel relieved,' she answered.

Actually, Imanishi himself felt at ease about this trip. All he had to do was to go to the Kameda area and make some inquiries. But if he didn't come up with results, he would lose face at investigation headquarters.

'Who will be going with you?'

Detectives never traveled alone. They were always paired up with a partner.

'I'll be going with Yoshimura,' Imanishi answered.

'Oh, Yoshimura-*san*, the young man who came by last year at New Year's. Will he be coming here?'

'No. We're getting on the train separately.'

Imanishi reached Ueno Station at 8:40 P.M. The limited express train bound for Akita was already at the platform. Imanishi took a stealthy glance around. He didn't see anyone who looked like a newspaper reporter. He continued to be cautious, going to the kiosk on the platform to buy a pack of cigarettes rather than entering the train right away. Yoshimura was nowhere to be seen. He smoked one of the cigarettes from the pack he had bought.

He felt a tap on his shoulder. 'Hey, Imanishi-*san*.'

Imanishi turned around in surprise. Yamashita, a reporter, was smiling at him.

'Where are you going so late at night?'

'I have a bit of business in Niigata,' Imanishi answered.

'Niigata?'

It might have been his imagination, but to Imanishi it looked as though Yamashita's eyes glittered.

'Did something happen in Niigata?'

'No, nothing.'

'That's strange. You're busy with that railroad yard murder, aren't you? For you to be going off to Niigata sounds fishy to me.'

'There's nothing fishy about it,' Imanishi retorted, acting

annoyed. 'My wife's family lives in Niigata. Her father died, so I'm on my way there. I just got the telegram.'

'Oh, really? My sympathies,' Yamashita said. 'But I don't see your wife anywhere.'

Imanishi recovered his composure. 'The telegram came about noon. So my wife went on ahead. I'm on my way now because I had some things to do first.

'What are you doing wandering around a place like this?' Imanishi asked Yamashita in return.

'I'm here to meet someone arriving from Niigata.'

'Well, that's nice of you,' Imanishi said. He waved good-bye and started walking slowly down the platform.

When Imanishi finally turned around, he could no longer see the newspaper reporter. He breathed a sigh of relief. Still taking precautions, he hid in the crowd and then jumped on the last car of the train. It was nearly full. Imanishi entered the second car. It was also packed. He moved to the next car, and spied Yoshimura, who was saving a seat for him with his suitcase.

'Did you get caught by a reporter?' Imanishi asked.

'No, I was all right.'

When the train's departure bell rang Imanishi breathed another sigh of relief.

'Have you ever been to the Tohoku region?' he asked.

'No, never.'

'It's the first time for me, too. Say, Yoshimura, wouldn't you like to take a relaxing trip with your family? We always take these trips for work, with no pleasure involved.'

'Unlike you, I don't have a wife.' Yoshimura laughed. 'I think it's more fun to travel alone. Any kind of trip is fine with me.'

'I suppose so.'

'You discovered Kameda, Imanishi-*san*. If we find out something, it'll be a gold star for you.'

'I don't know if my theory is correct. I might get criticized by the chief for spouting off and making them waste money on this trip.'

The two of them chatted for a while. It was hard to sleep. The lights from the scattered houses flowed past the dark window. They couldn't see the scenery, but it seemed that they could already smell the Tohoku region.

Daylight came. It was 6:30 when they reached Sakata. Imanishi woke early. Beside him Yoshimura was still asleep, leaning against the seat back with his arms crossed. After changing trains at Honjo they arrived at Kameda. It was close to ten o'clock.

The station was empty. The houses in front of the station were all old but built in a sturdy manner. A mountain rose up behind the town. The eaves of the houses were very deep in this area of heavy snowfalls. For Imanishi and Yoshimura this sight was unusual.

They went to a restaurant in front of the station. Only two or three customers were inside, and half of the space was taken by a souvenir shop. The second floor was an inn.

Imanishi ordered some noodles. They ate sitting side by side.

'Imanishi-*san*, this may sound strange, but I wonder how you feel about it,' Yoshimura said, wolfing down his tempura over rice. 'We go on various business trips like this. And afterward, rather than the scenery or problems I might have encountered, what I remember is the food. Our expense allowance is so small we can only afford rice with curry, or some meat on top of a bowl of rice, food you can get anywhere. Yet the flavoring is always different. It's the taste of each location that I remember first.'

'Is that so?' Imanishi said, sipping his noodles. 'After all, you're young. I prefer to remember the scenery.'

Yoshimura said, his chopsticks stilled for a moment, 'I hear that you write poetry. That's why you focus on scenery. Will you add to your haiku collection on this trip?'

'My poems aren't any good.' Imanishi laughed in self-deprecation.

'By the way, what shall we do? Should we go to the police station right after we eat?'

'Yes, let's do that.'

'Isn't it strange? We're here because you happened to look at the supplement in your wife's magazine. If it hadn't been for that, I wouldn't have seen this place. One's life can be changed by a chance happening,' Yoshimura said, pouring himself some tea. He'd polished off his bowl of rice leaving not a single grain behind.

The Iwaki police station was housed in an old building.

They entered and Imanishi presented his name card at the reception desk. A policeman looked at the card and led them into the station chief's room immediately.

The chief was seated, looking over some documents, but he stood up as soon as he saw the two visitors. He seemed to know who they were even before he had seen their cards.

'Please. Please, sit down.'

The heavy-set chief smiled at the visitors and had two chairs brought for them.

'I'm Imanishi Eitaro of the Homicide Division of the Tokyo Metropolitan Police Agency.'

'Yoshimura Hiroshi from the same division.'

'I appreciate your coming here,' the station chief said, urging them to be seated.

Imanishi offered their thanks for the cooperation they had already received.

'Not at all. I didn't know if it would be of any help, but I thought I should report the matter, just in case.'

A young staff member of the police station brought in some tea.

'You must have had a tiring trip,' the chief said, offering them the cigarettes on the table. 'Did you come to this station directly?'

'No, we got off at Ugo Kameda to see what the area was like. Then we took a bus here.'

'You're the first visitors we've had at this station who have come from the Tokyo police,' the station chief said. 'We've heard the outline of the case you are concerned with. But would you mind giving me more details?'

Imanishi gave an account of the investigation into the Kamata railroad yard murder case.

The chief listened intently. Then he started to explain. 'Kameda was a castle town in the olden days. It was a small domain of about twenty thousand *koku*. You must have seen that three sides of the town are surrounded by mountains. There is very little land that can be cultivated, so the main products of this area are dried noodles and cloth. This cloth is called Kameda weave, and it was valued up until before the war. Now there isn't that much production. Every year more and more young people leave town.'

The station chief was using the words of standard Japanese, but his accent was thick.

'That's why practically everyone would know a person who was a native of Kameda. I had my men go around with the photograph of the victim sent by your headquarters; it doesn't seem that the person is from this area. But . . .' he paused, and then continued, 'about a week ago, a strange man appeared in the town of Kameda.'

'When you say strange, in what way?' Imanishi asked.

'At first glance he seemed to be a laborer, wearing an old, worn-out suit, a man of about thirty or forty. He wasn't considered strange from the beginning, but when your inquiry came and we checked out the Kameda area, people recalled that a stranger had been around.'

'I see.'

'This man stayed at Asahiya, an inn in Kameda. This inn is an old house, and well regarded in this area. It's not strange that he stayed in that inn, but it seems odd that a laborer would stay in such an inn.'

'Yes, I see.'

'The inn at first refused to accept him. They didn't want him spending the night because of the way he looked. But the man said that he had enough money and would pay in advance. The innkeeper agreed to let him stay because they didn't have any other guests at the time. Of course, they didn't give him one of their good rooms.'

'What kinds of things happened?'

'Well, that's about all. Nothing happened in particular. He paid the inn for his lodging in advance as promised. He even gave a five-hundred-yen tip to the chambermaid. There aren't many people around here who would give such a tip to a maid. The innkeeper regretted having given him a bad room.'

'What did he do at the inn?'

'He arrived in the evening. After supper, he said he was tired and went to sleep without even taking a bath. That made the people think that he was quite odd.'

'Did anything else happen?'

'Something strange? Well, this is what happened. The man slept until after ten o'clock, and called a maid to ask how late the inn kept its doors open. When the maid answered that they were up until one o'clock, he said he had something to do and went out, wearing the inn's wooden clogs.'

'He went out after ten o'clock at night?'

'That's right,' the station chief answered. 'He returned to the inn just after one A.M.'

He continued, 'I forgot to mention this, but this man arrived with a shoulder bag. He left that bag at the inn when he went out. In this area all the houses close up early in the evening. So we can't figure out what this man was doing when he went out from after ten until one o'clock. It wouldn't be strange at all if he had gone out like that in a big city, but in our area, this is considered to be strange.'

'I suppose so. And when he came back, was there anything changed about this man's behavior?'

'There wasn't anything. It didn't seem that he had gone drinking, and he seemed to behave the same as before he left. When the maid asked where he had gone, he told her that he had gone to run an errand. But no one runs errands after ten at night.'

'I see. I suppose there is a record of his registration?'

'Yes, there is. We could have seized it, but since we knew you were coming, we've left it at the inn.'

'Thank you very much. Was there anything else that was strange?'

'That was all at the inn. The man left just after eight in the morning. When she served him breakfast, the maid asked him where he was going. He said he was getting on the train for Aomori.'

'What was the address he listed on the inn registration?'

'It's listed as Mito City in Ibaragi Prefecture.'

'So he's from Mito.'

'So it says on the inn registration. When the maid said Mito must be a nice place, he spoke about its famous sights. So it seems that he wasn't completely unfamiliar with Mito.'

'What about his occupation?'

'According to the inn registration, he put down company employee. But they didn't learn which firm he worked for.'

'So, it seems that what was strange was his leaving the inn for three hours late at night?'

'Yes. But if that were the only thing, I wouldn't have asked you to come all this way. There were a few other things that seemed unusual.'

'Yes, and what were those?'

'One was that this man was seen loitering in front of a dried noodle shop.'

'What is a dried noodle shop?'

'As I just explained, Kameda is famous for the dried noodles it produces. Rows of noodles are hung to dry next to the noodle-makers' houses. It was at such a house that this man appeared.'

'What did he do when he appeared in front of this dried noodle shop?'

'Well, it wasn't as if he *did* anything. He just stood there, in front of the place where they dry their noodles,' the station chief answered, with a strained smile.

'He just stood there?'

'Yes. He did nothing but stand there for twenty minutes or so, gazing at the noodles hung to dry.'

'Hm.'

'The shop owners were a bit concerned about this unkempt fellow standing in front of their drying area. But he went away after a while. That's about all there is to tell. But I thought it might be of some interest to you.'

'It certainly is interesting.' Imanishi nodded deeply. 'I assume that the man who stayed in the inn and the man watching the noodles were the same person?'

'I think so. There's also something else.' The station chief gave a little laugh.

'What is that?'

'There is a river that runs through the town of Kameda. It's called Koromogawa. A man thought to be this same person was seen lying on the bank of this river at noontime.'

'Just a minute,' Imanishi interrupted. 'Was that the day after he had stayed at the inn?'

'No, not the day after. It was the day he went to the inn. As I told you, he got to the inn in the evening, so this was noon of that day.'

'I understand. Please go on.'

'Well, there isn't much except that this man was lying at the edge of the river. But there aren't any men around here who can take things easy like that. There's a road at the top of the levee. A local person who was walking on that road thought it was a strange place for a man to be taking a nap. He thought the man was a drifter.'

'I see.'

'No one said anything about this. It's just that my men heard about it when they made their inquiries. When they asked if there were any unusual goings-on, they were told about this incident.'

'That means that this man was lying about in the grass around noon. That night he left the inn after ten and returned at about one o'clock . . . This does seem to be strange behavior.'

'You think so, too?' The station chief seemed relieved.

'Napping on the bank of the river during the day and leaving the inn in the middle of the night, that doesn't sound like a normal person, does it?'

'If you think he may have been a burglar, I thought of that, too. But there weren't any thefts reported around that date.' The station chief continued, 'If there had been any actual loss reported . . . but there was nothing, so it's hard to figure him out.'

'Was that the only day that the man was seen wandering about?' Imanishi asked.

'Yes, that's the only day. Imanishi-*san*, don't you think there's some connection to the case you were asking about?'

'Let me see,' Imanishi said and smiled. 'Let us look around the town a bit.'

'I'll have one of my men show you around.'

'Please don't bother. If you could just direct us, we'll go ourselves.'

Imanishi and Yoshimura got on the bus for Kameda. The passengers were all from that locality. Their accents were so strong that it was hard for the outsiders to make out their meaning.

Soon the row of houses ended, and the bus drove along a road through the fields. The warm season came to this area much later than to Tokyo. The color of the new green leaves of the hillside was beautiful.

They got off at the bus stop as instructed and went to the Asahiya inn. The station chief had said it was an old established house, and it looked it. The gabled entry seemed forbidding.

Imanishi presented his police identification to the maid who came to the doorway. The innkeeper, a man in his forties, appeared.

'I've come from the Tokyo Metropolitan Police,' Imanishi said. The innkeeper invited them to enter, but Imanishi preferred not to go inside. The maid brought seat cushions and some tea to the entryway.

Imanishi described what he had heard from the Iwaki police chief.

'Yes, we certainly had such a guest,' the innkeeper said, nodding.

'Can you tell me about him in more detail?' Imanishi asked.

The innkeeper agreed and recounted his version, which was no different from what they had heard from the station chief.

'I understand you have the guest register?' Imanishi asked.

'We do,' the innkeeper said.

'Could you show it to me?'

'Yes, certainly.'

The innkeeper asked the maid to bring the guest register. It was in the form of separate sheets of paper, each like a bill.

The entry the innkeeper showed them read:

'Hashimoto Chusuke, Number xx, xx town, Mito City, Ibaragi Prefecture.'

It was inscribed in a very poor hand, as if a grade schooler had written it. But this was not unnatural, since the man had seemed to be a laborer. Imanishi stared at the characters.

Imanishi asked what the man had looked like. About thirty years old, tall with a medium build, his face on the long side, and his hair short and unparted. His skin had been rather dark, but his nose was straight and his features even. The innkeeper said he had kept his face averted, and had not met anyone's eyes even when he spoke. That was why the maids' memories were vague.

Asked about the way he spoke, the innkeeper responded that the man did not have a Tohoku accent. His speech was close to standard Japanese and his voice was low. The general impression was that he had seemed to be a gloomy sort, and terribly tired. Everyone agreed on this point. He'd had neither a travel bag nor a suitcase, only the kind of shoulder bag people had used during the war with all his belongings in it.

The two detectives visited the dried noodle shop. Next to it, bamboo poles were set with noodles draped from them. This made the noodles appear like white waterfalls when the sun shone on them.

The woman of the house came out and showed them a narrow pathway about two hundred yards from the drying area, between the grass lots, that led to the main road. In this section of town the spaces between the houses were wide and overgrown with grass. The man in question had hung around this lot, squatting and standing, for about thirty minutes.

Imanishi and Yoshimura walked until they reached a wide river that flowed from the surrounding mountains. The grass grew tall on its banks. A farm woman walked along carrying a hoe on the opposite bank of the river.

'Imanishi-*san*,' Yoshimura asked, 'what do you think? Is it your feeling that this man is the one who was with the victim at the bar in Kamata?'

'I can't say either way. But there *is* something strange about this fellow.'

'There's nothing definite, though, is there?' Yoshimura looked disappointed. 'The name he used in the inn register is an alias, of course?' Yoshimura asked.

'Of course.'

Imanishi stated this so definitely that Yoshimura took the bait.

'How can you tell?'

'You saw the penmanship on that register, didn't you?'

'Yes, I did. It was very poor writing.'

'Of course it was poor, since he wrote it with his left hand on purpose.' Imanishi fished his notebook out of his pocket and took out the carefully folded sheet from the inn register. 'Look at this closely. See, there's no flow in the writing at all. No one writes such awkward characters. Remember what the maid said at the inn? He didn't fill in the register in front of the maid. She brought the register and left it in the room. When she came back later, it was filled in. The guest filled it in using his left hand to hide his handwriting while the maid was out of the room. So we can assume that the name and address are false.'

'But where did this fellow go from ten at night to one o'clock in the morning?' Yoshimura asked. 'From his behavior during the day, he didn't seem to have any pressing business.'

'That's it. I was just thinking about that myself.' Imanishi stood in the grass with both his hands stuck into the pockets of his slacks. Ripples spread in the river in front of his eyes. The sun shone on the mountains and cast deep shadows.

'This is a strange trip. The results are kind of disappointing, aren't they? Imanishi-*san*, what shall we do now?' Yoshimura asked.

'Since we don't have any more leads, shall we go home?'

'Don't we have to find out where else the man went?'

'I don't think we'll be able to. He was probably here in Kameda for only that one day.'

'Then what did he come here for?'

'I can't tell. Though he seemed like a drifting laborer, there's no evidence that he came to ask for work. But maybe we should make inquiries in the nearby towns just to be sure. After all, we've come all this way. Come on, cheer up,' Imanishi said, looking at Yoshimura's dejected face.

The following afternoon, Imanishi and Yoshimura visited the office of the Iwaki police chief once again.

'Thank you for everything you've done for us,' Imanishi said.

'You're very welcome. Were you able to discover anything?'

'Thanks to you we were able to get a concrete picture of what went on. It seems that the man didn't make an appearance in any other villages. Just Kameda. He must have gotten on a train at Kameda Station and gone to another area.'

'I see. That's too bad. But it seems strange that he got off the train only at Kameda.'

'That's true. So maybe this incident holds some promise.'

The two detectives chatted for a while with the station chief. After an appropriate length of time they took their leave.

They walked toward the train station by the deep eaved houses of the snow country.

They entered the small station and found the train schedule displayed above the wicket. The two men looked up to read the schedule.

At that moment they heard a commotion behind them. When Imanishi turned around, he saw four young men with suitcases surrounded by several men who looked like newspaper reporters. Some had cameras and were taking photographs.

Imanishi gazed at the four, wondering why the local newsmen were making a fuss over them. He could tell at first glance that the four were not from this region, that they had come from Tokyo. Although they were dressed casually, a closer look revealed that each item of their clothing had been carefully chosen. They were 'casually fashionable.' They wore their hair rather long, and seemed to be around thirty years of age. The youngest of the four men had a pale face and thin eyebrows, and was wearing a gray suit with the collar of his black sports shirt out. He was saying, 'I think it will be some time before Japan will be able to launch a rocket.'

'What are *they*?' Yoshimura asked Imanishi.

Imanishi had no idea who they might be. They seemed to him to be awfully young to have attained such importance.

The local people waiting for the train in the waiting room of this lonely country station were also watching this group. Some young girls went up to the four men and stuck out a notebook. One of the men took out a pen and wrote in it. The girl bowed and went to the next young man. He also scribbled something with a pen. It was clear that the girl was asking for their autographs.

'Could they be movie stars?' Yoshimura asked.

'I have no idea.'

'But I don't recognize their faces, and what they're saying doesn't fit.' Yoshimura pondered.

'I can't recognize the faces of the new movie actors,' Imanishi stated. 'They keep creating more and more new stars. Young girls know a lot more about that kind of thing.'

After a while, the group of young men went through the gate, toward the train bound for Aomori, in the opposite direction from the way Imanishi and Yoshimura were headed.

The newspaper reporters bowed their farewell and left the station.

'Shall I ask them?' Yoshimura said, his curiosity aroused.

'No, don't bother,' Imanishi stopped him.

'But I'd like to know who they are.' Yoshimura approached the young girl with the autograph book.

He bent over and asked her something. The girl answered, blushing slightly. Yoshimura nodded and returned to where Imanishi was seated.

'I've got it,' he said, smiling self-consciously.

'Who were they?'

'They are intellectuals from Tokyo. They are members of the Nouveau group. They often appear in newspapers and magazines.'

'What is this Nouveau group?'

'You might say it's made up of members of the younger generation who have progressive opinions: composers, academics, novelists, playwrights, musicians, filmmakers, journalists, poets – all types.'

'You're really up on all this, aren't you?'

'Well, I do read the papers and the magazines,' Yoshimura said, somewhat embarrassed.

'So those four are members of this group?'

'Yes. I just asked that girl. The one in the black shirt was Waga Eiryo, the composer. Next to him was the playwright Takebe Toyoichiro; then Sekigawa Shigeo, the critic; and the painter Katazawa Mutsuo.'

When he heard these names, Imanishi realized that they were vaguely familiar.

'Why did they come all the way out here?'

'She said that a university rocket research center is located here in Iwaki. They're on their way back from taking a tour of the center.'

'A rocket research center in this backwater?'

'When she told me, I remembered that I'd read about it somewhere.'

'A strange location for such a modern facility.'

'It sure is. They've finished their tour and are going on to see Lake Towada before they go home. The local press was all over them because they're mass media stars – opinion leaders. The spotlight of the new generation is on them.'

Imanishi was indifferent to them. The generation gap distanced him from this group. He yawned and said, 'Have you found us a train?'

'Yes. There's a limited express at seven forty-four P.M.'

'What time does it reach Ueno?'

'At six-forty tomorrow morning.'

'That early? Well, I guess it's all right. We can go home and sleep a bit before reporting to headquarters,' Imanishi said, and then added, 'There's no need to hurry; we're not going back with a breakthrough.'

'True. Imanishi-*san*, since we've come all this way, how about taking a look at the Japan Sea? We still have plenty of time.'

'You're right. Let's do it.'

Imanishi and Yoshimura walked toward the coast. The town gradually dwindled into a fishing village. Suddenly the air smelled of the sea. The beach stretched far along the shore. Not one island could be seen on the vast horizon. The setting sun created a sash of light across the sea.

'It's really boundless, isn't it?' Yoshimura gazed at the sea as he walked along the sand. 'The color of the Japan Sea is so dark,' Yoshimura exclaimed. 'The Pacific Ocean is much lighter. To me it looks like the color of this sea is more intense.'

'You're right. This color matches the scenery of the Tohoku region.'

The two men gazed out at the sea for some time.

'Imanishi-*san*, have you come up with anything?'

'You mean a poem?'

'You've probably come up with about thirty already.'

'It's not that easy.' Imanishi smiled ruefully.

A boy from the fishing village walked past them, carrying a large fish basket.

'Coming to a place like this makes you realize how hectic Tokyo is,' Yoshimura said.

'This *is* relaxing.'

'I suppose you'd feel washed clean if you spent several days in a place like this. I feel like our hearts are full of grime.'

'You're quite poetic yourself,' Imanishi said, looking at Yoshimura.

'No, I'm not.'

'I can see why you know about that group of young men. You've been reading those kinds of books.'

'It's not that I like them particularly. It's just part of common knowledge.'

'What did you call them? *Nouveau?*'

'The Nouveau group. They are all very smart. They expect to be the leaders of the next generation.'

'I remember hearing about another such group from my uncle when I was a kid.'

'You mean the White Birch group.' Yoshimura seemed to know about that movement, too. 'This group is more strongly individualistic. Mushanokoji and Arishima of the White Birch group turned out to be leaders, but most of them were pretty tame. Besides, the White Birch group limited itself to literature and art. These young intellectuals have political opinions as well.'

'That's the difference between the generations.' Imanishi had little interest, but thought he got the general idea.

'Shall we go back?' Yoshimura was starting to get bored.

'Since I can't sleep well on the train like you, I'd better get some rest now.'

The trains were not crowded. When they changed to a limited express in Honjo, the two detectives were able to sit together comfortably in the middle section of the third-class car.

As soon as they boarded, Yoshimura put his bags down and rushed off to buy their box lunches. Through the windows, passengers exchanged farewells with those who had come to see them off. Imanishi absent-mindedly listened to their conversations in the local dialect which he couldn't quite follow.

Presently, Yoshimura returned with box lunches and tea.

'Thank you, thank you,' Imanishi said as he accepted one of the little pots of tea.

'I'm starving. Shall we eat right away?'

'Let's wait until the train leaves. It'll be less frantic then.'

The lights on the platform were already lit. The station sign 'Ugo Honjo' blurred along with the platform as the train pulled out, picking up speed. Then the lights of the town flashed past them. People stood at the crossings, waiting for the train to pass. Imanishi felt sad, wondering if he would ever visit this town again. The lights of Honjo ended, all they passed now were black mountains.

'Shall we eat?' Yoshimura opened his box lunch.

'You know, Yoshimura,' Imanishi said as he opened his box, 'each time I eat one of these box lunches I'm reminded that it was my childhood dream to have one. It was almost impossible to get my mother to buy me one. They must have cost about thirty sen in those days.'

'Were they that cheap?' Yoshimura said, glancing at Imanishi.

He felt that he understood Imanishi better now. For a man of Imanishi's origins, the young men they had seen at the station must have seemed very well-off, sons of wealthy families who had all been to college. Looking over at Imanishi, Yoshimura couldn't help but compare those young men to his senior colleague, who had had a much harder life.

By the time Imanishi had finished eating, his spirits had improved. He poured some tea from the miniature teapot and drank it contentedly. He put the lid back on the box and carefully tied the string. Then he took out a cigarette he had cut in half and smoked as he relaxed. The pallor of fatigue could be seen under the stubble of his beard. When he had finished the cigarette, Imanishi rustled around in his coat pocket and took out his notebook. He looked at it, frowning in concentration. Yoshimura thought he must be studying the notes he had taken on the trip.

'Yoshimura, read this, would you?' Imanishi passed him the notebook with a sheepish chuckle.

> Drying noodles –
> flow among the young leaves –
> and glisten

> Trip to the north –
> the sea a dark blue –
> summer still young

'So, you reaped quite a harvest.' Yoshimura smiled and read the next haiku.

> The grass springs back –
> after a nap –
> at Koromo River

'Ah, this is about that strange fellow,' Yoshimura said.

'You're right.' Imanishi laughed self-consciously and turned toward the window.

Darkness flowed past the train, only an occasional light from a farmhouse drifting by in the lonely distance.

'Say, Imanishi-*san*,' Yoshimura said, 'wouldn't it be great if we could link the stranger to the suspect?'

'If we could do that, then our trip won't have been a waste,' Imanishi agreed.

'It'll be hard not to have a guilty conscience if we find out that there's no connection to the case after we've come all this way, and spent all this time and money.'

'We can't help that. If there's no connection, then we'll just have to ask the others to understand.'

'I suppose so, but it bothers me. While we're relaxing on this train, the rest of the team is running around investigating as hard as they can. That makes me feel bad.'

'Yoshimura, this is also part of the work. You don't have to feel bad about it.' Though he reassured the younger Yoshimura, Imanishi's feelings of responsibility for this trip weighed heavily on him, too. Looking out the window dejectedly, Imanishi muttered to himself, 'I wonder if they've found the shirt?'

Yoshimura overheard him and asked, 'Shirt?'

'Yes, the shirt the murderer was wearing. It had to have gotten bloody. He couldn't have continued wearing it, so he must have hidden it somewhere.'

'Suspects often hide such things in their houses, don't they?'

'Most of the time that's true. In this case, though, it seems that it might be different. What I mean, Yoshimura,' Imanishi continued, 'is that if there were a lot of blood on the shirt, he couldn't have worn it all the way home. He would have been afraid that people would notice.'

'But it was dark.'

'Yes, it was. But if the murderer's house was far away he couldn't have gotten on a train looking like that. Even if he took a taxi, the driver would have been suspicious.'

'He might have had his own car.'

'Yes, his own car. That could have been it. But I think there must have been some place where he changed his shirt.'

Outside the window, the darkness continued to pass by. Some of the passengers were already getting ready to go to sleep.

Yoshimura said, 'Such a place would have to be the suspect's hideout?'

'Probably,' Imanishi muttered. Looking into the darkness, he seemed to be thinking of something else. He pulled out another half cigarette and started smoking.

'Could this hideout be his lover's place?'

'I wouldn't know about that.'

'But if he went there to change his clothes, someone must have been living there. And it would still be impossible unless the suspect had a special relationship with that person.'

'That's true.'

'If it's not a lover, then it would have to be someone like a close friend or a brother.'

'Probably.' Imanishi didn't have much to say. Being a veteran detective, he preferred to think things over on his own.

Yoshimura was assigned to the precinct where the murder had taken place and did not work with Imanishi on a daily basis. They had worked together once before when they were teamed up to investigate a murder. That time Imanishi had been sent out from the central division. Since then Yoshimura had held Imanishi in high regard. Whenever he came across a difficult case, he would ask Imanishi for advice. He had gotten to know Imanishi's character and interests. He had even met his family.

It was not Detective Imanishi's style to tell even his colleagues when he came across a good lead. He usually reported things directly to the head of the Homicide Division.

Section One of the Homicide Division was in charge of all murder cases. This section was divided into eight subsections, each with approximately eight detectives assigned to it. When an investigation headquarters was set up, one of these subsections was dispatched. Each of the eight detectives had his own role on the team. They worked under the direction of the chief inspector, but if one came across a good lead, he would follow it up on his own because each of them wanted to get ahead. Detectives did not always reveal everything they had up their sleeves at the investigation meetings.

Imanishi had come this far by being discreet. At a certain point in an investigation, he would become as silent as stone.

'Let's go to sleep,' Imanishi said, stubbing out his cigarette.

Imanishi awoke. Pale light filtered into the train from around the edges of the window shade. Imanishi opened the shade a little.

Outside, mountains passed by in the milky whiteness, but these mountains looked different. He looked at his watch, it was four-thirty. Yoshimura was still asleep.

Imanishi wondered where they were. After a while, he saw a station go by. He read the name Shibukawa. He was smoking a cigarette when Yoshimura woke up.

The train descended from the mountains and ran along the plain. It became lighter outside. Imanishi opened the shade all the way. Here and there they could see an early rising farmer already out in the fields. The houses outside the window became clustered together as they approached Omiya.

'Yoshimura, could you please go get a newspaper?' Imanishi asked.

Yoshimura stood up and ran down the aisle to the platform. He returned to his seat just as the train was pulling out. Yoshimura had brought back three morning papers.

'Thank you.'

Imanishi immediately opened one of the papers to the city

news section. New developments might have occurred in the case while they were gone, but there was nothing about the murder. He opened the other two newspapers and found nothing in either of them, to his relief. Imanishi turned back to the front page and started reading slowly. In thirty minutes they would reach Ueno Station. Most of the other passengers on the train were awake now, some already starting to get their bags together.

'Yoshimura, he's one, isn't he?' Imanishi prodded Yoshimura with his elbow and showed him a photograph in the cultural section of the paper.

Yoshimura leaned over and saw the title 'Art in the New Age' and the author's name, Sekigawa Shigeo.

'Yes, he's one of the four men we saw at Iwaki Station,' Yoshimura said.

Imanishi stared at the picture. 'He must be quite something to be writing for a paper like this. I can't really understand what he's trying to say in this piece, but I suppose he's brilliant.'

'He must be.' Yoshimura was carefully reading the column in the paper that Imanishi had passed to him.

'Hey, we're here.'

The train stopped at Ueno Station. Yoshimura glanced out the window and folded the paper.

'Yoshimura, just in case, let's get off separately.'

3. The Nouveau Group

Club Bonheur was located in the back streets of the Ginza on the second floor of a multistory building. Although not very large, it was a popular spot where Tokyo's business and cultural elite gathered. There were already some customers even though it was early in the evening. After nine o'clock, it was usually so crowded that latecomers had to wait at the door.

An assistant professor of philosophy and a professor of history sat drinking in a corner booth. Two groups of executives were at other booths. It was still rather quiet. Most of the hostesses were sitting with one of these three groups. The executives told risqué stories while the professors complained about university life.

Five young men came into the bar. The hostesses turned toward them. 'Welcome,' they all said, and many of them drifted over to the newcomers.

A tall woman, the madam of the bar, left the side of one of the executives and greeted the new customers. 'Well, it's been a while since you've been in. Why don't you sit over here?' She gestured to a large, empty booth. As there weren't enough seats, extra chairs were pulled up. The customers sat facing each other in the booth, and several hostesses sat down next to them.

'You're all together this evening,' the madam said, full of smiles. 'What's the occasion?'

'We were at an uninteresting gathering. We decided to come by to wash away the bad aftertaste,' Sasamura Ichiro said.

Besides Sasamura, a stage director, the group included Takebe Toyoichiro, Sekigawa Shigeo, Waga Eiryo, and Yodogawa Ryuta, an architect. Katazawa Mutsuo, who had been at the earlier gathering, had gone elsewhere.

'What will you have to drink?' the madam asked, giving them each a charming smile. The five young men ordered.

'Waga-*sensei*,' the madam said, looking at the composer, 'it was wonderful to see you the other evening. How have things been going?'

'Fine, as you can see,' Waga said.

'No, I don't mean for you. I mean *with her*.'

'Waga,' Sasamura said, tapping him on the shoulder. 'You've been caught. Where did the madam spot you?'

'A nice place, wasn't it?' The madam smiled and winked.

'It was at a nightclub, wasn't it?' Waga said, looking at the madam.

'I can't believe it. He's admitting it,' Sasamura said.

'Yes, that's where I saw her. She is very lovely,' the madam smiled. 'I had seen her photograph in magazines, but she was much prettier in person. You are really lucky, Waga-*sensei*.'

'Am I?' Waga cocked his head and took a sip from his drink.

'To Waga's fiancée.' The stage director proposed a toast. Their raised glasses touched and clinked.

'What do you mean, "Am I"?' the madam said, frowning at Waga. 'Your work is brilliant. You're a leader of the younger generation. And you're about to marry a wonderful person. I'm so envious.'

'I'd like to have such good luck,' the bargirls said.

'I wonder,' Waga muttered, looking down.

'You still say that? You're just embarrassed.'

'I'm not embarrassed. I'm just skeptical – about everything. I look at myself objectively.'

'After all, you're an artist,' the madam said without hesitation.

'We would be drowning in our own happiness. That's the difference. We aren't able to analyze things the way Waga-*sensei* does.'

'That's why we make mistakes,' one of the hostesses said.

'But there's no denying that you're happy, is there, Sekigawa-*sensei*?' The madam turned toward the critic sitting beside her.

'I think it's best that people immerse themselves completely in the feeling when they're happy. I don't think excessive analysis is good,' Sekigawa said.

Waga looked at him, but said nothing.

'So, when is the wedding?'

'Oh, I read about it in a magazine. It's this fall. Their pictures were in the magazine,' a different hostess said. She was slim and pretty and wore a black silk dress.

'That's all made up. It's ridiculous,' Waga said. 'I can't take responsibility for the rumors they print.'

'But if you're taking her out to nightclubs, it must be quite a close relationship,' Yodogawa put in.

'I can vouch for that,' the madam concurred. 'I was watching them dance, and they seemed to be a perfect match.'

'Who are those young men?' the professor asked, turning around to take a look.

'They're members of the Nouveau group,' explained a hostess who had been watching them.

'I guess I have heard of them,' the elderly professor said. 'I think I read about them in the newspaper.'

'See the fellow with the long, messy hair sitting across from the madam? He's Waga Eiryo, the composer. His intent is to destroy the nature of conventional music,' the assistant professor said.

'You don't have to explain it all to me. Who's the one beside him?' the professor asked.

'The one sitting beside him is the stage director Sasamura. He's trying to start a revolution in the structure of dramatic production.'

'When I was young,' the professor said, 'we were excited by the Tsukiji Shogekijo. Is it that kind of movement?'

'It's a little different,' the assistant professor said with a puzzled look. 'How can I describe it? They're bolder, and more creative.'

'I see. And next?'

'That's the playwright Takebe, isn't it?' The assistant professor looked to the hostess for confirmation.

'Yes, that's Takebe-*sensei*.'

'Who's the one with his back to us?'

'That's the critic Sekigawa-*sensei*,' the hostess answered.

'And the one next to the girl?'

'The architect Yodogawa-*sensei*.'

'You call them all *sensei*, as if they were professors?' The professor let out a sarcastic laugh. 'They must be something to be called *sensei* at such a young age.'

'Anyone is called *sensei* these days. Even the leaders of underworld gangs,' the assistant professor said.

'What are they laughing about?'

'It must be about Waga-*sensei*,' the hostess said. She had overheard some of the conversation at the other booth.

'And what's so special about this Waga?'

'Waga-*sensei*'s fiancée is Tadokoro Sachiko-*san*. You know, the sculptor. She's also famous because her father is Tadokoro Shigeyoshi, the former cabinet minister,' the hostess explained.

'I see.' The history professor seemed to lose interest.

A similar conversation was taking place at the booth where the executives were seated.

'Oh, Tadokoro Shigeyoshi . . .' The executive did not know the names of the young artists, but his expression suddenly lit up when he heard the name of the former cabinet minister.

The bar gradually filled with customers. Most of those who arrived later came in twos and threes, so the group of young men continued to be the object of attention.

The door opened quietly and an elderly gentleman entered the bar. His hair was long and gray, and he wore thick-framed metal glasses. He started to walk in, but when he saw the young men seated at the large booth, he hesitated. The young men recognized him as well.

'Mita-*sensei*,' Sekigawa said, standing and greeting the new-comer. Mita Kenzo was a well-known cultural critic who wrote commentaries not only on literature but also on topics related to art and popular culture.

'Good evening,' Mita replied with a tentative smile. 'I didn't realize you fellows came here.'

'Yes, sometimes we do.'

Mita seemed to be at a loss for words and stood there hesitantly.

'*Sensei*, Mita-*sensei*, please sit with us,' the architect Yodogawa Ryuta said.

'Thank you. Maybe I'll join you later.' Mita walked off with a hostess, nodding good-bye to the young men.

'Escaped,' Sekigawa said. His voice was low, but the group let out a burst of loud laughter. Sekigawa had often voiced his scorn of Mita as a low-brow critic. He had secretly given him the nickname 'Jack-of-all-trades.'

The young men continued their conversation. The first one to suggest leaving was Waga Eiryo. 'I have to meet someone,' he said.

'Oh, Waga-*sensei*, you seem to be happy about it,' a slim host-ess said, clapping her hands.

'I'd better go home, too. I just remembered I have something to do,' Sekigawa said.

Taking this as their cue, they all stood up. The madam, who had been at another table, hurried over and shook their hands. They left the bar.

'Sekigawa,' Takebe asked, 'where are you going?'

'In the opposite direction. See you.'

Takebe stood looking after him, but gave up and went off with the architect and the stage director. Waga Eiryo waved to them and started walking toward the main street.

Sekigawa watched him go.

A young girl came up to him. 'Mister, how about some flowers?' Sekigawa brushed her aside. He spotted a telephone booth on the street corner, entered it, and without consulting his address book began to dial.

At eleven o'clock exactly Sekigawa got out of a taxi in front of an apartment house in a crowded residential area on a hill in Shibuya. As always, the gate was open. The entryway, lit by a dim lamp, was also left open all night. The hallway was faintly lit and on either side were apartments with locks on the doors.

Sekigawa never came here during the day. A card pasted on the farthest apartment door on the second floor indicated that it was rented to Miura Emiko. Sekigawa tapped lightly, barely grazing the door with his fingertips. The door opened a crack.

'Welcome home,' a young woman said.

Sekigawa entered the room silently. The slim hostess from the Club Bonheur had changed from her black dress into a casual sweater.

'You must be warm. Why don't you take your jacket off?'

Emiko helped Sekigawa off with his jacket and put it on a hanger.

The small, six-tatami-mat room was crowded with a wardrobe,

a dressing table, and a bureau set against one wall. It was neat and scented. Emiko always sprayed the air with perfume when she expected Sekigawa.

Sekigawa sat down, and Emiko brought him a moistened hand towel.

'When did you get home?' Sekigawa asked, wiping his face with the towel.

'Just now. I asked for permission to leave as soon as I received your call. I was in the middle of my shift, so it wasn't easy.'

'You should have made arrangements as soon as I came into the bar.'

'But you didn't say anything. You didn't even give me a sign.'

'I couldn't do anything with all those nosy guys around.'

'That's true. They're all so sharp. But I was so happy to see you unexpectedly.'

Emiko leaned toward Sekigawa, who put his arms around her shoulders. She collapsed into his arms.

Startled by a noise, Sekigawa pulled his lips away from hers and asked, 'What's that?'

Emiko opened her eyes. 'They're playing mah-jongg. It's the student across the hall. They play on Saturday night.'

'Do they play all night?'

'Yes. Normally he's just a quiet student, but he has his friends over every Saturday.'

'He's in the room diagonally across the hall, right?'

'Yes. At first the noise used to bother me, but he's young, so I put up with it. Now I've gotten used to it.' To change the subject she asked, 'Would you like something to eat?'

'I'm a little hungry.' Sekigawa took off his shirt and threw it on the floor. Emiko picked it up and put it on a hanger.

'I thought so. I suppose you haven't eaten anything since you left the bar?'

'All I had was a few bites of a sandwich at the party.'

'I made something light.'

Emiko brought out some sashimi, poached turbot, and pickles from the kitchen and placed them on the dining table.

'What is this fish?' Sekigawa asked, looking at the sashimi.

'It's sea bass. I went to a sushi shop and asked them to prepare it. They said it's the season for sea bass.'

Emiko scooped some rice into a bowl she kept especially for Sekigawa. Sekigawa ate silently.

'What are you thinking about?' Emiko studied his expression from across the table.

'I'm not thinking about anything.'

'But you're eating so quietly.'

'I don't have anything to say.'

'I feel lonely when you don't say anything. Where did you leave the others?'

'Just outside the Bonheur.'

'What about Waga-*san*?'

'He probably went to his fiancée's.'

Emiko glanced at his sullen face. 'Would you like another bowl of rice?'

'No, I've had plenty.' Sekigawa had her pour some tea. 'Is the bar busy?' he asked.

'It's been very busy recently. That's why it was so hard to get to leave early tonight.'

'Sorry about that.'

'I don't mind leaving for you.'

'No one at the bar suspects anything?'

'Don't worry. They don't suspect anything.'

'Didn't the person who answered the phone recognize my voice?'

'Don't worry. There's no way they would know. I get lots of telephone calls.'

'I bet you're very popular.'

'Don't talk that way. Of course, since this is my business, I'd feel humiliated if I didn't have a few customers of my own.'

Sekigawa smiled coldly. His face was very hard. But Emiko was bewitched by him.

They heard footsteps in the hall.

'It's so noisy. They'll be going back and forth to the toilet like that all night, won't they?' Sekigawa said, frowning.

'That can't be helped.'

'That student hasn't ever seen my face, has he?'

'Don't worry . . . I don't like it when you act so nervous.'

Sekigawa laughed and took off his undershirt.

Emiko switched on the lamp and turned off the overhead light. The soft light shone around the pillow. Emiko slid out of her slip.

Sekigawa turned over on the mattress and said, 'Hand me a cigarette.'

Emiko quickly threw something on and turned on the lamp. She took a cigarette from the cigarette box on the dining table, put it to her lips, and lit it. She then placed it between Seki-gawa's lips for him.

Sekigawa lay on his back and smoked.

Emiko returned to his side and lay down. 'What are you thinking about?'

'Hmm.' He continued to smoke.

'You're impossible. You've been like this all evening. Is it about work?'

There was no answer. The sound of the mah-jongg pieces could be heard from across the hall.

'They're so noisy.'

'It just seems that way to you because you're overly conscious of it. I'm used to it, it doesn't bother me . . . You're going to drop those ashes.' Emiko held up an ashtray and took the cigarette from Sekigawa's lips. She knocked off the ashes and put the cigarette back between his lips.

'How old do you think Waga-*san* is?' Emiko asked, looking sideways at Sekigawa.

'Twenty-eight, I think.'

'So he's a year older than you. How old would you say Sachiko-*san* is?'

'Twenty-two or -three, I guess,' Sekigawa muttered.

'Then they're a perfect match in terms of age, too. I read in a magazine that they're getting married next fall. I wonder if it's true.'

'No reason not to think so,' Sekigawa answered, sounding bored. The light from the lamp near the pillow lit his forehead and the tip of his nose.

'Waga-*san* is so lucky. You should get married to someone like that, too,' Emiko said, looking intently at Sekigawa's face.

'Don't be ridiculous!' Sekigawa spat the words out. 'I'm not like Waga. I wouldn't get married for political reasons.'

'Is it a political marriage? The magazines say they're in love.'

'There's no difference. Waga's an opportunist.'

'That's not the philosophy Waga-*san* and your group express.'

'Waga has his rationalizations. He says, "I won't compromise my integrity no matter whose daughter I marry." And although he considers Sachiko's father part of the opposition, he claims that by marrying her he'll be able to infiltrate their ranks and fight more effectively against the Establishment. But I see through him.' Sekigawa reached over and tossed his cigarette into the ashtray.

'Then you wouldn't marry someone like her?'

'No.'

'Really?' Emiko put her hand on his chest.

'Emiko,' Sekigawa said in a low voice, 'you took care of everything I asked you to, didn't you?' His eyes remained focused on the ceiling.

'Don't worry.'

He sighed and stroked her hair.

'Please trust me. I would do anything for you,' she said.

'You would?'

'Yes, anything. I realize that it's a critical time for you right now. You're on your way to becoming someone. I'll keep any secret you have. You don't have to worry at all.'

Sekigawa turned toward her, his hand caressing her neck. 'Are you sure?'

'For your sake I'd die if I had to.'

'Don't let anyone find out about us, understand?'

'Yes, of course.'

Sekigawa's expression hardened. 'What time is it now?'

Emiko looked at her watch, which lay next to the pillow. 'It's ten minutes past twelve.'

Without a word Sekigawa got up. Emiko watched him get dressed with a resigned look on her face.

'Are you going home? I know you have to, but I'd like you to stay over sometime.'

'Don't be impossible,' Sekigawa scolded as he put on his undershirt and his trousers. 'I've already explained it to you. I can't leave after it's light.'

'Of course, I understand. But I can't help asking.'

Sekigawa walked to the door and opened it a crack. No one was in the hallway. He sneaked out into the hall. He could hear the sound of the mah-jongg pieces as he passed by the student's door on his way to the toilet.

Sekigawa was cautious on his way back, too. He muffled the sound of his slippers. A door opened. The movement was so sudden, it took Sekigawa by surprise. A student stopped in his tracks, startled at seeing another person. The hallway was narrow with no place to hide. Sekigawa turned his head away and kept walking.

As he reached Emiko's door, he turned around. The student looked back at Sekigawa at the same time. Their eyes met.

When Sekigawa had returned to Emiko's room and closed the door, he stood very still.

'What happened?' Emiko asked, raising herself from the mattress. 'Why do you look so angry?'

He didn't answer. He sat on the tatami and, taking a cigarette, started to smoke. Emiko got up from the mattress and came over to him.

'Did something happen?' She looked closely at him.

Sekigawa whispered, 'The student saw me.'

His voice was so low, Emiko couldn't hear. 'What did you say?'

'He saw my face.'

Emiko's eyes widened. 'Who saw you?'

'The student across the hall.' Sekigawa pressed the hand holding his cigarette against his forehead.

Emiko watched him, saying, 'Don't worry. You just passed each other.'

'That's not all. When I turned around, he looked right at me.'

'Really?'

'He saw my face straight on.'

Emiko watched Sekigawa. After a while she said, smiling re-assuringly, 'There's nothing to worry about. He probably didn't really see your face. He couldn't recognize you from one glance and won't remember your face for long. Besides, the light in the hallway is terrible. If he'd seen you during the day that might be a problem. But you don't have to worry now.'

Sekigawa continued to fret. 'I just hope he didn't recognize me.'

'I'm sure he didn't. What did he look like?'

'He was round-faced, kind of stocky . . .'

Emiko nodded. 'Then it's not him, it's not the one who lives across the hall. He's tall and thin. You probably saw one of his friends. So he'd be even less likely to recognize you.'

'A friend of his?'

'Relax.' Emiko frowned at him reproachfully. 'You're too touchy, even about small things. We've been together for a year now, but you're always so edgy,' she sighed.

'I'm leaving,' Sekigawa said, standing up abruptly.

Emiko wordlessly helped him get his things together.

Sekigawa went out to the hallway. He crept quietly to the head of the stairs. No student appeared this time. He could hear the noise of the mah-jongg pieces mixed with the students' voices. He crept down the stairs and put on his shoes. He went out the entryway and closed the sliding door. Once outside the gate, he felt a sense of relief.

All the houses along the street had their night shutters closed. The street was empty. Sekigawa walked down the darkened street toward the main street to hail a taxi. He was still upset. Students these days were lazy. What did they mean by playing mah-jongg all night long? The student might not have recognized his face, but he was afraid that the student would remember him.

When he reached the main street, he saw a stream of taxi headlights. Few were empty. Most of the silhouetted passengers were couples. Finally an empty taxi came by, and Sekigawa raised his arm to stop it.

'Take me to Nakano.'

'Yes, sir.'

The driver sped down the road alongside the streetcar tracks.

'You're out late.' The driver tried to start up a conversation.

'Yeah, I was playing mah-jongg with some friends,' Sekigawa said, lighting a cigarette. 'How's business these days?'

'I'd say better than last year.'

'They say few cabs are empty these days. The economy must be good. Not long ago there were a lot of empty taxis except for rush hour and when it rained, but that's all over now. I hear the

Transportation Ministry has approved an increase in the number of cabs, so taxi companies must be happy.'

'No, they're not. My company is one of the bigger ones, but they're only getting ten more licenses. The company's pretty mad at the Ministry.'

'I understand they meant to make more licenses available to new companies rather than to the established companies.'

The taxi driver suddenly changed the subject and asked, 'Mister, are you from the northeast, from Tohoku?'

'How could you tell?' Sekigawa was caught off guard.

'By your accent. No matter how long you've been in Tokyo, I can tell. I'm from northern Yamagata myself. Listening to your accent, I'd say you're from Akita. How about that, am I wrong?'

'No, that's pretty close,' Sekigawa said, scowling.

4. Unsolved

The investigation had reached an impasse. Even with eight full-time investigators on loan from the Homicide Division of the Metropolitan Police Force helping fifteen local precinct investigators, not one concrete lead had turned up. Morale at headquarters hit bottom.

The two dozen investigators assigned to the Kamata case were all gathered in the gym room of the local precinct station. The chief of detectives of the Metropolitan Police, who was nominally in charge, did not appear at this meeting. The deputy chief, who was head of the Homicide Division, and the local precinct chief were there in his stead.

At each place was a cup filled with sake. Plates of snacks were scattered about the table. The detectives sat around looking depressed. When a case was solved, the final party to disband the investigation team was a happy occasion. But when the case was closed unsolved, the party became a wake.

The head of Homicide stood up.

'I want to thank each of you for all you've done during this long investigation,' he began in a discouraged voice. 'A month has passed since this investigation headquarters was established. Your efforts during that time have been extraordinary. Unfortunately, with no strong leads to follow, we must now close this headquarters. This is truly regrettable.' He looked around at the assembled men, who listened with downcast eyes. 'However, this does not mean that all investigation into this case must cease. We will continue to investigate on a voluntary basis. When I look back on this case, I think that we may have been too optimistic at the beginning. Because there was so much evidence at the scene of the crime, we felt sure of an early solution. Although the identity of the victim was unknown, I think we were too sure that, with so much evidence available, we would soon learn who he was. We found the murder weapon as well as witnesses who had seen the victim and the probable murderer. But despite your unstinting efforts, we have had no further results. Now it seems necessary to reevaluate our initial assessment.'

Imanishi Eitaro listened to the speech with his eyes on the floor. The division head was speaking forcefully, as if he were trying to encourage them. But after all, it was a speech about failure.

Imanishi felt more responsible than the other investigators. Now he even wondered if, as first suspected, 'Kameda' was a person's name after all. After going all the way to Kameda in Akita Prefecture, it seemed that 'the strange man' had nothing to do with the case. When an investigation folded, every uncertainty hounded the detectives. But there was no use going all over it again.

The main speech ended and the local police station chief said a few words. After that the detectives drank the sake in their teacups and broke into conversation. The talk was unenthusiastic. The dismal gathering soon broke up.

Imanishi started for home alone. He would no longer be coming to this station every day. As of tomorrow, he would return to headquarters. Imanishi walked toward Kamata Station. The street lights were on. Clear blue twilight lingered in the sky as the evening turned to night.

'Imanishi-*san*.'

He heard a voice calling him. He turned around and saw Yoshimura.

'Hey, it's you, is it?' Imanishi stopped.

'Since we're going in the same direction, I wondered if we could go together.'

'Sure.'

Side by side, they walked toward the station. The platform was crowded, as was the train. It was the middle of rush hour, and they couldn't stand together inside the train. Still, Yoshimura managed to grab a hand strap not far from Imanishi. From the window they could see the city of Tokyo below them. Neon lights were starting to shine across the stark cityscape.

'Yoshimura,' Imanishi yelled across the crowded car when they reached Shibuya Station. 'Let's get off here.'

Imanishi had pushed his way off the train and to the top of the stairs by the time Yoshimura caught up with him.

'What happened to you all of a sudden?' Yoshimura asked.

'I just wanted to talk to you some more. Let's have a drink somewhere nearby,' Imanishi said as they struggled down the crowded stairs. 'I hope that's all right.'

'It's fine with me,' Yoshimura said and smiled. 'Actually, I wanted to talk to you some more, too.'

'That's perfect. I just can't go straight home the way I feel now. It was like a funeral at headquarters. Let's go drown this bitter aftertaste in some beer.'

'Sounds good to me.'

The two men crossed the square in front of the station and turned down a narrow side street. This area was full of small bars with red lanterns hanging from their eaves.

They entered a narrow bar that served steaming hot *oden*, vegetables and dumplings simmered in a flavorful broth. It was early in the evening and there were few customers. They took two seats in the corner.

'Could we have some beer?'

The owner of the bar, who was tending the simmering pot with a pair of long chopsticks, nodded her head and said, 'Coming right up.'

The two men toasted each other with glasses nearly over-flowing with foam.

'That's better,' Imanishi said, drinking half the glass in one gulp. 'I'm glad I ran into you.'

'I was thinking the same. We won't be working together any-more, so this is good-bye, Imanishi-*san*.'

'Thanks for all you've done.'

'No, no, I'm the one who should thank you.'

'Why don't we order something?'

'I'd like some skewered *maruten*, please.'

'You like *maruten*, too?' Imanishi smiled. 'It's one of my favorites.'

Imanishi finished his beer and let out a big sigh; Yoshimura looked over at him. They weren't supposed to discuss their cases in public, but inevitably their conversation drifted back to it.

'You'll be at central headquarters starting tomorrow, won't you?' Yoshimura asked, tossing off his beer.

'Yes, I'll be going back to my home base,' Imanishi said, as he nibbled at the skewered *maruten*.

'You'll probably be assigned to another case right away, no?'

'Probably. One case after another, the work keeps coming. But even though you're assigned to something else, this kind of case stays on your mind. I've been a detective now for a long time, and I've been involved with three or four cases that were never solved. They're old cases, but they're always in a corner of my mind. Every now and then they pop up. It's strange. I don't remember anything about the cases that were solved, but I can recall clearly the faces of each of the victims of the unsolved cases. Well, now there's one more to give me bad dreams.'

'Imanishi-*san*,' Yoshimura put his hand on Imanishi's arm. 'Let's not talk about it anymore. Today is our farewell to working together. Let's drink to that.'

'You're right. I'm sorry.'

'You know, I have fonder memories of the time we went out of town together than of all those times we trudged around this city. It was the first time I'd ever seen the Tohoku area. I really liked the color of the sea.'

Imanishi smiled. 'It would be a good place to visit again just for pleasure after I retire.'

'I was just thinking the same thing.'

'What are you talking about? You're still young.'

'I'd like to walk around Kameda alone, without a care, with no worries.' Yoshimura's expression turned nostalgic, as if he were seeing the scenery again in his mind. 'That's right, Imanishi-*san*, you showed me three haiku that you wrote then. Have you come up with any more since that time?'

'Hmm, well, I did write a few more, about ten, maybe . . .'

'I'd like to hear them.'

'No.' Imanishi shook his head. 'Listening to lousy poetry would ruin the taste of this beer. I'll recite them for you another time. Well, shall we order one more beer before we go?'

By this time the bar was full and noisy. This made it easier for the two men to talk privately.

'Imanishi-*san*.' Yoshimura turned and leaned toward Imanishi. 'About the Kamata case . . .'

'Hm.' Imanishi glanced quickly right and left. No one seemed to be paying attention to them.

'Your theory that the suspect's hideout is not too far away . . . I think that must be right.'

'You do?'

'Yes, I do. The murderer had to have been covered with blood. So he couldn't have gone far. I think his hideout has to be somewhere nearby.'

'I've looked around with that in mind,' Imanishi muttered.

'The murderer couldn't take a taxi looking like that,' Yoshimura continued. 'The witnesses said he wasn't dressed well. In fact, you can tell he wasn't well off by the fact that he was drinking cheap whiskey in an out of the way place like Kamata. He wouldn't have the money to own a car.'

'Probably not.'

'Then, if he couldn't take a cab, he must have walked home. The streets would have been dark, so he could have walked without being noticed. If he could walk home, he had to live within a certain distance of Kamata.'

'That's true. Even if he walked till dawn, he still couldn't have gone very far. At most maybe five or six miles.'

'Here's what I think. If he went home looking like that, he would have to be living alone.'

'I see.' Imanishi poured Yoshimura some more beer and filled his own glass as well. 'That's a new idea.'

'Imanishi-*san*, you thought that the man lived somewhere else, and used a hideout after committing the crime, right?'

'I'm not confident about my deductions anymore.'

'Don't be so hard on yourself. If there was a hideout, it would most likely be his mistress's or a close friend's place. Since he isn't well off, I could go along with the friend theory; I can't see that he could afford a mistress.'

Imanishi said good-bye to Yoshimura and went home alone. His house was on a bus route in Takinogawa, and it shook every time a bus went by. His wife was tired of the noise and wanted to move, but they couldn't find anything they could afford. In the thirteen years they had lived there, the area had changed completely. Large new buildings had been built where old houses had been destroyed, and apartment houses now filled the empty lots. One of these apartment buildings had been built nearby, and because of it Imanishi's house had not gotten any sunlight for the last three years. When he turned down the narrow street to his house, he could see a moving van in front of the apartment building.

Imanishi tugged open his sliding front door, which tended to stick.

'I'm home,' he announced as he took off his shoes.

'Welcome home. You're very early today.' Yoshiko came to the entryway with a welcoming smile.

Silent, Imanishi walked to the back of the small house. In the tiny garden were miniature bonsai trees he had bought at outdoor markets.

'Hey,' Imanishi said to his wife as she folded his clothes to put away, 'I don't have to go to Kamata tomorrow. I'm back at police headquarters.'

'Oh, is that so?'

'I'll probably be home early from now on.'

Noticing his flushed face, Yoshiko asked, 'Did you stop off somewhere for a drink?'

'I stopped off at Shibuya with Yoshimura and had some beer.'

'That's nice.'

'Where's the boy?'

'My mother came by and took him home with her. Tomorrow is a holiday, so she'll bring him back before bedtime.'

Tying his obi around the kimono he wore at home, Imanishi went to sit on the veranda. He could hear the neighborhood children playing outdoors.

Imanishi asked, suddenly remembering, 'Did someone new move into that apartment building?'

'Yes, did you see something?'

'A truck was parked out front.'

His wife came and stood next to him. 'I heard the neighbors saying that the person who moved in is an actress.'

'That's an unusual type for this place.'

'You're right. I don't know who heard about it, but it's quite the talk around here.'

'If she's moving into that apartment, she can't be much of an actress,' Imanishi said, pounding his shoulder to get the kinks out.

'They say she's not a movie actress. She acts in plays. That's why she doesn't earn much.'

When they had finished supper, Imanishi suddenly asked his wife, 'What's the date today?'

'June fourteenth.'

'It's a day with a four in it, so it's the day of the temple fair at Togenuki Jizo in Sugamo. Shall we go, for a change?'

'Yes, let's.' Yoshiko started to get ready to go out. 'I suppose you're going to buy another bonsai plant?'

'I don't know if I will or not.'

'We don't have any space to put any more plants in the garden. Please don't buy any more.'

'All right, I won't.'

Imanishi intended to buy a plant if he saw one that he particularly liked. It might help put the case out of his mind.

At Sugamo they got off the streetcar, crossed the large square, and walked down a street lined with shops. Outdoor stalls were set up along the narrow street to the temple. Though it was late and many people were heading home, it was still crowded. The glare of bare light bulbs brightened the stalls, shining on people who had gathered to scoop for goldfish, or to buy cotton candy, bags, games, toys, or herbal medicines.

The Imanishis walked to the Jizo temple to offer a prayer. Then they took their time inspecting the festival activities.

There were several nurseries displaying a variety of potted plants. Imanishi stood in front of one of the stalls. His wife pulled at his sleeve, but the bonsai lover in him wouldn't let him leave. He squatted down in front of a row of plants. There were many interesting trees for sale. Remembering his promise to his wife, he chose only one. Yoshiko laughed as he walked over to her, carrying his plant in one hand.

'The garden is too crowded already,' she said on the way home. 'We can't line them all up unless we move to a house with a larger yard.'

'Don't complain so much.'

They had been out for only an hour, but they had had a pleasant time. When they reached the main street, they saw a group of people milling around staring at something near the edge of the road. It was easy to see that there had been a traffic accident. An automobile had plunged onto the sidewalk. Its rear end was smashed. A taxi was stopped ten to twelve yards behind the car. Half a dozen policemen were already there investigating the accident, shining their flashlights around on the ground. One of them drew several circles on the street with chalk.

'They've done it again,' Imanishi said, as he took in the scene.

'My, how dangerous.' Yoshiko grimaced as she looked.

Imanishi peered inside the car on the sidewalk. It was empty. When he looked in the taxi, he saw neither the driver nor his fare.

'It looks like they were all taken to the hospital,' Imanishi said. 'They must really have been hurt.'

'I hope no one was killed,' Yoshiko said, frowning.

Imanishi handed his plant to his wife and searched for a familiar face among the policemen. He walked over to one of them. 'Hello, you have quite a problem, don't you?'

The policeman, recognizing him, bowed respectfully. Imanishi had been involved in solving a case at the Sugamo police station.

'It's quite a mess, isn't it?' Imanishi asked.

'It's terrible.' The traffic policeman, who had been jotting down the main points in his notebook, pointed to the battered car. 'This one's a total wreck.'

'What happened?'

'The driver was speeding. And the taxi driver behind him was looking off to the side. He didn't even notice that the car in front of him had stopped and slammed into it without slowing down.'

'Any injuries?'

'The taxi driver and his fare were rushed to the hospital. But the people in the rear-ended car had only minor scratches.'

'And how badly injured were the people in the taxi?'

'The driver's head went through the windshield, so his face was badly injured.'

'And his fare?'

'His chest slammed into the back of the front seat when the taxi hit the car. He lost consciousness temporarily but regained it when he arrived at the hospital.'

'That's a relief.' Imanishi was glad there had been no worse casualties. 'Who was the passenger?'

'I heard that he was some kind of musician,' the policeman answered.

When Imanishi awoke the next morning he was grateful that he'd been liberated from the recent disappointing case. He looked at the clock. It was only seven, he would have plenty of time to get to work even if he got up at eight.

'Could I see the newspaper?' Imanishi called to the kitchen where he could hear noise.

Wiping her hands, Yoshiko brought him the morning paper.

The front page was full of political news. The headlines were bold and the articles were interesting. Still a bit drowsy, Imanishi turned the pages of the newspaper. There was a series of opinion pieces accompanied by small photographs of each commentator. Browsing through the pictures, Imanishi stopped at one. It was a photo of Sekigawa Shigeo.

Imanishi wasn't interested in Sekigawa's opinion. What had drawn his attention was his picture. He couldn't remember if the photograph resembled the face he had seen at Ugo Kameda, but he thought it was the same person. Yoshimura had said that he was a member of the Nouveau group. Seeing his young face among the photos of well-known figures in various fields, Imanishi realized that Sekigawa must be getting a lot of attention. He couldn't be thirty years old yet, he thought, impressed at such quick success.

Imanishi turned the page, but the sports news didn't interest him. On the city page, a large headline caught his eye: 'Composer Waga Eiryo Injured Last Night in Taxi Rear-end Collision.'

There was a photograph of Waga. Imanishi was startled to recognize another of the men he had seen at Ugo Kameda. He hurriedly read the article. It was about the accident he had come across the night before. Staring at yet another young face, Imanishi felt an odd connection.

Imanishi called to his wife, 'Hey, look at this.' He showed her the newspaper article. 'There's something in the paper about last night.'

'Oh, really? So there were no deaths after all.'

'It seems not. This man was taken to the hospital, but he wasn't that badly injured.'

'Well, that's good.' Yoshiko took the paper and skimmed the article.

'Do you know anything about him?' Imanishi asked, turning over on his stomach to smoke a cigarette.

'Just his name. Sometimes his picture appears in the women's magazines I read.'

'Really?' Imanishi found out once more how uninformed he was.

'There was a photo essay featuring him with his fiancée, a pretty sculptor. Her father is a former cabinet minister.'

'That's what I hear,' Imanishi responded. 'You know, I've seen this guy.'

'You have? In connection with a case?' Yoshiko asked.

'No, it wasn't. You remember, I went to Akita Prefecture a while ago? When we got to the station, he was there. I didn't know who he was. Yoshimura had to tell me.'

'I wonder why he went to a place like that?'

'We were in a town called Iwaki. He and some others were on the way back from visiting a rocket research center near there. Several local newspapermen were asking them questions,' Imanishi said. 'This fellow was one of them, too.' Imanishi flipped through the pages of the newspaper and showed her Sekigawa's photograph. 'They're quite something. They're even popular in the countryside.'

'Their names are in the magazines all the time.'

'That's what I hear.'

Imanishi continued to smoke. His wife left to cook breakfast. He looked at his watch. It was nearly time to get up.

Waga Eiryo's private room at the hospital was filled with flowers, baskets of fruit, and boxes of candy. The accommodations were luxurious and included a television set.

Waga sat on the bed in his pajamas. A newspaper reporter was interviewing him. A cameraman took photographs of Waga from various angles.

'By the way,' the reporter asked, looking around carefully, 'isn't Tadokoro Sachiko-*san* here today?'

'She called a while ago. She should be here soon.'

'I should leave quickly, then. Can we get one more shot of you with all these flowers in the foreground?'

'That's fine, go ahead.'

The photographer clicked away.

After they left, there was a knock at the door. A tall man wearing a beret entered.

'Hi.' He raised a hand holding a bouquet. 'How's it going?' It was the painter Katazawa Mutsuo. He wore his usual black shirt. Katazawa sat on the chair next to the bed and crossed his long legs. 'You were involved in quite a disaster.'

'Thanks for coming.'

The young artist looked around at the luxurious room. 'It doesn't seem like a hospital room at all. It must be really expensive.' Katazawa slapped his leg. 'I get it. You're not paying for it. I bet Sachiko-*san*'s father is paying for this,' he said, grinning.

Waga frowned. 'I have some pride. I'm not letting him pay for everything.'

'Why not? Let the rich pay.' Katazawa filled his pipe and asked, 'All right if I smoke?'

'Sure. It's not as if I'm sick.' Waga continued, 'I'm not depending on the bourgeoisie. You never know when something might happen to them. After all, the present-day capitalist system is rushing toward collapse. Do you think young artists like us can survive if we rely on such a system?'

'I agree with you. But I get discouraged at times. Critics say some nice things about my paintings. But when penniless critics say they like my paintings, it doesn't lead to the sale of a single canvas. You know I don't approve of Picasso, but I am envious that his paintings sell for so much money.'

'I'd expect you to feel that way,' Waga said. 'By the way, how is everyone doing?'

'They all seem to be very busy. Have you heard that Takebe is going to France?'

'Really? He is?' Waga looked surprised.

'It was decided a while ago. Then he's planning to travel around northern Europe. You know how he's always saying that northern European plays need to be reevaluated. He wants to study Strindberg and Ibsen. He wants to create a new direction for Japanese theater.'

'You think along the same lines as he does. You admire northern European painters. You say that the current fad for mere abstraction is over, that we should return to northern European realism as a new starting point. Who were those artists that you admire? Oh, yes, Van Dyck and Breughel, right?'

'But I can't ever hope to go abroad no matter how hard I work.'

'It's not set, so I haven't told anyone yet, but I may be going to America this fall,' Waga admitted. 'A music critic over there has heard about my music and has asked me to go to America to perform.'

'Really?' Katazawa looked surprised.

'It isn't sure yet, so I haven't told anyone.'

'You're lucky.' The artist slapped the patient's shoulder. 'Will you be taking Tadokoro Sachiko with you on this trip to America?'

'I don't know yet. Like I said, nothing has been settled.'

'Don't be so cautious. You're telling me about it, so your trip must be certain. I'm envious. That'll probably be your honeymoon. It looks like both you and Takebe are going abroad. It makes me feel that we're getting close to the artistic revolution in Japan that the Nouveau group wants.'

'Don't get too excited,' Waga cautioned him. Lowering his voice, he continued, 'Just between us, if Sekigawa hears about my trip to America, who knows how he might react? Hey, how is he doing?'

'Sekigawa?' Katazawa responded. 'He's doing quite well. He's written reviews for two big newspapers.'

'Yeah, I read those,' Waga said in a bored voice. 'They were typical Sekigawa.'

'It seems that there's a Sekigawa boom these days. He has several long pieces in magazines as well.'

'That's why some people put us down,' Waga said, spitting out his words. 'We're contemptuous of the popular media, but nobody is exploiting it as much as Sekigawa. He's always alluding to his contempt for publicity, yet he's the one who's making the most of it. Then we're criticized for Sekigawa's behavior.'

The young artist nodded in agreement. 'You're right. He's beginning to act cocky. His recent political opinions sound presumptuous to me.'

'Right. That statement he gave a little while ago, remember? He acted like he was our representative and collected our signatures to present somewhere. That's typical of the kind of gestures he makes. You could see right through him. His real intention was to get his name in the papers.'

'Others agree with you,' Katazawa said. 'Some even walked out of that meeting in protest.'

Waga nodded. 'He acts like he's the leader of the Nouveau group.'

They heard a knock on the door. It opened slowly. A young woman looked into the room.

'Oh, do you have a guest?' The bouquet she held wavered as the flowers brushed against her chin.

'It's all right, please come in.' Waga's eyes lit up as he spoke to his new guest.

'Excuse me,' she said as she entered.

The young woman wore a pink spring suit. Her face was round and she had dimples. It was Waga's fiancée, Tadokoro Sachiko.

Katazawa hurriedly pushed back his chair and stood up. 'I

hope I haven't overstayed my welcome,' he said, as he bowed to her in foreign fashion.

'No, of course not.' Sachiko smiled at him. Her teeth were beautiful and straight. 'Thank you very much for coming to visit him.'

'I was relieved to discover that his injury is slight.'

'There's no need for you to thank him so formally, since this fellow took his time in coming to see me,' Waga said.

'My, my,' Sachiko smiled, and gave the bouquet of flowers to Waga.

'These are very pretty,' Waga said, sniffing the flowers. 'They smell wonderful. Thank you.'

As Waga tried to find a place near his pillow to put the bouquet, Katazawa reached for it. He pushed aside a bouquet in order to place Sachiko's flowers in the center of the room.

'What lovely flowers,' Sachiko said looking at the bouquet that was swept aside. 'I wonder who sent those.'

'They're from Murakami Junko. She pushed her way in here a while ago and insisted on leaving them. She's been after me for a while, asking me to compose a song for her. So it probably has to do with that. She must be naive. She seems to think that I would write a piece for a singer like her,' Waga said.

Sachiko stifled a laugh.

'It's not just Murakami Junko,' Katazawa put in. 'All kinds of strange people are trying to use us. There are so many second-rate artists around who just don't know their limits. All they think about is how to use other people.'

'Is that so?' Sachiko asked demurely.

'Yes, it is. They think about how they can use people in order to improve their own reputations. You'd better be careful, too.'

'I don't think anyone thinks that I'm worth using,' Sachiko said.

'Quite the contrary.' Katazawa waved his hands exaggeratedly.

'If you're not careful, you might find yourself in a terrible situation. Your father is a special person, and your art is new . . .'

'You mean to say that because I come from a well-known family . . .' Sachiko said.

Katazawa became flustered. 'No, that's not what I meant at all. Since I've known you, I've never been conscious of your background.'

'I used to be concerned about that. It was very painful for me because I felt that as an artist I was burdened by my family background. But now it's different. Waga-*san* is very disdainful of family pride, and I've learned from him. I feel that my eyes have been opened.'

'I can understand that,' the artist agreed wholeheartedly. 'Waga's correct. We must constantly reexamine established concepts. We can't continue to reinforce present-day systems.' Katazawa's voice rose.

There was a knock at the door. A gentleman entered, led by a nurse. The nurse handed Waga the man's card, which indicated the magazine he represented.

'Please accept my sympathies for your recent accident.' He had brought a basket of fruit.

'Thank you.' Waga turned to face his new guest.

Katazawa stepped aside. Sachiko helped Waga move to a chair.

'I've come about the matter we arranged before your injury. We would be happy with just some informal comments. Could I trouble you for ten or twenty minutes? I'm sorry to have come while you are still recovering, but our deadline is pressing.'

The topic was 'On New Art.' The editor took down what Waga said, nodding and making agreeable responses. Finally, he stood up and bowed to Waga.

'Thank you very much. We also include brief biographical sketches of our contributors. Could I ask you for yours as well?

An abbreviated one is fine. It will appear in small type at the end of the piece.'

'Place of origin: Ebisu-cho, 2-120, Naniwa-ku, Osaka City. Present address: Denenchofu, 6-867, Ota-ku, Tokyo. Date of birth: October 2, 1933. Graduated from a Kyoto Prefectural High School. After coming to Tokyo, studied under Professor Kara-sumaru Takashige of Tokyo University of the Arts. Will that do?' Waga asked.

'Yes, that's fine. Could I ask why you went to a high school in Kyoto?'

'Well,' Waga said, laughing slightly, 'I was sick about the time I was to go to high school and was sent to some business friends of my father's in Kyoto to rest. I stayed on in Kyoto and went to high school there.'

'So that's the connection. I understand.' The editor nodded in comprehension.

Katazawa had been sitting in a chair reading a book. When he heard this, he looked over at Waga.

'Thank you very much.' The editor thanked both Waga and Sachiko and stood up. His attitude toward Sachiko was particu-larly deferential.

'I'll be going, too,' Katazawa said and stood up.

'Can't you stay longer?' Sachiko asked.

'No, I have an appointment.'

'That's just the kind of guy you are. You were just killing time here until your date,' Waga said, sitting on the edge of his bed.

'Is that so, Katazawa-*san*?' Sachiko's voice brightened and she smiled coyly at the artist.

'No, it's not like that. I'm meeting some artist friends.'

'You don't have to hide anything from us. We'd be happy for you,' she said.

'It's not that at all.' He walked to the door, then he turned around to face his friend. 'Waga, take care of yourself.'

'See you.' Waga raised his hand.

At this moment the telephone on the table rang.

Sachiko attempted to answer it, but Waga said, 'It's all right. I'll get it,' and answered the phone.

'Yes, this is Waga,' he said. 'No, I can't really.'

Sachiko stared into space listening to Waga's voice. On the wall was an oil painting of some flowers.

'I don't think I can make the initial deadline, but I'll make sure that I have it ready in time for the performance.' Waga put down the receiver and turned toward Sachiko.

'Something about work?' Sachiko was smiling.

'Yes. I've been asked to compose something for the Avant-Garde Theater. They're planning to use my music in a dramatic production. I agreed to it before the accident, so I can't refuse them now. They were asking about that. I took it on because Takebe asked me to.'

'Do you have a concept yet?'

'Yes, I have something vague in mind. But it hasn't progressed beyond that. That's the problem.'

'Couldn't you refuse, since it's Takebe-*san*?'

'No, just the opposite. If a friend asks me to do something, it's harder for me to refuse.'

'I see. But if it's a composition for a theater piece, wouldn't you have to do a lot of compromising?'

'Takebe told me to do something daring, but I probably can't go all out. And the theater group is poor, so my work will basically be donated.'

'I think you should refuse that kind of work. You should be concentrating on the work for your trip to America.'

'You're right, of course. Having my compositions recognized and played in America, that's my big chance.'

'I told Father about it. He was delighted. And he said he's willing to fund your trip.'

Waga's eyes shone. 'Really? That would be a big help. Please tell your father that I am counting on him. I think they'll be impressed with my work in America.'

'When do you think you might be going?'

'I'd like to leave in November.'

As Katazawa Mutsuo left the hospital for the parking lot, a taxi came through the hospital gates. It stopped beside him. He looked up in surprise to see Takebe Toyoichiro waving his hand out the window. Another man sat beside Takebe.

'Hi.' Katazawa raised his hand and smiled.

'Are you on your way back from seeing Waga?' Takebe asked, sticking his head out of the taxi.

'Yeah. Are you just going?' Katazawa approached the taxi.

'I thought I'd go see how he's doing.'

Katazawa shook his head. 'You'd better not go just now.'

'Why not?'

'Tadokoro Sachiko is there. She came when I was talking to Waga, so I took pity on them and left. You'd better wait a while or you'll interrupt them.'

Takebe opened the door and got out of the taxi. His companion got out, too. Katazawa didn't recognize him. He was slim and wore a beret.

'Let me introduce you,' Takebe said. 'This is Miyata Kunio, an actor affiliated with the Avant-Garde Theater.'

'Pleased to meet you.' The actor bowed to Katazawa.

'I'm Katazawa. I paint.'

'I've heard your name. Takebe-*sensei* and Waga-*sensei* have talked about you.'

'You know Waga?'

'I introduced them. Sekigawa was with us, too,' Takebe put in. 'It's no use just standing here. Shall we have some coffee somewhere nearby?'

Takebe looked around. There was a small coffee shop directly across the street. The three of them crossed the street and entered the shop. In the middle of the day the shop was practically empty.

'How's Waga doing?' Takebe asked, wiping his face with the moistened hand towel the waitress had brought him.

'It seems he hit his chest on the back of the front seat in the crash, but it doesn't seem to be too serious. He looked fine.'

'Waga has his own car. Why was he in a cab?' Takebe asked, drinking his coffee.

'You're right.' Katazawa thought for a bit and casually said, 'Maybe his car needed repairs.'

'Maybe that was it. Or maybe his license was suspended due to traffic violations. He does speed,' Takebe said. Thinking of something, he asked, 'Where was the accident?'

'They say in front of Sugamo Station.'

'Why was he going through a place like that?' Takebe asked.

'I didn't ask. You're right, though, I wonder why he was passing through an area like that.'

'Was Waga alone in the taxi?'

'It seems so. It would have been interesting if he had been with Tadokoro Sachiko.'

'No, it wouldn't. If Tadokoro Sachiko was riding in the cab, it would have been natural. It would be much more interesting if a different woman had been with him.'

'And if that woman had also been injured, Waga's engagement to Tadokoro Sachiko would most likely have been broken off. That really would make things interesting. Too bad he was alone in the taxi.'

The two of them laughed. Glancing at the actor by his side, Katazawa saw that he seemed deep in thought. Noticing Katazawa's glance, Miyata smiled.

Takebe motioned toward the actor and said, 'You'd better be careful. This fellow is quite popular with women.'

'Please don't make fun of me,' Miyata said, grimacing.

Although his coloring was dark, he was handsome and his manner pleasant.

Katazawa returned to the former conversation. 'Even if it was found out that Waga *had* been with another woman, I don't think his engagement to Tadokoro Sachiko would be broken off. On the contrary, the wedding might be speeded up.'

'Why do you say that?' the playwright asked.

'Because Sachiko is in love with Waga. She's much more infatuated with him than he is with her.'

'Really?'

'When a woman finds out that she has a rival for the man she loves, she becomes even more determined. First she gets angry and jealous. But the point is what she does after that. The woman who breaks off with a man isn't passionate about him. Women who are madly in love are the ones who want the man even more.'

'You sound like you're speaking from experience,' Takebe said. 'So, does Sachiko feel that way about Waga? Waga is a lucky guy. After all, behind her is Tadokoro Shigeyoshi. With his influence and financial power, Waga can do anything he wants.'

'But Sachiko herself says that Waga holds her father in contempt.'

'Sachiko is a bit naive. He's just saying that. Waga is depending on her father's backing.'

The actor in the beret listened silently.

Takebe looked at his watch. 'You think it's all right to go visit him now?'

'It's been a while since I left, so it should be all right.'

The two grinned at each other.

'See you, then.'

'See you.'

The actor in the beret also stood up. 'It was nice to meet you,' he said to the artist.

The three men went out to the sunlit road. Katazawa returned to the parking lot and walked to his car.

The playwright and the young actor walked through the park-like hospital garden and headed for the patients' wing. They walked down the hallway and stood in front of a private room. Checking the number, Takebe knocked on the door.

There was no answer. Takebe knocked again. There was still no answer. Takebe and Miyata looked at each other. At last the door opened.

'Yes?' Sachiko peeked out. Her face was flushed. Some of her lipstick had come off. Recognizing Takebe, she smiled and said, 'Oh, please come in.'

5. The Woman of the Paper Blizzard

Two months had passed since the murder when one day a man showed up at police headquarters. He handed over a business card that read: 'Miki Shokichi, Proprietor, General Store, xx Street, Emi-machi, Okayama Prefecture.' Miki's father had been missing for three months, ever since he had left on a pilgrimage to Ise Shrine. Miki wondered if his father might be the Kamata railroad yard murder victim.

The former head of the investigation team and Imanishi Eitaro met with Miki Shokichi. Miki seemed like an upright young man in his mid-twenties. He looked just like a country merchant.

'What were the circumstances surrounding your father's disappearance? Could you tell us in detail?' the section chief asked.

'Yes. My father is named Miki Ken'ichi. He turned fifty-one this year,' the young merchant began. 'As you can see from my card, I run a general store in a small town in Okayama Prefecture. In fact, I am not Ken'ichi's real son. I was adopted. Father lost his wife early and had no children. He hired me to work in his store, and then adopted me into his family. Then I married a local girl.'

'Hm, so it's what they call getting a son to gain a bride,' Imanishi said as he listened to Shokichi's simple explanation.

'Yes, that's it. My father had never been on a pilgrimage to Ise Shrine, and he said he wanted to go once in his life. He told us that he wanted to take his time and also visit Nara and Kyoto. We thought it was a good idea and urged him to go.'

'I see,' the section chief said.

'We encouraged him because he had worked so hard from the time he opened the store about twenty-three years ago to make it the best in town. I know the difficulties my father has faced, so I wanted him to take this time off. When he left, he said he didn't want to be tied to a schedule. He wanted to enjoy a lazy trip. He sent us postcards along the way.'

'But he never came home?'

'No, he didn't. Since he had said he didn't want to plan ahead, we didn't think anything of it when he didn't come home right away. But when it got to be three months, we started getting a little worried. So I filed a missing person report with the local police. When I filed the report, they checked their records, and the Kamata case turned up. I was shocked when I saw the police artist's sketch of the victim's face. I recognized my father right away. That's why I rushed to Tokyo. I'm sorry to cause you so much trouble, but I would like to identify the victim.'

Imanishi brought out the victim's clothing and other belongings and showed them to Miki.

Miki Shokichi's face twisted in pain. 'Those are definitely my father's things. Father was from the country, so he wore this kind of worn, inexpensive clothes.' His face flushed and his voice cracked.

'We'd like to show you some photographs, just to make sure. We're very sorry, but we have already cremated the body. We do have a written physical description, though.'

The photographs taken by the Identification Division showed the victim's battered face from every angle. Miki Shokichi was so shocked he couldn't breathe, but finally he found a few remaining identifying marks and stated that there was no mistaking his father. Then he bowed his head.

'About how much money did your father have with him when he left on his trip to Ise Shrine?'

Miki knew the amount. It was not a large sum, about eighty thousand yen, enough for one month's travel expenses and lodgings.

'Your father said that he would be traveling to Ise and Kyoto, but he died in Tokyo. Kamata is near Shinagawa. Did he have any business in that area?' Imanishi asked.

'I'm confused about that. I have no idea why Father would have gone to Tokyo when he said he was going to travel to Ise.'

'He never mentioned Tokyo?'

'No, never. Father would have told us if he had planned to visit Tokyo.'

'Since he died near Kamata Station, could he have visited someone in that area?'

'Not that I know of.'

'Was your father originally from the region where you now live?'

'Yes, he was from Emi-machi in Okayama Prefecture,' Miki Shokichi answered.

'You said he started his general store about twenty-three years ago. What was he doing until that time?'

'As I said before, I was adopted after he started the store, but Father said he had been a policeman.'

'A policeman? And where was that? Was that also in Okayama Prefecture?'

'I think so.'

'So he opened this general store right after he left the police force?' the section chief asked, smiling. He began to identify with the victim who had once been a policeman. 'And how is the business doing now? Is it going well?'

'Emi is a little country town in the mountains, and the

population is very small, but the store has been doing well since my father opened it.'

'Did your father have any enemies?'

The adopted son shook his head violently. 'There is no way that he could have. Everyone respected Father. As you can see from his adopting me, he was always helping others. He was so well thought of that he was forced onto the town council over his protests. There just aren't people who are as good as Father. He looked after people with problems and everyone said he was as kind as Buddha.'

'It is very sad that someone like that should have met with such an untimely death in Tokyo. We promise to find his murderer,' the section chief said to console the visitor. 'I'd like to ask you once more if your father had any plans to visit Tokyo when he left on his tour of Ise, Kyoto, and Nara?'

'No, he didn't.'

'Had your father ever come to Tokyo before?'

'Not as far as I know. I never heard that he had ever lived in Tokyo or even visited Tokyo.'

With permission from the section chief, Imanishi began to ask a few questions.

'Is there a place called "Kameda" near where you live?'

'Kameda? No, there isn't any place called that.' Miki Shokichi sounded certain.

'Then, did your father have an acquaintance named Kameda?'

'No, I've never heard of any such person.'

'Miki-san, this is a very important point, so I'd like you to consider it carefully. You're sure that the name Kameda means nothing to you?'

Miki thought for a few minutes, but then said, 'I don't recall ever hearing that name. Who could that person be?'

Imanishi looked over at the section chief. The section chief indicated that he could respond.

'Your father and the person we suspect of murdering him had been drinking together at a cheap bar near the scene of the crime. We have witnesses to that effect, and according to them the name Kameda was mentioned in the conversation between your father and this other man. We're not sure if Kameda is a person or a place, but they both knew the name.'

The shop owner thought some more, but his response was the same. 'I've never heard that name.'

Imanishi changed his line of questioning. 'Miki-*san*, did your father speak with a Tohoku accent?'

'What?' Miki Shokichi looked startled. 'No, Father didn't have a Tohoku accent.'

It was Imanishi's turn to be surprised by this answer. 'Are you sure of that?'

'Yes, I'm positive. As I told you, I was a shop clerk when I was adopted, but I've never heard that Father lived in the Tohoku area. He was born in Emi-machi in Okayama Prefecture, so there would be no reason for him to speak with a Tohoku accent,' Miki said definitely.

Imanishi exchanged looks with the section chief. The fact that the victim had spoken with a Tohoku accent had been one of the main clues. Relying on it, Imanishi had gone all the way to Akita Prefecture. Miki Shokichi's response had completely negated that lead.

'I'd like to ask you,' Imanishi pressed, 'whether your father's parents, your step-grandparents, were born in the Tohoku region?'

Miki Shokichi answered immediately. 'No, they weren't. Father's parents were from Hyogo Prefecture in western Japan. They have no connection to northeastern Japan at all.'

Had the witnesses in the bar been mistaken about the victim's accent? No, that couldn't be. The customers and the bar girls had all repeated that the victim had spoken with a Tohoku accent. Imanishi was puzzled.

'We'll probably be in touch with you again about this,' the section chief said to Miki.

'Will it be all right for me to go now?'

'Yes, that will be fine. We're very sorry about what happened to your father.'

'Thank you very much.' Miki asked, 'Do you have any idea who killed my father?'

'We haven't yet been able to identify him,' the section chief said gently. 'But now that we know that the victim was your father, it will be a great help to the investigation. We now have a clearer picture of the situation. I think we'll be able to arrest the murderer without too much difficulty.'

Miki looked down. 'But why did Father come to Tokyo?'

This was exactly what the detectives wanted to know.

Bowing many times, Miki Shokichi left police headquarters. Imanishi saw him to the front door. When he returned, the section chief was waiting.

'What a problem,' the section chief said when he saw Imanishi.

'Yes, it's a real mess.' Imanishi grimaced. 'All my assumptions so far have been completely invalidated. It's great that we've finally identified the victim, but now we're back to square one.'

Once the meeting with the section chief was over, Imanishi had meant to go back to his office. But now he did not feel like returning to the cramped, crowded detectives' room. He walked out to the back of the building. The thick leaves of the ginkgo trees towered over his head. Above the leaves was a bright white cloud filled with summer light. Imanishi stared blankly at the treetops. He was still thinking of Kameda and the Tohoku accent. Before he left for home, Imanishi called Yoshimura.

'Yoshimura, we've finally identified the victim in the Kamata railroad yard case.'

Yoshimura had already heard. 'I understand he was from Okayama Prefecture.'

'That's right.'

'That's totally different from what we'd suspected, isn't it?'

'We were way off base,' Imanishi responded dejectedly. 'But now at least we have the victim identified. I may be reassigned to your precinct again, so I might come bothering you.'

'I hope you do.' Yoshimura sounded glad. 'I can learn a lot from you if we get to work together again.'

'Don't say that. My theories on this case have been wrong from the beginning,' Imanishi said.

'This is a chance to start fresh.' Yoshimura tried to reassure him.

'I'd like to get together tomorrow.'

'I'll be waiting for you.'

Imanishi left police headquarters shortly after that. It was still light when he got home. The days were longer, but he had also gotten home earlier than usual.

'Why don't you go over to the bath?' his wife said.

'I'll take the boy and go for a long soak then.'

Ten-year-old Taro, their only child, ran around the house excitedly, happy that he was going out to the neighborhood bath with his father.

When they came back from the public bath dinner was ready.

While they were gone, Imanishi's younger sister had come over. She lived in Kawaguchi, on the outskirts of Tokyo. Her husband worked in a foundry, but they had saved up some money and owned a small apartment building.

'Good evening, Brother.' The sister poked her head out of the other room where she was changing out of her street clothes into some comfortable clothes she had borrowed from Imanishi's wife.

'I didn't know you were coming.'

'I just arrived.'

Imanishi made a sour face. His sister always involved them in her fights with her husband.

'It's hot today, isn't it?' she said as she plopped down beside Imanishi and started to fan herself.

Imanishi stole a glance at her. He could tell by her expression whether or not she had just come from having a fight with her husband. He was relieved. 'What is it? Have you two been at it again?' Imanishi talked this way on purpose when he knew that they *hadn't* been fighting. When it was obvious that there had been a fight, he tried not to refer to it at all.

'No, not today. Tonight he's on the night shift, and I'm tired from helping somebody move in all day. So I've come for a rest.'

'Who moved in?'

'A new tenant for one of our apartment units.'

'You mean the room that doesn't get much sunlight?'

His sister had been complaining that this room was hard to rent out.

'She's a single woman, about twenty-five years old. It didn't seem like she had anyone else to help her. I felt sorry for her and pitched in.'

'If she's a woman alone, could she be someone's mistress?'

'No, she's not. Although she does work in the entertainment district.'

'Is she a waitress at a *fancy* restaurant?'

'No, apparently a hostess in a bar in Ginza.'

'If she's moving into an apartment way out in Kawaguchi, she can't be working in a very profitable bar.'

Taking his comment as a slight, Imanishi's sister countered indignantly, 'Of course, the locations most convenient to Ginza would be Akasaka or Shinjuku. But apparently the bar customers are a real problem. They make up all sorts of excuses to see her home after the bar closes.'

'Really? So she moved to Kawaguchi to get away from that? Where was she living?'

'She said near Azabu.'

'Is she pretty?' Imanishi asked.

'Yes, very pretty. Why don't you come and take a look at her some time?'

At that moment Imanishi's wife entered the room with a bowl of watermelon slices. Imanishi's sister stuck out her tongue, embarrassed at what she had said.

'Please eat it while it's cold. Taro, come over here,' Yoshiko called out to Taro, who was playing in the yard, and set down the bowl. 'Oyuki-*san* says all the units in her apartment building are now rented,' she said to Imanishi.

'So she was just telling me.'

Sekigawa rode in a taxi with Emiko. It was almost midnight, and most of the houses along the route had closed up for the night. The only things that could be seen were what the taxi headlights picked up.

'I'm tired,' Emiko said. 'I was thinking of calling in sick today. But I forced myself to go in, since I had promised to meet you.' Emiko held Sekigawa's hand tightly as they sat in the back seat.

'When you moved in did you ask anyone to help you?' Sekigawa asked, looking straight ahead.

'No. The movers carried everything into the apartment. The hard part came after that. Luckily, the woman who owns the apartment building pitched in.' She leaned against Sekigawa. 'I wish *you'd* come to help.' Her voice was both scolding and seductive.

'But I couldn't possibly.'

'Yes, I understand. But I still wish you could have.'

Sekigawa was silent.

'After I moved out, I realized how convenient my other place was. There was shopping close by, and it was easy to get into town. The place I'm in now seems so far away, it's depressing. But since you insisted, I guess it couldn't be helped,' Emiko said.

'No, it couldn't. And it was your fault anyway.'

'What do you mean?' Emiko's grip on Sekigawa's hand tightened. 'It wasn't my fault. You were the one he saw. And even that . . .'

'Stop it,' Sekigawa said, jerking his head toward the driver.

The driver was speeding now. After they had ridden in silence for some time, they neared a lighted bridge spanning Arakawa River. Sekigawa stopped the cab after they had crossed it.

'Are you sure this is where you want to get out?' the taxi driver asked. Looking at the dark levee that extended along the river, he smirked.

'It's scary here. Let's not go too far,' Emiko said, hanging onto his arm.

Ignoring her, Sekigawa continued walking down toward the water.

'How far are you going to go?' Emiko leaned on him. Her high heels made it difficult for her to walk on the pebbled bank.

Across the river neon lights flickered in the distance. Stars glittered in the sky.

Sekigawa stood still and said out of the blue, 'Don't talk so thoughtlessly.'

'What do you mean?' Emiko asked.

'I'm talking about inside the cab just now. You can't tell what the driver overheard. He was listening to everything you said.'

'You're right,' Emiko said meekly. 'I'm sorry.'

'I've told you before. You shouldn't have said that I was the one he saw.'

'I'm really sorry, but . . .'

'But what?'

'I still don't think the student noticed anything.'

Taking a cigarette out of his pocket, Sekigawa cupped his hands to light it. For a moment, half his face was lit up.

'You're just trying to fool yourself,' he said in a dry voice, exhaling smoke. 'You told me the student across the hall asked you about me.'

'He doesn't know who you are. He just asked me what kind of man had come to my room the night before. He was curious. I don't think he meant anything by it.'

'See,' Sekigawa said, 'his asking you proves that his friend said something to him. I tell you, he recognized my face.'

'The way the student across the hall asked me about it, it didn't seem you were recognized.'

'My picture appears in newspapers next to my articles,' Sekigawa said, staring hard at the dark river. 'The guy is a student. It's very likely that he reads what I write. He might have remembered my photograph.'

The black surface of the river glinted in the dark. A train crossed a bridge at a distance, and a band of light trailed across the water.

'That makes me sad,' Emiko said.

'What does?' The tip of Sekigawa's cigarette glowed as he inhaled.

'Well, that you're so concerned. I feel like I'm becoming a burden to you.'

They could hear someone whistling across the river in the darkness.

'You still don't understand?' Sekigawa said, putting his hands on her shoulders. 'It's a crucial time for me right now. If my relationship with you is discovered now, people will say all kinds of terrible things about me. I have a lot of enemies because my job is to criticize people. If they found out about you, they'd be merciless.'

'It's because I'm a bar hostess, isn't it? If I were the daughter of a prominent family like Waga-*san*'s fiancée, you wouldn't have to be so concerned, would you?'

'I'm not Waga,' Sekigawa said, suddenly angry. 'Waga is an opportunist. I'm not like that. I don't say new and radical things and then behave in old and opportunistic ways. It doesn't matter at all to me that you work in a bar.'

'Then . . .' Emiko said hesitantly. 'Then, why are you so concerned about others finding out? I would like to be able to walk with you anywhere.'

'Why can't you understand?' Sekigawa clenched his teeth. 'You know the position I'm in.'

'Of course, I know. I know that your work is different from the usual occupation. I really respect that. That's why I feel happy that you love me. I'd like to brag about you to all my friends if I could. Don't worry, I won't tell anyone about us. But that's how I feel. I do understand, but it still makes me sad sometimes. Like this problem,' she continued. 'You told me I had to move right away because that student saw you. I feel I'm always going to be your hidden woman.'

'Emiko.' Sekigawa turned toward her. 'I understand how you feel, but I want you to see it from my perspective. Until the right time, I have to ask you to make this sacrifice for me. It's an important time for me right now. I'm just starting to make a name for myself. All my efforts up until now and all my hopes for the future could be destroyed by rumors. I don't want to lose out to any of my friends. My world is like that. It's a world where scandal can ruin you. Please be patient.'

Sekigawa took her by the shoulders and turned her toward him.

Murayama, an arts section editor of a newspaper, was walking alone at night down the back streets of Ginza. Many people were still on the streets. He had just left a bar and, as he walked toward some brightly lit store display windows, he passed a young woman walking on the sidewalk. The light from a display window shone in bands illuminating her profile. He thought he had seen her somewhere before.

He wondered if he had seen her in a bar. He kept walking toward central Ginza. He went into a bookstore and looked at the new releases. He wandered farther back into the shop, scanning the shelves aimlessly. His attention was caught by a book entitled *Have a Pleasant Trip*. The instant he saw the book, he remembered.

He had seen her not long before, on a train on his way back from Omachi in the Shinshu region. The second-class car had been rather empty. The girl had gotten on at Kofu and taken a seat next to the window facing him but across the aisle. She had a pretty face. Although she wasn't wearing expensive clothes, she wore her clothes with flair. He had gone to Omachi to report on the construction of the Kurobe Valley dam, so it must have been May 18 or May 19. It was a night train, and though it was not hot in the compartment she had opened her window half way as soon as they pulled out of Kofu. But if that were all, he might not have remembered her.

He was startled out of this recollection when he felt someone tapping him on the shoulder.

'Murayama.'

He turned around and saw Kawano, a university professor who also wrote for magazines.

'What were you thinking about? You looked as if you were far, far away.' Professor Kawano smiled, wrinkling up his eyes behind his glasses.

Murayama bowed hurriedly.

'How about having a cup of coffee with me, since I haven't seen you for a while?' The professor didn't drink alcohol.

Sipping coffee in the brightly lit coffee shop, Professor

Kawano asked, 'What were you thinking about so seriously in the bookstore?'

'I wasn't really thinking. I was trying to remember something,' Murayama said. 'I'd just passed a girl on the street that I had seen somewhere on a trip.'

'That sounds intriguing,' the professor responded. 'Was it a travel romance?'

'No, that wasn't it at all. It really isn't that interesting.'

'I'd like to hear about it even if it isn't interesting. Go on, tell me about it.' The professor's slightly bucked teeth showed as he smiled and urged Murayama to continue.

Murayama said he had been bored with the long train ride that evening. Perhaps it was because he was bored that his attention had been drawn to the young woman who had gotten on at Kofu. Besides her handbag she carried another small canvas bag, like the ones stewardesses use.

After leaving Kofu, the train ran through a lonely mountainous area. At first the girl read a paperback book. Then, when the train passed Enzan, she opened the window wide. He noticed this because it had let in a cold draft.

The girl stared out of the window. Because it was dark, she couldn't have been looking at the scenery. Other than the occasional lonely light from a distant house, there was nothing but a succession of black mountains. He thought that perhaps she hadn't ridden this train very often. Since she had gotten on at Kofu, he guessed first that she was from Kofu, traveling to Tokyo on a pleasure trip. But her clothing seemed too sophisticated. She had on an ordinary black suit, but she wore it stylishly. She had to be from Tokyo after all. From the side, her face was thin, and she had a slender figure.

Murayama had turned back to the book he had been reading. Before he could finish one page, the girl once again attracted his attention. She put the canvas bag on her lap and opened it, and then took something white out of it and began throwing it out the train window. The wind whipped in as the train rushed forward. The girl stuck her hand out the window and continued tossing something out. She did this all the way from Enzan to Katsunuma, the next station.

Then she went back to reading her book. But somewhere between Hajikano and Sasago, she put the book down and again started throwing away whatever it was she had in her bag. Murayama was curious. Pretending he was going to the rest room, he walked to the end of the car. He looked out from the back of the car and saw small, white pieces of paper being tossed by the wind, making a kind of blizzard. He thought she was fighting boredom by this innocent mischief and smiled at her childishness.

Murayama returned to his seat. He picked up his book and tried to continue reading, but the girl on the other side of the aisle kept distracting him. As the train neared Otsuki, she again put her hand in the bag and started scattering another paper blizzard.

The train reached Otsuki Station. Some new passengers entered the second-class car. Among them was a fat man about fifty years old who looked around the car. He finally sat down in front of this girl.

Casually, Murayama continued to watch the girl. She seemed a bit perplexed now that there was someone sitting in front of her. Yet she did not move to close the window. After the train had passed several small stations, she again began scattering small pieces of white paper out into the darkness. The man across from her grimaced because of the cold wind blowing on him from the window, but he just looked at the girl and said nothing.

Murayama resumed reading, and after a while saw that the girl had closed the window. She was now engrossed in her book. He noticed that the legs beneath the black skirt were lovely.

Thinking that they were finally nearing Tokyo, Murayama looked up, and saw that the man was talking to the girl. His attitude seemed a shade too amiable. It seemed that he was the one forcing the conversation, while she offered monosyllabic responses.

The two couldn't have known each other. The man had boarded the train long after the young woman. He seemed to be chatting with her just to pass the time. But to Murayama it did not appear to be a case of casual conversation. The man was very insistent. He took out a pack of cigarettes, but she shook her head. Next he pulled out some chewing gum, but she wouldn't take any gum either. The man took this refusal as mere politeness and pressed her again to have some gum. She finally gave in and took a piece, but didn't unwrap it. The man became increasingly obnoxious. He casually stretched out his legs toward hers. Startled, she drew her legs in. Pretending not to notice, the man kept his legs stretched out and continued talking to her.

Murayama had heard about young girls being bothered on trains by middle-aged men. He decided to interfere if the man continued to annoy her. Although he tried to read his book, he was unable to concentrate on it. He kept watching the situation across the aisle. She clearly looked irritated, but the man persisted.

Gradually the lights of Tokyo appeared. Some passengers started to take their bags down from the overhead racks. The obnoxious man was still talking. The girl didn't have to worry about her luggage because all she had was the small case. When the train passed Nakano, she bowed determinedly to the man and stood up. He stood up as well and quickly whispered something to her. She blushed and rushed toward the door. Heedless of Murayama watching, the man hurried after her.

Murayama closed his book and stood up. The train slid into

the platform at Shinjuku Station. Murayama walked to the door. The man was standing close behind her, right up against her. He was still murmuring in her ear. It was clear that he was trying to get her to go somewhere with him.

'That's why I remembered her,' Murayama said to Professor Kawano.

'What an interesting story,' the professor said and smiled. 'I've heard that there's an increasing number of such rude men.'

'I was appalled. I'd heard about them, but this was the first time I had seen one in action.'

'But I'm more interested in the young girl and the paper blizzard she was creating. You said it seemed mischievous, but to me it seems poetic.'

'Yes, perhaps it was,' Murayama agreed. 'I was more upset by the man's behavior.'

'It's interesting that you couldn't remember her when you saw her, but recalled this in the bookstore. I've been asked to write a piece for a magazine. It's supposed to be a light essay, but I haven't come up with a good topic. Could I borrow your story?'

'Will it work as an essay?'

'I'll put in a few flourishes and turn it into a five-page piece.' The professor took out his pocket notebook. 'Now, tell me again when did this happen?'

'Let me see. It was May eighteenth or May nineteenth.'

'Yes, yes. You said it wasn't hot enough to need the window open.' The professor jotted the date in his notebook.

'*Sensei*,' Murayama said, sounding concerned, 'you won't use my name, will you?'

'Don't worry. There'd be no point in bringing your name into this. This story wouldn't work well in the third person. I'll write it as if I had experienced it myself.'

'Fine. Readers will like it better that way. How about saying that you took a fancy to the girl yourself?'

'That'd be terrible.' The professor laughed. 'Then *I* would sound like a dirty old man. But Murayama, didn't you want to think of some reason to approach her when the two of you were alone in the train?'

'No, not really,' Murayama said, a bit bashfully.

'Was she beautiful?'

'I guess you'd say she was. She was on the slender side. And she had a charming face.'

'Yes, well.'

The professor contentedly wrote in his notebook.

Imanishi and his wife decided to walk his sister back to the train station.

'Oyuki-*san*, why don't you spend the night?' Yoshiko had asked. But Oyuki wanted to go home, saying that she had housework left to do.

'What did I tell you? You said you came here because you were free to do as you liked since your husband was working nights. But a woman can't forget about her household after all, can she?' Imanishi teased.

'I guess not,' his sister laughed. 'I guess I don't feel like staying over except when we've had a fight.'

It was late, and the streets were almost deserted. Soon they passed the new apartment building. Oyuki stopped to look at it.

'I'd like to own something even half the size of this building,' she sighed.

'You should save all you can of your rent income to use for a down payment,' Imanishi told her and laughed.

'I can't. That money goes to pay our living expenses. I'd never be able to save enough.'

The three of them started walking again.

A woman came toward them. The light from a shop lit her profile for only the second that she passed in front of it. She was young and slim. Avoiding the Imanishis, she quickened her pace to pass them.

When they had gone a half dozen steps farther, Imanishi's wife whispered to him, 'That's the girl.'

Imanishi wondered what she meant.

His wife continued, 'She's the girl from the theater company who moved into that apartment house. I told you about her, remember? They were saying she's an actress in the theater, but that was wrong. She works in the theater office.'

Imanishi turned around, but the girl had already disappeared into the apartment building.

'Since she has such a pretty face, everyone assumed she must be an actress,' Yoshiko explained.

'I wonder which theater group she's with.'

'They didn't say.'

'I wonder how much rent they charge for apartments there.' Oyuki's attention shifted back to the apartment building.

Imanishi's wife answered, 'I think they said it was around six thousand yen. But that's separate from the deposits, I assume.'

'It must be tough for a theater office girl to pay six thousand yen a month. I wonder if she has a patron helping her.'

They could now see the bright lights in front of the station.

Naruse Rieko, a clerk at the Avant-Garde Theater, entered her studio apartment on the second floor. It was dark inside, but it smelled like her own room. She had just moved in, but already the air inside felt different. She was relieved to feel it surround her. Her apartment was one six-tatami-mat room, newly built, and arranged for efficiency. Rieko turned on the radio, keeping the volume down. The radio helped to keep her company. She had looked in her mailbox on the way up the stairs, but there was nothing, not even a postcard.

She made some toast. The room that had seemed empty suddenly gained some warmth. On this small scale, the process of living had begun. She had some tea with the toast. When she finished eating, she sat idly for a while. The radio was pouring out music. It was not the kind she liked, but she felt too lonely to turn it off.

Rieko went to her desk and took out a notebook. She turned on the lamp but could not begin to write. She rested her chin on her hand, motionless. She could not shape her thoughts easily into sentences.

She heard footsteps in the hallway. They stopped in front of her door. She heard a knock.

'Naruse-*san*, you have a phone call,' the apartment manager's wife said.

Rieko frowned because it was too late to be receiving phone calls. 'I'm sorry. Thank you.'

She followed the woman down the hallway. The telephone was in the manager's apartment on the first floor.

'Excuse me,' she apologized. When the door to their apartment opened, she could see the manager reading the evening newspaper in his undershirt. Rieko bowed to him.

The telephone receiver had been left off the hook. Rieko put the receiver to her ear. 'Hello, this is Naruse speaking. Who's calling?' she asked. She did not seem pleased at the answer.

'What are you calling for?' She listened and then said, 'No, you can't. Please don't.'

With the apartment manager and his wife right there, she kept her voice low. The call was from a man. The manager and his wife were trying to be circumspect, but since they were sitting right next to her, they could overhear her conversation.

'That would present a problem for me.' Rieko sounded very

perturbed. It was unclear what the man at the other end was asking for, but from her responses, it seemed clear that she was refusing. Over the telephone, the man seemed to persist. She responded, 'I can't,' or 'That would be difficult for me.'

After about three minutes she hung up the telephone.

'Thank you very much,' Rieko said to the manager and left their room.

She returned to her room and stood listlessly, a sad expression on her face. Rieko stared out the window, thinking. The lights of Shinjuku blurred against the night sky. There were few stars. Rieko closed the curtain and returned to her desk. She opened her notebook, grasped her pen, and sat lost in thought for a while, her chin on her hand. She started to write, pausing often to think. She wrote a line, then crossed it out.

'Must love be a lonely thing?

'Our love has lasted for three years. Yet nothing has been built from this love. It will probably continue on in vain. Forever, he says. The futility of this love tastes empty and feels like grains of sand slipping through my fingers. At night, despair haunts my dreams.'

She heard someone whistle a tune, passing back and forth outside her window. She looked up from her notebook. She stood up. Without looking outside, she turned off the light.

The Imanishis were on their way home after seeing Eitaro's sister off at the station. Along the way they came across a row of stalls that were still open – among them was a nursery. Imanishi stopped in his tracks.

'I'm just taking a look. I won't buy anything,' Imanishi reassured his wife.

There were hardly any customers. The shopkeeper encouraged Imanishi, saying that he would give him a real bargain because he was about to close up. Imanishi looked the plants over, but luckily he didn't find any he wanted. Leaves and newspapers were scattered at his feet. Imanishi stepped down to the sidewalk.

He felt hungry. He spied a sushi shop that was still open. He asked his wife, 'Shall we have a few bites of sushi?'

His wife peeked into the shop and said unenthusiastically, 'Let's not. It's ridiculous to spend money like that. I'll cook something special tomorrow.'

He was hungry now. Tomorrow's dinner wasn't any help. But understanding how his wife felt, Imanishi kept his mouth shut. He continued homeward with a dissatisfied expression on his face. He imagined the texture of the tuna, but he restrained himself.

Now the doors to almost all the stores were closed, and the narrow street was lit only by the light from street lamps. In this light, Imanishi saw a man wandering around, whistling. He was right in front of the new apartment building. He was wearing a beret and a black shirt. It appeared that he had been whistling and wandering around for a while. When the Imanishis approached him, he stopped whistling and casually edged away toward the shadows, his head turned away.

Imanishi glanced at him as they passed.

'If you're hungry, shall I make some green tea over rice when we get home?' his wife asked.

'Hmm.' Still dissatisfied, Imanishi did not reply.

The man who had been whistling stopped as the couple passed by. He stood in front of the apartment building, staring at one of the lighted windows, but now the light had been turned out.

After the couple had passed by, the man with the beret whistled again toward the now darkened window. The curtain had been drawn. Next to the apartment building was a narrow alley lined with small houses. He could hear a baby crying somewhere. With deliberately loud footsteps, he walked back and forth several times. No one opened the apartment window. He kept this up for about twenty more minutes.

Finally he gave up and walked back to the main street, looking back at the apartment building. He headed for the station. He looked up and down to check for empty taxis, but didn't see any.

He saw the sushi shop across the street. Through the half-opened doorway he could see three customers seated inside. He crossed the street and entered the shop. Seeing him enter, one of them looked inquiringly at him.

He ordered some sushi.

After staring at his profile, the woman whispered to her companions. The woman searched inside her pocket and brought out a small notebook. Smiling, she approached the man in the beret.

'Pardon me,' she said modestly. 'Could you possibly be Miyata Kunio-*san* from the Avant-Garde Theater?'

The man in the beret abruptly swallowed the sushi he had been eating. Bewilderment briefly clouded his eyes, but he looked at the woman's face and reluctantly admitted, 'Yes, I am.'

'I thought so.' The woman turned around and smiled at her two male companions. 'Excuse me, but would you please autograph this for me?'

She held out her well-worn notebook. He grudgingly took out a pen and signed his name with a practiced hand.

6. The Distribution of Dialects

Imanishi couldn't put the Tohoku dialect and the word 'Kameda' out of his mind. It was possible that the witnesses had mistaken the accent, but he didn't think so.

He went out and bought a map of Okayama Prefecture. Miki Ken'ichi had lived in Emi-machi. Starting from there, Imanishi searched the map for Kameda. At first he looked for place names starting with the character 'Kame.' The name Kamenoko jumped out at him, but Kameda and Kamenoko didn't sound similar. He searched further, but could find no other locations beginning with 'Kame.' He felt teased by Kamenoko. It had leapt from the map to mock his frustration. He folded the map up. It was time for him to head to work.

The train was crowded. Imanishi was pushed up against the backs of the other commuters. He gazed absently at the posters in the train. One poster was fluttering in the draft from an open window. It was an advertisement for a magazine. He read the words 'Trip's Design' and wondered if trips really have designs. Recent advertisements were so strangely worded that it was impossible to figure out what they meant. Imanishi got off the train at Shinjuku Station and changed to the subway. He saw the same advertisement there. He suddenly thought of something completely unrelated to the posters.

When he arrived at police headquarters, Imanishi went straight to the Public Information Department, which served as headquarters' public relations arm. Because various pamphlets were published here, this office had a collection of reference books. The section chief was also Imanishi's former supervisor.

'Hey, it's unusual to see you here.' The Public Information section chief smiled at Imanishi, who bowed. 'I didn't think I'd see you in a place like this.' Then he joked, 'Oh, I know. You're looking for a book on haiku, right?'

'No, but I'd like to ask you something, if I may,' Imanishi said, a bit stiffly.

'What do you need?' the section chief asked.

'Well, I came to you, sir, because I know you are an expert on many things.'

'I'm not really much of an expert.' The section chief grinned. 'But if it's something I know, I'd be glad to help you.'

'It's about the Tohoku dialect,' Imanishi began.

'The Tohoku dialect?' The chief scratched his head. 'Sorry, but I was born in Kyushu, in the south. I don't know much about the Tohoku dialect.'

'What I'd like to know is if there are other places in Japan besides the Tohoku region where the Tohoku dialect is spoken.'

'Hmm.' The section chief cocked his head. 'You mean if they speak it in a certain locale, not if one individual might speak it. You mean if the population of a certain area speaks that dialect, right?'

'Yes, that's what I mean.'

'I wonder if that's a possibility.' The section chief thought it over as he puffed on his cigarette, but he looked doubtful. 'I think the Tohoku dialect is unique to the northeastern region. But I have something that might tell you more.'

He stood up and took from the bookshelf behind him a volume from a set of encyclopedias. He hoisted the heavy volume onto his desk and turned the pages. Finding an article, he skimmed through it.

'Read this part here,' he said, pushing the book toward Imanishi.

Imanishi read the article covering different theories on the distribution of dialects. It was of no help.

'You don't look very happy,' the Public Information chief commented. 'Weren't you satisfied with the article?'

'It's not that. I wanted to confirm something about dialects to see if I had a usable clue or not.'

'And what would satisfy you would be to find out that the Tohoku dialect is used in some other region. Is that it?'

'Yes.' Imanishi nodded. 'But from reading this, I'm convinced that there's no possibility.'

'Hold on a minute,' the Public Information chief said, thinking of something. 'This encyclopedia only gives summaries. It might be better for you to take a look at a more specialized book.' He drummed on the edge of his desk. 'A university classmate of mine is a Japanese language specialist at the Ministry of Education. He might be able to give you some information. I'll call him right now.'

After talking to his friend on the telephone he turned to Imanishi. 'He wants you to go to his office and talk to him directly. I'll write you an introduction if you want to see him.'

'Yes, I'd like to talk to him,' Imanishi said.

Imanishi got off the train at Hitotsubashi and walked toward the Imperial Palace moat until he came to a weathered white building. It was a small structure with a sign at the entrance identifying it as the National Language Research Center.

He gave his name card to the receptionist. A thin man in his forties came down the stairs, Kuwahara, the Ministry of Education specialist who was the Public Information chief's classmate.

'So you're wondering if the Tohoku dialect is used in some other region?' Kuwahara said.

'Yes. I've come to ask you if there is a region like that.'

'I wonder,' the specialist cocked his head. 'There are a few instances of the Tohoku dialect being used in areas settled by people from Tohoku. For example, there is an area in Hokkaido that was settled by an entire village from the Tohoku area, and so the dialect is spoken there. But I haven't heard of any places on the main island of Honshu. Just what is it that you are checking on? I assume that it's related to a case.'

Imanishi described the case briefly.

The specialist thought for a while and asked, 'Was it *really* the Tohoku dialect?'

'The witnesses said it sounded like it. The victim and his companion had only a short conversation, so we can't be certain, but all five witnesses said it seemed to be the Tohoku dialect.'

'Is that so? And yet they were not from the Tohoku region?' the specialist asked.

'We discovered later that one of the men – the victim – was not from that area at all. He was from Okayama Prefecture, in the opposite direction.'

'What? Okayama Prefecture?' The specialist muttered to himself. He thought hard for a moment, and said, 'Please wait a minute,' and stood up.

He walked over to a bookcase and pulled out a volume. He stood there reading for a while. When he walked back over to where Imanishi sat waiting, he was smiling.

'This book is about the dialects in the Chugoku region.' The specialist handed the thick volume to Imanishi. 'Here, why don't you read this section?'

From the look on the specialist's face, Imanishi could guess what he had discovered. He eagerly read the passage indicated.

The Chugoku dialect refers to the spoken language of the Sanyo and San'in routes composed of the five prefectures of Okayama, Hiroshima, Yamaguchi, Tottori, and Shimane. The dialect is subdivided into two groups. One is named Unho dialect from the three areas of Izumo, Oki, and Hoki; and the other, used in other areas, we shall term Chugoku main dialect.

Examples of Unho dialect include the existence of the labial sound in the 'h's'; the faintness of the sounds 'ie,' 'shisu,' and 'chitsu'; the existence of the sound 'kwo'; and the dominance of the 'shye' sound. This has caused scholars to expound various theories to explain the similarities in phonemic phenomena between two widely separated regions. One theory is that the Japan Sea coast region once was in a single phonemic unit that was invaded by the Kyoto area dialect, splitting the linguistic region . . . The phonemics of Izumo are similar to those of the Tohoku dialect.

When Imanishi had read this far, his heart started pounding. There *was* another region where the Tohoku dialect was spoken.

Kuwahara had found another source for Imanishi. This was called *Map of Japanese Dialects*.

'This map illustrates that hypothesis.' Kuwahara pointed.

The map used different colors to indicate the dialect regions. The Tohoku area was colored yellow. The Chugoku region was blue. But within the Chugoku region, one section of Izumo was colored yellow.

'It's amazing,' Imanishi said, letting out a big sigh.

'This is the first that I've heard of it. Thanks to your question, I've learned something myself,' the specialist said.

'Thank you very much,' Imanishi said and stood up.

'Has this been helpful?'

'Yes, it's been very helpful. Thank you for your time.'

It had been worth it to come all this way. Indeed, the results exceeded his expectations. Miki Ken'ichi was from Okayama Prefecture, which was right next to the Izumo area.

Before catching the streetcar, Imanishi stepped into a nearby bookstore and bought a map of Shimane Prefecture. Unable to wait until he reached headquarters, he went into the coffee shop next door to the bookstore. He ordered an ice cream that he didn't even want and spread the map out on the table. Now he was searching the Izumo area for the syllables 'Kame.' The map was full of tiny characters that looked like small insects. It was difficult for him to read each name. Going to the window he searched methodically from the right-hand edge of the map. All of a sudden he found it. There was a town beginning with 'Kame.'

Kamedake was west of Yonago, near Shinji. Deep in the hinterlands of Izumo, Kamedake was right in the middle of the *zu-zu* accent region he'd seen at the Language Research Center. It appeared from the map that Kamedake was a small area bounded on three sides by mountains with the only opening toward the Shinji side. Kameda and Kamedake sounded very much alike. The evidence was finally coming together.

Imanishi hadn't forgotten that Miki's adopted son had said, 'Father had been a policeman.' Had he been a policeman in Shimane Prefecture? He felt he was on the right track now. He felt a surge of excitement flow through him. When he reached headquarters, he hurried to his section chief. Showing him the map, he explained the linguistic theory in detail from the notes he had taken.

'You've made quite a discovery.' The section chief's eyes glowed. 'I think you're right. So what are you going to do about it?'

'I thought,' Imanishi responded, forcing himself to remain calm, 'that since Miki's son told us that his father had been a policeman before he opened his general store, it's possible that Miki was stationed in this Kamedake. I'd guess that Miki and the man with him in that bar had known each other when he was stationed there. Perhaps the other man had once lived in Kamedake.'

The section chief took a deep breath and said, 'You may be right. Let's ask the Shimane Prefecture police to find out whether a Miki Ken'ichi ever served as a policeman there. That's the next step.'

'I'd be grateful if you'd do that,' Imanishi said.

Three days later they received a response from the Shimane prefectural police. The section chief showed Imanishi the report as soon as he came in that morning.

As a result of the investigation concerning Miki Ken'ichi, we have discovered that said person served as a policeman in the Shimane Prefecture Police Department from 1928 until 1938. Said person's record was as follows:

February 1928: officially appointed as Shimane Prefecture policeman, assigned to Matsue station. June 1929: transferred to Kisuki station, Ohara county; January 1933: promoted to chief of police; March 1933: transferred to Minari station, Nita town, Nita county, assigned to Kamedake substation. 1936: promoted to assistant inspector, became chief of patrol at Minari police station. December 1, 1938: retirement at own request.

Imanishi sighed involuntarily.

'It's just what you thought, isn't it?' the section chief said, still at his side. 'Miki was a policeman in the hinterlands of Izumo for a long time.'

'That's right.' Imanishi felt as if he were half dreaming. This time, there was no mistake. For the first time, he felt that he could see the light at the end of a dark maze. He immediately took the map out of his pocket. Kisuki station and Minari station were both in the area where the Izumo dialect was spoken. Miki had spent ten years as a policeman there. No wonder he spoke with a *zu-zu* accent.

According to Imanishi's research at the language center, the people of this area swallowed the ends of words. What the witnesses had heard as Kameda had actually been Kamedake.

Imanishi boarded the Izumo limited express at Tokyo Station. It was scheduled to depart at ten-thirty P.M. Usually he traveled with someone, but this time he was alone. For a change, Yoshiko came to the station to see him off.

'What time will you get in?' she asked as they walked along the platform.

'Tomorrow night about eight, I think.'

'That's over twenty hours. It's a long way away, isn't it?'

'Yes, a long way.'

'I'm sorry that you'll have to be on the train for so long,' Yoshiko said sympathetically.

Yoshiko waved good-bye as the train pulled out of the platform. Imanishi leaned out the window and waved back.

The train was rather empty. Imanishi pulled out the small bottle of whiskey that Yoshiko had given him and took a few sips. In front of him sat a middle-aged woman and a child. She was already leaning against the back of the seat asleep. For a while he read the newspaper, but soon he, too, felt sleepy. There was no one sitting beside him, so he lay across the seat and folded his arms. He used the arm rest as a pillow for a while, but the back of his head started to hurt. He shifted around, but he still felt cramped. Eventually he fell asleep. In his sleep he heard them announce Nagoya Station. He shifted around again.

He woke up at seven-thirty. The train had just passed Maibara. From the window he could see the morning sun shining on a large expanse of fields. Now and then water glistened beyond the fields. It was Lake Biwa. It had been several years since he had come to this area. As he traveled, he thought about the cases that had brought him here.

Imanishi bought a box lunch in Kyoto and ate it for breakfast. His neck hurt from sleeping in a strange position. He massaged his neck and shoulders.

The trip went on and on. He ate lunch at Toyooka at one-eleven. The train stopped at Totton at two fifty-two, Yonago at four thirty-six. He could see the mountain Daisen out the left-hand window. Yasugi at four fifty-one, Matsue at five-eleven. Imanishi got off at Matsue.

If he continued straight to Kamedake, it would take another three hours, and by the time he arrived the police authorities would have left for the day. So there was no point in going all the way to Kamedake today. He went to an inn across from the station and asked for the cheapest room. His per diem was limited, so he couldn't be extravagant.

After supper, he went out to walk around the town. He saw a long bridge. Lake Shinji spread out into the night. Its shores were dotted by solitary lights. Gazing at the night scene, the lake, and the unfamiliar surroundings, he felt melancholy.

When he returned to the inn, Imanishi asked for a massage. It was too extravagant for his travel allowance, but he decided to treat himself to it. In his younger days, no matter what he had gone through, he would never have felt this tired. It must be age, he thought.

Imanishi paid the masseur in advance and said, 'I may fall asleep during the massage. If I do, feel free to leave.' He did start to feel sleepy as he was being massaged, his arms and legs stretched out on the bedding. Gradually, Imanishi stopped responding to the masseur's comments. He had fallen asleep.

Imanishi woke up once about four in the morning. He rolled over onto his stomach and smoked a cigarette. Then he pulled out his notebook and started thinking. He fell back to sleep as he was trying to compose a poem.

The next morning, Imanishi took the Kisuki Line at Shinji

Station. He had expected something old-fashioned, but it was a diesel train. The landscape along the way, however, fit Imanishi's vague expectations. The mountains closed and there were fewer fields. The river appeared and disappeared as the train moved on.

The passengers were mostly locals. Imanishi listened to them talk to each other. He could hear the rise at the end of phrases. But not the *zu-zu* accent.

Imanishi got off at Minari Station in Nita town. The train station was small, but it seemed to be the center of Nita. Descending the gentle slope from the station, he walked along a sleepy street lined with shops selling electric goods, general goods, and clothing. The signs advertising 'Yachiyo quality sake' had to be for the locally produced rice wine. He crossed a bridge. The row of houses continued. Some had tiled roofs, but most were thatched. After he passed the post office and the elementary school, he arrived at the Minari police station. The building was so substantial it seemed out of place in such a small town. The mountains pressed in behind the white building.

He walked into the police station and found only five people sitting at their desks. When Imanishi gave his business card to the uniformed policeman at the reception desk, a plump man in an open-necked shirt stood up from his seat in the rear and came over.

'You're from the Tokyo police?' he said, smiling. 'I'm the police chief here. Please, come in.'

He was led to the chief's desk at the rear of the room.

'I've heard about the case from the prefectural police.' The station chief took out a file from his desk drawer. 'I understand you're here for information on Miki Ken'ichi?'

Imanishi nodded and said, 'Yes. You've probably heard something about this, but Miki Ken'ichi was killed in Tokyo. I've been investigating this case, and we have found that Miki-*san* once served at this station as a policeman. That's why I've come to inquire about him.'

A staff member came over to serve them tea.

'That was a long time ago,' the station chief said. 'It's over twenty years ago, so no one now at this station knew Miki-*san*. I did ask around for you.'

'Thank you for taking time out of your busy schedule.' Imanishi bowed his head.

'No bother. But we weren't able to come up with much. As I said, it was quite a while ago. I don't know if this will be of any help. Miki Ken'ichi was transferred to Kisuki station in June of 1929, came to Minari station in March of 1933, and worked at Kamedake substation. He was already a police sergeant at that time. In 1936 he was promoted to assistant inspector and became chief of patrol here. He retired in December 1938.'

This confirmed what Imanishi had learned from the information sent to Tokyo by the Shimane prefectural police.

'Chief,' Imanishi said, 'I noticed from that brief résumé that he was promoted very rapidly.'

'That's right. It seems quite unusual,' the station chief nodded. 'As I understand it, he was committed to his work, but he was also a very kind person who did all sorts of good deeds.'

'Oh?'

'Yes. He was cited twice for outstanding work. Here's a copy of those commendations. Let me read from them,' the chief dropped his eyes to the file. 'The first one was when there was a flood in this area when the river overflowed due to a typhoon.'

Imanishi recalled the river flowing under the bridge that he had crossed.

'There was a landslide that caused a number of deaths and injuries. In that instance, Miki-*san* acted courageously and saved three lives. He saved one child who was swept downstream.

The others were a child and an old person that he saved by volunteering to go into a house that had been crushed by the landslide.'

Imanishi took notes on this.

'The other commendation was when there was a fire in this area. Miki-*san* stopped a mother who was trying to go back into her burning house and went in himself to save her baby.'

Imanishi noted this as well.

'He was exceptionally well thought of. Everyone who remembers him praises him. They all say that there was no one like him . . . Imanishi-*san*, I first heard of him after we got your inquiry. But I can't understand why such a good man as Miki-*san* met with such a horrible death in Tokyo.'

Imanishi had not expected to hear all these good things about Miki Ken'ichi, although he remembered the words that Miki's adopted son had spoken: that he was a good person, like Buddha.

'But you probably need more than just my report,' the station chief added. 'I know just the person you should talk to. He's not here, but lives in Kamedake, where Miki-*san* was stationed. I told him that you would be coming, so he's expecting you.'

'Yes, and who is this person?'

'Kamedake produces high-quality abacuses that are known throughout the country as Izumo abacuses,' the station chief explained. 'The person I mentioned is an abacus maker named Kirihara Kojuro. His is the top old-style establishment in Kamedake. Kirihara-*san* was close to Miki-*san* at one time. Since you've come all the way from Tokyo, I think it's best if you go and inquire directly.'

'I'd certainly like to meet Kirihara-*san*.'

'Kamedake is a ways from here. There is a bus that goes there, but it doesn't run very often. I've arranged for you to use the station jeep.'

'I'd like to ask you something that may seem a bit strange,' Imanishi said.

'Yes, what is it?'

'Listening to you talk, I don't hear any difference from standard Japanese. Forgive my impoliteness, but I can't hear any of the local accent in your speech.'

The station chief laughed and answered, 'That's because I'm not using the local dialect on purpose. The younger people these days use the local speech less and less.'

'Why is that?'

'The people of this region are ashamed of their countrified accent. That's why we speak standard Japanese when we talk to outsiders. And when we go to Shinji, we tend not to use the local dialect when we get close to town. I guess we have an inferiority complex. The local dialect has a terrible zu-zu accent. Nowadays, only elderly people or those from deep in the mountains speak it.'

'How about in Kamedake?'

'Let me see. Kamedake is probably different. Kirihara-san is elderly, so his accent is thicker than mine. But when you go to speak to him, he will probably avoid using the local dialect.'

Actually, it was the local dialect that Imanishi had come all this way to hear.

Riding in the jeep the station chief so thoughtfully provided, Imanishi headed for Kamedake.

Kamedake station was three miles from Minari station. The distance from Kamedake station to Kamedake village, though, was another three miles. When they entered the village, Imanishi saw that old, thatch-roofed houses lined Kamedake's central section. Some had stones on the roofs as did houses in the north.

The jeep drove on and stopped in front of the large estate that belonged to Kirihara Kojuro.

The driver preceded Imanishi through the gate. Imanishi was

surprised at the elegant landscaping of the garden attached to the house. As they slid open the front door, a man in his sixties wearing a gauze *haori* jacket came out to greet them as if he had been waiting for them.

The policeman introduced him to Imanishi, saying, 'This is Kirihara Kojuro-*san*.'

'It must have been difficult for you to travel so far in this heat,' Kirihara Kojuro greeted him graciously.

The old man's hair was white; he was as thin as a crane; and he had a long face with narrow eyes. 'I apologize for the poor condition of my abode but please come in,' he said in heavily accented tones.

'I'm sorry to impose on you.'

Imanishi followed the master of the house along the polished hallway that was also the veranda. From this hallway he could see the beautiful rock and water garden. The master led Imanishi into a tearoom. Imanishi was surprised once again – he had not expected to see such an elegant tearoom so deep in the mountains. On his way into the village he had seen only poor farmhouses.

The master indicated that Imanishi should sit in the guest's seat and proceeded to whisk a ritual cup of tea. It was the hottest time of day, and the pungently bitter taste of the tea eased some of Imanishi's fatigue. The tea utensils were of the highest quality. Imanishi, who had little knowledge of Tea Ceremony ritual, was stirred to comment on them.

'These aren't really worthy of your praise.' Kirihara bowed formally. 'In our countryside, we don't have much, but the custom of the Tea Ceremony is our heritage from times past. Matsudaira Fumaiko was the lord of Izumo, so the Way of Tea has stayed with us.'

Imanishi nodded. He now understood why the garden was landscaped in the Kyoto style, even in such a remote place.

'It's embarrassing for us to have someone from Tokyo see this – but this is all we have.' Saying this much, Kirihara Kojuro stopped as if something had occurred to him and peered at Imanishi's face. 'Well, I've been rambling on. The police chief has asked me to tell you all I know about Miki Ken'ichi-*san*.'

Imanishi had been listening closely to Kirihara for some time now and he could detect an accent in the elderly Kirihara's speech. Though slightly different from the Tohoku dialect, it sounded remarkably similar.

'I think the police chief must have already told you,' Imanishi began, 'Miki Ken'ichi-*san* recently met with an unfortunate death in Tokyo.'

'I still can't believe it!' The old man's delicate face filled with anger. 'Never in my wildest dreams would I have imagined that a person like Miki Ken'ichi would have been murdered. I can't conceive of the kind of hatred that must have caused it. You still haven't been able to find the killer?'

'Unfortunately, we haven't found a likely suspect yet. Knowing that Miki-*san* had been a policeman, we are determined to find his murderer. That's why I've come to find out about his past from you.'

Kirihara nodded seriously. 'Please avenge his death. A person who would kill such a man is unforgivable.'

'I understand that in the past you and Miki-*san* were close.'

'Miki-*san* served as a policeman at our substation for about three years. It's rare to find such an upstanding policeman. Even after he retired and opened up his shop near Tsuyama, we corresponded for quite a while, though in the last few years, we haven't kept up.'

Imanishi explained the situation to the old man, who listened attentively. 'We've concluded that, since there didn't seem to be anyone who hated him in Emi-machi where he was living, the cause might be here, in the distant past when he had been a policeman. You may think that something that occurred twenty years ago couldn't have any relation to the present, but we don't have any other leads. I won't be asking you for anything specific, I would just like you to tell me what you remember about Miki-*san*.'

Kirihara's face relaxed a bit. He was still sitting formally with his legs folded under him. 'Miki-*san* was still young when he came to our police station. Our ages weren't that far apart, so we became friends. I indulge in a little haiku poetry, and Miki-*san* joined me, composing some himself.'

Imanishi's eyes brightened in spite of himself. 'Hm. That's the first I've heard of this. He was a haiku poet, was he?'

'Well, there has been a lot of haiku written in this area. Every year, haiku poets from Matsue and Yonago, even as far away as Hamada, come all the way to our village meeting. A long time ago, Shikin, a haiku master who was a direct literary descendant of the famous Basho, came to Izumo and stayed for a long time in this house. His stay established Kamedake's reputation for haiku.'

'Yes, I see.' Imanishi's interest was obvious. But he wanted to get beyond his personal interests and hear more about Miki. The old gentleman, however, seemed reluctant to leave this topic and went on.

'At the time that Shikin was staying here, all the haiku poets in the Chugoku region would gather here in Kamedake. I still have the family heirloom, a box the poets used to put the topics in before they'd draw the one they'd have to write about. It was made by a carpenter named Murakami Kichigoro and built like a puzzle box, which can't be opened easily unless you know the secret. As you know, Kamedake is the source of Unshu abacuses, and Murakami Kichigoro was the original maker of these abacuses. There, excuse me for wandering from the point.' The elder Kirihara laughed at himself. 'We old folks seem to spend a long time talking about other things. I'll show you the puzzle box later. Anyway, Miki-*san* came over often for haiku and other reasons, and we were well acquainted. He was like a member of my own family. There aren't many like him.'

'Was Miki-*san* married when he came to Kamedake?'

'Yes, he was. His wife's name was Ofumi, if I remember correctly. Unfortunately she died when Miki-*san* was transferred to Minari. She was also a wonderful person. As a couple, they were like saints. Usually, policemen aren't popular, but everyone liked Miki-*san*. I don't know of anyone who cared so much for others.' The old man closed his eyes, recalling the past.

There was a splash, perhaps the sound of a carp diving in the pond.

'Miki-*san*,' the old man continued, 'was a very humble person. Nowadays the police are respectful, but in those days, especially in a police station like this one, there were those who acted high and mighty. Miki-*san* had no such arrogance, and he took care of everyone. As you probably saw, Kamedake hardly has any fields. All the farmers are poor. They make ends meet by making charcoal, or growing tree mushrooms, or cutting wood. That's about it. Others may work at the abacus factory, but life isn't easy.'

The strong sun beat down on the plants in the garden. No breeze found its way into the room.

'If they get sick, there's trouble paying the doctor's bills. In many households both husband and wife work. Families with children have their own problems. Miki-*san* saw this and collected donations to start a day-care center at the temple. Now we have a welfare commissioner, but there was no system like that in those days, so Miki-*san* filled that role. You can't imagine how many people he helped.'

Imanishi wrote down each point.

'A policeman's salary wasn't high, but from that small

amount, Miki-*san* would secretly pay for medicine for anyone who was sick and too poor to pay. The Mikis had no children, so his only indulgence was to drink a couple of small carafes of sake every evening. Yet sometimes he would even go without that small pleasure in order to help someone else.'

'I can see what a good person he must have been.'

'That's right. People today just aren't that good. I'm not heaping extra praise on him because he was my friend. He was truly a rare person. To give you an example, once a leper beggar came to this village. Let's see, when was that?'

'A beggar?'

'Yes, a beggar. This beggar came to the village with his son. Miki-*san* saw them and made a place for the boy in the temple day-care center. You've probably heard from the police chief that he rescued a baby from a fire and that he saved someone from drowning during a flood. There are more stories just like that from when he was here in Kamedake. One time a wood cutter fell ill in the mountains behind us. It was too steep and dangerous for the doctor to go up to him, so Miki-*san* carried the patient down from the mountain to the doctor. If there was any trouble in the village, Miki-*san* would show up and smooth things over. People went to him for advice on family quarrels, too. When Miki-*san* was transferred to the Minari station, the whole village tried to keep him here. The reason Miki-*san* was here for three years was because everyone begged him to stay.'

The old gentleman's long account ended. Imanishi couldn't help but be disappointed. The more he heard, the more upright Miki seemed. Imanishi felt a secret professional pride that there had been such a policeman in this hinterland. But along with gratification, he felt a sense of futility. He had come convinced that something in Miki's days as a policeman must have been the cause of his death, but Kirihara's discourse yielded not even a glimpse of a reason. Imanishi thanked Kirihara, but his expression was sad.

'I'd like to ask you one last question,' Imanishi said. 'Is there anyone from Kamedake who lives in Tokyo now?'

'Let me see.' The old man cocked his head. 'This is such a small village, quite a few have left for the city. Their relatives get letters, so I would naturally hear if someone were in Tokyo. I can't recall hearing about anyone moving to Tokyo.'

'A young man about thirty years old? Is there someone that age who has moved to Tokyo?'

'I haven't heard of anyone. I'm one of the old ones here and I run this shop, so I hear most things.'

'Is that so? Well, you must excuse me.' Imanishi started to stand up.

'Since you've come such a long way, please stay a little longer. I don't have anything more to add about Miki-*san*, but I'd like to show you the box for the haiku themes. Do you compose haiku?'

'I'm very interested in haiku.'

'In that case, you must stay. I'll have the box brought out to show you. There's no one now who can even pretend to do similar work. Since you've come all this way, you have to take a look.'

Kirihara clapped his hands together to call for a servant.

Imanishi spent some two hours at the old gentleman's house. Before he left, he had been shown the poetry theme box and the poems written on stiff-backed paper left by the haiku poets of old. The poems, too, were stored as family treasures.

Imanishi enjoyed seeing them and would normally have lost track of time, but he was troubled. The victim had been too fine a man.

He was driven back in the same jeep. When they reached the outskirts of the village, he saw the police substation. Imanishi asked to stop. Looking into the substation, he saw a young policeman at a desk, writing. In the adjoining living area, a blue rattan blind swung in the breeze. This was the substation where Miki had been posted. It looked as if it had remained unchanged from Miki's day. Imanishi felt as if he were visiting a memorial.

Imanishi had come back from Kameda in Akita Prefecture with something like a lead. But Kamedake yielded nothing.

7. Bloodstains

Imanishi Eitaro returned to Tokyo, his disappointment all the greater because his hopes had been so high. He reported his findings to his section chief and his department head. He criticized himself for having been so convinced about Kameda and the Tohoku dialect. His superiors tried to reassure him.

In order to shift his thoughts away from this case, Imanishi put his energies into new cases. Still, he couldn't get rid of his obsession. He felt guilty for having spent money from the limited investigation budget on two trips, one to the Tohoku area and the other to Kamedake.

Three months had now passed since the case was opened. A hint of autumn could be felt in the morning and evening air, but the summer days were still horrendously hot. One torrid day, Imanishi bought a weekly magazine on his way home from headquarters and opened it on the streetcar. An essay in the magazine happened to catch his attention. He read,

When one travels, one comes across various intriguing situations. This past May, I was traveling home from some business I had in the Shinshu region. I boarded a night train. At Kofu Station, a young woman boarded and sat across from me. She was quite a beauty.

That was not all. She opened the train window and started to scatter something.

Wondering what it was, I watched her and saw that she was scattering tiny bits of paper out the window. She did this not once, but over and over again, even after the train left Otsuki Station. This young girl reached into her bag to grab a handful of these scraps and tossed them bit by bit out the window. The pieces scattered in the wind like a paper blizzard.

I smiled in spite of myself. I didn't think that today's young girls, who are considered to be extremely pragmatic, would engage in such childish and romantic behavior. I was reminded of the short story 'Tangerine' by Akutagawa Ryunosuke.

Imanishi returned to his house. As soon as he arrived, he took his son, Taro, to the public bath. It was still early and the bath was not yet crowded. Seeing some neighborhood friends, Taro happily started to play with them.

Soaking in the large bath, Imanishi recalled the essay he had read on his way home. He thought it interesting. From the way the piece had been written, the girl seemed to be traveling alone from Kofu to Tokyo. Loneliness might have motivated her. Imanishi had not read the short story by Akutagawa Ryunosuke to which the author referred, but he felt that he could understand such a young girl's feelings. He could see the bits of paper dancing in the darkness and falling onto the tracks.

Imanishi splashed his face with water. Then he got out of the tub to scrub his body. He caught hold of Taro and washed him. He felt relaxed. His mind was still riveted by the image of the girl scattering a paper blizzard.

He sat outside the tub for about ten minutes. Then he went back in to soak. He sat up with a start when the water reached his shoulders. His expression changed, his relaxed face was now tense.

He was unaware of toweling off. Forcing his son, who was playing with his friends, to hurry, he rushed home.

'Where did you put the magazine I brought home today?' he said to his wife.

Yoshiko answered from the kitchen. 'I'm reading it right now.'

Imanishi grabbed the magazine out of her hands. He opened the magazine to the essay. The title was 'The Girl of the Paper Blizzard.' The author was someone named Kawano Hidezo, a university professor who often wrote for magazines.

Imanishi looked at the clock. It was after seven. There should still be someone at the magazine's office. He rushed out of the house to the nearest pay phone and dialed the magazine's number. In response to his questions, he was told that Professor Kawano lived in Gotokuji, Setagaya Ward.

The next morning, Imanishi paid a visit to Professor Kawano. The professor was slightly surprised to receive a visit from a police detective.

'I read your essay in a weekly magazine, Professor; it was entitled "The Girl of the Paper Blizzard,"' Imanishi began.

The professor laughed with some embarrassment.

'As a matter of fact, I've come to ask you about the young woman you saw on the train.'

'Do you mean the person I wrote about in that essay?'

'Yes. I'm concerned about something related to a certain case, so I'd like to ask you about that woman's appearance and clothing.'

'I'm a bit embarrassed.' The professor gave a confused laugh. 'Actually, I'm not the one who saw that girl.'

It was Imanishi's turn to be surprised. 'Then what about your piece in the magazine?'

'Well,' the professor said, waving his hands, 'I'm afraid I've been found out. I heard that story from a friend of mine, but to make it more interesting I wrote it as if it were my own eyewitness account. I didn't dream that I'd be ambushed like this. I've really made a mess of it.' Professor Kawano put his hand to his forehead.

'But Professor, your friend's story, it's not a fabrication, is it?'

'No, it's a true story. He's not the type to make things up, so I'm sure it really happened.'

'Professor, could you please introduce me to your friend?'

The professor agreed.

That afternoon, Imanishi telephoned Murayama, the editor. Over the telephone, Murayama offered to meet Imanishi at a coffee shop near the newspaper.

Murayama laughed when he heard Imanishi's question. 'It happened just the way I told Professor Kawano. He wrote it up for the weekly right away. He promised to treat me when he receives his fee, but I didn't think it would become a police matter.'

'That's not it. Sometimes cases that seem to be at a dead end are solved unexpectedly. If you hadn't told your story to Professor Kawano, he wouldn't have written that essay, and I wouldn't have thought of a clue. I'd like to thank you for telling your story to Professor Kawano.'

'You're certainly welcome, then.' Murayama rubbed his head sheepishly.

'What did the girl look like?' Imanishi asked.

'Let me see. She was in her mid-twenties and was a petite girl with a pretty face. She didn't wear heavy makeup. And her clothes were stylish.'

'What was she wearing?'

'I don't know much about women's clothing, but she was wearing an ordinary black suit and a white blouse.'

'I see.'

'The suit didn't seem to be of high quality, but she knew how to wear it, so that it looked good on her. Besides her black handbag, she also had a blue canvas bag.'

'That's quite helpful. And quite detailed.' Imanishi was satisfied. 'Could you tell me something more about her face?'

Murayama closed his eyes halfway and said, 'Her eyes were rather large and her mouth was demure. It's hard for me to describe the girl's face, but if I think of an actress she resembles, I'd say she looks like Okada Mariko.'

Imanishi was not familiar with this actress's face, but he made a note to look at a photograph of her later.

'Was the location where you saw the paper fragments the same as the place Professor Kawano described in his essay?'

'Yes. There's no mistake. I watched her, thinking that she was doing something strange.'

'When did this happen?'

'It was on my way back from the Shinshu region, so it must have been May nineteenth.'

Imanishi got on a train on the Chuo Line. His destination was Enzan. On his way there, he opened a window on the right side of the train and stuck his neck out like a child. After the train had passed Lake Sagami, he started to look intently along the tracks. The hillsides were overgrown with summer grass and in the fields the rice plants were green. Imanishi watched carefully, but there was no way he could see what he was searching for as the train sped past.

Over three months had gone by since the girl had scattered the paper blizzard. It was doubtful if the bits of paper would still be there. But there was a possibility that some fragments might remain in the tall grass.

Imanishi alighted from the train at Enzan Station and sought out the stationmaster to ask permission to walk along the tracks. Then he started walking slowly toward Katsunuma along the narrow path beside the railroad tracks with his eyes on the ground. It was a hot day. He had to look carefully among the small stones wedged in between the railroad ties as well as among the blades of grass on the cutting alongside the tracks.

Imanishi had realized his task would be difficult. But once he had actually begun it, he discovered how truly hopeless it was. If he wanted to do a complete search for the paper fragments, he would have to hire some laborers to mow the grass along the tracks. Even so, since the area was so large, it was like searching for a diamond in a desert. His only hope was that the pieces might still be white so that they would stand out from the green of the grass.

He became disgusted at all the garbage discarded along the tracks. Yet he had come all this way; it would be a shame to give up and go home. He was determined to discover just one piece no matter what it took. A lizard, flashing its blue back, darted in front of Imanishi.

He walked in the direct heat of the sun, staring at the brightly lit ground. Soon it made him dizzy. The steel tracks were scorching.

From Enzan to Katsunuma his effort was wasted.

At Katsunuma Station, Imanishi drank some water. After resting a while, he started out again. The distance from Katsunuma to Hajikano was also long. Eventually he passed Hajikano. As Imanishi walked he wiped the perspiration out of his eyes. Unless he continued to look carefully at the ground, he was afraid he might miss something. After all, he was searching for only a tiny fragment.

During his trek, several trains passed him in both directions. There was a breeze immediately after they passed, but then the sweltering heat returned. His body was tired, but it was his eyes that gave out first. Imanishi plodded along, but he didn't find what he was looking for. He started to give up. So much time had passed that finding something now would take a miracle. The tracks began to slope upward toward the mountain. He could see the entrance to the Sasago Tunnel in the distance. The steep mountainside dropped off toward the tracks from either side. The bright white of the concrete restraining wall hurt his eyes. He couldn't search inside the tunnel; he hadn't brought along a flashlight.

Imanishi was now close to the tunnel and was about to turn back. Then he saw something in the grass beside the tracks, two or three small, dirty brownish fragments, stuck on the ground as if caught on something. Imanishi crouched down. Carefully he picked up one fragment by the edge and examined it closely.

It was a piece of cloth about one inch square. The color had changed, but the material had obviously come from a cotton shirt. The rain and sun had changed the color to a dirty gray, but he could see some spots, as if brown paint had splattered it. Imanishi picked up another piece. On this, the brownish area was larger and covered about half of the fragment. Imanishi picked up more. In all there were six pieces. In each case the size of the brownish spots varied and the cloth had turned dark gray.

Imanishi put his collection carefully into the empty cigarette pack that he was carrying and closed the flap.

The cloth fragments looked like they had been cut with scissors. Imanishi could tell that the material was of good quality. He couldn't be sure, but it seemed to be a cotton-synthetic blend. Imanishi thought back. The man who had appeared in the bar in Kamata had been wearing a light gray sports shirt. The cloth fragments were dirty, but it seemed that the original color could have been a light gray.

Encouraged, Imanishi walked back to Hajikano Station to catch the next train. He rode the train through the tunnel and got off at Sasago Station. Here, too, he walked along the tracks.

The pieces he had recovered had given him something definite to look for. Judging from the way the fragments he had discovered had fallen, he figured that there would be a greater chance of finding them in the grassy areas.

Imanishi walked five hundred yards and stopped to rest, then he walked three hundred yards and stopped again. Otherwise, he got dizzy. When he had walked about a thousand yards, resting off and on, he saw another bunch of fragments lying next to a lunch box discarded on the grass. Imanishi slid down the slope and carefully picked up the pieces. This time the fragments were mostly whitish, but they were unmistakably the same as those he had already placed in his cigarette case. Imanishi spent about an hour searching this area, but he was unable to discover any more pieces.

Imanishi walked all the way to Otsuki Station. The bustle of the town became louder, and the railroad tracks were intersected by crossings. Imanishi entered a restaurant in front of the station and poured some water over his head. If he had continued plodding in the sun, he would have fainted from sunstroke.

Next was the section between Saruhashi and Torizawa. It would be quicker for him to walk than wait for the next train. Crossing the railroad bridge, he looked to his left and saw Saruhashi bridge, which the woodblock print master Hiroshige had drawn. He again followed the tracks and was struck by the sickening aroma of the grass. The burning sun was finally moving toward the west, but the heat had not diminished. The heat waves rising from the ground nearly overpowered Imanishi's eyes and nose. He continued to walk. The railroad tracks curved ahead of him and glinted in the sunlight. Imanishi felt that his investigation had finally gotten on track.

He returned to Tokyo police headquarters. He had been able to gather thirteen fragments of cloth along the tracks between Enzan Station and Lake Sagami Station. He established that they were all of the same cloth and had been cut into bits.

Imanishi went to the Identification Division. He turned over the cloth fragments to the technician Yoshida, who said, 'In view of the efforts you've made to find these, I'll try to get the results as soon as possible.'

The testing procedure involved ascertaining whether the stains were blood; if they were bloodstains, whether they were human blood; and if they were human bloodstains, isolating the blood type.

'Imanishi-*san*,' Yoshida reported, 'the bloodstains on these cloth fragments are type O.'

Imanishi had noted Miki's blood type in his notebook. Miki had type O blood.

Imanishi reported this finding to his superiors. They were generous with their encouragement. Imanishi gave a little jump for joy. The next step was to find the girl who looked like the actress Okada Mariko. Imanishi promised himself that he would find the girl, just as he had found the cloth fragments along the railroad tracks.

Imanishi had no clue other than that the girl had taken a night train to Tokyo on the Chuo Line over three months ago. There were hundreds of thousands of young women in Tokyo who fit her description. But Imanishi was sure she had helped Miki's murderer. The murder had been committed in the middle of the night of May 11, and the fragments had been scattered from the train window on May 19, so there was a gap of about one week. During that time, the girl had hidden the murderer's bloodstained clothes.

Armed with a general description of the woman, detectives targeted rental rooms and apartments along the Mekama and Ikegami lines, but no clues surfaced from their inquiries. Suspecting that this girl might be a hostess at a bar or nightclub, the investigation was extended to the entertainment districts.

One morning, as Imanishi was drinking his tea after his breakfast before he had to leave for work, Yoshiko came running back from the tobacco stand where she had gone to buy her husband some cigarettes.

Imanishi lowered his teacup. 'What is it?'

'Someone's committed suicide in that apartment house.'

Imanishi wasn't much interested in suicides. But Yoshiko continued, her eyes bright with excitement. 'It's the girl we saw once who works for the theater group, remember?'

'Eh?' Imanishi was surprised. 'That girl?' Imanishi remembered the slim girl they had passed on the street. 'That's surprising.'

'Isn't it? I was shocked when I heard. To think that she would commit suicide. You really can't tell.'

'When did she die?'

'The apartment owner discovered her at seven this morning. Apparently she had taken two hundred sleeping pills. There's a crowd of people gathered in front of the apartment house now.'

'Hm.' Imanishi recalled the face he had seen under the dim streetlight. 'Why did she commit suicide?'

'I don't really know; but since she was young, it may have been a love affair.'

'I wonder. It's a shame; she had her whole life ahead of her.'

Imanishi took off his kimono and changed to his street clothes. As he was buttoning his shirt, something occurred to him.

'Hey,' he called to his wife. 'Did you see that girl very often?'

'Yes, I did.'

'What did she look like?'

'Well, she had a pretty, slender face with big eyes.'

'Did she look like Okada Mariko?'

'Let me think.' His wife stared off into space. 'Now that you mention it, she did look a bit like Okada Mariko. Yes, that was the general impression she made.'

Imanishi suddenly frowned and hurriedly put on his jacket.

'I'm off.'

'Have a good day.' His wife saw him to the door.

Imanishi walked quickly to the apartment house. Some neighbors were standing outside, looking at the apartment. A patrol car from the local police station was parked at the entrance. Imanishi walked up the stairs. The suicide had occurred in Number 5 on the second floor. A policeman from the local station was standing outside the apartment. He recognized Imanishi and nodded a greeting.

'Thanks for your efforts,' Imanishi said and stepped into the room.

Policemen stood around as the medical examiner squatted to examine the body.

Imanishi recognized all of the men there. 'Could I take a look at the body?'

Imanishi peered at the body from above. Her hair was nicely styled and she had on makeup. She had known that she would be seen by others after she died. She seemed to be wearing her best clothes. The room was tidy and clean.

Imanishi stared at the dead girl's face. It was a pretty face. There was no doubt that she was the girl he had passed on the street. Her face was slender and her shapely lips were slightly open. Her eyes were closed, but judging from the shape of the sockets, they would have been large if opened. The medical examiner was dictating information to his assistant. Imanishi waited until he was finished.

'Was it sleeping pills?' Imanishi asked one of the policemen in a low voice.

'Yes. She was discovered this morning, and we estimate that the time of death was about eleven last night,' the policeman responded.

'Any suicide note?'

'Not really. But there's a journal that could be taken as such.'

'What was her name?'

'Naruse Rieko, age twenty-five. She's a staff member at the Avant-Garde Theater,' the policeman answered, consulting his notebook.

Imanishi looked around the room. Everything was put away carefully, as if she had been expecting guests. Imanishi's gaze fell on a small wardrobe in the corner of the room.

'There's something I'm concerned about,' Imanishi said to the policeman. 'Is it all right if I open the wardrobe?'

'Please, go ahead.' The policeman agreed at once. Since this wasn't a murder case but an obvious suicide, the regulations were not that strictly observed.

Imanishi stepped quietly to the wardrobe and opened the door. Several pieces of clothing hung on hangers. Imanishi focused on one of them. It was a black suit. He stared at the suit. Then without a word, he closed the door.

He scanned the room, and his eyes alighted on a blue canvas bag set between the desk and a small bookcase. It was the type of bag carried by stewardesses. Taking out his notebook, Imanishi jotted down a description of the bag.

About this time, the medical examination was finally finished. Imanishi knew the examiner from other cases.

'Thank you very much, Doctor,' Imanishi said, bowing.

'Oh, it's you. What are you doing here?' The doctor looked suspicious. This was not the kind of case to involve a homicide detective from headquarters.

'I live in the neighborhood. So I just stopped by to take a look. I've seen her several times, so I feel some sort of connection.'

'That's kind of you. Please say a prayer for her.'

The doctor stepped aside. Imanishi knelt beside the body and pressed his hands together in prayer. The light from the window shone on Naruse Rieko's face, giving it a bright and pure look.

'Doctor,' Imanishi said, turning toward the medical examiner, 'you're sure it was suicide?'

'There's no mistake. She'd taken about two hundred sleeping pills. The empty bottle was by her pillow.'

'So there's no need for an autopsy?'

'Absolutely none. It's clearly a suicide.'

Imanishi stood up. Then he walked over to the policeman. 'You said that there was no note, but there was a journal. Could I take a look at it?'

'Please, go ahead.' The policeman went over to the desk. The top of the desk was cleared off. He opened the drawer. 'This is it.' It was a lecture notebook and had been left open. 'She seems to have written her thoughts in it every now and then.'

Imanishi nodded in silence and read the words on the page. They were written in a cultured script.

Must love be a lonely thing?

Our love has lasted for three years. Yet nothing has been built from this love. It will probably continue on in vain. Forever, he says. The futility of this love tastes empty and feels like grains of sand slipping through my fingers. At night, despair haunts my dreams. And yet I must be strong. I must believe in him. I must protect this lonely love. I must persuade myself to be content with this loneliness, to find happiness within it. I must cling to this hopeless thing. This love always demands sacrifices of me. I must feel the joy of a martyr as I make sacrifices. Forever, he says. As long as I live, he will continue to demand that I make sacrifices.

Imanishi flipped through the notebook. All that was described were abstract feelings. It was written so that only the writer herself could understand it.

Again, with permission from the policeman, Imanishi picked up the bag that he had seen. He unzipped it. The contents had been cleaned out, and nothing remained in the bag. Imanishi searched in the corners, but he did not find any cloth fragments.

'So, she committed suicide because she was heartbroken,' the policeman from the local station said to Imanishi. 'You can tell from what she wrote in the journal. Young women her age are so susceptible.'

Imanishi nodded. His thoughts were elsewhere. It did appear as if this young woman had been disappointed in love. Could it be that, in addition, she had a sense of guilt and that guilt had driven her to her death? Imanishi envisioned her scattering to the wind the small fragments of a man's bloodstained shirt. He left the room and descended the stairs.

The woman who managed the apartment house was pale, still tense from the unexpected incident. Imanishi recognized her.

'You've got a terrible situation on your hands,' he said sympathetically.

'I never expected . . .' she responded, her voice faltering.

'I didn't know her really, but it's too bad. She seemed like a nice girl. Did she seem sad all the time?'

'She's only been here a short while, and she didn't say much, so I don't know. But she seemed like a well-mannered young woman.'

'I understand she worked as a staff member at a theater?'

'Yes.'

'Then did she have men friends or a lot of young people coming to visit her?'

'No.' The woman shook her head. 'There was never anything like that. It's been about two and a half months since she moved in, but no one came to visit her.'

'I see.' Imanishi thought a bit, and asked, 'Even if she didn't let him in her room, did you see her with a young man near the apartment house?'

'Let me see.' The woman cocked her head. 'I don't think so.'

'Did you ever see her talking to a young man wearing a beret?'

'No, I never saw anyone like that.'

Imanishi remembered the young man wearing a beret who was loitering one night outside the girl's window. He'd been whistling some tune.

'Was there a man wandering about whistling? Whistling to signal or invite the girl out.'

Her answer was negative as to this as well, 'I can't remember anything like that.'

Then perhaps it had only been that one night. If it had been more frequent, this woman would have heard it and remembered it.

Imanishi went outside. Had the girl he had been searching for been living so close to him? Was the girl of the paper blizzard the theater staff member living in his neighborhood whom he had seen several times? It was hard for him to believe.

In his mind's eye he saw the tall, young man in a beret who had been hanging around outside her window. He had let it go at the time. He regretted not having made more of an effort to find out who the young man was. Now it was too late.

The woman who managed the apartment said that Rieko was always alone and never had visitors, so the young man in the beret must have been trying to call her out by whistling to her.

All of a sudden, Imanishi remembered the young man who had wandered around acting strange at Kameda. It was just a thought. He decided to go to the Avant-Garde Theater and ask about Rieko.

Imanishi came out of the back street. The sushi shop was getting ready for business. A young man was hanging the shop curtain outside to let customers know that it was open. The

man with the beret might have stopped in there to have some sushi. Imanishi walked across the street.

'Good morning.'

The young man turned around and bowed to Imanishi. They knew Imanishi at this shop. He sometimes called to have sushi delivered to his home. 'We're not open yet,' the young man said.

'No, no, I haven't come to eat. I'd just like to ask a few questions. Is the master in?'

'Yes, he's inside preparing the fish.'

Excusing himself, Imanishi went inside the shop.

The shop master put down his knife when he saw Imanishi. 'Welcome.'

'Good morning.' Imanishi sat on a stool at the counter while the shop was still being cleaned. 'Sorry to bother you when you're so busy. I came in because I wanted to ask you something.'

'Yes, sir, what is it?' The sushi master took off his headband.

'It was quite a while ago, so you may not remember. Did a tall man in a beret come here to eat some sushi toward the end of last month, late at night?'

'A beret, you say.' The sushi master thought a while.

'A tall young man.'

'What did he look like?'

'I don't know what his face looks like, but he may be an actor.'

'An actor?'

'Not a movie actor, a stage actor. In modern dramas.'

'Ah.' When he heard that, the sushi master nodded energetically, indicating that he understood. 'Yes, yes, there was someone like that who came in. I definitely remember an actor who wore a beret. It must have been toward the end of July.'

'Hm. Did he eat some sushi?'

'Yes. It was around eleven. He dropped in alone. There were three other young customers already eating. One of them, a girl, went right up to the fellow with the beret and asked him for his autograph.'

'Did you get his name?'

'It was Miyata Kunio. He's known as a young leading man in the Avant-Garde Theater.'

'He's not a leading man,' the young worker put in from the side. 'He's a character actor, he plays any kind of part.'

'I see, Miyata Kunio.' Imanishi noted it down. 'Does he come here often?'

'No, that was the only time.'

Imanishi got off the streetcar at Aoyama Yonchome. The Avant-Garde Theater was located less than two minutes from this stop. In front were posters announcing its current production. The front door was the main entrance to the theater. Imanishi asked for directions to the office at the ticket booth.

Inside, the office was cramped, barely room enough for the five desks. The floor was covered with boxes. Colorful posters from the theater's productions plastered the walls. There were three staff members in the room, one young woman and two young men.

Imanishi went to the counter and said, 'I'd like to inquire about something.'

Hearing this, the girl stood up.

'Is Miyata Kunio-san here?' Imanishi asked.

'Is Miyata-san here now?' the girl turned around and asked one of the men.

'Yeah, he showed up a little while ago. He should be in the rehearsal hall.'

'Could I give him your name?' she asked.

'Please tell him it's Imanishi.'

'Wait a moment, please.'

The girl left the office by going through a glass door that separated the office from the rehearsal area. Imanishi took out a cigarette and began smoking. The two staff members worked on their abacuses and examined the ledgers, ignoring Imanishi. Imanishi waited, gazing at the words 'People from the Underground' on one of the posters.

After a while the door at the back of the office opened. The girl reappeared, followed by a tall man.

Imanishi studied him closely as he came nearer. He was about twenty-seven or -eight. His hair was long, and he wore a short-sleeved print shirt and a pair of slacks.

'My name is Miyata,' the actor said and bowed. His attitude was that of someone used to dealing with people he did not know.

'Sorry to bother you when you're so busy,' Imanishi said. 'My name is Imanishi. I came because I want to ask you something. Could you step outside with me for a minute?'

Miyata Kunio looked displeased at first. But when Imanishi discreetly showed him his police identification, his expression turned to surprise.

'I just want to ask you a few questions, and this is probably not the right place,' Imanishi said, looking around the office. 'So shall we go to a coffee shop?'

Miyata Kunio nodded submissively and followed Imanishi outside. They went to a nearby coffee shop together. As it was still morning, there were no other customers. An employee was washing the windows. The two men took seats at a table toward the back of the shop. Miyata Kunio's face, lit by the sunlight streaming in from the window, was apprehensive.

In an attempt to make him relax, Imanishi started off by making small talk. 'I know absolutely nothing about contemporary drama,' Imanishi began. 'Do you play leading roles?'

'No, I'm only a beginner.'

'I see. It must be hard.'

Imanishi offered him a cigarette. The two drank their coffee.

'Miyata-*san*, I'm sorry to have disturbed you during your work. Were you in the middle of rehearsing?'

'I'm free right now.'

'Good. Excuse me for being so abrupt, but do you know a young woman named Naruse Rieko, a staff member at the theater?'

It seemed that Miyata's face twitched when he heard the question. Imanishi had thought when he visited the theater office that the theater members, including Miyata, must not have heard yet about Naruse Rieko's suicide. But Imanishi thought Miyata flinched for a different reason.

'Miyata-*san*, Naruse-*san* has committed suicide.'

'What?' Miyata's eyes opened wide. After staring at the detective for a while, he stammered, his face changing color, 'Is . . . is that the truth?'

'Yes, last night. I was there this morning. There's no mistake. Hasn't the theater been notified yet?'

'I didn't know anything . . . Oh, yes, I did hear that the staff director went rushing out for some reason. I wonder if it was because of this?'

'It could be. Were you close to Naruse-*san*?'

A fly crawled up the window.

Miyata Kunio looked down and took a while to answer.

'Well, were you?' Imanishi repeated.

'I certainly knew her well.'

'I see. What I wanted to ask you, Miyata-*san*, is whether you might have any idea as to the reason behind Naruse-*san*'s suicide.'

With a mournful expression, the actor put his fingers to his chin. Imanishi watched his expression intently.

'This isn't a murder, so it may not be my place to inquire.

Even though it may be impolite to the deceased, we would like to know any hidden reason for Naruse-*san*'s suicide. I say this because there is some connection with another case. I'm sorry I can't go into details about that, but I can tell you that is why I'm asking you these questions.'

'But, I . . .' Miyata answered in a low voice, 'I don't know why Naruse-*san* would commit suicide.'

'We have found a journal that gives some explanation. I don't know if you'd call it a suicide note. From what she had written, it seems that she was in despair over a love affair. She had written some tragic lines to that effect.'

'Is that so. Did she write the man's name?' Miyata looked up at Imanishi.

'As a matter of fact, she gave no name. Probably Naruse-*san* didn't want to cause any embarrassment after her death.'

'So that was it, after all.'

'What do you mean "after all"? Is there something else you know about?' Imanishi watched intently so as not to let any change in Miyata's expression escape him.

Miyata Kunio did not answer. Looking down again, he bit his lip to keep it from trembling.

'Miyata-*san*, I think you know the reason behind Naruse-*san*'s death.'

'What do you mean?' Miyata looked up.

'Do you wear a beret when you go out?' Imanishi asked, looking steadily at the face of the long-haired man across from him.

'Yes, I do.'

'A while ago you went to a sushi shop near Naruse-*san*'s apartment, didn't you?'

The actor was startled again.

'At that sushi shop you obliged a fan who wanted your autograph, didn't you? That's not all. You tried to call Naruse-*san* out from her apartment by whistling, didn't you?'

The actor grew pale. 'No, that wasn't me. I never called her out.'

'But you were whistling beneath her apartment window to try to get her to come out. Miyata-*san*, I saw you there. I heard you whistling that night as I passed by.'

When Imanishi said he had seen Miyata near the apartment, Miyata's face lost all color. The actor was silent for a while. His face was full of pain.

'How about it, Miyata-*san*,' Imanishi pressed. 'I'd like you to tell me everything you know. That doesn't mean that I intend to do anything to you. Naruse Rieko's death was a suicide. The police don't act unless it's a murder. But we are interested in Naruse-*san* in connection with another case.'

Miyata looked afraid, but he still didn't answer.

'This is just my personal opinion, but I think the reason for Naruse-*san*'s death is connected to what we wanted to question her about. How about it, Miyata-*san*. Can't you tell me the truth? Why would she commit suicide?'

The actor kept silent.

Imanishi leaned on his elbows across the table. 'You must know. You seem to have known her very well. That is neither here nor there. All I want you to do is to tell me frankly what you think caused Naruse-*san* to commit suicide.'

Imanishi continued to stare at Miyata. Imanishi had a look that seemed to pierce to the depths of one's soul. Miyata began to fidget.

Imanishi observed this and said, 'Miyata-*san*, how about it? Will you cooperate?'

'Yes.' Miyata took out a handkerchief and wiped the perspiration off his brow. 'I'll tell you what I know. But I can't talk to you now.'

'Why not?'

'Nothing is clear to me right now. As you say, I know

something that might be of help in terms of Naruse-*san*'s suicide. But that's not all. I'd like to tell you about something else, but . . . I can't do that right now.'

Imanishi nodded, never taking his eyes off Miyata. It seemed clear that Miyata knew a lot about Rieko, that he knew secrets she kept from others, that Miyata felt something more than friendship for her. Now was not the time to insist on answers. He was so upset that it was unlikely he would say anything if pressed. His instinctive reaction to his suffering would be complete silence. Imanishi knew, if he was to learn more, he would have to give Miyata time.

'I understand. Then when can we talk?' Imanishi asked.

'Please give me two or three days,' Miyata said.

'Two or three days? Couldn't you make it sooner? I need to hear what you have to say about Naruse-*san* as soon as possible.'

'Inspector,' Miyata asked, 'are you sure Naruse-*san* had something to do with your case?'

'We're not sure yet, but we hope that there's some tie-in.'

Miyata stared intently at Imanishi. He said, 'It's very likely that I can help your investigation. I'll tell you everything I know about Naruse-*san* tomorrow.'

Grateful, Imanishi said, 'Where shall we meet?'

'I'll wait for you at the Company S Tearoom in Ginza at eight o'clock. I'll have my thoughts straight by then,' Miyata said.

8. A Mishap

Imanishi entered the Ginza tearoom the next evening promptly at eight o'clock. It was crowded with customers, but he did not see the actor. He took a seat along the wall, ordered a cup of coffee, and took a weekly magazine out of his pocket. Each time the door opened he looked up. He sipped his coffee as slowly as he could, but the actor hadn't shown up by the time he had finished.

Imanishi grew impatient but realized the actor might have been delayed. He would give it another twenty minutes.

Imanishi continued to skim the magazine. The tearoom became more and more crowded; newcomers left when they saw that the shop was full. Imanishi could tell from the look on her face that the waitress wanted him to leave. Reluctantly, he ordered again, this time a cup of tea. He took his time sipping this as well. At eight-forty Imanishi became concerned. The telephone rang, and a customer was paged, but it was not for Imanishi. His teacup was empty. Next, Imanishi ordered a fruit punch. He couldn't even finish half of it.

An hour passed. Imanishi waited, determined to hear Miyata's story about the girl who had cooperated with the murderer, the girl who had cut up and scattered the bloodstained shirt.

Imanishi became annoyed. Finally, he left the tearoom and went on waiting outside, sure that as soon as he left for home

Miyata would arrive. Imanishi called the theater, but there was no answer. He had to give up.

Imanishi woke up at six o'clock the next morning. For some reason, no matter how late he had gotten to sleep, or how occupied he had been on a case, he woke up at six o'clock. Yoshiko and Taro were still asleep.

He smoked a cigarette and crawled out of the futon to go to the front door. The morning newspaper had been slipped between the lattice work of the door. He returned to his bed, taking the newspaper with him.

One of the pleasures in his life was to lie in bed and read the newspaper as he smoked. He turned first to the city page out of professional interest. Articles on unimportant cases filled the page. Imanishi stopped suddenly at a small headline: 'Modern Drama Actor Dies at Roadside – Heart Attack on Way Home from Rehearsal.'

Imanishi looked at the photograph next to the headline. It was Miyata Kunio. He read:

At approximately eleven P.M. on August 31, Sugimura Isaku, 42, a company executive, discovered a dead body as he drove to his home near Number xx, Kasuya-cho, Setagaya-ku. He reported his discovery immediately to the Seijo police station. As a result of an inspection of the man's belongings, the deceased was identified as Miyata Kunio, 30, an actor with the Avant-Garde Theater. The cause of death was tentatively given as a heart attack. Today there will be an autopsy at the Tokyo police medical center.

Miyata had finished rehearsals at the Avant-Garde Theater at approximately 6:30 P.M., and had left the building at that time. According to Sugiura Akiko of the Avant-Garde Theater, Miyata was an actor with a bright future. Recently, he had become quite popular.

Imanishi was shocked. Kicking off his bedding, he got up again. He hurried Yoshiko to prepare breakfast and ate quickly.

'Is something the matter?' Yoshiko wondered.

'Nothing, nothing.'

Imanishi dressed in a rush, like a firefighter called to a fire. He left the house at 8:30.

Miyata's body would no longer be at the Seijo police station. The Tokyo police medical center in Otsuka started its workday at nine A.M. It would be quicker to go there.

It was slightly after nine when he reached the medical center located only a ten-minute walk from Otsuka Station. In front of the medical center was an attractive garden, but inside the building it was dingy and dark. Two men, someone's next of kin, sat uncertainly in the waiting room. Imanishi went directly to the medical center chief's office.

'It's been a while since I've seen you,' the medical center chief greeted him.

'Doctor, I'll get right to the point. Has the body from Seijo station been delivered here yet?'

'Yes, it came in late last night.'

'When do you plan to open it up?'

'We're in a bit of a crunch, so I expect it will be this afternoon.'

'Doctor, could you manage to do it earlier?'

'That's a death from illness, isn't it? We're just doing a routine autopsy. Is there something suspicious?'

'I have a strange feeling about it.'

'You mean, the death may not have been natural?'

The medical examiner knew Imanishi's skill as a detective. He agreed to do this autopsy first.

Imanishi looked through the file sent over from Seijo while he waited for the coroner to get ready. A young examiner came out to guide Imanishi to the autopsy room. They went down a narrow hallway and a flight of stairs. At the entrance to the autopsy room, they put slippers over their shoes. The autopsy room could be seen from the waiting room through a set of glass doors. Five medical examiners wearing white laboratory coats were already gathered inside.

In the center of the concrete-floored room stood the dissecting table on which a man's naked body was laid out. The body was pasty white; long, tangled hair lay spread out on the table. The eyes were open, the mouth was slightly ajar. There was a look of pain on the face. Imanishi pressed his palms together in prayer as he faced the body.

The medical examiners took their respective places around the table. The coroner began with his observations on the exterior condition of the body. An assistant took down the information. When this dictation was over, the coroner inserted a scalpel into the chest cavity and cut downward in a Y-shaped line through the center of the body. He sliced the body open in one swift movement. Blood ran out.

Imanishi watched without flinching. The stench filled his nostrils, but he was used to it. An assistant had cut open the stomach to inspect its contents. Another assistant was slicing the brownish-tinted liver. Finally the scalp was opened. Miyata's long hair flopped onto his face.

Imanishi left the autopsy room. His brow was beaded in perspiration. He could see the green leaves swaying in the breeze outside the corridor window. The sunlight was bright, the air fresh and full of life.

As he was looking out the window, he felt a tap on his shoulder. It was the coroner.

'Thank you very much for your efforts, Doctor,' Imanishi said.

'You're welcome. Could you come this way, please.'

The coroner escorted Imanishi to a room.

'Imanishi-*san*, I'm sorry to say,' the coroner said, smiling, 'the cause of death is unmistakably a heart attack.'

'Is that so, after all?' Imanishi looked at the doctor.

'We examined everything with particular care, but there were no external wounds, and no traces of any assault. We also examined the stomach, but there was no indication of a reaction to poisonous substances, no abnormalities in the abdominal organs. There was some enlargement of the heart, leading me to think that this person may have suffered from a mild case of valvular disease. We came to the conclusion that it was a heart attack. In each organ there was coagulated blood, which backs up this finding.'

'So you would say that it was death from natural causes?' Imanishi became lost in thought. He seemed to be terribly disappointed.

The doctor asked, 'Imanishi-*san*, what were you suspicious of?'

When asked point-blank, Imanishi had no suitable answer. He could not say that he was suspicious because the man had died before he could hear his evidence.

'The man didn't die at home. His dead body was discovered on the roadside, wasn't it?'

'Yes, is there something strange in that?'

'If he had become ill and died at home, I wouldn't be so suspicious. I'm concerned because he died at the side of the road.'

'But Imanishi-*san*, there are occasionally such cases. You can't choose where you're going to have a sudden heart attack.'

Imanishi had no reply. 'I'm afraid I've got a bad habit of suspecting that every death is related to police work,' Imanishi said.

He continued to ponder. At eight P.M., Miyata was to have met him at the tearoom in Ginza. Why had he been walking around in the Setagaya district? Imanishi was still convinced that Miyata had intended to meet him. Could he have been lured to Setagaya against his will? Had he visited someone in the Setagaya area and lost track of the time?

Imanishi decided to view the place where Miyata's body was

found. By bus, it was not far from the Seijo police station. There were very few houses. The area still retained a rural feeling. He walked over to where the actor's body had been discovered, following the diagram drawn for him by one of the men at the Seijo station. It was in a field, one yard away from the main bus route. Plumes of the pampas grass near the wooded area had already turned to autumn white.

As he stood there, Imanishi noted that there were many cars but few pedestrians passing by. At night it would be a lonely place. Had Miyata been walking here? If he had meant to keep his appointment with Imanishi, he would have taken a taxi. Suppose he had visited someone nearby and had waited here to hail a taxi. Who would Miyata have come to visit out here?

Imanishi stopped by the Avant-Garde Theater. When he made it clear that he wanted to ask about Miyata Kunio, a member of the office staff escorted him to Sugiura Akiko's room. Her name was familiar to Imanishi; he'd seen her photograph in newspapers and magazines. She greeted him pleasantly. The famous actress – the leader of this theater group – smoked a cigarette while she answered.

'Miyata-*san* was at the theater rehearsing our new play until six-thirty. He didn't seem to be in pain. That's why I couldn't believe it when I heard that he had died.'

'Do you know if he had some kind of heart condition?'

'Now that you mention it, he wasn't very strong. Sometimes we rehearse all night before an opening, and he did seem to tire easily.'

'Did he happen to mention where he was going after the rehearsal ended?'

'No, I really wouldn't know,' she said and pushed a buzzer to call in a young actor, a good friend of Miyata's. 'This is Yamagata-*san*. Did Miyata-*san* say where he was going after he left here last night?'

The young actor stood at attention, his hands clasped together in front of him. 'Well, yes. He did say that he had to meet someone in Ginza at eight.'

'At eight in Ginza?' Imanishi interrupted. 'Is that really what he said?'

'Yes, that's what he told me,' Yamagata turned toward Imanishi and answered. 'I invited him out, and that's the reason he declined.'

So Miyata Kunio *had* intended to keep his appointment with Imanishi.

'Where did he live?'

'In an apartment in Komagome.'

'Komagome?' It was in the opposite direction from where his body had been found.

'How did Miyata-*san* seem when you parted?'

'He seemed to be his normal self. Oh, yes, he did say something – that he wasn't looking forward to the meeting in Ginza.'

'I'd like to ask you about a different matter,' Imanishi turned toward Sugiura Akiko. 'A young woman named Naruse Rieko used to work here, didn't she?'

'Yes.' Sugiura Akiko nodded. 'She was a quiet, gentle girl. She recently committed suicide.'

'Do you have any idea why she committed suicide?'

'No. I didn't know her well at all, so I asked the office staff, thinking they would have more of an idea about what had gone on. But everyone said they had no idea why she committed suicide.'

'Could she have been heartbroken?'

'Well.' Sugiura Akiko smiled. 'I wouldn't know anything about that. If only she had left a suicide note or something.'

'This may sound strange,' Imanishi said, 'but could Naruse Rieko have been on intimate terms with Miyata Kunio?'

'No, I can't imagine that they were . . . Have you heard anything like that?' Sugiura Akiko looked around and asked the young actor standing near her.

He smiled faintly. 'Actually, there were rumors about that.'

'What?' The actress's eyes brightened.

'It wasn't that the two of them were particularly friendly,' the actor said. 'Naruse-*san* didn't seem to have special feelings for Miyata, but he was quite serious about her. You could tell by watching him.'

'I'm amazed,' Sugiura Akiko said.

This explanation made sense to Imanishi. Rieko had died leaving a journal full of longing. It was clear that the object of her love was not Miyata. Then who was Rieko so in love with that she decided to die for him? Imanishi asked if Rieko had had another boyfriend.

'No, I don't think there was anyone special. But I really wouldn't know,' the actor replied. 'Naruse-*san* was very reserved. If her suicide was from a broken heart, it must be over someone we don't know.'

The boyfriend none of the theater members knew about – was he the killer in the Kamata murder case? Imanishi wanted to find him.

At eight-thirty, Sekigawa Shigeo left the restaurant where he had been attending a meeting sponsored by a literary magazine. A large black car waited for him in the shadows.

'Sekigawa-*sensei*,' the magazine editor called out, 'will you be going straight home?'

'No.' Sekigawa smiled. 'I have to visit someone.'

'Then where shall we have the car take you?'

'If you could drive me to Ikebukuro, that would be fine.'

At Ikebukuro Station, he changed to a taxi and ordered the driver to go toward Shimura. Sekigawa smoked a cigarette.

After a while, the street started to slope uphill. Sekigawa alighted from the taxi and turned the corner, walking away from the streetcar tracks.

A young woman, standing in the shadows, rushed over to him. It was Emiko.

'Darling? You've finally come. I'm so happy.' She pressed herself against Sekigawa's side.

'Have you been waiting long?'

'Yes, about an hour.'

'The meeting ran late.'

'That's what I thought. I was worried that you might not come.'

Sekigawa did not answer. Emiko reached out and took his arm.

'Did you skip work at the bar tonight?' Sekigawa asked in a low voice.

'Yes, because I was coming to meet you. It's awful to have a night job.'

'How is your new apartment?'

'I like it. The woman below is nice to me. It's much better than the other place.'

'That's good.'

The two of them walked in silence. The streetlights grew fewer.

'I'm so happy,' she said. 'The only time I'm happy is when I'm with you. That's the only time I feel fulfilled.'

Sekigawa was silent.

'I know you don't feel the same. Are you seeing someone other than me?' Emiko asked.

'There's no one else.'

'Are you sure? Sometimes I can't help thinking that there is someone else.'

'You're just being jealous.'

'Whenever I start thinking that, I try to stop my thoughts, but I can't.'

'Is it that hard for you to trust me?'

'No, I trust you, of course. I don't care if I'm not your only woman. It doesn't matter to me even if you love someone else. Only, please don't leave me.'

Emiko walked clinging to Sekigawa's arm. The road was dark. Beyond the darkness they could hear the lonesome sound of the streetcar.

'The streetcars are still running,' Emiko said, leaning her cheek against Sekigawa's shoulder.

'It must be the last run.' Sekigawa tossed his cigarette. The small red flame glowed on the ground.

Emiko looked up at the sky. It was full of stars.

'It's gotten late. Orion is all the way over there,' Sekigawa said.

'Which is Orion?'

'See, it's that one.' Sekigawa pointed his finger at the sky. 'See the three stars lined up sideways as if they were on a ship's mast? And around them are four stars that box them in.'

'Yes, those?'

'In the winter, that constellation shines brightly in the sky. When I see Orion, I realize that autumn has already come.'

'You know so much about stars, too.'

'Not really. I knew someone when I was a boy who taught me all kinds of things. He's dead now. He taught me about the stars, too. The place I come from is surrounded by mountains so you can't see much of the sky,' Sekigawa said. 'He would take me up to the top of a nearby peak at night and teach me about the stars. When we reached the mountaintop, the sky would open up.'

'What area do you come from?'

'You wouldn't know even if I told you.'

'Oh, yes, I remember reading somewhere that it was in Akita Prefecture.'

'Yes, that's what they say.'

'What do you mean, that's what they say?'

'It doesn't really matter.' Sekigawa changed the subject. 'Tomorrow night I have to review a concert.'

'You're so busy. Which concert?'

'Waga's. A newspaper asked me to review it, so I accepted.'

'Waga-*san*'s music is very new, isn't it? What do they call it, avant-garde music?'

'He calls it "musique concrète." Others pioneered this form, Waga picked it up and started doing it himself. He's not capable of going much further. He has no originality. He just steals from what others have done.'

A scarlet curtain was the backdrop. The only stage decoration was a weirdly shaped sculpture placed in the center. The sculpture was as white as fallen snow. The contrast between the white and the scarlet was stark. A sculptor from the Nouveau group had decorated the recital stage for his comrade Waga Eiryo.

This concert differed greatly from the usual musical performance. Speakers had been placed at different locations to create a three-dimensional effect. Sound came from beyond the curtain hung behind the sculpture, from above the audience and from beneath it. The hall was full and most of the audience was young. The last work was entitled 'Nirvana,' based on the myth of Buddha's death, when all the animals lamented and heaven and earth wailed in mourning. The piece at times moaned, then quavered, howled, and vibrated. Metallic sounds and voices like loud laughter were combined to create tension, relaxation, pause, and climax. It could not be said that the audience was enraptured. They were trying to make sense of this new music.

The music stopped. A loud round of applause welled up. There was some confusion as to whom the audience was applauding as there was no orchestra on the stage. Eventually, the recipient of the applause, Waga Eiryo, dressed in a black suit, walked on stage from the right wing.

Sekigawa went backstage to Waga's dressing room, which was jammed with people. In the center of the room were three tables pushed together loaded with beer and plates of hors d'oeuvres. Cigarette smoke and voices filled the room.

'Hey, Sekigawa.' Someone tapped him on the shoulder. It was Yodogawa Ryuta, the architect. 'You're late.'

Sekigawa nodded, squeezing sideways between people.

Waga stood smiling in the center of the throng. Beside him stood Tadokoro Sachiko in a pure white satin cocktail dress. Encircling her slender white neck was a necklace of three strands of pearls. She looked gorgeous enough to take the stage herself.

Pushing his way through the crowd, Sekigawa went up to Waga. 'Congratulations.'

'Thank you,' Waga responded.

'Sachiko-*san*, congratulations.'

'Thank you very much. Sekigawa-*san*, how did you like the concert?' Sachiko looked up at Sekigawa with smiling eyes.

'You'd better not ask the opinion of the critic tonight,' Waga interjected. 'At least he congratulated me.'

'Sekigawa-*sensei*, it's because the music is so fascinating that there was such a large audience.' The singer Murakami Junko spoke up from directly behind Sekigawa. As usual, she wore a red suit. She had strong features, the kind that showed to advantage when she was on stage. Secure in her looks, she smiled boldly.

'I suppose you could say that,' Sekigawa agreed, with a laugh.

'*Sensei*, please let me pour you a glass.'

Sekigawa allowed the singer to pour him some beer. With an

exaggerated gesture, he raised his glass and looked from Waga to Sachiko. 'Congratulations on your success.'

Many well-wishers circled around Waga. The door was left open to accommodate the crowd.

'It's an incredible number of people,' Yodogawa whispered to Sekigawa. 'I'm envious of musicians. No matter how many houses I design, no one throws such a party for me.'

The architect's envy was understandable. Not only music lovers, but also those who had nothing to do with the arts, surrounded Waga. And many of them were older men.

Yodogawa spoke in an undertone. 'They're all Sachiko's father's connections.'

'Don't be so envious.' Sekigawa turned his back on Waga and moved away. 'It's probably annoying to him as well.'

'No, look at Waga's face. He doesn't look annoyed at all,' Yodogawa continued.

'No, that expression means he's pleased that his art has been recognized.'

'How many people in tonight's audience understood Waga's "musique concrète"? I couldn't understand it very well myself.'

'You, an avant-garde architect?'

'I don't have to cover up my ignorance in front of you.'

'The masses,' Sekigawa said, 'are always dumbfounded by the unintelligibility of pioneering efforts. But after a while, they get used to it. This accommodation leads them into understanding.'

'Are you saying this describes Waga's case?'

'Let's not get into individual cases,' Sekigawa answered. 'Here it is necessary to act politely. If you want to know what I have to say, take a look at the newspaper tomorrow.'

'To get your honest opinion?'

'Right. We say all kinds of things about each other, but Waga is impressive. He's doing just what he wants to do the way he wants to do it.'

'Isn't it just that he's lucky? He's made such quick progress. Even if he didn't create anything, the media would pay attention to him because he's the future son-in-law of former Cabinet Minister Tadokoro.'

Imanishi managed to read one-third of the newspaper review of Waga Eiryo's recital. He did not have the patience to read the rest. To him, the piece was totally incomprehensible. The reason he had read that far at breakfast was because he recognized the photo of Sekigawa Shigeo, the critic who had written the piece.

Imanishi got off the streetcar at Kichijoji-machi. The apartment building where Miyata had lived was quite old. The wife of the building owner answered the door. When he said he was from police headquarters, she looked worried.

'I'd like to ask you a bit about Miyata-*san*,' Imanishi said.

'I appreciate your concern. Was there something Miyata-*san* had done?'

Imanishi had refused to go inside so they stood talking in the doorway. 'No, it's not that Miyata-*san* did anything,' Imanishi said, putting the woman at ease. 'I was a fan of his. I'm disappointed that he died so young. How long did he live here?'

'Let me see. It's been about three years.'

'Actors tend to have a life-style different from what we imagine when they're off the stage. What was he like?'

'He was a very nice person. He was quiet and neat.'

'Did he ever bring over friends and have rowdy parties?'

'No. Apparently he had a weak heart, so he didn't drink much, and he was very careful about his health. For an actor, he seemed to be a very quiet person.'

'By the way, did Miyata-*san* go on a trip to the Tohoku region about mid-May?'

'Yes, he did,' the housewife answered immediately.

Imanishi's eyes lit up. 'You're sure?'

'I'm sure I'm not mistaken. He brought me back some presents from Akita, some sweets and a wooden *kokeshi* doll.'

Imanishi concealed the joy he felt.

'About how long was Miyata-*san*'s trip to the Tohoku region?'

'Let me see. I think it was about four days.'

'Did Miyata-*san* say anything to you at that time?'

'He said he had a break from the theater's performances, so he thought he'd go on a little trip. I only found out after he returned that he had gone to Akita.'

Leaving the apartment house, Imanishi went to a telephone booth and called detective Yoshimura. The two men met at Shibuya Station. It was just noon, so they went into a noodle shop.

'You look as if you've come up with a big find,' Yoshimura said, looking at Imanishi's face.

'Is it that obvious?' Imanishi grinned. 'Actually, I finally figured out the reason for our trip to the Tohoku region.'

'Really?' Yoshimura opened his eyes wide. 'Did you find out who that man was?'

'I did.'

'I'm amazed. Give me all the details.'

The cold noodles they had ordered were served.

'A few days ago an actor died of a heart attack.'

'Yes, I read about it in the newspaper. It was Miyata Kunio, wasn't it?'

'That's right. Did you know him?'

'I knew his name. I don't go to see many contemporary dramas. But I remember reading the article about his death. It said that he was a new actor for whom they had had high hopes in the future.'

'He was *that guy*.'

'What?' Yoshimura nearly dropped his chopsticks.

'Miyata was the strange man in Kameda.'

'How did you find that out?'

'I'll tell you, give me time.'

For a while, there was only the sound of the two men slurping *soba* noodles.

'As a matter of fact,' Imanishi said, after taking a sip of tea, 'in this morning's paper there was a piece by one of those people we saw at Kameda station. That Nou . . .'

'The Nouveau group, you mean?'

'That's it. One of them was in the paper. One's train of thought is a strange thing. I had been keeping my eye on this fellow Miyata. I'll tell you the reason later. Anyway, I was checking on him when he died. There's no reason to be suspicious about his death, because it was a heart attack. But I remembered that he was an actor when I read the piece in the paper this morning. And you know how much I've been thinking about the Kamata case. I realized that Miyata would be used to disguises, especially since he acts in contemporary dramas. I had a flash that maybe *he* was the one who had gone to Kameda.'

Yoshimura looked intently at Imanishi. 'And was that what had happened?'

'I went over to his apartment building and talked to his landlord's wife. Miyata went to Akita for four days from about May eighteenth. It was at the end of May that we went to Akita, right? So the dates match up pretty well. The dead can't talk, so we can't ask Miyata himself, but I'm sure there's no mistake.'

Imanishi ate the rest of his noodles.

'I'm impressed.'

'That's what I mean about train of thought. I remembered when I read that complicated article by the guy in the Nouveau group. And the reason I read that piece was because I remembered seeing him at Kameda Station. Then suddenly the two strands fit together: Miyata, whom I'd been checking on for a while, and Kameda.'

'So your hunch was right on target.'

'That's fine so far. But the question is, why did Miyata go to Kameda?'

'That's true.'

'He wandered aimlessly in that town dressed like a laborer. Those weren't his normal clothes. And all the people there said that he kept his head down and didn't look directly at anyone, didn't they?'

'Yes, they did.'

'And yet, in such a small country town he was sure to be noticed. One of the hotel maids described him quite accurately as being "dark-skinned but handsome."'

Imanishi and Yoshimura stared intently at each other.

'I can't figure it out. What brought him to Kameda in disguise?'

'I don't know. At any rate, he didn't do anything. All he did was walk around. He hung around near some houses and lay around at the riverside. And that's all.'

'Wait a minute,' Yoshimura put his hand up to his forehead. 'What if that was why he went?'

'That's it!' Imanishi nodded. 'He behaved in such a way as to leave an impression on the local people.'

'Why did he do that?'

Imanishi did not reply directly to Yoshimura's question. 'The rumor about the strange man found its way to the local police. And we found out because we requested information about the Kamata killing. We were taken in.'

9. Groping

Yoshimura had asked Imanishi to guide him to the spot where Miyata had died.

'This is the place,' Imanishi said.

'I see.' Yoshimura looked where Imanishi pointed. 'The bus stop is right over there, isn't it?' Yoshimura asked. In fact, passengers were getting off a bus that had stopped not three feet from where they stood. 'The theory that Miyata was waiting for the bus is a possibility.'

'That's true. Oh, yes, Yoshimura,' Imanishi said, thinking of something, 'would you ask the conductor the exact times buses stop here around eight o'clock at night?'

Yoshimura ran for the bus and asked the conductor. He came back as the bus pulled away.

'There's a bus to Seijo at seven-forty,' Yoshimura said. 'At eight o'clock the bus for Kichijoji goes by, and ten minutes later another bus for Seijo. Then nothing for about twenty minutes until the bus from Chitose Karasuyama passes through on the way to Seijo. After that buses in both directions come by at twenty-minute intervals. So a bus comes by here every ten minutes or so.'

Imanishi listened to this and muttered, 'They come quite often, don't they?' He continued, 'Miyata died at about eight o'clock. If we assume that he was waiting near the bus stop, his heart attack must have occurred during the ten-minute span between buses. It's not certain that the buses in both directions pass by at exactly those intervals, so there is some leeway. But in any case, he couldn't have been waiting long. If Miyata had his heart attack during the ten-minute wait, he was really unlucky.' Imanishi was thinking out loud.

Yoshimura could not hear him. He was walking across the field near the road.

'Imanishi-*san*,' Yoshimura called out, bending over. 'Look at this.' Yoshimura pointed to the ground. In the grass there was a piece of paper some four inches square, torn, with ragged edges.

'What could it be?' Imanishi picked it up.

'It looks like a list of figures,' Yoshimura said, peering over Imanishi's shoulder.

The sheet of paper listed the following:

Total Amounts of Unemployment Insurance Disbursed

1949	_____
1950	_____
1951	_____
1952	_____
1953	25,404
	_____
	_____
1954	35,522
	_____
	_____
	_____
1955	30,834
	_____
	_____

1956	24,362
	————
	————
1957	27,435
1958	28,431
	————
	————
1959	28,438
	————

It appeared that this sheet of paper was one section of a larger report that had been torn apart.

'I wonder if there's someone in this area interested in these figures?'

'Maybe someone from the Labor Ministry lives around here,' Imanishi responded.

The statistics were of little interest to the two men, but the piece of paper had been dropped about ten yards from where Miyata had collapsed.

'I wonder how long this paper has been here?' Yoshimura said.

'It's not very dirty, Yoshimura. When did it rain last?'

'I'm quite sure it rained four or five days ago.'

'Then this paper was dropped after that. It hasn't been rained on.'

'Miyata died three days ago. Could it be from about that time?'

'I wonder.' Imanishi thought. 'I can't imagine why Miyata would be carrying around something like this.'

'Should we ask at the Avant-Garde Theater just to be sure? It might be a prop for a play or a part of a script.'

In response to Yoshimura's suggestion, Imanishi said, 'It could also be a piece of paper blown here by the wind.'

'Yes, sir. I think we should take that possibility into account.'

'You suspect that someone other than Miyata dropped this?'

'Yes,' Yoshimura answered. 'I'm speculating that someone Miyata knew might have written these statistics down, someone who was interested in labor relations.'

'Then you think that person might have been here with Miyata?'

'Maybe. Or Miyata may have been given that piece of paper and had it in his pocket. When he collapsed, it may have fallen out. Then later the wind blew it over here. That's another possibility.'

Imanishi laughed. 'It's probably unrelated. Miyata wouldn't have been given something like this. It would have been of no interest to him. But your idea that there might have been someone with Miyata is interesting.'

Imanishi looked the piece of paper over again.

'I wonder what this is?' he asked, pointing to a figure. 'See, this chart starts at 1949. But for 1949, 1950, 1951, and 1952, there are no numbers.'

'That must be because those numbers were unnecessary, or unclear, one or the other.'

'I can see that. But look at this. Between 1953 and 1954, here, there are two lines drawn. And between 1954 and 1955 there are three lines. There are no notations of the year before these lines. What do these blanks mean?'

'I wonder.' Yoshimura was craning his neck to look at the piece of paper. 'I can't figure it out. I wonder if a different number is supposed to fit there. For example, maybe they intended to put in the number of insured people or the number of people receiving insurance?'

'If that's the case, you'd think those categories would be filled in, but they're not. It may be that this is a reminder to the person who wrote down these figures.'

'The handwriting isn't good, is it?'

'Right, it's not. It looks like a junior high school student wrote it. But these days even college graduates have terrible handwriting.'

'What shall we do with it?'

'Well, it might be of some use later. I'll keep it.'

Imanishi placed the piece of paper in his pocket.

'Sorry to have had to drag you all the way out to a place like this,' Imanishi said to Yoshimura. Apologizing for inconveniencing even a younger colleague was natural to Imanishi.

'I don't mind. It's better for me to have seen it. I'm glad I came along,' Yoshimura was equally polite.

The two men walked back to the bus stop.

Imanishi returned to police headquarters and sat, staring absentmindedly for a while. Then he went to the Public Information Department.

'Are you wrapped up in another complicated investigation?' the section chief asked Imanishi.

'I'd like to find out something about "musique concrète,"' Imanishi said seriously.

'What on earth is that?' The section chief looked at Imanishi, baffled.

'Apparently, it's some kind of music. Do you have something that I could look it up in?'

'Last time it was dialects, and now music.' Shaking his head, the section chief stood up and brought out a reference book. 'There must be something in this.'

Imanishi opened the thick volume. He read the small print of the encyclopedia and soon closed it. The article was full of difficult terminology, and it was hard for him to take it in. He could tell that it must be a very complicated form of music and that it was different in style from traditional music. However, none of the intricate points was comprehensible to him.

'Thank you very much.' Imanishi returned the heavy volume.

'Did you get the meaning?' the section chief asked.

'No, not very well. It's a bit over my head.' Imanishi smiled ruefully.

'I'm not surprised. What on earth brought you to this topic?'

'Well, there was something I was thinking about.' Imanishi kept his answer vague and left the room.

He had become curious about all of the members of the Nouveau group. He could not imagine the connection between this group and Miyata Kunio. Yet he was impelled to find out about this 'musique concrète.'

That evening Yoshimura called Imanishi, who was still at work. 'Remember we were wondering why Miyata had gone to Kameda? I've got an idea.'

'Really? I'd like to hear it.'

'I thumbed through the newspapers from around the time of the Kamata murder. About three or four days after the murder, articles appeared saying that the police were pursuing a lead, that the murderer and victim had been talking in Tohoku dialect, and that the name Kameda had come up.'

'I see. And?' Imanishi swallowed hard.

'I think these newspaper articles led to Miyata's going to Kameda. You see, I think that since investigation headquarters was concerned with Kameda and the Tohoku dialect, the murderer thought that Kameda in the Tohoku region would attract the attention of the police. The killer figured out that sooner or later the police would discover a location named Kameda and investigate it. Couldn't it be that the killer's aim was to focus attention on that area?'

'Yes, that could be it,' Imanishi shouted into the telephone. 'You've really hit upon something.'

Yoshimura's excitement was heightened by Imanishi's praise. 'To keep the attention of the police on Kameda, there had to be something strange happening there. I think that's what the killer calculated. I think the killer performed a sleight-of-hand trick. He's *not* from the Tohoku region. He's from somewhere else.'

'Then what about Miyata?'

'He was sent by the killer of course. He could have played his role without knowing the reason behind it.'

'Then the killer must have been acquainted with Miyata.'

'He may even have been on close terms with Miyata since he asked him to go there.'

'Thank you,' Imanishi said to Yoshimura. 'You've come up with a very good point. I'm impressed that you thought of it.'

Yoshimura's voice sounded a bit embarrassed. 'I just happened to think of it. I might be wrong.'

'No, no. You've been very helpful.'

'I'm glad to hear that. Let's get together some time and talk it over.' Yoshimura hung up.

Imanishi pulled out half a cigarette from his desk, stuck it into a battered old bamboo cigarette holder, and lit a match. While he smoked he thought over what Yoshimura had said on the telephone.

It was no doubt as Yoshimura had suggested. He had found out why Miyata had gone to Kameda. This brought the murderer into clearer focus. The murderer knew Miyata; he was not from the Tohoku region, but was from somewhere else.

Miyata had wanted to tell Imanishi about something important. Imanishi had asked Miyata about Rieko's suicide. But in addition, Miyata might have wanted to talk of another important matter. As he thought, Imanishi made notes on a piece of paper. With his hands on his forehead, he stared at his notes.

Miyata's death had created a problem. If he had been murdered, there would be clues pointing to his killer. But he died of a heart attack. Those around Miyata had known that his heart was weak, and this fact had been substantiated by the medical examiner. Yet Imanishi's suspicion of foul play wouldn't subside. The actor's death seemed too well timed. But it *could* be a coincidence. As the coroner had said, heart attacks don't choose their time and place.

Various theories contended within Imanishi's head. He thought of Kamedake, an area located in the opposite direction from Tohoku. And yet what had he found there? Nothing. He had not discovered a shred of a motive for the crime.

He considered facts about Naruse Rieko. It had been Rieko who had scattered the bits of the murderer's bloodstained shirt. She and the murderer must have had a special relationship, and Miyata must have known about it.

When Imanishi returned home, he found that his younger sister was visiting. She and Yoshiko were chatting gaily.

'Good evening, Brother,' she greeted him.

Imanishi changed from his office clothes into a kimono.

'What have you been up to today?' Imanishi said, sitting down in front of his sister, sipping a cup of tea.

'I got some passes to the Nichigeki theater, so I stopped by on my way home.'

'No wonder you look happy. At least you haven't had a fight with your husband.'

'We haven't been fighting,' his sister assured him. 'You look very tired.'

'I do?'

'Are you busy at work?'

'That's right.'

'Isn't this early for you to be home?' Yoshiko asked.

'I must be getting old, I'm exhausted.'

'You should be more careful,' his sister said.

Imanishi felt depressed. He wasn't able to join his wife and sister's cheerful chatter. He went into the next room and sat at a small desk. The plain bookcase housed books related to police work. He was not the kind to read novels. Imanishi took out his notebook. Turning the pages, he read over what he had written about his trip to Kamedake. He had written down what he had heard in Kamedake about Miki Ken'ichi's days as a policeman. There were no dark shadows in Miki's life, not even a speck of dust that would have caused him to be hated.

Imanishi lay back on the tatami. He folded his arms under his head to form a pillow and looked up at the sooty ceiling. From the next room he could hear Yoshiko and his sister still chatting. The sound of a bus passing by rumbled in his ears. He thought of something and got up and went into the next room.

'Why don't you sit down and join us?' his sister urged.

'No, I have something I need to do.'

Imanishi took a piece of paper out of the pocket of his suit jacket, which was hanging from a hook.

He returned to the other room with the piece of paper Yoshimura had picked up in the field near where Miyata had died. According to the figures on the scrap of paper, Japan's unemployment insurance disbursements were steadily rising, indicating that the economic situation was worsening. Nineteen fifty-two was the year after the end of the fighting in the Korean War. The boom in special procurements had ended, forcing the closing of many smaller factories. The rise in unemployment must have been due to that. The figures reflected this. But they had nothing to do with the case.

Yoshimura had suggested that the person who'd made the chart might have been with Miyata. That was possible. At any rate, he would save this piece of paper for the time being. Whether it would end up being useful or not was another matter. Folding it carefully, he put it in his notebook.

Yoshiko came to call him to supper. Taro had gone to bed early, so Imanishi ate with his wife and sister.

'I hate to eat and run, but it's getting late, so I must go home. I've been out since morning,' his sister said.

'Then I'll see you off and go for a walk,' Imanishi said.

'You don't have to do that.'

'No, I need the walk.'

In fact, he felt wretched. He wanted to walk the evening streets to shake off his bad mood. Yoshiko said she would go as well, so the three of them set off toward the station. When they came to the nearby apartment building, Yoshiko told Imanishi's sister about the recent suicide.

'That's a real problem for a landlord,' she said, speaking from her own perspective. 'We have a young woman renting from us. I hope *she's* all right.'

'Oh, you mean the one who recently moved in?' Yoshiko asked. 'Didn't you say she was a bar hostess?'

'That's right. She comes home late every night, but she seems to be quite respectable.'

'Do her customers ever see her home?'

'I don't really know. At least when she comes into the building she's always alone. Even if she might be a little tipsy, she seems to pull herself together.'

'Even so . . .'

'Yes, but it's her job, you know. I hope there's no trouble. I worry when I hear about things like this suicide.'

They passed under a streetlight.

'You know, though, that hostess is quite admirable,' the sister said. 'She reads difficult books.'

'What do you mean?'

'Some sort of theoretical books. Just a couple of days ago I went to her room on an errand and she was clipping something from the paper. I peeked at the article, and it was a music review.'

'Is she musical?'

'No, she said she wasn't interested in music at all.'

'Then why was she clipping the review?'

'It caught her interest. She let me read it, but I couldn't make heads or tails of it.'

Imanishi overheard them.

'Was that the review about "musique concrète"?' he asked his sister.

'Yes, yes, I think it was. Do you know about it?' His sister was surprised.

'Just a little. But she was reading it even though she said she wasn't interested in music?'

'Yes, she said the person who wrote the review was a very brilliant, impressive man.'

'Did she mean Sekigawa Shigeo?'

'I'm amazed. How could you know that?'

Imanishi was silent. He wondered if young people in general admired Sekigawa Shigeo that much.

'What difficult books has she?'

'Well, there were two or three books by this Sekigawa.'

'Does this bar hostess read a lot of books?'

'No, not really. She mainly reads popular magazines.'

'What's her name?'

'It's Miura Emiko.'

'I think I'll come visit you some time,' Imanishi said. 'And you can casually introduce me to this bar hostess.'

Imanishi went to his sister's house in Kawaguchi the following day. The apartment building had been built two years before. The two-story building was divided into eight units. His sister and her husband lived on the first floor.

Oyuki was surprised to see him. 'My goodness, you came right away.'

'Right. I was nearby in Akabane, so I decided to come over. Is Sho at work?' he asked about his brother-in-law.

'Yes. I'll pour you some tea.'

'I've brought you something.' Imanishi gave her a box of cakes.

'You know, last night you were talking about the bar hostess who lives here. Can you arrange for me to meet her casually?'

'You're really persistent. Is she connected with a case?'

'No, not really. It's nothing, I just want to meet her. You haven't told her your brother is a detective, have you?'

'Of course not. I wouldn't talk about that. If I told my tenants my brother was a detective, they'd all get nervous and move away.'

'I'm decent at heart.'

'That's true. But for those who don't know you, it might make them uncomfortable.'

'I guess so. At any rate, can you invite her for tea? Is she still here?'

'Yes, she's probably doing her laundry about this time. She leaves for Ginza about five.'

'Okay. I'll watch the kettle.'

Shooed out by her brother, Oyuki left the room. Imanishi felt nervous. He changed seats twice while he waited. After a while, he heard two sets of footsteps in the hallway.

'Brother, I've brought her here.'

Behind his sister stood a young woman in a cream-colored sweater.

'Please come in.' Imanishi put on his kindest expression.

'This is my older brother. He hasn't come by for ages. We were just about to have some tea.'

'Excuse me.' Emiko entered the room. She then greeted Imanishi saying that she would always be grateful to his sister.

'Please, come in. I'm sure that my sister is a bother to you.' Imanishi observed the bar hostess. She had a pretty face. She was about twenty-five, but her rounded face still retained a childish quality. 'Are you busy with chores?' he asked.

'No, not really.'

'It must be hard. Are you off to work soon?'

'Yes, in a little while.'

'It must be a problem returning home late at night.'

'Yes, but I've gotten used to it.'

'Where were you living before you moved here?'

'Well . . .'

Emiko hesitated. She started to answer, but suddenly thought it over and said vaguely, 'Well . . . I've moved around quite a bit.'

'I see. Was the place you lived in before closer to Ginza?'

'Well . . . it was in the Azabu area.'

'Oh, yes, Azabu. That's a nice area. And it's near Ginza.'

'But the owners of the building decided to sell it. That's why I moved here. Even from here, it doesn't take that long on the train, so it's more convenient than I thought it would be.'

'But,' Imanishi continued, sipping his tea, 'aren't there times when you can't make the last train?'

'That's hardly ever a problem. The bar owner knows that I live out here, so she lets me out in time to make the last train.'

'I see. But there must be times when you have problems with a drunken customer who won't let you leave.'

'Yes, occasionally. But then friends fill in for me.'

'I've never been to a bar like that. I don't have that kind of money, so I really wouldn't know,' Imanishi said, with a rueful smile. 'I hear that at bars and cabarets these days, unless you're on an expense account, you aren't really welcome.'

'That's not so. It's just that expense account bills are paid without fail, so the managers prefer them. With regular customers, the bills mount up, collecting becomes a problem, and they're the responsibility of the hostess assigned to a particular customer.'

'I see. You have interesting and witty conversations with customers, but there's a difficult side to your work, too.' Imanishi changed the topic. 'By the way, are you interested in music?'

'Music?' Emiko looked surprised. 'Not especially. I don't understand it very well. Jazz is the kind of music I like.'

'I don't understand music at all. It seems like there are all kinds of new forms of music these days. Have you heard about "musique concrète"?'

'I've heard the term,' Emiko answered without thinking. For an instant, her eyes lit up.

'What kind of music is it?'

'I don't really know,' Emiko said. 'I've just heard the term.'

'I see. We're both the same, then. Actually, I came across the term in yesterday's newspaper. When you get to be my age, it's hard to keep up with the new foreign terms that they use. I had a little time, so I read the piece, wondering what this "musique concrète" was. It seemed to be a critique. But I couldn't understand it at all. The sentences were complicated.'

'Oh, yes, that was written by Sekigawa-*san*,' Emiko said, her voice suddenly more lively. 'I read that article as well.'

'Oh, you did?' Imanishi showed surprise. 'But I bet you could understand it.'

'No, it was too difficult for me to understand. But I try to read everything that Sekigawa-*sensei* writes.'

'Hmm. Do you know him?'

Emiko's eyes held a confused expression. It took a while for her to reply.

'He comes to the bar where I work every now and then. I know him slightly.'

'Is that so? Actually, I know him also.'

'Oh?' Emiko was surprised. 'How do you know him?'

'I've never talked to him, and he wouldn't know me. It's just that I saw him coincidentally at a train station in Akita Prefecture. He was with several other friends. But somehow I feel a special closeness to people I see on a trip like that.

'I'm envious of young people,' Imanishi continued, reminiscing about the trip. 'There were four or five of them at the station. Apparently they were on their way home from looking at a rocket research center. They were full of energy.'

'Is that so?' Emiko listened, her eyes shining.

'One of those young men was Sekigawa-*san*. After that I saw his face in newspaper photos. And each time I felt nostalgic about that trip. That's why I read that review though I couldn't understand it.'

Emiko sighed.

'What kind of person is Sekigawa-*san*? You said he goes to your bar sometimes.'

'He's very different from other types of customers,' Emiko said, in a lilting voice. 'He's quiet and one learns so much just listening to him.'

'You're lucky to have such a good customer at your bar,' Imanishi said. 'Are you very friendly with him?'

'No, I don't know him that well.' Emiko looked troubled. 'I just know him as one of our customers.'

'I see. I wonder what kind of life an artistic person like that leads. I suppose he's always reading books, and thinking?'

'Probably. In his type of work it's important to keep up with everything.'

'I agree. I'm just a layman, so I don't know, but I suppose a critic has to write about other things than music?'

'Oh, yes, all kinds of things. Particularly in Sekigawa-*sensei*'s case. He started off with literary criticism. Since his talents are so wide-ranging, he writes about painting, music, and society, too.'

'I see. He's so young and yet has studied so much,' Imanishi said, sounding impressed.

His sister brought out some early tangerines. 'This is nothing special, but please have some.'

'Oh, please don't bother.' Emiko looked at her watch in a flurry. 'I should be getting ready to go.'

'Don't say that. Please stay.'

Emiko took one of the tangerines offered her. 'This is so delicious,' she said, as she ate it.

The conversation continued, but they did not talk further about Sekigawa.

'Thank you so much,' Emiko said politely and stood up to leave.

'See, I told you,' his sister said, sitting next to him. 'She's a quiet young woman. You'd never guess she was a bar hostess.'

'I suppose not. But she's really fond of that Sekigawa.'

'I guess so. I could tell that, too.'

'She said he just came to her bar every now and then, but I think there's more to it than that. Didn't you notice?'

'What?'

'She's pregnant.'

'Oh?' his sister looked at him with surprise.

'That's what I think. Am I wrong?'

The sister did not answer right away, but looked at him in amazement. 'Brother,' she said with a sigh, 'you're a man, how can you tell?'

'So I'm right, aren't I?'

'She hasn't said anything, but I've been thinking she must be. How did you figure it out?'

'I just felt it somehow. It's the first time I've seen her face, but I imagine that normally she must have a softer expression. Besides, she ate the whole tangerine. It was so sour, I couldn't eat mine at all.'

'That's true. The tangerines aren't sweet yet.'

'You suspected, too?'

'Yes, I did. She seemed to be throwing up the other day. I thought it might have been something she ate, but since then, too, there've been some other indications.'

'I see.'

'Whose child do you think it is?'

'I wonder.' Imanishi sat thoughtfully as he smoked a cigarette.

'That Sekigawa-*san* might be the one,' his sister said.

'How are we to know that?' Imanishi said reprovingly. 'You can't just gossip like that.'

'You're right. This is just between us.'

A short while later they heard a soft knock on the door. It was Emiko dressed up for work, kneeling in the hallway. 'I'll be going out now. It was nice to meet you,' she said to Imanishi.

'Well, thanks for coming by,' Imanishi said, sitting more formally. 'Have a good evening at work.'

After seeing Emiko off at the door, his sister turned around to Imanishi and said, 'It may be just because we think she is, but it really does seem like it, doesn't it?'

10. Emiko

In the back streets of Ginza was a coffee shop that stayed open until two A.M. After eleven-thirty at night, its customers were mainly hostesses from the nearby cabarets and bars who, after they finished work, would stop by for coffee and pastries before making their way home, relaxing after a tiring night. Some people waited in this coffee shop until after midnight, when the rush to hail taxis after the bars closed subsided. Others came here to meet hostesses with whom they had private arrangements.

Pushing the door open, Emiko entered; she was wearing a kimono. She looked around the shop until she spied Sekigawa, who was sitting in one of the last booths with his back to the entrance.

'Sorry to keep you waiting.' Slipping off her black lace shawl, Emiko smiled happily at him. 'Did you wait long?'

Sekigawa glanced briefly at Emiko and looked away. In the dim light his face seemed morose.

'I've been waiting for twenty minutes.'

His coffee cup was nearly empty.

'I'm so sorry,' she said and bowed her head as if to a stranger. 'I was impatient to get away, but there was a customer who just wouldn't leave, so I couldn't escape. I'm sorry.'

A waitress came to take her order.

'I'd like a lemon tea.'

When the waitress left, Emiko continued, 'I hope I haven't

caused you any trouble asking you to come and meet me like this.'

'I'm busy, you know,' Sekigawa said gruffly. 'I wish you wouldn't do this sort of thing.'

'I'm sorry,' Emiko apologized again. 'But I really need to talk to you.'

'What about?'

'I'll tell you later.'

'Can't you tell me now?'

'No. I'll tell you later. Oh, yes, there's something I've been meaning to mention to you. I met someone who said he saw you in Akita Prefecture. It must have been about a month ago . . .' This was a topic that she did not consider to be very important.

'In Akita?' Sekigawa suddenly raised his eyes. They showed more concern than Emiko had anticipated. 'Who was that?'

'Remember, a while ago you went to Akita with Waga-*san*?'

'Oh, yes, we went to see the rocket research center.'

'Yes, that was the time. This person says he saw you at a train station there.'

'Is it someone I know?' Sekigawa asked.

'No, you don't know him. It's someone you have no connection with.'

'Why did this topic come up?'

'Apparently he read your piece in the newspaper. He saw your name and photo and said he remembered seeing you there.'

'Is he a customer at your bar?'

'No, that's not it. He's my landlady's brother.'

'Why did such a person mention that to you?'

'We started out talking about "musique concrète." So I happened to say that I knew you, and we began talking.'

'You told him you knew me?'

'Don't worry,' she said. 'I told him that you were just a customer who comes to the bar.'

'He doesn't suspect anything between us?' Sekigawa said with a serious expression.

'No, no.' She smiled to placate him. 'How could he know?'

'Don't talk about me to anyone at all.' Sekigawa's voice thickened with displeasure.

'Of course, I'm very careful about that.' She looked contrite. 'But when your name comes up in conversation, I feel so happy. I'll be more careful in the future.'

'And what does this landlady's brother do for a living?'

'I asked her that,' Emiko answered, 'but she didn't give me a definite answer. He seemed to be a very nice, kind man.'

'And you have no idea what he does?' Sekigawa pressed.

'I found out. Not from the landlady, but I asked around at the apartment house. I was a bit surprised.'

'What was it?'

'He's a detective at police headquarters. But he didn't seem like that at all. He was very friendly and seemed to enjoy talking.'

Sekigawa didn't respond to this. He took out a cigarette and lit it, silently thinking.

'Let's go.' He grabbed the bill.

Looking at her unfinished tea, Emiko said, 'Why don't we stay here a little longer?'

'If you want to talk, I'll listen somewhere else.'

'All right,' she said docilely.

'You go out first and hail a taxi.'

Nodding, Emiko quietly stood up from her seat and left the coffee shop.

Two minutes later Sekigawa stood up. He walked to the register with his head bent down so as not to be recognized by people sitting in the other booths.

When he got outside, Emiko was waiting with a cab. Sekigawa entered the taxi first. The two of them sat silently for a while, looking ahead. Emiko quietly stretched out her hand and grasped Sekigawa's fingers, but he gave no response.

'Was it unwise of me to mention you? If that's what's made you angry, please forgive me,' Emiko apologized, looking at his darkened profile.

'You're going to have to move from that apartment,' Sekigawa said eventually.

'What did you say?' Emiko asked, thinking she might have misunderstood his words.

Sekigawa repeated, 'You'll have to move from that apartment.'

'Why?' Emiko asked, her eyes wide. 'I just moved in. I've only been there two months,' she said in a dejected voice. 'Did I do something bad by chatting with the people there? Is that why I need to move away?'

Sekigawa did not give her an answer. Instead, he continued to smoke as if he were displeased.

After a while, he asked, 'Has that detective been there often?'

'It seemed like it was the first time since I moved in.'

'When you had your conversation, was it you who started it?'

'No, it wasn't. The landlady invited me in for a cup of tea. When I went to her apartment, her brother was visiting. We started talking while we were having tea.'

'So the detective had her call you over.'

Emiko had not expected these words. 'I'm sure it was a co-incidence. I don't think you should be so suspicious.'

'It doesn't matter which it was,' Sekigawa said. 'At any rate, I want you to move out of that apartment. I'll find some other place for you.'

Emiko knew what he was thinking. Sekigawa was always worried that his relationship with her would become known to others.

'If you don't like my present apartment, I'll move,' she said, giving in.

Sekigawa stubbed out his cigarette in the ashtray.

He was in a bad mood and she wanted to coax him out of it. Emiko needed him to be in a good mood, especially tonight.

'The nights are already so chilly,' she said.

Sekigawa was still silent.

They could see the neon lights of Akasaka. On the right was a large new hotel.

'Oh, look.' Emiko had been looking out the window, and suddenly poked Sekigawa's knee. 'Isn't that Waga-*san*?'

Next to the hotel was a nightclub with its entrance lit up. Luxury cars were parked in front of the club. Among the customers leaving the club was Waga Eiryo.

'Hmm,' Sekigawa said, looking out.

'He's with a pretty woman. Is she his fiancée?'

'Yes. That's Tadokoro Sachiko.'

Their attention was held by Waga and Sachiko, who stood waiting for a car. Their taxi sped by the standing figures.

'They seem so happy,' Emiko said with a sigh. 'They're getting married soon, aren't they? And before they do, they're enjoying going out together,' Emiko said with envy.

'Who knows,' Sekigawa said.

'What do you mean? They seem so happy together.'

'Right now, yes. But no one knows what will happen tomorrow.'

'You shouldn't say such things. He's your friend; why can't you be happy for him?'

'Of course I'd like to be happy for him. It's because I'm his friend that I don't want to say the standard, trite things.'

'Did something happen?' Emiko looked at Sekigawa's profile with a worried expression.

'No, nothing,' Sekigawa answered. 'But Waga is quite ambitious, so who knows if he really loves her. His target may be her father, Tadokoro Shigeyoshi, and his own road to glory with that man's backing. Do you think that will make her happy?'

'If there is love, then wouldn't it be all right?'

'I wonder.' Sekigawa seemed not to like what he was hearing. 'If that kind of love lasts, I suppose it could be called happiness.'

'But I'm envious. Even if you're right, the two of them can go anywhere they like together. You and I are always meeting in secret.'

Without replying, Sekigawa watched the darkened scenery of the Aoyama district go by outside the window.

The other side of Roppongi intersection was dotted with restaurants specializing in Russian, Italian, Austrian, Hungarian, and other cuisines. As they were operated by foreigners, journalists had nicknamed the area 'the international settlement.' Some of these restaurants stayed open until three o'clock in the morning.

Sekigawa ordered the taxi to stop in front of a restaurant with its light on. Up a red-carpeted set of stairs there was a spacious dining area.

'Welcome.' A waiter guided them to the back.

The dining area was divided into two rooms. Several young couples were seated in the rear section.

Sekigawa ordered a highball.

'What about you?'

'I'd like to have an orange juice,' Emiko answered.

The waiter departed.

'What is it that you want to talk to me about?' Sekigawa asked, his gaze fastened on Emiko.

The other couples were also talking in low voices. At this hour, there was no music and no sound from the street. The late night restaurant was enveloped in its own special atmosphere.

Pressed by Sekigawa, Emiko couldn't at once come out with the next words. She bowed her head and fidgeted.

'You called me during the day, so I thought it was something important and made a special effort to come out tonight. I wish you'd hurry up and tell me what it is.'

'I'm sorry.' It was about telephoning him that she apologized. Sekigawa often told her that he did not want her to call him. Even so, Emiko did not continue. The waiter served them; she sipped her juice through a straw, eagerly.

'Did you have too much to drink tonight?' Sekigawa asked, watching her face.

'No.' Emiko shook her head slightly.

'You seem to be awfully thirsty.'

'Yes.'

'Are you hungry?'

'No.'

As Sekigawa drank his highball, the waiter brought over an appetizer. It was a plate of smoked salmon. Emiko stared at it.

Noticing her gaze, Sekigawa offered the dish to her. 'Eat some if you like.'

'Thank you. I'll just take this.' Emiko pierced the slice of lemon on the plate with a toothpick. Putting it into her mouth, she ate it as if it were delicious.

'Does such a sour thing taste good to you?' Sekigawa asked, watching her.

At this moment, Sekigawa's expression changed. He had realized something. He glared at Emiko. Suddenly shifting his chair around, he moved close to sit next to her.

'You,' he said softly in her ear, 'can't possibly be . . .'

Emiko turned bright red. Her hand stopped moving. She sat perfectly still.

'So that's it.' Sekigawa was still looking at her intently.

Without uttering a word, Emiko nodded.

Sekigawa said nothing further. Looking away from her, he tightened the grip on his glass.

'It's really true? There's no mistake?' he asked after some time.

'Yes,' Emiko said.

'How far along is it?'

The answer to this question also took a while. Calling up her courage, Emiko answered, 'It's almost four months.'

Sekigawa clenched the glass so tightly that it nearly broke. 'You fool.' He spoke in a deliberately low voice. 'Why didn't you say anything about it before now?'

He focused on the hair of her downcast forehead.

'I was afraid that it would end up like the last time,' she said.

'Of course,' he said, drinking a mouthful of highball. 'That's the obvious solution.'

'No, it's not.' Emiko raised her head. Her eyes showed a determination she had not displayed so far. 'I did as you said before, but now I regret it.'

'Regret it?'

'Yes. You wouldn't listen to what I said. You don't know how disappointed I felt. But this time . . . this time I'm going to do what I want.'

'You can't,' Sekigawa said. 'What are you saying? Where's your common sense? It was because you did as I said that nothing happened that time before. If we acted according to your selfish wishes, it would have been a tragedy.' Sekigawa let out his breath and continued, 'It's not something to be decided on the basis of temporary sentiment or excitement. You have to be more realistic. For one thing, think about the child that will be born. How unfortunate that child will be . . .'

'No,' she resisted strongly. 'This time I'm going to have my way.'

There was something so determined in her voice that Sekigawa could not continue.

'Please, just this once listen to what I want,' she pleaded, despite the harsh expression on his face. 'It's the second time. The first time I did as you said. But now I know that it was wrong. No matter what happens, I'll take responsibility.'

'Responsibility?' Sekigawa looked at Emiko in a displeased manner. 'What are you saying?'

'I'll raise the child all by myself.'

'Don't be unreasonable,' he said in a disagreeable voice. 'Do you think you should act out of such sentimentality? It will only lead to misfortune.'

'I don't care. I don't have to be happy. I'll be content just having the proof of your love and raising the child.'

Sekigawa looked aside, exasperated. Then he swallowed the rest of his highball. The pieces of ice clinked against each other.

Emiko was looking downward sadly.

Sekigawa said, 'I'll never agree. I want you to do as I say. You're just being silly. You haven't even thought of what will happen in the future. If you do this, you're the one who'll regret it.'

'No, I never will,' Emiko said, looking stubborn. 'That won't happen. I intend to have it.'

Sekigawa adopted a placating tone. 'Emiko, I can understand how you feel. But you can't solve anything with love alone. What you think you want can turn out to have unexpected, opposite results.'

Emiko asked sadly, 'Do you love me?'

'You know how I feel.'

'Then . . . then you shouldn't say such things.' Her shoulders heaved up and down as she breathed and her face was pale. 'You should agree to what I want.' Her low voice wavered as tears welled up in her eyes.

'Emiko.' Suddenly gentle, Sekigawa patted her shoulder. 'Let's go. Let's go and talk this over as we think about it together.'

Emiko pressed her handkerchief to her eyes.

The area was absolutely silent with no people around. It was a quiet street even in the daytime. On either side stretched the long walls surrounding large houses. The street was a steep hill laid with cobblestones. Street lamps etched patterned shadows onto its surface.

Sekigawa stuck both of his hands deep into his coat pockets. Emiko was close at his side, her hand through his arm. Their two shadows moved slowly down the sloping street. Occasional taxi headlights passed, lighting up the couple.

'You say you can't give it up?' Sekigawa was very displeased.

Emiko pressed her cheek against his shoulder. 'I'm sorry.' Her apology did not hide the inner strength of her conviction. 'This time I won't change my mind.' Knowing that Sekigawa would be annoyed with her words, Emiko repeated, 'I won't ever cause any problems for you.' Her voice was full of entreaty.

'Problems?' Sekigawa walked facing straight ahead. 'I'm not talking only about the problems it would cause me. I'm also thinking about you.'

The sloping street went downhill and then started to rise again. This area housed foreign embassies hidden behind trees.

'Are you really sure?' Sekigawa asked her.

Emiko was silent. Her silence told him that her mind was made up.

Sekigawa sighed in the darkness.

'I'm sorry,' she said, her voice quavering. 'I'll never mention your name.'

'I guess it can't be helped,' Sekigawa said simply.

'What?' Emiko raised her head in surprise.

'I'm saying it can't be helped.'

'What do you mean?'

'I guess I'll have to go along with you.' Sekigawa said this as if he were speaking his thoughts out loud.

'Then you'll forgive me for my selfishness?' Emiko breathed more freely, but she still curbed her happiness.

'I lose,' he spat out. 'I've been defeated by your stubbornness.'

For the first time, Emiko squeezed his arm with all her might. She suddenly became lively.

'I'm glad.' She grabbed Sekigawa's arm and swung it back and forth. 'I'm so glad.'

She clung to him with her body. Then she buried her face in his chest. Her shoulders quivered.

'What are you doing? Are you crying?' Sekigawa put his hand on her obi and embraced her. The tone of his voice had softened.

She actually was crying softly. Her head, cheeks, and shoulders were shaking with her emotions. A sweet odor rose from the back of her white neck, which showed against her collar.

'I'm sorry,' Sekigawa said gently. 'If you're so determined, I won't say any more. I'll cooperate with you as much as I can.'

'Really?' she asked in a tearful voice.

'Yes, really. I was probably too harsh in the way I spoke to you.'

'No, you weren't.' She shook her head vigorously. 'I understand very well how you feel. That's natural, I think. But, just this time, I want to protect my own life, actually the life that will pass on from you . . .' Emiko could not continue, because she was so wrought up, and her lips quivered.

With a sudden motion, Sekigawa pulled her shoulders toward him and pressed his lips to hers. The tears flowing down her cheeks felt cold to him.

The tall trees trailed over the wall beside them. In the darkness of the shade of the trees, they stood embracing for a long time. Suddenly automobile headlights swept the figures of the couple. The two pulled apart and began walking.

'You don't have to worry,' Sekigawa encouraged Emiko. 'I'll do all that I can. But in exchange,' he continued as he walked along, 'could you do as I ask? You'll have to quit the club right away.'

To Emiko, these words seemed an unexpected kindness.

'But I feel fine,' she responded cheerfully.

'No, now is the most important time. You don't want to take any chances. What would you do if you became ill?'

'Well, yes.' Emiko took out her handkerchief and wiped her tears.

'You should tell the madam at the club tomorrow and quit. You can give as your reason something else and say that you want to stop working there.'

'Yes, I'll do that.' Emiko's step became brisk, a complete change from five minutes before.

'So, it's all set. Now that it's decided, it'll work out,' Sekigawa said.

When Imanishi arrived home early for a change, he heard his sister's voice in the back room.

'Welcome home,' his wife greeted him at the entrance. 'Oyuki-*san* is here.'

Imanishi took off his shoes without a word and stepped up into the house.

'Brother, I've come for a visit,' his sister greeted him.

'Right. Thanks for having me over the other day.'

He changed his clothes with his wife's help.

'That's what I've come about today.'

'What do you mean?'

'That bar hostess you were asking about, she suddenly moved out of her apartment.'

'What?' Imanishi stopped untying his necktie. 'She's moved? When was that?'

'It was yesterday afternoon.'

'Yesterday afternoon? She's not at your place anymore?'

'No. I was surprised, too. She brought it up yesterday, all of a sudden. I've never seen anyone move like that.'

'Where did she go?'

'She said she was moving to the Senju area.'

'Where in Senju?'

'I didn't get details.'

'You fool,' Imanishi unexpectedly yelled at his sister. 'You should have told me earlier. Why didn't you contact me right away at headquarters?'

'Was she that important?' His sister was surprised.

'You wouldn't understand. It would have been much more helpful if you had told me while she was in the middle of moving than telling me about it now. And if you don't know where she moved to, what good is that?'

Having been scolded by her brother, Imanishi's sister looked unhappy. 'You didn't say anything, so I thought it would be all right if I told you about it later.'

Imanishi had not expected Emiko to move again only two months after she had moved into his sister's apartment building.

'Which moving company did she use?'

'I don't know.' It seemed that his sister had not paid much attention.

'You're really hopeless.' Imanishi tightened the knot on his necktie that he had loosened. 'Hey, my jacket.'

'Are you going out again?' Yoshiko asked, looking at him in surprise.

'I'm going right to her house.'

'My goodness.' His wife and sister exchanged looks. 'I'm getting supper ready. Oyuki-*san* just arrived a little while ago. Why don't you go later?'

'I'm in a hurry. Oyuki,' Imanishi said to his sister, 'let's go to your place right away. I want to find out where she moved to.'

'Did that woman do something wrong?' his sister asked.

'No, it's not that she did something wrong. But there's something that's bothering me. And we might be able to find out where she went if we make the effort right now.'

★

Oyuki showed Imanishi to the second floor, which was divided into five units. Emiko's had been the one farthest back. Oyuki opened the door and turned on the light. It was a room that got the afternoon sun from the west, fading the tatami. The areas that had been covered by furniture were a darker color. All that was left in the room were the things Emiko no longer needed. In the corner of the closet she had left empty cosmetic and soap boxes, old folded newspapers, and old magazines. She had left the room neat and tidy.

'She was a quiet, nice girl,' Oyuki told her brother. 'When I heard that she was a bar hostess, I thought she might be sloppy. But she was much more concerned about neatness than most people.'

Imanishi spread the old newspapers and magazines on the tatami. There was nothing unusual about them. The magazines were reviews usually read by intellectuals. Taking one of them, Imanishi flipped through the pages. He then opened it to the table of contents and scanned it. He looked at the other magazines. He opened them to the tables of contents and read through them. He nodded. Next, he looked at the empty boxes. Inside were sheets of old wrapping paper that had been neatly folded. These also showed how tidy Emiko was.

As he was checking through the boxes, he discovered a box of matches. It was from a bar. Imanishi read the name on the label, 'Club Bonheur.'

'Is that where she worked?' Imanishi showed his sister the matchbox, printed in yellow letters on a black background.

'It might be. She never told me the name of the bar.'

Imanishi put the empty matchbox in his pocket. He didn't find anything else.

'Which moving company came to pick up her things when she moved out yesterday?'

'I didn't notice which one.'

'But you saw the movers, didn't you?'

'Yes, I saw them. She and a man carried her things from this room to the van outside.'

'Where are the closest movers?'

'There are two near the station.'

Imanishi went downstairs. He went straight to the entryway and put on his shoes.

'Are you leaving already?' his sister said in surprise.

'Yes,' he said as he tied his shoelaces.

'You've come all this way. Why don't you have some tea at least?'

'I can't take the time.'

'Are you in that big a hurry?'

Finishing with his shoelaces, Imanishi straightened up.

'If Miura-*san* comes back, shall I ask her anything?' his sister said.

'Hm,' Imanishi said, without much enthusiasm. 'I don't think she'll come back here.'

'Really?'

'She found out that I work for the police. That's why she moved out so suddenly.'

'But I didn't say anything to her.'

'Then she must have heard from someone in the building.'

'Does that mean that she has something to hide?' his sister asked, her eyes wide.

'I can't tell one way or the other yet. On the off chance that she does come around, find out what you can.'

Imanishi walked quickly to the station. He first went to the Yamada Moving Company.

Imanishi showed his police identification. 'Did you go to a house called Okada to pick up some items yesterday afternoon? It's an apartment building, and the person who was moving is named Miura.'

'Let me check.' The clerk went into the back room to ask one of the employees.

'It doesn't appear to have been us,' the clerk answered, returning to the front. 'If we had done the job, we should be able to tell right away, since it was only yesterday. It may have been Ito Movers just down the street.'

'Thank you very much.'

Imanishi entered the other shop and asked the same question.

'Yesterday, you say? I don't remember anything like that,' the clerk said. 'Just to make sure, let me ask our workers.'

The clerk returned. 'We didn't take that job. But one of our men saw someone moving things out when he passed by that address.'

Imanishi asked the young mover, 'Do you know which moving company it was?'

'Yes, I do. Their name was written in big characters on the side of the van. It's one in Okubo called Yamashiro Moving Company.'

'Do you know where in Okubo?'

'It's right in front of the station. You'll see it right away if you go out the west exit.'

According to his sister, Emiko had said she was moving to Senju. Senju and Okubo were located in entirely different directions.

Walking out the west exit of Okubo Station, Imanishi saw a large sign for the Yamashiro Moving Company half a dozen storefronts down the main street, just as the young mover had said. It was nighttime, but when he approached the shop, he could see that there were still people inside.

A woman clerk, who had been examining a ledger, stood respectfully as she listened to Imanishi's question.

'Oh, yes, Miura-*san*,' she responded.

'Do you know where her things were taken?'

'I'm afraid we didn't deliver them to the new location.'

'What does that mean?'

'At her request, we brought her belongings here.'

'Here?' Imanishi looked around the dimly lit space, but did not see anything.

'Yes, but then someone came to pick up her things.'

'You brought her things here and unloaded them, and then someone came to pick them up again?'

'Yes, that's right. It was a bother for us, too, so we weren't happy about it. Fortunately, her belongings were called for right away.'

'Was it this woman named Miura who came to pick them up?'

'No, it wasn't a woman. It was a man of about twenty-seven or twenty-eight.'

'Did he come in a van?'

'Yes, he did. But it was a small van, so he had to make two trips.'

'Was there a name written on the van?'

'No. It wasn't from a moving company, it was a private van.'

'You said the man was twenty-seven or twenty-eight?' Imanishi asked, 'What did he look like? For example, was he thin or fat; what was his hair like?'

'Let me think . . . I seem to remember him as being very thin,' the woman clerk answered after a few moments.

'No, he wasn't that thin,' a man who was in the room put in. 'He was quite stocky.'

'Was he?' The woman clerk was unsure now.

'No, he wasn't. He wasn't that stocky.' Another man put in his opinion. 'His hair was carefully parted. His coloring was light and he wore glasses.'

'He wasn't wearing any glasses,' the woman clerk retorted immediately.

'Yes, he was.'

'I don't think he was wearing any.' She turned toward the other man, asking for confirmation from him.

'He could have been wearing glasses, but then again maybe he wasn't.'

Each of them gave a different description of the man's features. The move had taken place just the day before, and already their memories were contradictory.

Imanishi changed his line of questioning. 'You said he came to load up twice?'

'Yes, he did.'

'Where did he say he was taking the things?'

'I didn't hear anything about that.'

'Then about how much time passed between the time he left with the first load and the time he came for the second load?'

'Let me see. I think it was about three hours.' On this point, there was no disagreement.

'Thank you very much.'

Imanishi boarded a streetcar at Okubo Station and went to Ginza. On the tram he did some thinking.

Imanishi arrived at Club Bonheur at about nine o'clock. The writing on the matchbox in his pocket had given him the address. When he pushed open the door, the dim light was hazy with cigarette smoke.

'Welcome.'

Imanishi took a seat at the bar.

The booths were packed with customers. It appeared to be a popular spot. Ordering a highball, Imanishi casually glanced around the room. There seemed to be about ten hostesses, wearing either Western clothes or kimonos. He couldn't tell which one was Emiko. Because he was sitting at the counter, no hostess came to take care of him.

Imanishi asked the bartender. 'Is Emiko-*san* here?'

'She quit yesterday,' the bartender answered, with a polite smile.

'What? Yesterday?' Imanishi was shocked.

'Yes.'

'That was sudden,' Imanishi muttered. He had counted on finding her here.

'That's right. We were very surprised. But she insisted on giving notice, so, finally, the madam accepted it.'

'Did she say anything about going to a different bar?'

'No, it wasn't that. She said she wanted to go back to her family for a while.'

'Is that true?'

The bartender grinned and replied, 'I wonder. But I wouldn't know.'

'Is the madam here?'

'Yes, she is.'

'Could you please call her over?' Imanishi said in a low voice, as he showed him his police identification.

The bartender's demeanor changed. He bowed to Imanishi, then he hurried around the end of the bar and went toward the booths. The bartender returned with the madam. She was a tall, sexy-looking woman of about thirty. She was wearing a stylish kimono.

'Welcome,' she said in a charming tone of voice.

'Sorry to interrupt your work. I'd just like to ask a few questions. I understand that one of your girls, Emiko, quit yesterday?'

'Yes, she did.'

'Do you know what caused her to leave?'

'She said that she planned to go back to her hometown. It was so sudden, I was really surprised. She's been at this club for quite a while and had many customers, so it puts me on the spot to have her leave. When I told her that, she pleaded with me, nearly in tears, so I finally agreed to let her go even though she hadn't given proper notice. Is Emiko in trouble?'

'No, it's not that. I wanted to ask her some questions. Do you know where she lives?'

'She mentioned something about Kawaguchi.'

'She moved out of there yesterday.'

'Really? I didn't know that.' She seemed truly surprised.

'What kind of customers did Emiko have?'

'Let me see. She had all kinds. She was quiet, and seemed to be naive, so her customers were mostly quiet ones.'

'Was there a Sekigawa-*san* among her customers?'

'Sekigawa-*san*? Oh, you mean of the Nouveau group?'

'Yes, that's the person.'

'He used to ask for Emiko by name quite a while ago, but not recently.'

'When you say "quite a while ago," how long ago do you mean?'

'It must have been about a year ago, now.'

'Hasn't he been in at all since then?'

'He hardly ever comes now. Maybe once every two months or so, and usually with other people.'

'Was there anything special between this Sekigawa-*san* and Emiko?' Imanishi asked the madam.

'I wouldn't know. He did ask for her once, but I don't know what happened after that.'

'Could it be that he stopped coming because their relationship was secretly becoming more intimate?'

'I suppose so. The girls who work at places like this often have their lovers avoid their bars. So that may have been the case with Emiko as well.' The madam said this much and then asked Imanishi, 'Was Sekigawa-*sensei* really on close terms with Emiko?'

'I don't know.' Imanishi didn't want to be pushed on this point.

'Did something peculiar happen between Sekigawa-*sensei* and Emiko?' the madam continued to ask.

'No, not that I know of. It's not anything Emiko-*san* did. As I said before, I came here because I just wanted to ask her some questions.'

'I can't believe that Sekigawa-*sensei* had something going with Emiko,' the madam said doubtfully.

'Well, it isn't clear that he did,' Imanishi said to prevent the conversation from becoming more confused. 'If she comes by, please let me know her new work place and address.'

He left Club Bonheur feeling that he had been put in a difficult position. As he walked Ginza's back streets, he realized his own contradictory thoughts. Neither Emiko nor Sekigawa was the object of his investigation. It was absurd for him to be pursuing them. Yet he could not figure out Emiko's sudden move from his sister's place. He connected this hurried move to the fact that she had found out he was a detective. The elaborate precautions she took in moving were suspicious. She appeared to be hiding something. But strange behavior wasn't reason enough for a detective to pursue her.

He did, however, feel a certain foreboding regarding Emiko's whereabouts. He didn't have any specific reason, just a premonition. In terms of crime prevention, the police were absolutely powerless. It was only after the damage had been done that the police could move in. He couldn't investigate on premonition alone.

ii. A Woman's Death

It was eleven-fifteen P.M. The nurse who took the telephone call remembered the time exactly because she was just about to go to her room to sleep. It was a man's voice on the telephone.

'Is this Uesugi Clinic?'

'Yes, it is.'

'Dr Uesugi's, the obstetrics and gynecology clinic?'

'Yes, it is.'

'There's an emergency patient here. Could the doctor come right away?' The man's voice sounded young.

'May I ask who's calling?'

'It's a first-time patient.'

'What is the problem?'

'A pregnant woman has collapsed suddenly. She's bleeding and has fainted.'

'Are you sure she's pregnant? How far along is she? It's late. Can it wait until tomorrow?'

'She might be dead by tomorrow morning.' The man sounded as if he were threatening the nurse.

'Wait a moment, please. I'll ask the doctor.'

The nurse put the receiver down beside the telephone and walked along the corridor to the doctor's residence at the back of the clinic.

'Doctor,' the nurse called through the paper shoji door, as she stood in the hallway. 'Doctor.'

She could see a light through the shoji. The doctor must still be awake.

'What is it?'

'There's a telephone call about an emergency patient.'

'An emergency? Who is it from?'

'It's a first-time patient. Apparently a pregnant woman has fallen and is bleeding.'

'Couldn't you refuse?' The doctor seemed reluctant. He hated to be called out late at night by a stranger who was probably overreacting or confused.

'But he says it's a severe case and she may die if it's left until tomorrow morning.'

'Who's saying this?'

'It's a man's voice. It sounds like the patient's husband is alarmed.'

'Well, I guess it can't be helped.' The threat that she might die seemed to affect the doctor as well. 'Make sure you get the exact address.'

The nurse returned to the telephone. 'We'll be there right away.'

'Thank you so much.' He sounded relieved.

'Your address?'

'There is a wide road leading north from the streetcar stop at Soshigaya Okura. Follow that road and you'll see a shrine called Myojinsha. If you turn left at the edge of the shrine you'll see a name plate for Kubota Yasuo at a house with a cedar fence.'

'Are you Kubota-*san*?'

'No, I'm renting the Kubotas' cottage in the back. The entrance is through a wooden door.'

'Could I ask your name?' the nurse asked.

'It's Miura. Miura Emiko. That's the name of the patient.'

'I understand.'

'Um, will you be able to come right away?'

'Yes, we'll be there.'

'Please hurry.'

The nurse was not in a good mood. She had been interrupted just as she was about to go to bed. As she was sterilizing the needles, the doctor appeared from the back of the house, coughing from a cold.

'Have you prepared everything?'

'Yes, I just finished sterilizing the needles.'

The doctor went to the pharmacy to collect the necessary medicines.

'Room number three is open, isn't it?' the doctor asked, coming out of the room.

'Yes.'

'Depending on her condition, we may bring the patient here. Could you go back to the house and tell my wife to get the room ready?'

The doctor packed his bag. He drove while the nurse sat in the passenger seat.

'Let's see, he said near the shrine?'

'It's in back of Myojinsha.'

The doctor drove along the empty streets. Eventually the headlights lit the black woods ahead of them and the torii gate to the shrine.

'It has to be this way.' The nurse pointed to a narrow road to the left. 'That must be it,' she said, spotting the cedar fence.

Approaching the house, the doctor flipped on his bright lights to read the name plate, 'Kubota Yasuo.' He stopped the car and they got out.

'He said they're renting the back house, and there's a separate wooden gate that leads to it.'

They found the gate. The doctor turned on a flashlight and pushed it open. The cottage was easy to find. It was a small unit about six yards away from the main house. When he trained the flashlight on its entrance, they saw a piece of paper with 'Miura' written on it pasted onto the side of the doorway in place of a name plate. A dim light shone from inside the house.

'Excuse me,' the nurse called as she stood outside the latticed sliding door. 'Excuse me.'

No one came out.

'They might be in the back. Don't worry about it, open the door,' the doctor said.

The door slid open easily. The nurse had the doctor go in first.

'Excuse me.'

Still no one came out.

The doctor was annoyed. It was unheard of to have been summoned by telephone in the middle of the night and not even be greeted at the door.

'Go on inside,' he ordered the nurse.

The nurse was reluctant, but she slipped off her shoes resignedly and stepped up from the small entryway into the house.

'Excuse me, excuse me,' the nurse continued to call out.

There was still no answer. They could not even hear anyone's footsteps.

'Doctor, no one is coming.'

'All right, I'll go inside.'

The doctor took off his shoes. A light was on in the main room. There must be someone there, he thought.

The doctor opened the sliding door. Out of consideration for the patient, a towel had been placed around the lamp shade, which made the room quite dark. It was a six-tatami-mat room, with the bedding laid out in the center. A woman was lying there covered by a futon. Her hair trailed out at the side of the pillow.

At first they thought the husband had gone out, perhaps to buy ice. But they could not wait around aimlessly for his return. The doctor turned back the futon. The woman lay with her face toward the wall.

'Hello,' the nurse said in a low voice, 'Hello.'

There was no answer.

'Could she be asleep?' the nurse asked the doctor, turning around.

'If she's asleep, it can't be that serious.'

The flashlight still in his hand, the doctor walked around the bedding and sat facing the patient.

'Miura-*san*,' he said to her, focusing on her face.

Even when the doctor called her, she didn't move. Her expression was full of pain. Her brow was furrowed, her mouth slightly open.

Suddenly he said in a different tone of voice, 'Look around the place for someone else.'

The nurse gathered the seriousness of the patient's condition from the tone of the doctor's voice. She went toward what appeared to be the kitchen.

'Isn't anyone here?' she called out two or three times. Still there was no answer. 'No, Doctor, no one is here.' The nurse returned and stood behind the doctor.

The doctor had already turned back the covers and placed his stethoscope on the patient's chest. His concentration in listening for a heartbeat seemed to be more intense than usual.

The nurse went to call the people from the main house. They were a couple in their fifties, who came in, having just been awakened, in confused haste.

'Has something happened?' the wife asked.

'I'm a doctor named Uesugi.'

'Yes, I recognize you.'

'I was just called to this house by telephone. I'm examining a patient. Is her husband here?'

'Her husband?' the man of the house responded. 'There's no husband. She moved in alone.'

'Alone? But some man called me on the telephone a little while ago.'

The doctor looked at the nurse.

'Yes, it was a man. He asked that we come here right away.'

'Well, we didn't call. We didn't even know she was ill.'

'Doctor, what seems to be the problem?' The couple fearfully entered the room and peered at the patient from the edge of the bedding.

'She's in critical condition,' the doctor said.

'What? Critical?' The couple stared, amazed.

'Her heart is still beating, but it's faint. I don't think she can make it.'

'What . . . what happened?'

'She's expecting.'

'Expecting?'

'Yes, she's pregnant. I think she's about four months along. I can't tell unless I examine her more closely, but she's had a miscarriage.'

The doctor had hesitated before he used the word 'miscarriage.' He had a different opinion. He had chosen to use a softer expression. The couple looked at each other.

'Doctor, what shall we do? This is really distressing,' the wife said.

'Under normal conditions, she should be hospitalized. But in this situation, there's nothing to be done.'

'What a terrible problem,' the landlord said. His way of stating this revealed the inconvenience he was aware would result from having a person die on his premises.

'Doesn't she have any family?' the doctor asked.

'No, we know of no one. She just moved here yesterday.'

The doctor looked at the patient's face again. He ordered the nurse to prepare an injection and quickly gave the patient a cardiac stimulant.

'Is she conscious?' the landlord asked, looking at her.

'No, I don't think she's aware of anything anymore.'

Just as the doctor said this, the woman's lips moved. The doctor watched her tensely.

'. . . Stop it, please. Oh, no, no. I'm afraid something will happen to me. Stop it, please, stop, stop . . .' Then the words ceased.

'Imanishi-*san*,' a young detective called out, 'you have a telephone call.'

Imanishi was at his desk writing a status report. He had been put in charge of an unimportant case.

'All right.' He pushed his chair back and stood up.

'It's from someone named Tanaka.'

'Tanaka?'

'It's a woman.'

Imanishi could not place the name. 'This is Imanishi,' he said, taking the receiver.

'Thank you for coming by yesterday,' said the woman's voice.

'Yes?' Imanishi was taken aback since he couldn't tell who it was.

'I don't think the name Tanaka means anything to you. I'm the madam at the Club Bonheur, which you visited yesterday. I wanted to inform you about Emiko, but perhaps you've already heard?'

'No, I haven't heard anything. Where is she?'

'Emiko's dead.'

'She's dead?' Imanishi was shocked. 'Is that true?'

'So you haven't heard yet. Actually, after you left the bar, I had a telephone call from Emiko's new landlord. He said Emiko had died and that he wanted to contact her parents. He asked me if I knew where they were.'

'I see. How did she die?' Imanishi was still astonished. He

thought at first that Emiko had been killed. But if it had been murder, there would have been a report filed with the Homicide Division.

'Apparently she was pregnant; she fell and hit herself in a bad place. I was completely unaware that she was pregnant, so I was shocked when I heard.' The madam seemed more surprised about Emiko's pregnancy than about her death.

'Where did this fall occur?'

'At her new place. It seems she'd just moved in.'

'And the address?' Imanishi picked up a pencil.

'I'll tell you exactly what the landlord told me. It was Kubota Yasuo's house, Number xx, Soshigaya, Setagaya Ward. She had rented a cottage in back of the main house.'

Imanishi hurriedly thanked her.

Imanishi introduced himself to Kubota Yasuo, who seemed to be a good-natured man of about fifty.

'We were very surprised,' Kubota said in response to the detective's questions. 'It was almost midnight when a doctor called to us from the house in back. He said that the woman who had just moved in was dying. We rushed over, but she was almost gone.'

'So you hadn't called the doctor?'

'No. But someone had telephoned him.'

'Did she come to rent the cottage herself?'

'Yes, she did. We always list our cottage with the real estate agent across from the station. She said she heard about it there and came to see it.'

'I see.'

'I never expected anything like this to happen. She said she lived alone, so I thought she would be a quiet tenant, and gladly offered her a lease.'

'Did she say that she worked as a bar hostess?'

'No, she didn't tell us that. She said that she was planning to go to a dressmaking school during the day, so I had no idea that she was a bar hostess. When I looked through her things after she died, I found something from a Club Bonheur. That's why I called there last night.'

'Can you tell me about the day she moved in?'

'I can't really tell you much. Her things were delivered the night before last. As you can see, our rear house has its own entrance. I heard the moving van and thought that her things were probably being unloaded. But it was dark, and I didn't bother to go and watch.'

'How many deliveries were there?'

'It seemed like the van made two trips.'

This agreed with what the employees at Yamashiro Moving Company had said. The times also matched.

'Did she move in the same day she signed the contract?'

'Yes, she did. She came to sign the lease in the morning. And then her things were delivered that night.'

'Did you hear the voices of anyone helping with the move?'

'Well, there's a garden between this main house and the cottage. When the night shutters are closed, we can't hear anything from the back house. So I'm afraid I didn't notice whether there was anyone else helping other than the mover.'

Imanishi asked to see the cottage. The body had already been removed.

'Actually, I was relieved that the police took the body away,' the landlord said, as he guided Imanishi to the house. 'I was worried that it might have to be left here since no one came to claim it.'

Imanishi studied the belongings that Emiko had left. A chest of drawers, wardrobe, mirror stand, desk, suitcase, a wicker trunk still sealed up . . . He checked each item, opening doors and drawers, except for the wicker trunk. He didn't discover anything new. Almost nothing had been unpacked.

'Her futon was covered with blood, so I wrapped it up in a straw mat and stuck it in the storage shed out back. I'd like to get rid of that as soon as possible, too.' The landlord was upset. 'What will happen after the autopsy?' he asked Imanishi.

'I suppose that unless someone comes to claim the body, her remains will be buried in a communal grave.'

'What about her things?'

'There should be some instruction from the police. Please bear with us for a little while longer.'

Imanishi put on his shoes.

It was about a twenty-minute walk from the Kubota residence to the Uesugi Clinic, which was set back inside an impressive gate. It looked like a recently renovated mansion. The approach to the entrance was flanked by a garden landscaped with rocks and plants.

Dr Uesugi came out of his office to talk to Imanishi. 'It was a real surprise. When I got there the situation was already beyond help. There was nothing I could do for her.'

'What was the cause of death?'

'She fell and hit her abdominal area very hard, resulting in a sudden miscarriage. The fetus, however, was dead before she miscarried. The direct cause of her death was loss of blood due to excessive internal hemorrhaging.'

'When you saw her, Doctor, was she unconscious?'

'She was unconscious when I arrived. But she regained consciousness just before she died and said something strange.'

'What? Something strange?'

'She wasn't completely conscious, she was speaking deliriously. Her words were something like "Stop it, please. Oh, no, no. I'm afraid something will happen to me. Stop it, please, stop, stop."'

'Wait a minute.' Imanishi hurriedly took out his notebook. 'Please say that again.'

Dr Uesugi repeated the words. Imanishi carefully wrote them down in his notebook.

'Doctor, why did you decide to report this to the local police station right away?'

'She wasn't my patient. So it wouldn't be proper for me to write out a death certificate. I didn't want to encounter any problems later. That's why I reported it to the police and requested an official autopsy.'

'That was a good way to deal with the situation,' Imanishi commented. Imanishi certainly wouldn't have wanted the body taken directly to the crematorium, leaving nothing for the investigation but ashes. 'By the way, Doctor, I understand that it was not the landlord who called you about the patient.'

'That's right. I was summoned by a telephone call as I was about to go to bed. I was finishing a nightcap just after eleven when the nurse came and told me about the telephone call. She asked me whether I was willing to make a house call.'

'Was the caller a man or a woman?'

'Just a minute. I'll call the nurse in.'

The nurse looked tired and washed out.

Instructed to by the doctor, the nurse answered Imanishi's query, 'It sounded like a young man's voice. I refused to bother the doctor at first, but he pleaded for a house call because she had collapsed suddenly and was bleeding heavily.'

'Did he say he was the patient's husband?' Imanishi asked.

'No, he didn't say that, but I assumed he was her husband. I asked if it could wait until morning, and he said "she may die before then."'

'She may die.' Imanishi thought for a while about those words.

'The patient's heart stopped beating at twelve thirty-four A.M. I took care of a few things after the death and went home. Early the next morning I called the police. So I think the body must have been taken to the police medical examination center.'

'Thank you so much for your help.' Imanishi bowed and left the clinic.

At Soshigaya Okura he boarded a train for Shinjuku. He planned to head directly for the police medical examination center in Otsuka. The train left the station, and he could see the woodlands passing by outside the window. In between the woods were open fields. As he was staring at the woods, Imanishi suddenly remembered that he had been in this area only last month. The place where Miyata Kunio had died was not far from here.

When he realized this, Imanishi took out his notebook and leafed through it. Miyata's body had been found at Number xx, Kasuya-cho, Setagaya Ward. It was very close to the Soshigaya house he had just left. No wonder the scenery looked familiar.

'I see you're back again,' the coroner said when Imanishi arrived at the medical examination center. 'What is it this time?' he asked.

'Doctor, I know it's not a homicide, but I've come about Miura Emiko, who was sent over here for an official autopsy.'

'Oh, that one?' The doctor looked at him with surprise. 'Is there something the matter with that case?'

'No, it's not a criminal case. I'd like to ask a few questions about the body, that's all. Who performed the autopsy?'

'I did.'

'Oh, good. And what was your opinion after the autopsy?'

'She died from excessive hemorrhaging. She was pregnant,' the doctor said casually.

'Ah ha, so it was death from an illness?'

'Yes. I'd say death from an illness, but she fell carrying a four-month fetus. The fetus died and the fall caused the miscarriage. The fetus was stillborn.'

'There's no mistake in that?'

'Well, that's the way it looked to me. But does the great detective have some doubts?'

'I'd have to explain it to you, but there are several strange points about this death.' Imanishi described what he knew about Emiko.

He explained that the accident took place just after she had suddenly quit her job and moved, that a man had telephoned the doctor, but that this man did not appear even after Emiko's death.

'That does sound strange.' For the first time, the genial expression left the coroner's face and he became serious. 'It's certain that a man called the doctor on the telephone?'

'Yes. And yet he never showed up.'

'Hmm.' The doctor thought for a while and said, 'Someone was on intimate terms with the woman. He might even be the child's father. But when she died, as so often happens, he thought about his own reputation and disappeared.'

'That's my theory, too.' Imanishi went on to ask, 'Are you sure she wasn't murdered?'

'No, it wasn't murder.'

'Are there many cases in which pregnant women die from falling down?'

'I can't say there are none. But she was an extremely unlucky woman.'

'You said that there was internal hemorrhaging in the abdominal area from a fall. There's no mistake?'

'No, there's no mistake.'

'Can you tell from the injury what she fell on?'

'It appears that she bumped into something. It must have been something like a rock. Since there were no skin lesions, it must have been a smooth boulder, without sharp corners.'

'What about the fetus?'

'When I saw it, it was on the futon bedding. So we brought it over and examined it as well. The fetus had died while it was in utero. I would say it was a miscarriage. In cases where the fetus is stillborn, we check to see if the stillbirth was the result of a shock to the mother, or if the fetus had died and caused the miscarriage. In this woman's case, she had the double misfortune of having the fetus die and then falling. That's why there was excessive bleeding.'

'I'd like to ask you again,' Imanishi persisted. 'When you performed the autopsy, you found no special changes in any other internal organs?'

'Imanishi-*san*, in your position, I know you have to question everything, but unfortunately, as far as I could tell, there were no symptoms of poison.'

'I see,' Imanishi said, looking downcast. 'What gender was the fetus?'

'It was a girl,' the doctor answered, his face clouding for a moment.

Imanishi felt as if an unforeseen shadow had passed before his eyes. 'Thank you very much for everything.'

'If you ever have any doubts, don't hesitate to come to me.'

'I may be calling on you again with more questions.'

'Are you on a case that involves this woman?'

'Well, it's not that definite yet. But there are some things that I am not satisfied about concerning the circumstances surrounding her death.'

'Imanishi-*san*, do you know when her relatives will come to claim the body?'

'Hasn't there been any word from the local police?'

'No, we haven't heard anything yet. They said they were making inquiries in her hometown.'

Imanishi felt his initial sadness return. As he left the medical examination center, he could not put the doctor's words that the fetus had been a girl out of his mind. Imanishi could picture

Emiko as a mother. When he had met her at his sister's place, he couldn't picture her as a bar hostess. He had seen only the unsophisticated innocence of a young woman. She had been polite and quiet.

Why had Emiko moved right after she had met Imanishi? Despite his sister's protestations, Imanishi thought that it was because Emiko had found out that he was a police detective.

The way she had moved was not usual. Probably the man with the moving van was the man who had called Dr Uesugi. No one knew what this man looked like. The employees at the moving company agreed that he was young, and the nurse at Uesugi Clinic also said that the voice on the telephone was young. Why did he phone the doctor about Emiko and then disappear? He acted just like a murderer even if it was clear from the autopsy that Emiko wasn't murdered.

It was also a strange coincidence that the distance between the house in Soshigaya where Emiko had died and the lonely field where Miyata had died was not great. If measured in a straight line, these two locations were a little over a mile apart.

Miyata had died just before he was to meet with Imanishi. Emiko's death had taken place when Imanishi was searching for her. Imanishi had been trailing both of them and now they were both dead.

The locations and the circumstances of these two deaths were too similar. But both seemed to have been from natural causes. Imanishi was deep in thought as he swayed with the motion of the streetcar. He took out his notebook. He looked at Emiko's last words, the words Dr Uesugi had said she'd spoken in delirium: 'Stop it, please. Oh, no, no. I'm afraid some-thing will happen to me. Stop it, please, stop, stop . . .'

To whom was she speaking? And what was she crying out to stop?

*

Three days later, Imanishi visited Nakamura Toyo, who lived in Nakameguro in a small house at the end of an alley. Her husband had passed away ten years ago, and now she lived with her son and his family. She had been hired by Sekigawa to look after his house during the day. Imanishi went to see her after nine o'clock at night.

'I've come from an inquiry agency,' Imanishi said to Nakamura Toyo when she came to the entryway. 'I'd like to ask you about Sekigawa-*san*.'

'What kind of questions?' Nakamura Toyo looked at him in surprise.

'I understand that you go to his house every day to do the housekeeping?'

'Yes, I do. I've just now returned.'

'Actually, it's about a marriage possibility.'

'What? A marriage?' Toyo's face lit up with curiosity. 'You mean a marriage for Sekigawa-*san*? What kind of proposal does he have?'

'I'm not at liberty to tell you. My clients have requested that it be kept strictly confidential. That's why I'd like to ask you various questions about him.'

'Well, for a happy reason like that, I'd be glad to tell you everything I know.'

He could see the figures of her son and daughter-in-law in the sitting room that led off the entryway. 'It might be a bit difficult here, so could I trouble you to go somewhere nearby with me? We could talk over a bite to eat.'

Taking off her apron and wrapping a shawl around her shoulders, Toyo followed Imanishi outside. There was a Chinese noodle shop two or three doors down on the main street.

'How about some won ton soup here?' Imanishi asked Toyo.

'That would be fine.' Toyo smiled.

The two of them opened the glass door to a store, which

displayed a red paper lantern hung from its eaves. The shop was steamy inside. They sat at a corner table facing each other.

'Hey, two won tons,' Imanishi ordered and pulled out his cigarettes. 'Please.'

It seemed Toyo liked to smoke. She nodded her head and took a cigarette. Imanishi lit it for her.

'It must be quite difficult for you,' Imanishi said, 'working at the Sekigawa house from early morning until late at night.'

Toyo pursed her lips and exhaled. 'Actually, it's a rather care-free job for me. Sekigawa-*san* is single, as you know. And there's no sense in me just sitting around at home. It lets me earn some spending money.'

'You're lucky to have your health. I guess it's probably better for our bodies if we work for as long as we can.'

'I agree. I haven't been sick at all since I started going to work at Sekigawa-*san*'s.'

While chatting in this way, Imanishi was deciding how he would elicit the information he wanted.

After a while, the two soups were served.

'Please go ahead.'

'I won't stand on ceremony.' Toyo gave a big smile and split a pair of chopsticks. She sipped the soup noisily, making appetizing sounds.

'Is Sekigawa-*san* a difficult person to work for?' Imanishi began.

'No, he's not very difficult,' she answered as she ate. 'Since there aren't any other family members, it's quite easy for me.'

'But don't they say that most writers have difficult personalities?'

'Well, when he's writing an article, he closets himself in his study and doesn't allow me to enter it. That's easier for me to deal with.'

'Does he leave his door closed while he's working?'

'Yes. He doesn't go as far as locking his door, but he closes it tight from the inside.'

'Is that for very long stretches of time? I mean, that he stays in his study?'

'It depends on the day. Sometimes he doesn't come out for five or six hours.'

'How is the study set up?' Imanishi asked.

'It's a Western-style room. It's about the size of eight tatami mats. There's a desk at the window that faces north. He also has a bed that he can sleep on, and there are bookcases lining the walls.'

If it were possible, Imanishi would have liked to see the study. However, his sense of ethics did not allow him to search a person's house under a false identity. Unless they had a search warrant police officers were not allowed to enter a house without permission. Imanishi was already feeling somewhat guilty for having lied about being a private inquiry investigator, but this had been unavoidable. If he had told her that he was a police detective at the outset, Toyo would not have told him anything.

'What are the windows like in the house?' Imanishi asked.

'There are two windows on the north side and three on the south side. Also two on the west; on the east side is the front door.'

'I see.' Imanishi drew a mental diagram of the layout.

Toyo looked at Imanishi's face quizzically as she chewed her won ton. 'Is that kind of information necessary for an inquiry for marriage purposes?'

Imanishi was taken aback slightly. 'Well, actually, um, after all, my client wishes to know how Sekigawa-*san* lives on a daily basis.'

'Is that so? I suppose the parents of a young woman would like to know the details about whom their daughter will marry.' Toyo nodded easily. 'This what I gather,' she offered. 'He's quite a popular writer now, even though he's so young. He's actually quite busy. He once laughed and told me that his income was at about the level of a section chief if he were a regular company employee.'

'I see. He earns that much?'

'Yes, and he's always working. He does a lot of extra jobs, like taking part in panel discussions for magazines and the radio. It's all too complicated for me to understand, but my son tells me that he is a very popular young critic.'

'I've heard that as well.'

'So if he were to get married, his livelihood is very well assured.'

'I understand. My clients will be relieved to hear that. I'd like to have them feel at ease about another thing as well. Does he have girlfriends?'

'Well.' Toyo gulped down the soup. 'He's still young, and he's not bad-looking, and he does have a good income and is famous. So it would be strange if he didn't have a girlfriend, wouldn't it?' Finishing the last of the soup, Toyo wiped her mouth with her handkerchief.

'So he does have a girlfriend?' Imanishi leaned forward.

'I think he does.'

'Doesn't Sekigawa-*san* bring this woman to his house?'

'No, he's never done that.'

'Then how do you know he has a girlfriend?'

'He gets telephone calls occasionally.'

'Have you listened to these calls?'

'There are two telephones, and the calls can be switched over to his study. I've heard calls that have come from her. She seems to be young and has a nice voice.'

'I see, and her name?'

'She never gives her name. She says Sekigawa-*san* will know who she is. That's why I think she's more than a casual acquaintance.'

'I see. And have there been calls recently from this woman?'

'No, I haven't taken any. Now that you mention it, there haven't been any for a while. Of course, these calls don't come that often. I'd say, maybe two or three in a month's time.'

'That's not many at all. Have you ever heard Sekigawa-*san* talking on the phone with this woman?'

'No, I haven't. He always takes those calls in his study.'

'But can't you tell something from the way he behaves? For example, if they are on intimate terms, or if she is just a friend?'

'I think they must be on very intimate terms. But this is just my guess. I can't be sure about it.'

'Is she the only woman who telephones him?'

'No, she's not the only one. There are several others, but those seem to be work-related, and he talks to them in front of me. The only one he talks to in his study is that one woman. Of course, I don't know about his previous relationships. Would this sort of thing hinder his marriage prospects?' Toyo began to worry.

'I'll make sure that it's presented to my client in the right way. His relationship with that woman is probably over.' Imanishi unthinkingly let this slip out.

'How do you know that?' Toyo asked, surprised.

'I just feel somehow that it is. Oh, yes, I'd like to ask you one more thing,' Imanishi said, as he drank his tea. 'This month on the evening of the sixth, was Sekigawa-*san* at home, or was he out?'

'The sixth, you say. That's five days ago. I wonder . . . After all, I leave his house at eight o'clock,' Toyo responded, 'so I wouldn't know about after that time. But I think on the sixth he went out about two hours before I left.'

'How can you be sure? Do you have that date, the sixth, fixed in your mind?'

'That day my daughter-in-law's parents came for a visit. I remember because my son and his wife asked me to be home early that evening.'

'Ah, I see. Then Sekigawa-*san* had definitely left the house by six P.M. on the sixth?'

'Yes. Is that kind of information also necessary for your investigation?' Toyo became quite suspicious.

'No, there was just something I was concerned about, so I asked you. But it's nothing, really. By the way,' Imanishi changed the subject, 'you said that there was only one woman's calls that Sekigawa-*san* takes in his study. You also said you didn't know about his previous relationships.'

'Yes.'

'Isn't there more than one woman whose calls he takes in his study? How about it?'

The woman thought for a bit. 'Since we're talking about an auspicious occasion like marriage, it probably wouldn't be good for Sekigawa-*san* if I say anything that wouldn't be advantageous.'

'No, please tell me everything without any hesitation. I'll separate out what I think will be good to tell my client and what I should leave out.'

'You will? Actually, it's just as you suspect,' she admitted. 'But there haven't been any calls from that woman for a while.'

'When was it that those calls stopped?' Imanishi asked.

'I'd say it's been over a month.'

Imanishi heard this with a start. That was just about the time that Naruse Rieko had committed suicide. 'Do you know what that woman's name was?'

'I don't know. She just asked to speak to Sekigawa-*san*. I think, though, that she was a bar hostess.'

'A bar hostess?' This was not the answer Imanishi had expected.

Toyo continued, 'Her way of speaking was very common. And the words she used were quite rough.'

This did not fit. Why would Naruse Rieko have used such language? Yet the time frame fit. Imanishi reconsidered, thinking that the way Toyo had heard Rieko's voice over the telephone might have misled her.

'You're quite sure that the calls from that woman stopped about a month ago?'

'Yes. Recently, it's just been the woman with the nice voice, as I said before.'

A silence fell over the table. Toyo stared at Imanishi while he appeared to be deep in thought.

'Does Sekigawa-*san* have friends over to his house to entertain them?' Imanishi resumed his questions.

'No, he doesn't do that sort of thing. I don't know why, but he seems to be the antisocial type. He hardly ever has any friends over. The only guests are editors from the magazines.'

'I see. But he must go out a lot. I suppose he often comes home late at night?'

Toyo responded, 'I'm only there until eight o'clock, so I don't know anything about after that time. But apparently he does come home late at night. The people in the neighborhood say they've heard the sound of a car stopping at about one o'clock in the morning.'

'He is young, after all. By the way, I'm changing the subject again, but do you know where he was born?'

'He really doesn't tell me much about himself,' Toyo answered, a bit miffed. 'Can't you get that kind of information from his family register?'

'Yes, we can. I did get a copy of it. It lists Meguro in Tokyo as his registered domicile.'

'Tokyo, you say?' The woman thought for a bit. 'I wonder. I don't think he was born in Tokyo. I was born in downtown Tokyo, so I don't know much about the countryside, but his accent isn't that of a Tokyo native.'

'Then where do you think he's from?'

'I can't tell. It really says on his family register that his place of origin is Tokyo?'

'Yes, it does.' Imanishi already knew that Sekigawa had not been born in Tokyo. He had gone to the Meguro Ward office and had seen his family register, which had noted that the registered domicile had been transferred from elsewhere. 'Thank you so much for your time.' Imanishi bowed politely to Toyo.

'Not at all. Thank you for the snack.'

Parting from her, Imanishi walked up the slope leading to the streetcar stop. The wind swirled dust around his feet. Imanishi walked away with his shoulders hunched and his head down.

Four days went by. Imanishi returned to police headquarters to find two letters on his desk. One was from the Yokote city hall, and the other from the Yokote police station. Imanishi opened the one from the city hall.

This is in response to your inquiry about Sekigawa Shigeo's registered domicile.

In 1957, Sekigawa Shigeo transferred his registered domicile from Number 1361, Aza Yamauchi, Yokote City, to Number 1028, Kakinokizaka, Meguro Ward, Tokyo.

This confirmed the reported transfer of registered domicile recorded in the family register at the Meguro Ward office.

Next he opened the one from the police station.

Regarding your inquiry, our response is as follows:

In investigating Number 1361, Aza Yamauchi, Yokote City, we ascertained that the residence is now owned and occupied by Yamada Shotaro (age 51), a distributor of agricultural machinery.

When we inquired of Yamada-*san* about Sekigawa Shigeo, and said person's father Sekigawa Tetsutaro and mother Shigeko, he responded that he had no knowledge of these three persons.

According to Yamada-*san*, he came to this address, which was owned at that time by Sakurai Hideo, general goods merchant, in 1943, and he knows nothing about the previous owners or residents.

Investigating said Sakurai Hideo, we have found that he has moved to the Osaka area. Should you require further investigation regarding Sakurai Hideo, please contact him at Number xx, Sumiyoshi, Higashi-nan Ward, Osaka City.

Regarding the Sekigawa family, we inquired of several citizens, but found no one who knew of them, and thus terminated the investigation.

Imanishi Eitaro was disappointed. With this response, the investigation into Sekigawa Shigeo's past in Yokote City, Akita Prefecture had reached a dead-end. Yet Imanishi made one more effort. The merchant Sakurai, who had moved to Osaka, might have known Sekigawa Shigeo's father Tetsutaro. Imanishi determined to follow this thread as far as it would lead. He took out stationery and carbon paper and began to write yet another inquiry.

He had finished writing and was addressing the envelope when a young detective came over.

'Imanishi-*san*, a package has come for you.'

'Oh, thanks.'

The package was a thin rectangle. On the address label were the words 'Imanishi Eitaro, c/o Homicide Division, Tokyo Metropolitan Police' and on the reverse side was printed 'Kamedake Abacus Company, Nita Town, Nita County, Shimane Prefecture' with the name Kirihara Kojuro written in brush ink alongside.

Imanishi opened the package at once. Inside was an abacus in a case. On the cover of the case were the words 'Unshu Specialty

Kamedake Abacus.' Imanishi took out the abacus. It was a comfortable size. The frame was made of ebony, and the counter beads were slick and heavy. The entire piece had a shiny black gloss. Imanishi tested the counters with his fingers and found that they glided beautifully.

Kirihara Kojuro was the old gentleman Imanishi had met the previous summer when he went to Kamedake to hear the Izumo dialect. Imanishi had forgotten about Kirihara, but the old gentleman had not forgotten Imanishi. He had no idea why Kirihara had sent him such a gift at this time. There seemed to be no letter enclosed, so he could not be sure of the old man's intentions. But as he was putting the abacus back into its case, a folded piece of paper fell out. Imanishi unfolded the letter. It was written in the old-fashioned, polite language of a bygone era.

My Dear Imanishi-*san*,

Greetings. I wonder how you have been faring since our meeting last summer. I have been keeping myself quiet in the mountains of Unshu, as usual. We have manufactured a new model of abacus at our factory. It is slightly smaller than previous abacuses, and has been redesigned with office use in mind. My son has given me one of the test models, and I hope that you will not consider it too impolite of me to present it to you. If it might remind you of your visit here this past summer, it would please me greatly.

> *The palm of the hand*
> *Holding the abacus feels*
> *The autumn village cold*

Kojuro

Imanishi recalled the garden of the tearoom-style house in Kamedake. A haiku aficionado himself, Imanishi was touched by the old man's letter.

He had gone all that distance and returned without accomplishing anything. But as a by-product, he had become acquainted with the old gentleman. He recalled the *zu-zu* dialect, which had been hard to understand and had been the cause of much confusion. Putting the Kamedake abacus carefully in his drawer, Imanishi rested his chin on his hand.

Sekigawa seemed to have been born in the Tohoku area, famous for its *zu-zu* dialect. As a child, Sekigawa Shigeo had been put in the care of Takada Tomijiro, who lived in Meguro. In Sekigawa's school records, Takada was listed as a relative, but this was not noted in the family register. Checking to see if Takada Tomijiro was from the Tohoku region, Imanishi had found that his original registered domicile was Tokyo. Unlike Sekigawa's, this was not a transferred registration. What was the connection between Takada Tomijiro, who had been born in Tokyo, and Sekigawa, who had been born in Yokote City, Akita Prefecture?

If only someone in Yokote had known Sekigawa's father, he might be able to find out about this family. But the reply from the Yokote police station had betrayed that hope. The only remaining chance, and it was a slim one, was that Sakurai Hideo, who had lived in Sekigawa Tetsutaro's house after him, knew something. He might provide a clue. Yet given the outcome of the investigation so far, Imanishi was not optimistic.

12. Bewilderment

Imanishi had established several circumstantial facts involving Sekigawa Shigeo.

The prime suspect, the man who was seen with Miki Ken'ichi before his murder, had a slight northeastern accent. Sekigawa was born in Yokote, Akita Prefecture, in northeastern Japan.

The murderer probably lived not too far from Kamata. Perhaps he murdered Miki in the railroad yard because he was familiar with that area. Sekigawa lived at Number 2103, Naka-meguro, Meguro Ward. From Meguro, he could easily take the Mekama Line to Kamata.

The murderer must have been covered with blood after he killed Miki. If so, he probably did not take a train afterward. The murderer might have taken a taxi without attracting the attention of the driver, particularly since it was dark. It was also possible that he could have used a private car. Sekigawa did not own a car, but he had a driver's license.

The murderer had to dispose of his bloodstained clothes. Naruse Rieko had cut a bloodstained shirt into bits and scattered the squares out the window of a night train. She must have had some connection with the murderer. So far nothing tied Rieko to Sekigawa. Yet since she was a quiet person who wasn't gossiped about, one couldn't be certain there was nothing between them. It was conceivable that Sekigawa and Rieko had met because the Nouveau group was a supporter of the

Avant-Garde Theater. They could have been seeing each other without anyone knowing about it. Could her suicide have been caused by guilt over her cooperation with the murderer, and not by grief over a love affair?

Sekigawa had been involved with Miura Emiko, who had been four months' pregnant when she died. Perhaps Rieko's despair began when she found out about Emiko.

Miyata seemed to have been attracted to Rieko. He may have suspected that there was something between Rieko and Sekigawa. Miyata had wanted to tell Imanishi something, and it seemed to be so important that he had asked for twenty-four hours to think it over. Then he had died suddenly in a lonely place in Kasuya-cho, Setagaya Ward. It was only twenty minutes by taxi from Sekigawa's house to the place where Miyata had collapsed.

There was no way to corroborate Sekigawa's alibi for the night Miki was murdered in the Kamata railroad yard. Five months had passed, and everyone's memory was hazy. But according to the statement from Sekigawa's housekeeper, he was not at home when Emiko died.

The next problem was Emiko herself. She left her apartment in Imanishi's sister's building in Kawaguchi late in the afternoon and arrived at her new place in Soshigaya at about eight o'clock. But her landlord had just assumed that Emiko had arrived when they heard her belongings being delivered. They hadn't actually seen Emiko in person.

It was about eleven o'clock the following night when a mysterious telephone call from a man summoned the doctor. By then, Emiko was already dying. It was conceivable that only her belongings had arrived at eight o'clock and not Emiko herself. If this were the case, where had she gone after she left the Kawaguchi apartment and stopped by the bar to inform the madam that she was quitting?

The coroner's examination revealed that Emiko died from

loss of blood after a miscarriage, and that she had suffered a fall. Where had she fallen? The coroner told Imanishi that she had fallen against something like a round boulder. But he had seen nothing like that at the Kubota cottage.

The more Imanishi thought, the more confused the situation seemed. As he tapped his chin with his pencil, he realized with a shock that he was obsessively reconstructing a death that wasn't even a murder. His mood changed. He grabbed the telephone on his desk and dialed a number.

'Is this Yoshimura?' he asked.

'Yes, it is. Oh, Imanishi-*san*? How have you been? I'm sorry that I've neglected to call you.' Yoshimura's voice was friendly.

'How about getting together on the way home from work tonight?'

'I'd be glad to. At the usual place?'

'Good.' Imanishi put the receiver down.

When his shift at headquarters was over, Imanishi headed straight for the small *oden* bar in Shibuya. At six-thirty the area around the station was full of people, but the *oden* shop was not crowded.

'Welcome.' The woman who owned the shop smiled at Imanishi. She recognized the faces of these two who always dropped by as a pair. 'He's waiting for you.'

'Over here.' Yoshimura smiled, waving from the corner.

Imanishi took the seat next to him.

'It's been a long time,' Yoshimura began.

'It certainly has. Could you warm some sake for us, ma'am?' Imanishi turned toward Yoshimura and said, 'How's it going?' Then in a much lower voice, 'Anything new on the railroad yard case?'

Imanishi didn't like to talk about their work in this kind of environment, but when he saw Yoshimura's face, he couldn't help asking. He had been thinking about the case incessantly.

Yoshimura shook his head slightly. 'Nothing has turned up. I'm trying to follow up leads in my spare time.'

Imanishi touched his sake glass to Yoshimura's. The two lapsed into silence for a while.

'How's it going from your side?' Yoshimura asked.

'I'm doing a bit here and there. But like you, I'm not making much progress.'

He intended to confide in Yoshimura eventually. It felt good to be drinking with this young colleague with whom he was on familiar terms. The brooding feelings he had were lightened during their time together.

'It's been five months since we took that trip to the northeast, hasn't it?' Yoshimura broke the silence.

'That's right. It was almost June . . .'

'I remember it being quite warm. I thought the northeast would be cooler, so I wore winter underwear.'

'Time goes by quickly.' Imanishi sipped his sake.

Just then a young man tapped Yoshimura on the shoulder.

Yoshimura turned around and smiled at him. 'Hi. I haven't seen you for a while.'

Imanishi looked at the man, but he didn't know him. He seemed to be about Yoshimura's age.

'How've you been?' Yoshimura asked.

'All right.'

'What are you up to now?'

'I'm in insurance sales, but I'm not doing that great.'

Yoshimura whispered to Imanishi, 'He's a friend of mine from grade school. Would you excuse me for five minutes or so while I talk to him?'

'Sure, I don't mind. Take your time,' Imanishi said.

Yoshimura went off to talk to his friend. Imanishi sat alone. He must have looked slightly forlorn, because the shop owner reached over and handed him a newspaper.

'Thanks.'

It was the evening paper. Imanishi opened it up. There weren't any major stories, but he glanced at the headlines to pass the time. The arts and culture section had columns on music and art events.

As Imanishi was looking at these columns, his eyes rested on a familiar name: Sekigawa Shigeo. Imanishi put down his sake and squinted at the article. The title of the piece was 'The Work of Waga Eiryo.'

Imanishi could no longer read small print without reading glasses. He hurriedly drew a pair of glasses out of his pocket and put them on.

In the world of avant-garde music, Waga Eiryo can no longer be called an up-and-coming composer. Those critics who glanced curiously at 'musique concrète' and electronic music a few years ago saw Waga Eiryo's efforts as merely a direct translation of foreign trends.

Now, however, Waga has graduated from direct translation and has become a creator of original compositions. Naturally, individual pieces have certain shortcomings, which critics have pointed out. In fact, I, too, have criticized his works quite sharply.

When an art form is a direct import from abroad, the first examples of it will naturally be a translation of the foreign technique. This limitation does not discredit Waga Eiryo. Most of the paintings of the early twentieth century were merely copies of Cézanne's style. The paintings of the seventh-century mid-Asuka period in Japan were nothing more than imitations of China's Sui and Tang Dynasty works. Even music cannot avoid the fate of imitation. The issue is how to internalize new, foreign techniques, and how individual creativity can emerge from this process.

Gradually, yet in a definitive way, Waga has gone beyond the influence of the West and is in the process of giving form to his own inherent creativity.

Many are struck by his new art form and rush to follow in his wake. But they have no hope of reaching the level of this composer who has based his work on a solid foundation. I am impressed at what he has achieved in such a short time. I anticipate further great rewards from Waga Eiryo's rich talent and his ceaseless efforts.

Imanishi was perplexed. He didn't understand a thing about music. Still, it seemed to him that this piece was written in quite a different tone from Sekigawa's previous criticisms of Waga's work.

Imanishi had just started to go over the column from the beginning to reconfirm his impression when Yoshimura rejoined him.

'Forgive me,' he said as he sat down beside Imanishi.

'Look.' Imanishi showed the newspaper to Yoshimura.

'Hm, it's Sekigawa Shigeo, is it?' As Yoshimura finished the piece he said, 'I see,' and rested his elbow on the counter.

'What do you think? I can't follow the arguments too well, but wouldn't you say he's praising Waga Eiryo?'

'Of course he is,' Yoshimura stated unequivocally. 'He's showering him with praise.'

'Hm.' Imanishi thought for a moment. Then he muttered, 'I wonder why critics change their opinions so quickly. I read something before that Sekigawa had written about Waga Eiryo's music. He didn't praise him like this.'

'Really?'

'I can't remember the wording, but he didn't sound that impressed. This is completely different from that other piece.'

'Critics sometimes change their minds,' Yoshimura said. 'I have a friend who is a journalist who told me that there is a lot of behind-the-scenes politics. Critics are human, too.'

'I wonder.' Imanishi's face looked as if he couldn't quite understand.

Imanishi had finally reached the point where he was about to tell Yoshimura that Sekigawa might be a likely suspect, but he changed his mind after reading the newspaper piece. He decided to wait.

'Imanishi-*san*, shall we call it a day?'

They had drunk four or five orders of sake.

'Sure. I've had enough. Shall we go?' Imanishi was still thinking about Sekigawa's review. 'Could we have our bill?'

When Imanishi said this, Yoshimura hurriedly offered, 'No, no, I'll get it this time. You're always treating me.'

Imanishi stopped him. 'You're supposed to let your elders take care of these things.'

The shop owner pulled an unwieldy large abacus toward her and began figuring their bill. Watching her, Imanishi remembered the Kamedake abacus in his coat pocket.

'Yoshimura, let me show you something interesting.'

'What is it?'

Imanishi pulled his coat toward him. 'This.'

'So, it's a Kamedake abacus,' Yoshimura said reading the label on the box.

'Your total comes to 750 yen. Thank you very much.' The owner presented the bill.

'Hey, ma'am, look at this.' Imanishi pointed his chin at the abacus Yoshimura was holding.

The glossy back beads reflected the light. Yoshimura was flicking the beads in a comfortable way.

'They slide very smoothly.'

'They told me they make the best abacuses in Japan. That's the advertising slogan of the local manufacturer. When you see the real thing, it doesn't seem to be empty boasting.'

'Where are they made?' The shop owner leaned over to look.

'In the mountains near Izumo in Shimane Prefecture.'

'May I see it, too?' The shop owner flicked the beads as if to test them, just as Yoshimura had done.

'This is a wonderful abacus,' she said, looking at Imanishi.

'This summer I went to the part of the country where they make these. Someone I met there sent it to me,' Imanishi explained.

'Is that so.'

'Oh, did it come recently?' Yoshimura asked.

'Yes. It came today. The old man I met, Kirihara, sent this to me as a present. He said it was made in his son's factory.'

'I remember hearing you talk about him.' Yoshimura nodded. 'People in the countryside are sincere, aren't they?'

'They really are. It surprised me to receive this; I had only met him briefly.'

Imanishi paid the bill.

'Thank you very much.' The owner bowed her head.

Sticking the abacus back into his coat pocket, Imanishi left the *oden* shop with Yoshimura.

'It's funny,' Imanishi said as he walked along with Yoshimura, 'this abacus came just when I had forgotten all about Kamedake.'

'You went there full of anticipation, didn't you?'

'I went thinking "this time for sure." It was during the peak of the heat. I'll probably never go to that mountain area again.'

They walked along the raised tracks.

'Oh, yes, Kirihara-*san* enclosed a haiku he had written. "The palm of the hand holding the abacus feels the autumn village cold." '

'I see. I can't tell whether a haiku is good or bad, but this one makes you feel the scene. Speaking of haiku, you haven't shown me any of yours recently.'

'I've been too busy to write any.'

What Imanishi said was true. These days the pages of his haiku notebook remained blank.

'I'm glad I could see you tonight,' Imanishi confided.

'Really? You didn't say much.'

'Just seeing you has made me feel a little better.'

'You're still working on that case, aren't you? And I suppose you've come up against a stumbling block.'

'That's about it.' Imanishi rubbed his face with his hands. 'I'd like to talk to you, but, to be honest, right now I'm confused.'

'I understand.' Yoshimura smiled. 'Knowing you, I'm sure things will start falling into place soon. I'll look forward to hearing about it then.'

It was ten o'clock when Imanishi returned home.

'I'd like some rice with green tea poured over it,' he told Yoshiko. 'I stopped off to have a drink with young Yoshimura.'

'How is he?' she asked as she helped Imanishi off with his jacket.

'Fine.'

'He should come visit us some time.'

'Look what I was given.' He took the abacus out of his coat pocket.

'Oh, my.' She took it out of the box. 'It's a beautiful abacus. Who gave it to you?'

'An old gentleman that I met last summer who owns an abacus factory in Shimane.'

'Oh, from that trip?'

'I'd like to give it to you,' Imanishi said. 'Use it to keep the family accounts so that we won't waste any money.'

'This elegant abacus would cry if we used it for our meager household finances,' Yoshiko said as she put it carefully away in a drawer.

Imanishi had taken out his stationery and was thinking about how to word his thank-you letter to Kirihara Kojuro when Yoshiko called him saying, 'Your food is ready.'

On the dining table were plates of simmered radish and some dried fish.

'It's getting to be the season for radishes,' Yoshiko said as she poured hot tea over Imanishi's rice.

'Mm.'

Imanishi put his lips to the bowl and slurped the rice into his mouth.

'So it's Kamata . . .' Imanishi muttered.

'What's that?' Yoshiko looked over at him and asked.

'No, it's nothing.'

Imanishi chewed the dried fish and ate the radishes. He hadn't meant to say Kamata out loud. He had a habit of concentrating on what was on his mind while he ate his meal. As he put his food into his mouth he would meditate on one thought. The meal would give a certain rhythm to his thoughts. At these times he would mutter things out of context. This helped to clarify his thinking process. He had muttered 'Kamata' because he was ruminating about the case.

The late meal ended. Imanishi moved to his desk and started writing his thank-you letter.

I am sorry I have taken so long to write to you.

Thank you very much for an unexpected gift of such superb quality. In looking at the abacus, I can tell, even though I am unfamiliar with such pieces, that it is of exquisite make. I hope to preserve it for a long time. I only regret that I have no use that will do justice to such a piece.

I will, however, inform people whenever the opportunity arises that these precious abacuses are made in your district.

When I look at the Kamedake abacus, memories of my visit there come back to me. Thank you so much for all you did for me at that time. I also read with fond memories the wonderful haiku you wrote for the abacus.

I recall the mountains surrounding your town, which must now be beautiful in their autumn colors . . .

Having written this much, Imanishi paused to read the letter over. How should he continue? He could close here, but it was too short for a proper thank-you letter.

He wondered if he should take the old gentleman's lead and enclose a haiku of his own. But no good ideas came to mind. Since he hadn't written any poems recently, his brain seemed to have grown dull. As he was going over these thoughts, Yoshiko brought in some tea.

'A thank-you letter?' She peered at his desk.

Imanishi lit a cigarette.

'Shouldn't we send him something in return?' Yoshiko asked.

'I guess so. What would be good?'

'There isn't anything very special we can send from Tokyo. Asakusa seaweed is probably a safe gift.'

'Could you go to the department store and have them send some tomorrow? Won't it be expensive?'

'Even if it is, for a thousand yen we should be able to get something appropriate.'

'Then go ahead and do it.'

Imanishi thought he would write at the end of the letter, 'I have taken the liberty of sending something to you by separate post. I would be happy if you would accept this token of my gratitude.'

Although his cigarette ash grew long, no poem came to him. The memory of Kirihara Kojuro's expression as he spoke was the only image in his thoughts.

It was at that instant Imanishi felt as if he had been hit by an electric current, jolting his brain into awareness. He sat still while the ashes from his cigarette fell on his knees. He didn't move for some ten minutes. Then, suddenly, as if he had awakened from a dream, he continued his letter in a flurry. The ending was completely different from the one he had intended to write.

★

Waking early the next morning, Imanishi realized there was another person he should write to as well.

Miki Ken'ichi had come to Tokyo immediately after making a pilgrimage to Ise Shrine. This was what his adopted son, Shokichi, had stated when he had come to Tokyo police head-quarters. At that time Imanishi had thought that Miki had simply decided to come to Tokyo to see the sights before return-ing home. But perhaps there had been something that had made Miki change his plans. There may have been a pressing reason that couldn't be explained as a mere change of heart. It could be that Miki's change of plans, his coming to Tokyo after Ise, had been connected to his murder.

Stubbing out his cigarette in the ashtray, Imanishi got out of bed, washed his face, and sat at his desk. The letter he had writ-ten the night before to Kirihara Kojuro had been left there inside its envelope. He began to write a letter to Miki Shokichi.

I hope you have been well.

You may not remember me, but I am the detective you spoke to when you came to Tokyo to inquire about your father's whereabouts.

As you know, we have been unable to locate the person who killed your father. I feel a deep sympathy for the memory of your father. Even though the investigation team has been disbanded, that does not mean we have stopped searching for the criminal. We are determined to find this despicable killer to appease your father's soul. We intend to pursue every lead, to take any measure to arrest the murderer. We will not allow this case to remain unsolved.

The case has reached a very difficult crossroads. In order for any progress to be made toward a solution, we feel we need your cooperation.

Toward this end, would you please inform me of the places your father visited from the time he left on his pilgrimage to the Ise Shrine until the time his body was discovered at the Kamata railroad yard?

It would be most helpful if, for example, you knew which days he spent at which inns. When I asked you about this matter, you mentioned that you had received a few picture postcards from his trip. If you have any further information, I would greatly appreciate hearing any details.

Five days passed. During those five days, Imanishi was involved in a few new cases, which were easily solved. On the fifth he found an envelope on his desk. Turning it over, he read the carefully written return address: 'Miki Shokichi, xx Street, Emi-machi, Okayama Prefecture.'

Imanishi had been waiting for this reply. He opened it at once.

Thank you very much for your letter. I am sorry to cause you so much trouble on account of my late father.

I was deeply grateful to learn from your letter that you and others are working incessantly to apprehend my late father's killer. As a member of the family of the deceased, I would like to help in the investigation as much as possible, but regret that my incompetence does not allow me to be of much assistance.

It may be presumptuous for me to say this, but my late father was a person who had great compassion for others, and never incurred the hate of anyone. As I said before, he was a virtuous man. There is no reason that his killer should not be found, and I believe that Heaven will not let this case go unsolved. Each morning and evening we burn incense at the family altar and pray for the arrest of his killer.

In reply to your questions, here are my answers.

My father sent us a total of eight postcards during his trip.

- April 10: Omiya Inn, in front of Okayama Station
- April 12: Sanuki Inn, Kotohira-cho, Shikoku Island
- April 18: Gosho Inn, in front of Kyoto Station

- April 25: at Mt Hiei, outside Kyoto
- April 27: Yamada Inn, Aburakoji, Nara City
- May 1: at the Yoshino mountains
- May 4: Matsumura Inn, in front of Nagoya Station
- May 9: Futami Inn, Ise City

These are all of the postcards we received. He wrote about how he was enjoying his trip.

My father had planned to return home as soon as he finished his Ise Shrine pilgrimage. In fact, in his postcard from Nagoya, he wrote that he would be able to come home in four or five days. There was no word about going to Tokyo.

Imanishi received another letter the following day.

It was from Kirihara Kojuro. This was written with a brush in bold strokes on stationery of elegant handmade Japanese paper that made the black characters stand out in contrast. Imanishi read the contents of the five-page letter that was the response to his questions about Miki Ken'ichi.

Imanishi read the letter over several times. It was a detailed account of former policeman Miki's good deeds. Kirihara's letter gave more concrete information about the deeds Imanishi had heard about on his visit to Kamedake.

Imanishi spent the whole day deep in thought. Even while at work, his thoughts of the Kamata murder stayed with him. He sent off another letter of inquiry. In the evening, he went to see his supervisor to ask for two days off.

'That's unusual.' The supervisor looked at Imanishi's face and smiled. 'I don't think you've ever asked for a two-day leave.'

'No.' Imanishi rubbed his head. 'I'm feeling a bit tired.'

'Take care of yourself. You can take three or four days if you like.'

'No, two days will be enough.'

'Are you going somewhere?'

'I was thinking of going to soak in some hot springs on the Izu peninsula.'

'That's a good idea. You've been working straight through. Unless one gets some rest, one can get really sick from overwork. Go soak in the baths and ask for a massage and get some sleep.'

The supervisor put his seal on Imanishi's leave request and submitted it to the section chief.

Imanishi left police headquarters early and rushed home.

'I'm off on a short trip and I'm leaving right away. Would you help me get my things ready?'

'Is it a business trip?' Yoshiko asked, seeing that Imanishi was impatient.

'No, it's not for work. I'm taking a short break. I feel a sudden urge to get on a train and go somewhere.'

'Are you leaving on tonight's train?'

'Yes. I want to leave as soon as possible.'

'Are you going alone?'

'Yes, alone.'

'It sounds strange. Are you sure you don't have some work there?'

'No, I'm not going on work. I'm just going to pay my respects at Ise Shrine.'

Yoshiko laughed in amazement. 'I wonder what brought this on?'

The train arrived in Nagoya the next morning. Imanishi changed to the Kintetsu Line for Ise. It took another two hours to reach Ise City. He had come here once, before the war, and the city didn't seem much changed. He found the Futami Inn right away. It was a five- or six-minute walk from the station. He looked inside, but it seemed very busy as a large group was just leaving. It would be better if he visited the inn a little later. The slowest time for the inn would be around noon. That would be the best time to ask questions.

Imanishi decided to visit Ise Shrine in the meantime. He could not go home without paying his respects to this national Shinto shrine after coming all the way here. The inner shrine did not look different, and there were many worshipers. What was different was the result of the recent typhoon. It had broken branches and destroyed some of the trees in the shrine grounds. Imanishi felt amazed that he could be here at Ise Shrine today when he hadn't even thought of coming until yesterday.

Normally, on this kind of trip, he would go to the local police and ask for their cooperation. But he had already taken two official trips, to the northeast and to the Japan Sea area, with nothing to show for them. Unsure if he could come up with any useful results, he had felt unable to request permission from his supervisor for another official trip.

When he returned to the Futami Inn, the entranceway was quiet and the cleaning had been completed. Imanishi stood in the entry, which had been sprinkled with water. A young maid, still in her cleaning clothes, came out to the entrance. She greeted him with a bow when she saw him there. 'Welcome.'

He was taken to a room in the back of the inn on the second floor. The front of this new wing faced the main road, which led directly to the station, but the back rooms had unimpressive views of the cluttered roofs of the city. In the sky above, an airplane flew by. Another maid brought him some tea.

Imanishi gave her his name card. 'Would you tell the proprietor of this inn that I'd like to see him?'

The maid took the card and seemed a bit surprised when she read it. It stated that he was from the First Investigation Section of the Tokyo Metropolitan Police.

'Please wait just a minute.'

Imanishi smoked as he waited for the innkeeper to come up to his room. From his window, all he could see were roofs. The largest one seemed to cover a movie theater. An ink painting of the woods at Ise Shrine hung in the *tokonoma* alcove. On the other wall was a painting of the 'Wedded Rocks' at Futami-gaura Bay. Twenty minutes passed while he gazed at the view and the paintings.

'Excuse me.'

He heard a voice from the other side of the sliding doors.

'Come in,' Imanishi answered, still seated.

A bald-headed man of about fifty opened the door and came into the room. 'Welcome.' After closing the door, the man bowed formally. 'I'm the owner of this inn. I'm sorry that you had to come such a long way.'

'Please sit over here.' Imanishi invited the innkeeper to sit in front of him.

'Thank you very much.'

The proprietor showed by his respectful demeanor his deferential attitude toward the police. It was not the attitude shown a regular guest.

'When did you arrive?' he asked Imanishi.

'I left last night, and got here just this morning.' Imanishi made himself look as amiable as possible.

'Then you must be tired.'

The innkeeper bowed his head each time he spoke. He seemed to be uneasy. All kinds of people spent the night at inns as guests. Burglaries might occur. Wanted criminals might hide out. These things caused all sorts of problems for innkeepers.

'As a matter of fact, I've come from Tokyo to ask for some information,' Imanishi began calmly.

'Yes, is that so?' The innkeeper looked at Imanishi.

'It's nothing for you to worry about. I just want to ask some questions for background information.'

'Yes?'

'I'd like to know about a guest who stayed here on the night of May ninth. I'm sorry to cause you trouble, but could you let me see your guest register?'

'Yes, yes, certainly.'

The innkeeper picked up the telephone receiver on the table and asked that the guest register be brought up.

'My, it must be hard for the police.' Becoming a bit more relaxed, the innkeeper made small talk.

'Well, yes, but it's part of our work.'

'It's the first time we've had someone from the Tokyo police here. Being in this kind of business, we often have to deal with the local police.'

A maid came in while they were talking. The innkeeper took the guest register from her.

'Let's see, May ninth, was it?'

'Yes, that's right.'

The innkeeper leafed through the bound bills.

'What was the name?'

'A man named Miki Ken'ichi,' Imanishi replied.

'Miki? Let's see, yes, here he is.'

The innkeeper passed the register to Imanishi. Imanishi took it and looked intently at the page:

Present address: xx Street, Emi-machi,
Okayama Prefecture.
Employment: General Store.
Name: Miki Ken'ichi.
Age: 51.

The penmanship showed uprightness; the characters were written clearly with no abbreviations. Imanishi stared at the words. This was the writing of the unfortunate Miki Ken'ichi.

No matter how he tried, Imanishi could not connect the style of these characters with the man's brutally beaten body.

Miki had no way of knowing that a tragic fate awaited him when he signed this guest register. He had left the mountains of Okayama Prefecture to make a trip he had always dreamed about; he had fulfilled his goal of a pilgrimage to Ise Shrine and had seen the sights along the way. At the edge of the entry, the name 'Sumiko' was noted, identifying the maid who had waited on Miki.

'It seems that Miki spent only the night of the ninth?' Imanishi asked the proprietor.

The innkeeper also looked at the register. 'Yes, it does.'

'Do you remember this guest?'

'I'm usually in the back office, so I can't recall him.'

'It looks like Sumiko was the maid in charge.'

'Yes, she was. I can call her here if you have any more questions.'

'Please.'

The innkeeper picked up the telephone again and told the maid to come to the room.

Sumiko was a young maid who seemed like a hard worker. Her appearance was not very tidy, and she had red cheeks.

'Sumiko, this guest has questions he'd like to ask about a guest you took care of. Tell him all you can remember,' the innkeeper told the maid.

'You're Sumiko-*san*?' Imanishi asked, smiling.

'Yes.'

'I wonder if you remember. It says in the guest register that you waited on this guest. Do you remember him?'

Imanishi showed the register to the maid. Sumiko looked at it for a while.

'That was the Bush Clover room,' she said to herself and continued to think. 'Oh, I remember. Yes, I'm sure I waited on him,' she said with certainty.

Imanishi asked her to describe his looks and mannerisms. Without a doubt, the maid described Miki Ken'ichi.

'How did he speak?' Imanishi asked.

'Let me think. It was a bit unusual. It sounded like *zu-zu* dialect, so I thought he was from the northeast.'

Imanishi was absolutely sure now. 'Was it that hard to understand?'

'Yes. The sounds weren't clear. In the guest register it said he was from Okayama Prefecture, so I asked him if he was from the northeast. He laughed and said people often made that mistake. He said the people in the village he lived in for a long time also have this accent.'

From the way the maid spoke, it seemed that Miki had been quite friendly to her.

'Was there anything unusual about his behavior when he stayed here?'

'Well, now that you mention it, he came here after he had worshiped at Ise Shrine during the day, and said he was going home the next day. But the next morning he suddenly told me he would be going to Tokyo.'

'Hmm, so it was the next morning that he said he was going to Tokyo?'

This was the crucial part.

'Yes, it was.'

'What time did he arrive at the inn?'

'It was in the evening. I think it was about six o'clock.'

'Once he arrived, did he go out at all?'

'Yes, he did.'

People from all over Japan came to worship at Ise Shrine. Miki might have bumped into someone he knew on this evening excursion. A chance encounter might have been what caused Miki to decide to go to Tokyo.

'Did he go out just for a stroll?'

'No, he said he was going to see a movie.'

'A movie?'

'He said he was bored, and that he wanted to see a movie. He asked me where the movie theater was, so I told him. Look, you can see it from this window. It's that tall building.'

'What time did he return from the movie theater?' Imanishi asked the maid.

'Let me see. I think it was about nine-thirty. I'm sure it was about that time.'

'You mean right after the movie ended.'

'Yes.'

Imanishi was a bit disappointed. If Miki had met someone on his way to see the movie, the time that he returned to the inn would have been either earlier or later. Imanishi had to conclude that Miki had not met anyone.

'How did he seem when he came back to the room? Since it was so long ago, you may not remember, but please try to recall.'

'Let me think.' The maid glanced at the innkeeper and tilted her head.

'This is important, so think it over carefully, and don't make any mistakes,' the innkeeper added.

The maid's expression became tense.

Imanishi felt a bit disconcerted. 'Don't think about it so intently. Just tell me what you remember.'

The maid finally answered, 'I didn't notice anything different about the guest when he returned. He just asked to have his breakfast served later the next morning.'

'You mean the next day, the day he was to depart?'

'Yes. Earlier, he had said that since he was going home on the nine-twenty train he wanted breakfast at about eight o'clock.'

'How did he change that?'

'He said he wanted his breakfast at ten. And that he might stay until the evening.'

'The evening, huh?' Imanishi sat forward. 'Did he say why he changed his plans?'

'No, nothing particular. But he did seem to be deep in thought. Since he didn't say much to me, I just told him good night and left the room right away.'

'I see. And the next morning, was everything on time as he had asked?'

'Yes. I served him his breakfast at ten.'

'So he spent the rest of the day until evening in his room?'

'No, he didn't. He went out just after noon to the movie theater.'

'To the movie theater?' Imanishi was surprised. 'He must have really liked to see movies.'

'But he went to the same theater. I know, since I had an errand in that direction and went part of the way with him.'

'You mean to say he went to see the same movie he had just seen the night before?'

This time it was Imanishi's turn to think hard. Why would Miki see the same movie twice while he was on a trip – it wasn't as if he were a child or a teenager. What about the movie had piqued Miki's curiosity?

'So after Miki came back from seeing the movie, he checked out that evening?' Imanishi asked the maid.

'Yes, that's right.'

'Do you know which train he took?'

'I know,' the innkeeper said. 'I looked up the train schedule for him in the office and gave him the departure time. He called the desk from his room, and I told him that the Kintetsu train connects with an express for Tokyo that leaves Nagoya at ten-twenty P.M.'

'What time does that train arrive at Tokyo Station?'

'It arrives in Tokyo the next morning at five. Many of our guests use this train to go to Tokyo, so I have it memorized.'

'Did Miki say anything special or strange when he left the inn?' Imanishi again turned his gaze to the maid.

'No, I didn't notice anything. I did ask him why he was going to Tokyo when he had said that he would return home to Okayama the night before . . .'

'Yes, yes. And . . . ?'

'He said he had suddenly decided to go.'

'Suddenly decided to go. Is that all?'

'Yes. He didn't say anything more.'

'So that was all.' Imanishi thought for a bit, then asked, 'What movie was it that the guest went to see?'

'I don't remember.'

'That's all right. I can check that out. Thank you so much for taking time when you're so busy.'

'Will that be all?' the innkeeper asked.

'Yes. You've been very helpful. Could you bring me my bill?'

'Are you leaving already?'

'I think I'll go back to Tokyo on that same train. There should be enough time for me to catch it.'

Imanishi paid his bill and left the inn. But instead of going directly to the station, he went to the movie theater. It was located in the middle of an avenue of shops. Several garishly painted posters were displayed outside advertising the two historical movies that were playing.

After he showed the woman at the box office his card and asked if he could see the manager, he was led inside. At the back of the theater they came to a closed door. When the door was opened Imanishi saw a worker painting a poster for a coming feature. The manager stood with his hands clasped behind him watching the painter. When he read Imanishi's card, he welcomed him pleasantly.

Imanishi came directly to the point. 'Excuse me for asking this abruptly, but could I find out what movies were playing at this theater last May ninth?'

'The films we showed on May ninth, did you say?' The manager responded with surprise.

'Yes, I'd like to know the names of the films,' Imanishi said.

'Hmm, is it related to a case or something?'

'No, I just need to know for reference. Can you find out immediately?'

'It's no problem to look it up for you.'

The manager led Imanishi out of the room. They went to the office next to the projection booth. Posters were plastered all over the walls, and the desk was piled high with paper. A young man sat alone figuring, flicking the counters on his abacus.

'Hey, what were the movies we showed on May ninth? Can you look it up?'

The young man pulled the ledger toward him. He flipped through the pages and found it at once.

'One was *Windy Clouds of Tone* and the other *One Man's Rage*.'

'Those were the ones,' the manager said to Imanishi standing beside him. 'One was a period piece and the other a modern movie.'

'Which production company were they from?'

'We show Nan'ei films exclusively.'

'I'm sorry to trouble you, but do you have a pamphlet or anything that would list the actors in those movies?'

'It was quite some time ago, so I don't know if we still have anything. Let me have someone look around.'

The manager ordered the young man to look. He searched the drawers of the desk and the shelves and finally pulled a sheet of paper out from under a pile of posters.

'We've found something.' The manager took the sheet and gave it to Imanishi. 'This is the cast.'

For your reference, the following is a copy of the information in our records.

Father: (unnamed) deceased

Mother: (unnamed) deceased

Head of household: Motoura Chiyokichi (eldest son)

    Date of birth: October 21, 1905

    Date of death: October 28, 1957

Wife: Masa

    Date of birth: March 3, 1910

    Date of death: June 1, 1935

    (Wife, Masa, was second daughter of Yamashita Chutaro, Number xx, Yamanaka Town, Enuma County, Ishikawa Prefecture. Date of marriage: April 16, 1929)

Eldest son: Hideo

    Date of birth: September 23, 1931

The records state the above.

                      General Affairs Section Chief, Jikoen

Imanishi stared at the letter as he slowly smoked an entire cigarette. Being conscientious, he immediately wrote a thank-you letter, then another request for information, asking for the names and addresses of any living relatives or close acquaintances of Yamashita Chutaro, Number xx, Yamanaka Town, Enuma County, Ishikawa Prefecture. He addressed this to the police station in Yamanaka, Ishikawa Prefecture. After rereading the request, Imanishi added, 'As we are in urgent need of this information, please expedite this inquiry.'

It was about eight o'clock when Imanishi returned home. The house was dark, and the front door had been locked from the inside. There was an extra key left under a potted plant for Imanishi to use when his wife was out. Opening the door, he turned on the light and saw the note left on the table.

Oyuki-*san* has come over, and we have gone out to see a movie. Taro is at my parents' house in Hongo. We should be back by 9:00. There is some food in the kitchen cupboard if you'd like something to eat.

Still in his suit, Imanishi opened the cupboard. There was some sashimi purchased at the local fish store, along with a plate of meat and radishes. Steam rose from the thermos container for the rice, a recent purchase. He carried the dishes to the dining table. Since his wife was not at home, he was not distracted. As he ate, he thought over the content of the response he had received that day from Jikoen in Okayama Prefecture.

He had changed his clothes and was skimming the evening paper with a toothpick in his mouth when he heard the front door open.

'Oh, he's back,' he heard Yoshiko say. 'I'm home,' she said as she entered the room. His sister came in after her, smiling. 'I'm sorry. Since Oyuki-*san* came, I asked her if she wanted to go out.'

'That's not true. I was the one who asked Yoshiko-*san* to go out.'

They were covering for each other. The two women continued to talk while they changed their clothes in the next room. Imanishi's sister was a movie fan and she was talking about the performance of one of the actors. His wife came out in her house clothes.

'Did you eat some supper?'

'Yes, I did.'

'We expected to be back before you.'

'Here, Brother, a present.' Imanishi's sister held out a bag of roasted chestnuts.

'Hey, aren't you going home tonight?'

His sister was wearing one of his wife's house dresses.

'No, my husband is away on business again.'

'You come over when you have a fight with your husband,

Oyuki-*san* has come over, and we have gone out to see a movie. Taro is at my parents' house in Hongo. We should be back by 9:00. There is some food in the kitchen cupboard if you'd like something to eat.

Still in his suit, Imanishi opened the cupboard. There was some sashimi purchased at the local fish store, along with a plate of meat and radishes. Steam rose from the thermos container for the rice, a recent purchase. He carried the dishes to the dining table. Since his wife was not at home, he was not distracted. As he ate, he thought over the content of the response he had received that day from Jikoen in Okayama Prefecture.

He had changed his clothes and was skimming the evening paper with a toothpick in his mouth when he heard the front door open.

'Oh, he's back,' he heard Yoshiko say. 'I'm home,' she said as she entered the room. His sister came in after her, smiling. 'I'm sorry. Since Oyuki-*san* came, I asked her if she wanted to go out.'

'That's not true. I was the one who asked Yoshiko-*san* to go out.'

They were covering for each other. The two women continued to talk while they changed their clothes in the next room. Imanishi's sister was a movie fan and she was talking about the performance of one of the actors. His wife came out in her house clothes.

'Did you eat some supper?'

'Yes, I did.'

'We expected to be back before you.'

'Here, Brother, a present.' Imanishi's sister held out a bag of roasted chestnuts.

'Hey, aren't you going home tonight?'

His sister was wearing one of his wife's house dresses.

'No, my husband is away on business again.'

'You come over when you have a fight with your husband,

For your reference, the following is a copy of the information in our records.

Father: (unnamed) deceased

Mother: (unnamed) deceased

Head of household: Motoura Chiyokichi (eldest son)

    Date of birth: October 21, 1905

    Date of death: October 28, 1957

Wife: Masa

    Date of birth: March 3, 1910

    Date of death: June 1, 1935

    (Wife, Masa, was second daughter of Yamashita Chutaro, Number xx, Yamanaka Town, Enuma County, Ishikawa Prefecture. Date of marriage: April 16, 1929)

Eldest son: Hideo

    Date of birth: September 23, 1931

The records state the above.

                      General Affairs Section Chief, Jikoen

Imanishi stared at the letter as he slowly smoked an entire cigarette. Being conscientious, he immediately wrote a thank-you letter, then another request for information, asking for the names and addresses of any living relatives or close acquaintances of Yamashita Chutaro, Number xx, Yamanaka Town, Enuma County, Ishikawa Prefecture. He addressed this to the police station in Yamanaka, Ishikawa Prefecture. After rereading the request, Imanishi added, 'As we are in urgent need of this information, please expedite this inquiry.'

It was about eight o'clock when Imanishi returned home. The house was dark, and the front door had been locked from the inside. There was an extra key left under a potted plant for Imanishi to use when his wife was out. Opening the door, he turned on the light and saw the note left on the table.

'Thank you. I'm sorry to cause you all this trouble.' Imanishi rose from his seat.

The outdoor light was so bright that he had to shield his eyes for a while.

Miki Ken'ichi had seen *Windy Clouds of Tone* and *One Man's Rage* twice when he was in Ise. There must have been some scene in the movies that had made him curious enough to see these movies twice. The maid at the inn had said that when he returned from the theater Miki was deep in thought. Yet Imanishi had not come across anything that would have prompted Miki's second viewing of either of the two feature films or the newsreel.

Imanishi returned to headquarters and found a brown envelope on his desk. The return address on the back of the envelope was Jikoen, xx Village, Kojima County, Okayama Prefecture. Imanishi opened the envelope at once. This was what he had been waiting for impatiently. After reading Kirihara Kojuro's reply he had written a letter of inquiry to Jikoen.

To: Chief Inspector Imanishi Eitaro
   First Section, Homicide Division
   Tokyo Metropolitan Police Headquarters

This is in response to your inquiry regarding Motoura Chiyokichi.

Motoura-*san* entered our sanatorium in 1938 through an introduction from the town hall of Nita Town, Nita County, Shimane Prefecture. He received treatment and lived here until his death in October 1957. His death was reported to his registered domicile. (Registered domicile: Number xx, xx Village, Enuma County, Ishikawa Prefecture.)

During the time Motoura-*san* was a patient in our facility, he received no letters and had no visitors.

went on to social events, then scenes of horrendous traffic jams, the opening ceremony for a local train line, and finally sports topics. Next was *Windy Clouds of Tone*. It was a period film about fights between two gangs of gamblers featuring some spectacular sword-fighting sequences.

Imanishi watched the action on the screen with unblinking eyes, scrutinizing the faces of all the actors, even the extras.

Windy Clouds of Tone was over in one and a half hours. When the lights came on, Imanishi let out a sigh. Imanishi had examined carefully all who had appeared on the screen – petty gang members, passersby, and lawmen.

After a five-minute rest, the projectionist said, 'I'm starting the next one.'

The room darkened and the title *One Man's Rage* flashed on the screen. Imanishi knew the cast from the program notes, but he was unable to connect the names with the faces. When he was younger, he had often gone to the movies, and he knew the faces of the older actors, but none of the younger stars looked familiar.

One Man's Rage was a modern gangster film with much use of pistols. Imanishi peered at the faces of passersby, bar customers, and gangster henchmen. Because it was a contemporary film, the settings showed many parts of Tokyo: the bar areas in the back streets of Ginza, the crowds in Yurakucho, the interiors of large office buildings, and even the warehouses at Harumi Wharf. This meant that there were many people in the background. Imanishi's objects of study were not the featured actors. On the contrary, he was focusing on the bit players and the extras.

When the film ended, Imanishi sat back in his seat, dumbfounded. He had not seen a single face that meant anything to him.

'We've finished showing everything. How was it?' the person in charge asked.

13. A Thread

After his return to Tokyo, Imanishi asked the Nan'ei Film Company for a screening of *One Man's Rage* and *Windy Clouds of Tone*, along with the newsreels that had been shown at the theater. The film company did not grant his request readily. There was no problem about pulling the films out of storage, but the screening room was always booked. New films were completed twice a week, and invitational screenings of these films took precedence. The company was also reluctant to show two films, totaling three and a half hours, at one person's request.

'Do these films have some relevance to a crime?' Imanishi was asked.

'Not directly. If they were being shown in the movie theaters, I'd go there to see them. They aren't showing anywhere, so I have no choice but to ask you to screen them for me.'

'We'll let you know when the screening room becomes free.'

Imanishi waited impatiently three or four days. Finally, he received a telephone call. 'The screening room will be open this afternoon.'

Imanishi rushed over. He felt apologetic at having the films shown just for him, but he had to see them.

The Nan'ei Film Company's screening room was located in the basement of a theater. The screen was about half the width of those in commercial theaters, but the sound was clearer.

The first film was a newsreel. Starting with political news, it

'Thank you.'

Both *Windy Clouds of Tone* and *One Man's Rage* featured currently popular actors. The sheet listed supporting actors and minor actors as well. It even listed the names of the actors playing maids and children.

Imanishi carefully folded the pamphlet and put it into his pocket. 'Are these movies showing anywhere now?'

'Let me think. Since they came out quite a while ago, I don't think they're showing even at theaters specializing in second runs.'

'In that case, were the films returned to the film company?'

'Yes. When we're finished with them, we send them back to the company. These movies are probably in the company warehouse.'

'Thank you very much.' Imanishi bowed.

'Oh, is that all I can do for you? Just a minute, are you on a case related to those movies?'

But by that time Imanishi had turned and left the office.

and you come to stay when he's off on business. What can I do with you? How was the movie, was it good?'

'So-so.'

Imanishi's wife and sister continued discussing the movie.

'Actually, I saw some movies today, too,' Imanishi said.

'Oh, did you really?' his sister said, surprised.

'Is that why you were late?' Yoshiko asked.

'Hardly. I went to see the movies for work.'

'Hmm. Do detectives see movies for their work?'

'Depending on the circumstances, yes.'

'What did you see?'

'*One Man's Rage* and *Windy Clouds of Tone.*'

'Oh,' his sister laughed, 'they came out quite a while ago.'

'Have you heard of them?'

'I saw them. It must have been about six months ago. They weren't any good, were they?'

'I suppose not.' Imanishi turned his eyes back to the newspaper.

His wife sat beside him, peeling roasted chestnuts and placing the pieces on the newspaper Imanishi was reading. The articles were not very interesting, but there was nothing else to read:

Revolution in Boring Holes through Ultra Hard Metal Alloy – Using Extra Strength Ultrasonics.

Far East Metallurgy Company has succeeded in applying the principle of extra-strength ultrasonics to boring holes through a hard metal alloy, something that had been considered impossible until now. This process will allow for a tenfold increase in manufacturing and has been hailed in various areas as a revolutionary technical accomplishment.

A characteristic of this method is that, because the cutter is not rotated, the hole created is not circular. Ultrasonics is considered to be a process having a . . .

It was an uninteresting article. Imanishi was easily distracted. His ears picked up the conversation between his sister and his wife.

'The previews are more interesting than the movies, aren't they?' his wife said.

'That's true. After all, they pick the most interesting parts to show in the previews,' his sister said.

Imanishi put down his newspaper. 'Do they always show previews at movie theaters?'

The answer was, 'Of course.'

When Imanishi went to the film company the following day, the staff member he had come to recognize leafed through the booking ledger to find this information. 'Oh, yes, we did show a preview. We showed a preview of the next week's film and a preannouncement of a coming feature.'

'What is a preannouncement?'

'When we release a major feature, we start advertising about a month in advance. The next week's preview is, as the name says, a trailer of the film that will be shown the following week.'

'What was the following week's movie?'

'It was *The Distant Horizon*. It was a contemporary film.'

'And the preannouncement?'

'That was for a foreign film.'

'A foreign film? Do any Japanese appear in that film?' Imanishi asked to make sure.

'Of course not. It's an American movie, so all the scenes are foreign . . . But there is some snapshot footage of opening night scenes taken in Tokyo. It was a major film and a prince and princess attended the premiere.'

'I see. The preannouncement has shots of that event attached to it?'

'Yes.'

'I'm sorry to ask you again, but could I see both of them?'

'I don't know,' the staff person cocked his head doubtfully. 'We don't keep the films of the previews in our warehouse forever. When the time comes, we get rid of them. I'd have to check to find out if we still have that piece of film.'

'When you say get rid of, how do you do it?'

'We cut up the film and sell it to a scrap collector.'

'Could you please check to see if you still have the film?'

Imanishi stepped outside. He walked around for about an hour, then returned to the film company.

'I was able to find out,' the staff member said. 'We have the preview of the following week's movie, but we got rid of our preannouncement about the foreign feature. It's too bad. We sold it to the scrap collector just three days ago.'

Imanishi was able to see the preview, but it was not informative. It was just a collection of scenes from *The Distant Horizon* with the director and the cameraman wandering about as well. It lasted only three minutes.

'You said the preannouncement was for a foreign film?'

'Yes.'

'What was the name of that film?'

'It was called *The Road of the Century*.'

'In addition to scenes from the movie, the preannouncement also had shots from opening night? I hope I've understood correctly.'

'Yes, it did.'

'There must have been several prints. Would there be one, perhaps, that might still be left somewhere?'

'I can't imagine that that would be the case. We usually get rid of all of them at once. But if I find out that there is still a print somewhere, I'll let you know.'

'I would really appreciate that.' There was nothing else that he could say.

★

Imanishi telephoned Yoshimura. 'Thanks for joining me the other night.'

'No, thank you for treating me,' Yoshimura said.

'Yoshimura, do you like movies?'

'Why are you asking all of a sudden? Yes, I like movies.'

'Did you see one called *One Man's Rage*?'

Yoshimura laughed. 'No, I didn't see that one.'

Imanishi was disappointed. 'How about a foreign movie called *The Road of the Century*?'

'Yes, I saw that one.'

'Did you see the preannouncement film?'

'You mean the one they show ahead of time to advertise the movie?'

'That's the one.'

'Let me think . . . Yes, I did, I saw it.'

'You saw it?'

'Yes, the one with the scenes from the opening night, right?'

'Yes, that's it,' Imanishi cried out. 'I'd like to meet you right away to ask you details about that film.'

'About the film?'

'Yes. Please remember as much as you can about it before we meet.'

Imanishi hurried to the Kamata police station. Yoshimura was working in the detectives' office, but he joined Imanishi as soon as he spotted him.

'We could have tea here, but the others would be curious, so we wouldn't be able to talk much.' They entered a small coffee shop across the street from the police station.

'Welcome back,' Yoshimura said to Imanishi. It was their first meeting since Imanishi's trip to Ise. 'How were things there?'

'That's just what I wanted to talk to you about.' Imanishi told Yoshimura what had happened in detail. 'So I haven't made any progress since I've gotten back. The problem is, what did Miki see that made him change his plans? The only thing I can think of is the preannouncement of the foreign film, but the movie company says it's already been thrown out. Can you remember the content and tell me about it?'

'Give me a moment,' Yoshimura said, crossing his arms. 'It was quite a while ago, so I've pretty much forgotten . . . The main portion was the introduction of the movie. They showed scenes from the film.'

'I heard that there were some shots of the premiere in Tokyo.'

'Yes, there were. The prince and princess were there together to see the film, so there were many shots of them.'

'What other scenes were there? I mean other than those of the movie itself.'

'Otherwise . . .' Yoshimura looked down in an effort to remember.

'What about some celebrities? Maybe in the shots of the theater . . .' Imanishi said, giving him a lead.

'Yes, there were, there were.' Yoshimura raised his head at once. 'There were definitely some shots like that. I can't remember exactly who they were.'

'Were there any members of the Nouveau group in those shots?'

'Wait a minute. That's just what I'm trying to recall.' Once again, Yoshimura lowered his head. 'There were lots of them. Novelists, directors, movie stars . . .' he said slowly as if talking to himself. 'The words "Nouveau group" weren't used, but I have a feeling they may have been there. I think there were some young artists. My memory is vague though.'

Imanishi thought he had the general picture. He would assume that the members of the Nouveau group had appeared on the screen. Miki had suddenly decided to go to Tokyo after seeing the face of one of the members of the group. The question was, which member of the Nouveau group had that face belonged to?

★

Imanishi was still concerned about the latest review by Seki-gawa Shigeo. As a detective he was suspicious about everything. Sekigawa's piece had been fairly easy to understand but Ima-nishi wasn't sure whether he should take it at face value. It seemed to be necessary to read between the lines to comprehend what critics really meant.

Sekigawa was not the only member of the Nouveau group upon whom Imanishi's attention was focused. Imanishi had received two responses to his inquiries about Waga Eiryo. One was a copy of his family register, which had been sent from the Family Register Section of the Naniwa Ward Office in Osaka.

Number 120, 2 Ebisu-cho, Naniwa Ward,
Osaka City
Father: Eizo
    Date of birth: June 17, 1908
    Date of death: March 14, 1945
Mother: Kimiko
    Date of birth: February 7, 1912
    Date of death: March 14, 1945
Himself:
    Date of birth: October 2, 1933
Mother, Kimiko, was second daughter of Yamamoto Jiro, registered domicile: Number 47, San-ban-cho, Higashi, Sendai City; marriage to Eizo recorded on May 20, 1929

The other response was from the prefectural high school in Kyoto Prefecture. According to this information, Waga Eiryo had withdrawn from the school in 1948.

Imanishi sat deep in thought. Then he looked at his calendar. The next Monday was a holiday.

'I'll be going to Ishikawa Prefecture Saturday night,' he told Yoshiko on his return home that evening.

'Are you off again?' She made a face.

'This isn't a pleasure trip. I can't take so many days off. So I'm taking advantage of the holiday.'

'Can't you make it a business trip?'

'I don't feel I can ask again since I don't know if I'll get any results. Do we have enough money?'

'I have some tucked away. Where are you going in Ishikawa Prefecture?'

'Near a hot spring called Yamanaka.'

'Well, that's a nice place you're going to. Be sure to bring me back a present.'

Imanishi had never taken his wife to a hot spring. Her comment stung him.

'Sure, I'll bring you something. I'm sorry to be using the money you were saving up.'

'It's all right. It can't be helped since it's for your work.'

Imanishi was determined to come back this time with something in his grasp.

The following day, he telephoned Yoshimura. 'I'm going to Yamanaka in Ishikawa Prefecture tomorrow night.'

'To Yamanaka?' Yoshimura said, surprised. 'You mean the Yamanaka in the song "the hot springs of Yamanaka, Yamashiro, or Awazu"? What kind of work is it this time?' Yoshimura asked.

'It's that same case,' Imanishi answered, a bit abashed.

'There are so many connections all over the place, aren't there?'

'I guess so.'

'Imanishi-*san*, if there's anything I can do to help, let me know.' Yoshimura's voice was earnest.

'Let me see,' Imanishi said. 'I'm leaving tomorrow night from Tokyo Station. The train leaves at nine-forty.'

'I'll be there to see you off.'

On Saturday night Imanishi stood on the platform at Tokyo

Station with his suitcase in hand. Yoshimura approached through the crowd of people seeing off the travelers.

'You came after all.' Imanishi smiled.

'Thank you for all your efforts.' Yoshimura bowed. 'It's not a business trip this time?'

'I can't ask to be sent on another expense-paid trip. Luckily, Monday's a holiday. So it looks like I'm off to enjoy myself. My wife let me use her savings, so I'm grateful. But she's not too happy about it.'

'I'm sure that's not the case. Your wife is very supportive.'

'That doesn't matter, really. Actually, I'd like to ask you to do something for me,' Imanishi said, looking around to either side. 'Let me tell you.' Drawing Yoshimura close, Imanishi whispered to him.

Yoshimura opened his eyes wide. 'I understand. I'll make sure that's done before you return.'

'Thanks.'

Just five minutes before the train's departure time, Yoshiko appeared from the crowd of people.

'Dear, this is for you to eat on the train.' She held out something wrapped in a cloth.

'What is it?'

'Look forward to being surprised when you open it.'

'Sorry to make you spend money like this,' Imanishi said in an unexpectedly formal way.

When the train had left the platform and had become a small speck in the distance, Yoshimura turned to Yoshiko standing beside him and said, 'It must be tough on you, too. There aren't many like him, though.'

'He really loves his work,' Yoshiko responded.

Dawn came at Sekigahara. Imanishi changed to the Hokuriku Line at Maibara. The morning sun glinted on Lake Yogonoumi.

Snow had already fallen in the mountains of Shizugatake. It was just before noon when he changed at Daishoji to a small electric train that headed for the mountains. Yamanaka hot spring was at the end of the line, where the plain narrowed and came up against the mountains. Half of the passengers had come to take the cure at the hot spring. In this distant area, the sounds of the Kansai dialect of the region around Osaka grated on his ears.

Taking out his notebook, Imanishi asked for directions near the station. His destination was a village at some distance, near the mountains. Imanishi hailed a taxi that followed a country road beside a stream.

'Is this the first time you've been here, sir?' the middle-aged driver asked. When Imanishi answered yes, he asked, 'Did you come here for the hot springs?'

'Yes, I did, but I also want to visit someone I know,' Imanishi answered.

The cloud over the mountain looked cold.

'I hardly ever take passengers to this village.'

'Really? Is it that remote?'

'There's nothing there. It's called a village, but there are only about fifty houses. And they're all scattered. Only farmers live there, so no one uses taxis.'

'Is it that run-down a village?'

'It's a poor area. In Yamanaka and Yamashiro there are lots of visitors from the Osaka area who liven things up, but just five miles away, there are people who have trouble getting enough to eat. It's a strange world. Oops . . .' the driver caught himself, 'do you have relatives in this village?'

'No, I don't have any relatives there. I'm visiting someone named Yamashita.'

'Yamashita-*san*, you say. About half the people in that village are named Yamashita. What's his given name?'

'It's Yamashita Chutaro.'

'I could ask about him.'

The road climbed into the mountains from the plain. Narrow fields dotted the valleys between the mountains. The poor condition of the road made the taxi pitch like a boat as it navigated two passes.

'Mister, that's the village. As you can see, you can hardly call it a village.'

Small roofs, placed haphazardly, appeared in the direction the taxi driver pointed. The driver offered to ask for directions, but Imanishi stopped him. He got out of the taxi near half a dozen farmhouses separated by fields. This was an area with considerable snowfall so the eaves of the houses were very deep.

A young woman stood in front of a house, carrying a baby on her back. She stared at Imanishi as he walked toward her.

When Imanishi bobbed his head in greeting, she did not even smile. 'I'd like to ask you something. Which house belongs to Yamashita Chutaro?'

'Yamashita Chutaro, oh,' she uttered slowly, 'it's on the other side of the mountain.' She pointed with her chin to the ridge line of the mountain. Her face was rough and freckled from outdoor physical labor.

'Thank you,' Imanishi said and started to walk away.

'Mister, wait,' the woman stopped him. 'Yamashita Chutaro is no longer in this world.'

Imanishi had half expected this. If he had been alive, he would have been quite old.

'I see. When did he pass away?' Imanishi asked.

'Let me see. It was about twelve or thirteen years ago.'

'Is there someone at his place now?'

'Now? His daughter Otae-*san* lives there with her husband who was adopted into the family.'

'I see. So his daughter is called Otae-*san*? And what's her husband's name?'

'He's Shoji-*san*. They may not be at home now. They may be out working.'

'Thank you very much.'

Imanishi returned to the taxi. When he told the driver that he wanted to go to the other side of the ridge, he looked unhappy.

'Mister, that's a terrible road.'

The road was so narrow it was unclear whether a car could drive through, and it was even more rutted than the road they had come on. But for Imanishi it was essential that the taxi take him there.

'Sorry, but won't you try? I'll make sure to give you a good tip.'

'I don't need a tip.' The driver grudgingly agreed to go.

Rounding the ridge, they came across some different scenery. If it had been the sea, the area would have been an inlet. Some four or five houses lay scattered at the base of the foothills.

Alighting from the taxi, Imanishi walked along the footpath toward an old woman working her field.

'Excuse me, could I ask you something?' he called to her politely. 'Where is Yamashita Chutaro-*san*'s house?'

The old woman straightened up, leaning on her hoe. 'Chutaro died many years ago.' She seemed to be suffering from trachoma and had bleary eyes.

'I understand that the house now belongs to his adopted son, Shoji-*san*.'

'Shoji's house is that one.' The old woman stood up even straighter and pointed a finger caked with dirt to the farthest of the half-dozen houses. It stood on the hillside, so its thatched roof appeared taller than the others.

When Imanishi thanked her and started to walk on, she called after him, 'You won't find Shoji there now.'

'Oh, is he away?'

'I hear he's gone to the Osaka area. We don't need any men

to work the fields here until the spring. So they go away to find other work.'

'Who's living there now?'

'Shoji's wife is there. Otae-*san*.'

Imanishi continued along the path. The farmhouses all looked poor. They were small, decrepit, and dirty. As Imanishi walked by, several old people stared at the outsider from their doorways. Stone steps led to the highest house. Imanishi followed the path between the barren fields until he reached the house. A dirty board with the name 'Yamashita Shoji' was nailed to an old pillar.

There was no answer to his knock, so he tried the door. It opened.

'Hello? Excuse me,' Imanishi called into the darkened interior.

He caught a glimpse of a small figure that walked slowly toward him without uttering a sound. In the bright light he could see that it was a skinny boy of eleven or twelve years of age, dressed in dirty clothes. He had a large head.

'Is anyone home?' Imanishi asked the boy.

The boy raised his eyes in silence. Imanishi gave a start. One eye was completely white. The iris of the other eye was small.

'Isn't anyone home?' Imanishi said in a louder voice. He heard a sound from inside the house.

The boy continued to look up silently at Imanishi. The eerie eyes of the boy were repugnant to Imanishi, who did not feel pity right away even though it was a child. What he felt most strongly was a sense of abnormality as he gazed at the boy's pale face.

A woman in her mid-fifties appeared from the dark interior. Her hair was thin and balding in the front. Her face was pale and puffy.

'Is this the home of Yamashita Shoji-*san*?' Imanishi asked, bowing to the woman.

'Yes, it is,' she nodded gloomily.

The woman looked at Imanishi with clouded eyes. She seemed to be the mother of the one-eyed boy.

'I'm an acquaintance of Motoura Chiyokichi-*san*.' As he said this, he watched her face. The sleepy eyes did not move a bit. 'I got to know Chiyokichi-*san* in Okayama Prefecture. I heard that this was the home of his wife's family. I happened to be in the area, so I thought I would drop by.'

'Is that so?' Otae nodded her head slightly. 'Please sit down here.'

This was her first expression of greeting. The boy was still staring at Imanishi with his white eye.

'Boy, go away,' she waved the boy away. Without saying a word, the boy walked to the back of the house. 'Please,' Otae urged Imanishi, who had been watching the boy retreat. She indicated a thin cushion.

'Thank you.' Imanishi sat down. 'Please don't bother with anything,' he said, as she started to prepare some tea.

Otae offered a cup of tea on a tray to Imanishi. The tea cup was soiled, but Imanishi gulped down the liquid.

'I understand that your husband, Shoji-*san*, is away,' he said.

'Yes, he's off to Osaka.' Otae sat facing Imanishi.

'Through a quirk of fate, I got to know your brother-in-law, Chiyokichi-*san*. He was a good man.'

'I'm sure you were kind to him.' Otae bowed her head.

It appeared that Otae thought that Imanishi was a staff member or a doctor from Jikoen in Okayama. She had assumed that that was where he had become acquainted with Chiyokichi.

'I heard a lot about Yamanaka hot spring from Chiyokichi-*san*. I had always wanted to visit, and this time I was able to come. So I thought I would drop by.'

'Is that so?'

'I heard that your younger sister Masa-*san* passed away in

1935, but what happened to her son? I mean the boy who was born to your sister and Chiyokichi-*san*.'

'You mean Hideo?' Otae asked.

'Yes, his name was Hideo. I often heard about him from Chiyokichi-*san*. I remember hearing that Hideo and his father were separated before Chiyokichi-*san* entered Jikoen.'

'Yes. Did Chiyokichi say anything to you about that?'

'No, not really. He just always wondered what had happened to Hideo.'

'I suppose so. My sister died four years after she gave birth to Hideo. She probably never had a chance to see him again before she died.'

'What do you mean? Didn't your sister return home after she and Chiyokichi-*san* separated?'

'You seem to know all about them, so I'll tell you without hiding anything. My sister parted from Chiyokichi as soon as he got that disease. My sister may have been coldhearted, but it couldn't be helped, because of the kind of illness he had. But Chiyokichi was so fond of Hideo that he took him on his travels.'

'What year was that?'

'It must have been about 1934.'

'Did Chiyokichi-*san* have somewhere to go to?'

'He went around to visit temples to try to cure his disease.'

'So he went all around the country, did he? Like a pilgrimage?'

'Yes, I think so. He didn't send any word to the boy's mother, my sister,' Otae answered, looking down. 'My sister became a maid in a restaurant in Osaka after she parted from Chiyokichi. But that lasted for only a year or so. She got sick and died there.'

When he first saw her, Imanishi had thought that Otae was a woman without any feelings, but as they talked he realized that she was quite able to express her emotions.

'So your sister died without knowing what became of Chiyokichi-*san* and Hideo?'

'Yes. My sister wrote me some letters that said she had no idea where they had gone.'

'What about now? I mean, Hideo. He's your nephew, isn't he? He should be thirty years old this year.'

'Would he, now?' Hearing that, Otae seemed to be calculating the years. 'Has it been that long?'

'You haven't heard anything about him?'

'No, nothing. I don't even know if he's dead or alive.'

'Chiyokichi-*san* told me that he had entered Jikoen in Okayama in 1938 and that he had parted with his son in the countryside in Shimane Prefecture.'

'Is that so? I didn't know anything about that.'

'He didn't know what had happened to Hideo after that. That was what Chiyokichi-*san* was concerned about. You haven't heard anything about Hideo's whereabouts?'

'No, we haven't.'

'Have there been any requests from any local offices for Hideo's registry of residence or copies of his family register?'

'No, there haven't. I know the village official. He says that if Hideo had died somewhere, the notice would come to the village office.'

'I see.'

Otae sighed. 'My sister was unfortunate. She married Chiyokichi without knowing that he had such a cruel disease. When he became ill, she was shocked. She was worried that Hideo might catch the disease because Chiyokichi dragged him around with him on his travels. My sister died after suffering a lot.'

'I'd like to ask you one more question,' Imanishi said. 'Have you occasionally seen a young man, a stranger, wandering around here?' Imanishi asked this question, thinking that Hideo might have come back to his mother's home.

'No, I've never seen anyone like that.'

At the end of his visit Imanishi showed Otae a photograph he had cut out of a newspaper.

'I don't know,' Otae said, cocking her head in doubt after gazing at it a while. 'He was only four years old when I saw the boy last, so I can't say one way or the other whether he looked like this person.'

'Does he look at all like your sister or Chiyokichi-*san*?'

'Well, he doesn't look like his father. Now that you say so, perhaps he looks a bit like my sister around the eyes, but I can't be sure.'

Imanishi left the Yamashita home. Otae saw him off at the doorway. She watched, standing with her back to the dark doorway, as Imanishi drove off in the taxi.

Imanishi turned around twice to wave to her. This house and the entire village were dreary. As the taxi drove off, he saw the one-eyed boy standing by the roadside, looking up at him. Imanishi felt depressed. The boy was about the same age as his son, Taro.

At Yamanaka, Imanishi left the taxi and entered the first restaurant he saw.

'Give me a bowl of *soba* buckwheat noodles.' As he sipped the soup in the bowl, he heard the financial news on the radio.

. . . We now bring you the stock market report. First the major trends. In the morning Tokyo market, encouraging factors caused trading to progress smoothly, with a gradual increase in profit-taking and mixed changes in prices. Next, in general issues, there was selective buying of stocks in chemicals, automotive machinery, metal industry, late-issue coal, and paper. High-yield electrical stocks were also traded . . . Nagoya Sugar 188 yen, unchanged. Osaka Sugar not traded. Shibaura Sugar not traded. Toyo Sugar not traded. Tensai Sugar 205 yen, unchanged. Yokohama Sugar 340 yen, unchanged. Snow Brand Dairy

Products 148 yen, unchanged. Kirin Beer 550 yen, unchanged. Takara Brewing 163 yen, unchanged . . .

Unchanged, unchanged . . . he thought. Imanishi felt that these words described his achievements, too. He had moved around a lot, but how much progress had he made?

Imanishi imagined the curve of the stock market figures, with its large and small valleys. Suddenly he thought of the piece of paper he had picked up near the location where the body of the actor Miyata Kunio had been discovered. That had also been an arrangement of statistics. When he finished eating his noodles, he took out his notebook and reread the numbers he had copied down.

1953:	25,404
1954:	35,522
1955:	30,834
1956:	24,362
1957:	27,435
1958:	28,431
1959:	28,438

Did these figures have anything to do with Miyata's death?

Imanishi closed his notebook. He intended to board the night train. He had done what he had come here for, and he did not feel like spending a leisurely night soaking in the hot spring. He left the noodle shop. Shops lined the street, all with similar souvenirs for sale, mostly towels and sweets. He bought some sweets for Taro. Then he saw a Wajima lacquerware obi clip in a display case. Seeing that he was gazing at it, a saleswoman came over to him.

'Welcome. About what age is the lady it is for?'

Somewhat embarrassed, Imanishi answered, 'She's about thirty-seven,' giving his wife's age.

'Then, these would be most appropriate.' The saleswoman placed five or six obi fasteners on the counter.

Imanishi chose one from among them and asked to have it wrapped. This was the only present he bought for his wife at Yamanaka hot spring.

14. Soundless

The day after Imanishi returned from his trip, he reported to work at headquarters. From his office he telephoned Yoshimura.

'Welcome back.' Yoshimura was surprised at Imanishi's early return.

'I took the night train both going and coming.'

'You must be tired.'

'I rested for a day, so it's not that bad. Yoshimura, I'd like to talk to you. Could you come over to my house tonight?'

'Are you sure? Aren't you still tired from your trip?'

'No, that's no problem. Let's eat some sukiyaki.'

'In that case, I'd be glad to come over.'

Imanishi did not have any pressing cases. He was able to reach home at six-thirty.

'Young Yoshimura is coming over tonight,' he told his wife. 'Could you get things ready? I promised him that we'd have some sukiyaki.'

'Is that so? It's been a while since he's visited us, but dear, aren't you tired?'

'Yoshimura said the same thing. I'm all right. I rested yesterday. He'll be coming soon, so could you hurry?'

Yoshiko started out for the market, but returned and said, 'I showed the obi clip to the woman next door. She complimented me on it, saying it was lovely. I thought it might be a bit flashy for me, but she thought it was just right.'

About an hour later, Yoshimura arrived.

'Welcome.' The voices of Yoshiko and Yoshimura could be heard from the doorway. 'He's here.'

A smiling Yoshimura entered the room.

'Sorry to drag you out like this when you must be tired.'

'It's you, Imanishi-*san*, that should be tired. It's exhausting to take the night train both ways.'

'I guess so. My back still hurts. It didn't bother me when I was younger. I'm feeling my age.'

'We younger ones can't take that kind of discomfort either. I'm always surprised at how energetic you are.'

'Don't flatter me too much.'

Yoshiko brought in the sukiyaki pan. 'This isn't much of a dinner, but please help yourself.' She put a carafe of sake and some tiny cups on the table.

'Thank you for your hospitality,' Yoshimura said.

Yoshiko poured some sake into each of their cups.

'Let's have a toast, anyway. To our good health,' Imanishi proposed.

Yoshimura raised his sake cup. Imanishi prepared the suki-yaki, poking at the pan with his chopsticks, adding some water, sprinkling in some sugar, and checking the taste.

'How was it there?' Yoshimura asked, after sipping two or three cups of sake.

'I met the person I wanted to see.' Imanishi recounted what had happened at the village near Yamanaka hot spring. Yoshimura listened intently, nodding his head and making agreeable responses.

'So that's about it. It didn't result in much, but I went through all the questions I had intended to ask.'

'Even that is quite a bit of corroboration.'

'Go ahead and eat. The meat will get too tough.'

'Yes, thank you.'

'The meat's from a neighborhood shop, so it's probably not very good . . . By the way, how were things at your end, Yoshimura?'

'After you left, I went around right away. It's only been one day, so I haven't been able to get much information. But I heard about a curious episode.'

'Hmm, what was that?' It was Imanishi's turn to show interest.

'Our man doesn't have many dealings with his neighbors, so I didn't get that much from them, but his reputation isn't bad.'

'I see.'

'That area is full of large houses, so neighbors don't see each other constantly. Since he's an artist, he probably doesn't have much in common with his neighbors.'

'What's this interesting information?'

'It's like this,' Yoshimura said, emptying his sake cup. 'That area gets a lot of those pushy door-to-door peddlers. It's about these peddlers . . . One of them went to that house. He stayed for about half an hour, then left with a sickly pale face.'

'A peddler left the house with a pale face? I wonder why. Did he get yelled at?'

'No, that wasn't it. He went into the entryway and spread out his goods and started delivering his pitch – the usual kind, full of threats. The person who dealt with the peddler was the owner of the house himself. After a while, the peddler gathered up his things on his own and left the house without a word. The neighbors heard about this from the housekeeper.'

'I see.'

'Apparently the story spread because it was so unusual for one of those peddlers to retreat in silence.'

'Was it because he realized that there was no chance for a sale?'

'No, that wasn't it. Those guys don't give up easily. They force the householders to buy even a hundred yen worth of goods.'

'I wonder what happened.'

Yoshimura's story of the peddler continued. 'I don't understand it much myself, but the fact is that the peddler left without a word. That's not all. Two or three days later, another peddler went to the same house. Interestingly enough, this peddler hurriedly gathered up his things in the middle of his sales pitch and left the house, too.'

'Hmm. Why was that?'

'That's what I can't figure out. It sounded interesting to me, so I thought I would bring it up when I saw you.'

Imanishi added some water to the pan. Yoshiko brought in some more sake.

'I'm enjoying the meal,' Yoshimura said to her, bowing his head.

'I'm sorry, it isn't very much.'

When Yoshiko left the room, Imanishi looked up from his sake cup. 'That story about the peddlers is very interesting. When did this happen?'

'About ten days ago.'

'Is there any way we can find those peddlers?'

'The peddlers? I suppose we could check them out.'

'I'd like to find those two peddlers and ask them what happened.'

'If you say so, I'll try to find them. They aren't independent peddlers. They're an organized gang. So if I ask around, I think I'll be able to get hold of them.'

'I'd like you to do that, and I'd like you to hurry it up.'

'I'll start on it tomorrow, right away.'

Resting from his sake drinking, Imanishi smoked a cigarette. He seemed to be deep in thought.

'Oh, yes, there was one more thing you asked me to do. About the film.'

'Oh, yes, that.'

'They're looking for it right now. The ones that have been sent around the country are mostly all collected, but there may still be one left somewhere. I should have a definite answer in two or three days.'

'Yes. Thank you.'

'It's taken a long time, but I feel as if we're starting to close in on this case, little by little,' Yoshimura said.

'Do you?'

'Yes, I do. Nothing's definite yet, but that's my intuition. I feel we've come to the moment just before the solution.'

Two days passed. Imanishi waited in the usual *oden* bar for Yoshimura, who came with another man in tow.

'Sorry to keep you waiting. This is Tanaka.'

'Good evening.' Tanaka bowed his head politely. He was about thirty and wore a leather jacket. From the start, he was both overly courteous and unduly familiar.

'Thanks for coming. Why don't you sit here?' Imanishi seated the man beside him, and Yoshimura sat on the other side.

'Some sake, ma'am,' Imanishi ordered.

'Tanaka here,' Yoshimura explained, 'is a member of the Sakurada group in Asakusa. There's another fellow named Kurokawa, but since he's off somewhere else right now, I asked Tanaka to come along by himself. I was able to get hold of him through an introduction by a colleague of mine at the station.'

'Well, shall we have a drink first?' Three glasses of sake had been served.

'Thanks. I'll gladly drink some.' Tanaka raised his glass and bobbed his head.

'Well, thanks for coming. I'm sure you're busy, so I appreciate it,' Imanishi said, smiling.

'No bother. We're always beholden to the police, so if there's anything I can do for you, boss, I'm glad to,' Tanaka said.

'You've heard about it from Yoshimura here. I understand you went to sell something and had a strange experience?'

'Yeah,' Tanaka said, scratching his head. 'It was a real surprise. I'm amazed that you heard of it.'

'It's a curious incident, so I wanted to ask you about it in detail. I heard that something strange happened when you spread out your wares at that house. Is that right?'

'Yes, that's true. But boss, I wasn't the first one. It was that rascal Tsune who was the first one to go there.'

'Tsune?'

'That's the other fellow, Kurokawa,' Yoshimura explained.

'I see. And what did Tsune-*san* say happened?'

'Tsune came back and said something weird,' Tanaka responded to Imanishi's question, staring at the sake in his glass. 'He said he was doing the area around there that day. He went into a house and spread out his goods and was giving his pitch. Then a young man who seemed to be the master of the house came out. He listened to Tsune's threats quietly. After a while, Tsune felt light-headed and started feeling sick. He got a bit spooked and left the house quickly. That's what he said.'

'So you decided to go there in place of Tsune-*san*?' Yoshimura asked.

'That's right, boss. I thought Tsune was a coward, so I said I'd go and check that house out. Since my friend had such an awkward experience, I went there, not really to get back at them, but to defend his honor.'

'When did you go to that house?'

'It was two days later. I took some socks.'

'You're sure it's the house that Tsune-*san* had gone to?'

'There's no mistake. I got directions from Tsune.'

'Then what happened?'

'First a maid came to the door. While I was putting out my goods, she went to the back and returned with the master. He was a young one, twenty-seven or so, wearing a flashy shirt and slacks. When I realized that this was the guy who had made Tsune cower, I made my pitch even more threatening than usual. I said all kinds of things. Usually, the customers flinch when they hear me, but this fellow just stood there calmly listening to me. Then' – Tanaka shook his head – 'I started feeling strange, light-headed, like you feel when you're going down in an elevator. I felt really sick.'

'When you say you felt sick, in what way?'

'I felt sick to my stomach, like throwing up. I could feel my face getting green. I couldn't take it anymore and wrapped up the socks and rushed out of that house. I couldn't snicker at Tsune after that.'

'Was there anything unusual going on in the house when this happened?'

'No, that's just it, there was nothing. It was really quiet.'

'Hmm. It is a strange story,' Imanishi said, putting down his glass.

'It sure is, boss. It was the first time I came across anything like that.'

Three days later, a policeman came to see Imanishi at headquarters.

'Hello.' Imanishi asked him to sit down. 'Sorry to have made such a bothersome request the other day,' he said, bowing his head.

'That's no problem.' The policeman was stationed at a police box under the jurisdiction of the Higashi Chofu police station. He was a stocky man, just over thirty. 'I've come about that inquiry you made.'

'Yes, yes.' Imanishi leaned forward in his chair.

'I went to that house. I met with the master of the house under the pretext of asking whether he had been victimized by peddlers.'

'Thanks so much for taking the time.'

'I said that we had arrested a peddler and had heard that he had come to the house so I was investigating. The master said he hadn't bought anything from peddlers, so he had no damage claims.'

'Yes.'

'In making this inquiry, I stayed as long as I could in the entryway.'

'How long were you there?'

'I must have stayed at least fifteen minutes. I started off with just general chitchat and then slowly went through the case.'

'Did you notice anything out of the ordinary?'

'I was watching out, but I didn't notice anything unusual.'

'How was it inside the house?'

'I didn't hear any voices or any other sounds. Oh, yes, the maid or someone was washing dishes in the kitchen.'

'Did you start to feel sick?'

'No, nothing like that. Since you'd mentioned it, I was trying to notice everything, but I didn't feel strange at all.'

'I see.' Imanishi tapped his fingers on his desk. His gaze turned contemplative. 'Let me ask you once more, there was nothing unusual that you could see inside the house?'

'No, there wasn't. It's a normal house and I didn't feel sick at all.'

'Thank you so much.' Imanishi bowed his head.

'Is that all?'

'Yes, thank you . . . I may ask you to do something again.'

'Certainly. My duty at the police box is quite light unless there's an accident, so ask me any time.'

Imanishi saw the policeman out to the main entrance of the

headquarters building. The policeman went out to the street, where a cold wind was blowing. Imanishi returned to his room.

'Imanishi-*san*, you have a telephone call,' a young detective called out.

'Is this Detective Imanishi?' The voice was that of a young man. 'I'm calling from Nan'ei Film Company.'

'Oh, yes. I've been causing you a lot of trouble.'

'That's quite all right. We've found just one copy of the pre-announcement of *The Road of the Century*.'

'What, you've found it?' Imanishi asked excitedly. 'I would really like to see it.'

'We were finally able to call in the one that was sent out to theaters in the Tohoku region. The screening room is available today. I could show it anytime.'

'Thank you so much. I'll be over right away.'

'I'll make sure we're ready for you.'

Imanishi rushed out of headquarters. The swans swimming in the moat around the Imperial Palace looked cold. The branches of the trees lining the streets were shivering in the wind, scattering yellow leaves.

'Welcome.' The staff member who had been helping Imanishi smiled at him when he entered the building housing the Nan'ei Film Company. 'Please come right into the screening room. It's all ready for you.'

Once again, Imanishi sat alone in the screening room. As the room became dark, his heartbeat quickened. What had Miki discovered in the film? Trying to identify with Miki, Imanishi watched the screen.

The Road of the Century was a major American spectacle film set in the ancient Orient. The preannouncement film began with an explanation of the production. Next, there was a newsreel-like section showing scenes of the premiere held in Tokyo. An Imperial prince and princess entered the hall and bowed as they passed by the receiving line made up of those connected with the film. The faces of the film company officials flashed by in a second, but Imanishi saw none that might have drawn Miki's attention.

The next scenes were informal shots of prominent guests who had attended the premiere. Faces of people who were familiar from newspapers and magazines smiled and chatted in the theater. There were some business leaders, but most were from cultural and entertainment fields. Imanishi watched, holding his breath. A narration accompanied the film. Each time a different face appeared on the screen, the voice gave the person's name. There were no faces that Imanishi recognized.

The prince's face came on again. Beside him sat a man explaining the film. For three or four seconds the screen switched to the famous people in the audience. The screen changed color and showed scenes from *The Road of the Century*.

The lights came on in the screening room. Imanishi sat there vacantly.

'How was it?' the staff member asked, standing beside Imanishi.

Imanishi rubbed his eyes. 'I'm sorry, but could you run through that once again?'

The film was only four or five minutes long. If he had been slightly inattentive, he might have missed something. Imanishi wanted to reconfirm what he had seen, just as Miki had gone to see the same film twice in Ise. The projectionist started the film once again.

Imanishi concentrated once again. He could feel the perspiration in his clenched fists. He was once again unable to discover anything new. He had thought this would be a sure winner. But his hopes were completely dashed.

Imanishi left the screening room and walked outside. What was it that Miki had seen in the movie theater in Ise? It had not been the preannouncement film for *The Road of the Century*. Imanishi was sure of that now.

Miki had arrived in Tokyo from Ise City and had met the murderer at the cheap bar in Kamata. There had not been much time between those two events. He had arrived in Tokyo on the morning of the eleventh and had been killed that very night. His movements during those nineteen hours were still completely unknown.

Why had Miki gone twice to the movie theater in Ise? Three possible reasons for this had to be considered. First, there might have been a scene that only Miki could comprehend. Second, Imanishi had missed seeing the critical scene. Third, there was some item of interest other than the movies.

Of these, Imanishi was confident that it was not the second reason. He believed that he had not missed the slightest detail in the films.

Imanishi was not as confident about the first reason. However, he could not conceive of a scene that could only have been understood by Miki and not by anyone else.

Finally, was there something other than the films? He had deduced that Miki had seen the films because he had gone to the movie theater. He wondered if that conclusion had been too hastily arrived at. Miki might have gone twice to the movie theater to confirm something else. Could it have been a person? Someone in the audience? Did someone Miki knew work at the theater?

Imanishi returned to headquarters.

The vital link remained Ise City. Imanishi decided to inquire whether any employee at the theater knew Miki. He would also ask if any of the employees had quit after Miki visited the theater, and he would request information about the background of the manager himself. Perhaps Miki had gone to see him. He wrote a request to the investigation section at the Ise police station.

Imanishi waited impatiently for the reply, which came four days later.

This is in response to your inquiry.

The movie theater you inquired about is the Asahi Theater. The owner is Tadokoro Ichinosuke, 49 years old. We asked Tadokoro-*san* to check with his employees, but none of them had met or talked with the person in question. On the day you indicated, the theater did show the two movies you mentioned, previews of the next week's films, and the preannouncement of *The Road of the Century*. There were no other short films or PR films shown. Tadokoro-*san* said he does not remember meeting Miki-*san* that day.

Tadokoro-*san* has lived in Ise City for some time. He is a self-made man who started out as an employee in a movie theater. He was born in xx Village near Nihonmatsu City in Fukushima Prefecture. He has lived in our city since he left home at a young age and settled here. He has one son and one daughter.

It seemed that Miki's two visits to the movie theater had not been to meet anyone. Then was the reason hidden in those four films, after all? It couldn't be. But Miki must have seen something. Otherwise, there would be no reason for him to go there twice, or for him to change his travel plans and go to Tokyo. What was it that had beckoned him to Tokyo?

Imanishi was also concerned about the house that had been visited by the door-to-door peddlers. He wondered if he should go there to check it out himself. The two peddlers had started to feel sick to their stomachs in the entryway. Yet nothing had happened to the policeman. Imanishi saw a problem in his going there himself. If he did, his face would become known. He did not want to show his face for a while yet, nor Yoshimura's either.

Imanishi's mind was getting cluttered. It was just about the end of the workday. He tidied up the top of his desk.

It was dark when he stepped outdoors. The lights of the streetcars and the headlights of the cars glared brightly. Several darkened silhouettes walked toward him.

'Hi,' someone called out. It was a group from the security section.

Imanishi recognized them. 'Thanks for your hard work,' he said. 'It must be tough, day after day.'

'It's only another two or three days,' the other fellow said, smiling.

Tokyo was in the midst of a political reshuffling. The cabinet had resigned en masse, and a new cabinet was about to be formed. The men from the security section had been assigned to guard the prime minister's residence.

The next morning Imanishi read his newspaper in bed. On the front page was the lineup of the new cabinet. The newspapers had been full of this news for a while, but the new cabinet had just been confirmed late the previous night. Imanishi picked out one of the names printed in large characters: 'Agriculture and Forestry Minister: Tadokoro Shigeyoshi (Fukushima Prefecture representative, 6th term; 61 years old).'

This was the first time that Imanishi had realized that Tadokoro Shigeyoshi's district was Fukushima Prefecture. He continued to stare at the print.

'Dear.' Yoshiko's voice came through the sliding doors. 'You'd better get up soon. It's time.'

Imanishi put down the newspaper. Whether a new cabinet was formed or the opposition gained power, it had nothing to do with lower-level civil servants like Imanishi. He rose and washed his face. As he brushed his teeth he could smell miso soup and scallions.

During breakfast Yoshiko talked to him, but he did not even respond. In glum silence, he was not really listening, he was just eating. He muttered to himself . . . So Tadokoro Shigeyoshi was from Fukushima Prefecture.

'Fukushima Prefecture . . . Wait a minute.' Imanishi cocked his head to one side. Something sounded familiar about that location.

'Did you sleep on your neck wrong?' Yoshiko asked from across the table, seeing him cock his head.

Imanishi remained silent.

'Oh, that's it.' He put down his teacup. The owner of that movie theater in Ise was from Fukushima Prefecture, too.

The residence of the new minister of agriculture and forestry was located on a rise in the Azabu area. That evening, Tadokoro Shigeyoshi, still in his cutaway, was accepting the congratulations of his family and followers after returning from the cabinet swearing-in ceremony. He had an impressive head of white hair and an upright bearing. His healthy face was continually smiling. This was his second time as a cabinet minister, but he seemed to find pleasure in the occasion.

Because of the arrival of so many well-wishers, it was nearly nine o'clock before he could take a rest. He moved to the dining table where his wife had laid out a congratulatory dinner. The inner circle had gathered to toast the occasion.

Tadokoro Sachiko had been helping her mother, but when Waga Eiryo arrived, she turned her attention to him.

'Congratulations,' Waga said as he bowed to his future father-in-law.

'Thank you.' Tadokoro narrowed his eyes. He was in a good mood. 'Please, everyone, sit down.'

Tadokoro's younger brother and his wife, his wife's niece, and Sachiko's younger brothers all sat down with them at the table. Tadokoro sat at the head of the table with his wife beside him. Waga and Sachiko sat across from the new cabinet minister and his wife. On the table were impressive dishes catered from a first-class restaurant. The only nonfamily member was Tadokoro's private secretary.

'Does everyone have some wine?' Tadokoro's wife asked, looking around the table. 'Let's toast Father.' Her face was the most excited.

'Father, congratulations.'

'Congratulations, Uncle.'

The way those at the table referred to the man varied, but their glasses were all raised to eye level.

'Thank you.' The new minister beamed with joy.

'Father, please do the best you can,' Sachiko said from across the table in a loud voice after everyone had taken a sip of wine.

'I'll try.'

The newspapers said that it was rumored that the post of minister of agriculture and forestry was not what Tadokoro had hoped for, but the man still seemed to be in good spirits.

This small dinner party started off full of laughter.

Tonight, Waga wore a charcoal gray suit with white pin-stripes, a bright white dress shirt, and a burgundy-colored necktie with a black design. He wore his fashionable clothes well, and his good looks complimented the luxuriously dressed men and women at the table. Beside him sat Sachiko in a crimson dress and a white orchid corsage.

Gazing at the couple sitting across the table, Tadokoro smiled and whispered to his wife, 'Tonight seems more like a wedding party for the young couple than a celebration for me.'

About halfway through this enjoyable meal, the maid came to Sachiko and, in a low voice, announced some visitors. Sachiko gave the message to Waga, who looked across at Tadokoro.

'What is it?' her father asked Sachiko.

'Some members of Waga-*san*'s group have come to give

you their congratulations. It's Sekigawa-*san*, Takebe-*san*, and Katazawa-*san*.'

'Well, that's thoughtful of them,' the minister said affably. 'Sachiko, you know them, too?'

'Yes, I see them all the time. When Waga-*san* was in the hospital after his accident, they came to visit him.'

'So the Nouveau group has a strong sense of duty.' Tadokoro smiled.

'Why don't you show them into the living room?' his wife said.

'Why not have them come here? They're not official guests, so it will be more informal if we invite them in here.'

The table was large enough to accommodate the extra guests. Mrs Tadokoro ordered the maid to bring three more place settings at once. The young men, with Sekigawa in the lead, entered the room, guided by a maid. Seeing the gathering, they hesitated a bit, puzzled as to what they should do. Waga stood up and smiled at his friends.

'Congratulations on your new appointment.' The newcomers greeted their host and bowed.

Tadokoro pushed his chair back and stood up. 'Thank you for being so courteous.'

Mrs Tadokoro said, 'Thank you for coming. Please join us.'

The children stared curiously at the newcomers who had intruded upon the family gathering. Sekigawa tapped Waga on the shoulder and took a seat. Extra glasses were brought in.

'Congratulations,' said Sekigawa in a toast. The other two also raised their glasses.

'Thank you.' Tadokoro bowed politely.

Waga stood up and moved behind the chairs of his three friends and said, 'Thanks for coming.'

Sachiko also greeted them familiarly. 'You're all so busy, thank you for taking the time to come over.'

'Well, it is an occasion on which congratulations are in order. So we came right over,' Sekigawa responded, representing the others. 'It looks like tonight might be a rehearsal for Waga's wedding,' he said jokingly.

The small family party grew livelier with the addition of the three new guests. From the start, they talked a lot and drank a lot. Smiling broadly, Tadokoro listened to the young men's discussion of art. The most animated speaker was Sekigawa. The other two were artists, so they did not reach the level of Sekigawa's eloquence. Sekigawa explained the new artistic theory in terms that the elderly bureaucrat Tadokoro could understand.

The family dinner party ended about an hour after it had begun. The older people and children left. The others retired to the living room. Coffee and fruit were served.

Waga and Sachiko chatted quite naturally with their three friends. The talk was an extension of the artistic theory discussed in the dining room. In their eyes, leading figures of the establishment were nothing more than targets of denunciation. Tadokoro and his wife sat near them, listening. The lively young people spoke with animation. The older adults were quite overwhelmed.

More well-wishers came to the mansion. Newspaper reporters were among them, asking for photographs.

'It's a perfect occasion for you to take some photos of me with these young people,' the new minister said, and stood informally with the others. Tadokoro and his wife were flanked by Waga and Sachiko, with Sekigawa, Katazawa, and Takebe included along with members of the family.

'Well, shall we take our leave?' It was Sekigawa who still took the lead.

'Why not stay a little longer?' Waga was acting like a member of the family already.

'No, it's getting late.'

'Why don't you stay and talk some more?' Sachiko tried to detain them.

Sekigawa said for the others, 'Thank you so much for the delicious dinner.'

Waga and Sachiko saw them off at the front door.

The three young men walked away together.

'It was quite a gathering,' Takebe said.

'Right. Waga is already behaving like a son-in-law,' Katazawa said.

They took a taxi to Ginza.

'I know a bar near here. Let's stop off and drink some more,' Takebe suggested. Katazawa agreed to go with him.

'Sekigawa, how about you?'

'No, I'll beg off this time.'

'Why?'

'I've remembered something I have to do. Driver, let me off at Yurakucho.' Sekigawa stepped out and waved at the others. 'So long. See you soon.'

'Sekigawa's acting a bit strange,' Katazawa said to Takebe. 'Why did he get off alone there so late at night?'

'He may have been a bit upset about things tonight.'

'What do you mean?'

'It might have been a shock for him to see the way Waga was acting this evening.'

'Hm.' Katazawa felt that he understood what his friend meant. They had both felt oppressed by Waga's behavior at the Tadokoros'.

'He's been really close to Waga recently. Tonight, too, he was in a good mood and talking up a storm.'

'That's human nature for you,' Katazawa responded. 'You go overboard acting lively at that kind of occasion. Then you feel lonely afterward.'

'Well, let's drink, then,' Takebe said. 'Let's get drunk.'

Sekigawa walked alone. He appeared to have nowhere in particular to go. Turning away from the neon lights of Ginza, Sekigawa walked slowly down a side street, deep in thought. He entered a brightly lit *pachinko* hall.

'Give me two hundred yen worth.'

He scooped up the small metal balls in his hands and stood in front of a board. His thumb flipped the lever, sending the balls across the face of the machine. He did not seem to care at all whether he won or lost. He just kept on flipping the lever.

15. On the Track

A letter arrived for Imanishi from the head of the investigation section of the Ise police station.

The following report is in answer to your inquiry.

We went immediately to question Tadokoro Ichinosuke, manager of the Asahi Theater. Tadokoro-*san* says he does not know any Miki Ken'ichi, nor did he meet him during the period you indicated. This is as we reported to you in answer to your last inquiry.

Tadokoro-*san* is from the same village as Tadokoro Shigeyoshi, who was recently appointed minister of agriculture and forestry. Tadokoro-*san* holds Tadokoro Shigeyoshi in the highest regard. Each time he visits Tokyo, he stops by at Tadokoro Shigeyoshi's residence to pay his respects and to deliver some special items from this area. He also mentioned that he has received many favors from Tadokoro Shigeyoshi.

Tadokoro-*san* has at his home many letters, calligraphic works, photographs, and other items that he has received from Tadokoro Shigeyoshi. Furthermore, to show his respect for Tadokoro Shigeyoshi, he has occasionally displayed at the Asahi Theater commemorative photographs taken of himself with Tadokoro Shigeyoshi. When we inquired about May 9, he indicated that at that time there was an enlargement of a photograph taken with the Tadokoro Shigeyoshi family placed on the wall of the hallway leading into the auditorium of his theater. This photograph was taken down at the end of May, and is now at Tadokoro-*san*'s private home.

I have borrowed the original photograph from Tadokoro-*san* and am sending it under separate cover. Please return it when you are finished with it. I have signed a receipt for this item in my own name and request that the utmost care be taken so as not to lose the photograph.

Impatient to see the photograph, Imanishi left home early the next morning and reached headquarters at nine A.M. Only two young detectives had arrived so far.

'Hey, has the mail come?' Imanishi asked right away.

'No, sir, not yet.'

Imanishi could not sit still. He had never wished so hard for a new case *not* to break. If a murder occurred, he would have to rush out.

The section chief arrived just before ten o'clock.

'Imanishi,' he called from his desk.

Imanishi shuddered. But after talking with the chief, he was relieved that he would not need to leave the office. He returned to his desk to find that the mail had been delivered, but there was nothing for him.

'Hey, didn't I get anything?' he asked the young detective who had distributed the mail.

'No, sir, there was nothing.'

'When does the next delivery come?'

'Usually about three.'

Imanishi sipped the tea that a junior detective served him. He could hardly wait for the next delivery. As the long hours stretched slowly into the afternoon, he sat at his desk filling out reports. He kept looking at the clock. One of the young detectives picked up the mail from the reception desk. At three-fifteen, he came through the door, waving a manila envelope.

'Finally, it's here.' Imanishi jumped up from his chair.

Inside the envelope was a photograph protected by two sheets of cardboard. Imanishi looked at the photograph so intently that he no longer heard the voices around him. In an elegant garden of a grand residence half a dozen people were standing in a line. Imanishi focused his attention on one of them, staring at his face for a long time.

'Could you lend me a magnifying glass?' he asked a young detective.

The detective brought over a magnifying glass, and Imanishi placed it over the face in the photograph. So this photograph was what Miki had seen. The enlargement displayed on the wall at the Asahi Theater in Ise must have been nearly poster size.

Miki had focused on one face, and he must have gone back to jot down the name of that person from the label beneath it. Even without an address, he was the sort of person who would be easy enough to find in Tokyo. Miki had changed his plans and suddenly decided to go to Tokyo. There was someone he wanted to see again before he took leave of this world. That person was one of the people in the photograph. Miki arrived in Tokyo early on May 11 and looked up the address of the person in the photograph, perhaps in the telephone directory. He telephoned.

Imanishi telephoned Yoshimura to arrange a meeting at Kamata Station at six-thirty.

'Where shall we talk?'

'Let me see.' Imanishi looked down the long, narrow shopping street and led the way into a tearoom. The customers were mainly women who came to eat bean paste sweets, which made it a good location for their confidential conversation. They sat at the table farthest from the door.

'This is it.' Imanishi took the photograph out of his pocket.

'Please let me have a look.' Yoshimura gazed at the photograph, which he, too, had been eagerly awaiting. His eyes held the same expression as Imanishi's had when he first saw the picture.

'Imanishi-*san*,' Yoshimura said, 'you've done it.'

'Hm,' Imanishi answered. 'Finally.'

He was thinking that he had taken many detours before he had been able to identify the face that had drawn Miki to Tokyo.

Neither Imanishi nor Yoshimura mentioned the photograph again. The remaining task was how to solve the rest of the case.

Imanishi had theorized from the start of this case that the murderer's hideout was close to Kamata Station and that he had walked there to change his bloodstained clothes. So the murderer's lover probably lived near Kamata. Naruse Rieko, who had destroyed the evidence, had been in close contact with the murderer.

She had moved into an apartment in Imanishi's neighborhood soon after the crime. Where had she lived before? He had asked the manager of the apartment building, but had been told that it was unclear where she had come from. Yoshimura had searched the area around Kamata thoroughly, carrying with him a photograph of Rieko. He had not been the only one. Many detectives had taken part and the local policemen also had searched the area, but to no avail.

'Yoshimura,' Imanishi said. 'We were wrong. Rieko was brokenhearted and committed suicide. There is no mistake in that. But we had the wrong lover.'

'I guess so,' Yoshimura agreed.

'Now that we know that, let's try one more time to find Rieko's address at the time of the murder. Your station still has her photo?'

'Yes, we do.'

'We did that investigation once, but there may be something we overlooked. She must have lived within a twenty-minute walk from Kamata. The murderer walked to this hideout after he committed his crime at the railroad yard. If he had walked for a long time, he would have risked being noticed.'

'I agree.' Yoshimura nodded over and over. 'I understand. I'll check it out once more. This time we'll keep it to an area within a twenty-minute walk from Kamata.'

Three days later there was an interim report from Yoshimura. 'My investigation section head was enthusiastic when I told him about your finding. He pulled together a special investigation team.'

'That's gratifying.' Imanishi was satisfied. No matter how he might have fretted about it, if the local police station was un-enthusiastic, he could not hope for any success.

'The newspaper reporters have started to suspect something, so it's getting difficult.'

'Make sure they don't find out anything.'

'Of course we're doing all we can, but those fellows are quick to notice things. They won't leave us alone. They're after me to talk to them, and they're really persistent.'

'That's a problem,' Imanishi said, his expression clouded.

'We're giving them various excuses. Imanishi-*san*, I'm afraid that we won't have an answer for quite a while.'

'I'm not expecting anything right away. How far has the investigation proceeded?'

'We've practically finished the area a mile and a quarter around Kamata Station.'

'That's a lot of work for you.' Imanishi thought for a bit and said, 'My hunch is that the areas to the north and west of Kamata Station are the most likely.'

There was something else that Imanishi was looking into, but his best hope was that the Kamata police station would find Rieko's former address. Imanishi became impatient. He wanted to go to each house, photo in hand, but his work schedule did not permit it.

One morning, Imanishi came across the following report in the cultural section of the newspaper.

Composer Waga Eiryo has announced that he will be visiting the
United States by invitation of the Rockefeller Foundation. He will
depart on November 30 from Haneda Airport for New York, where he
will reside for a while. Mr Waga's stay in America will last approximately three months, during which time he will present performances
of his electronic music compositions. Afterward, he plans to travel in
Europe to observe developments regarding electronic music. He plans
to return to Japan at the end of April. Soon after that, Mr Waga will
wed his fiancée, Tadokoro Sachiko, the daughter of Agriculture Minister Tadokoro Shigeyoshi.

Imanishi read through this article twice.

Arriving at headquarters in low spirits, Imanishi found
Yoshimura waiting for him. 'You're awfully early.'

'Yes, sir.' Yoshimura's face showed fatigue, and Imanishi realized that the investigation had not been successful.

'So, nothing's been found?'

'We've come up with nothing.' Yoshimura was dejected.
'The section chief gave us all the support he could, but . . .'

'How many days has it been since you started the search?'

'Almost a week. We've searched everywhere we could.'

'I see . . .' Imanishi placed his hand on the shoulder of his
young colleague. 'Thanks for all your efforts.'

'I'm so sorry that we couldn't come up with anything.'

'Don't let something like this get you down. Keep up the
good work.'

'Yes.'

'You've given so much to this investigation. I'm sure there
was no oversight. I feel that there must be something that we
don't see yet – a blind spot.'

'Imanishi-*san*, it makes me relieved when I hear you say that.
As you say, there may be something like a blind spot.'

'Right, let's think about it some more.'

'Yes, I'll think about it.' Yoshimura's expression regained some of its energy.

'Please give my best to your section chief.'

'Yes, I will.'

Imanishi saw his young colleague out to the front door of police headquarters. He watched as Yoshimura crossed the brightly lit avenue.

That day Imanishi did not go home directly, but took the streetcar to the Avant-Garde Theater. It was dusk, but there was still a light shining in the office where three of the staff were putting posters and tickets in order. One of them recognized Imanishi.

'Welcome.' The clerk guided Imanishi to the reception area.

'Thanks so much for your help before,' Imanishi said, as he took off his raincoat and sat down.

'Have you been able to find Naruse-*san*'s previous address?' the clerk asked, lighting a cigarette. He seemed to welcome a break from his work.

'I'm afraid we haven't been able to locate it yet.' Imanishi also lit a cigarette. 'I don't suppose you've heard anything here?'

'Nothing at all,' he replied. 'But I'll keep my ears open.'

Imanishi chatted for a while with the clerk. He had come to ask about Rieko's previous address, but he felt he could not be so curt as to leave right away.

'Why are the police still trying to find Naruse-*san*'s previous address?' the clerk asked with a puzzled expression. The theater company had no idea that there was some connection between Naruse Rieko and the Kamata railroad yard murder case.

'We're just looking into the circumstances.' Imanishi avoided a direct reply. 'Naruse-*san* committed suicide, so we treat it as an unnatural death, not as a normal death from illness. That's why we need to find out more about the circumstances.'

'Oh, I see what you mean.' The clerk was impressed. 'If the police are that careful about finding things out, one can't commit suicide lightly, can one?'

'I suppose not.' As they were talking, Imanishi heard shouting in the distance. 'What is that?' Imanishi asked, straining his ears.

'Oh, that? They're rehearsing for our next production.'

'Oh, I see.'

'How about it? If you have the time, would you like to take a peek?'

Imanishi had never seen a contemporary play. As its name indicated, the Avant-Garde Theater was currently noted for staging the most progressive dramas.

'Well, perhaps I could take a look if I wouldn't be in the way.'

'That's no problem. It's a dress rehearsal. It's really no different from seeing a regular performance. You could sit there and not be noticed by anyone.'

Opening the door of the theater office, the clerk walked ahead of Imanishi along a hallway. The clerk quietly opened the closed door at the end of the hallway, and Imanishi followed.

Suddenly they could hear the voices on the stage where many people were moving about. The clerk showed Imanishi to a chair placed against a dark wall. There were four or five others sitting in the dark, watching the stage.

The stage set seemed to be part of a factory in which were gathered about twenty people dressed as factory workers. They were surrounding one man, also dressed as a factory worker, and arguing with him.

As Imanishi watched, the director, standing below the stage, occasionally corrected the delivery of the dialogue. Imanishi gazed at the stage. It was no different from watching a real stage performance. All of the actors were wearing workers' uniforms. Imanishi thought that it must be quite a task to gather so many costumes. As he watched the progress of the play, his eyes began to shine. Soon he was merely following the action with his eyes while his thoughts were running elsewhere.

He left quietly and returned to the office, where the three staff members were still preparing posters for mailing.

'How was it?' the clerk who had shown Imanishi to the rehearsal hall asked.

'It was very interesting,' Imanishi responded, smiling.

'I'm glad you thought so. If you'd like, you're welcome to watch until the end.'

'Thank you.'

'That's a play that our troupe is premiering, so we're putting all our efforts into it. The advance notices are very favorable.'

'Is that so? They're all putting a lot of spirit into their performances.' Imanishi went over to the clerk and said in a low voice, 'I'd like to ask you something. I noticed that you need many costumes.'

'Yes, we do. Just making those costumes takes quite a bit of money.'

'Do you save the costumes after you finish with a performance?'

'Yes, we usually save them.'

'Then there must be someone who oversees the costumes?'

'Yes, there is.'

'I'm sorry to trouble you, but could I see that person?'

'The wardrobe mistress?' The clerk looked at Imanishi's face with a quizzical expression.

'Yes, I'd like to ask her some questions.'

'I see. Please wait a minute. I'll see if she's in.'

Soon the clerk returned and led Imanishi toward the rear of the building. 'This is our wardrobe mistress.' She was a plump woman of about thirty-five, wearing a coat and preparing to leave.

'I'm sorry to hold you up just as you're about to go home.' Imanishi bowed his head.

'What is it you'd like to ask me?' The short woman looked up at Imanishi.

'There must be an incredible number of costumes. Do you ever lose any?'

'No, that hardly ever happens.'

'Hardly ever?' Imanishi took that phrase as his cue. 'Then that means that sometimes they do disappear?'

'Yes. It almost never happens, but there are times when one or two pieces might be missing. But that's only once every several years.'

'I see. That must be because you're careful about overseeing the costumes. But there must be forces beyond your control. No matter how careful you are, with so many items, there must be times when the numbers aren't complete.'

'Yes. Then it's my responsibility.'

'I see. Did a man's costume disappear this past spring?'

The wardrobe mistress looked surprised at Imanishi's specific question.

'Yes, one did.'

'And when was that?'

'We presented *Flute* by Kawamura Tomoyoshi-*sensei* in May. During that time a man's raincoat disappeared, and we couldn't find it.'

'A raincoat?' Imanishi opened his eyes wide. 'When was that?'

'That play was on for the month of May, so I think it was around the middle of May that we lost it. Since we couldn't find it anywhere, I rushed around and got another one to take its place.'

'I'm sorry to ask you, but could you tell me the exact date?'

'Please wait a moment. I'll look in my work journal.'

She hurried back to her own room.

'I suppose things do go astray,' Imanishi said to the clerk. Despite his nonchalant manner, his heart was pounding with excitement.

'I've found it,' the wardrobe mistress said, as she returned. 'It was May twelfth that we lost it.'

'You said May twelfth?' Imanishi thought, This is it!

'That's right. It was on the twelfth that I searched for another raincoat to take its place.'

'What time did the previous performance end?'

'It was at ten P.M. on May eleventh.'

'The location?'

'It was at the Toyoko Hall in Shibuya.'

Imanishi's heart pounded again. Shibuya was close to Gotanda. From Gotanda the Ikegami Line went to Kamata. Furthermore, Meguro was even closer to Shibuya. And from Meguro the Mekama Line went to Kamata.

'What color was that raincoat?'

'It was a darkish gray.' Having said this much, the wardrobe mistress's expression became puzzled. 'We didn't report it as a burglary; was it wrong not to?'

'No, that's not a problem at all. This has nothing to do with any burglary report.' Imanishi smiled. 'Was there a burglary?'

'No, we don't think so. But it is certain that it disappeared.'

'Was it kept in the dressing room?'

'Yes, it was. At the end of a play's run, we store things in the costume warehouse, but during a run we leave them in the dressing rooms.'

'That's strange. Do you have burglars who steal from the dressing rooms?'

'I can't say we never do, but I can't imagine that a burglar would take a worn-out raincoat. Although sometimes money has been stolen.'

'It was the twelfth that you realized the raincoat was gone? That means the raincoat was there the evening of the eleventh and was used for the performance, but on the next day, the twelfth, you found that the raincoat had disappeared before the performance began.'

'Yes, that's the way it was. Since Miyata-*san* was tall, I had a hard time finding a raincoat that was long enough.'

'What! It was Miyata-*san*?' Imanishi's voice rose involuntarily. 'That raincoat was for Miyata-*san*'s part?'

'Yes, it was.' The woman was surprised at his loud voice.

'You mean Miyata Kunio, of course?'

'Yes.'

Imanishi's rapid breathing showed his excitement. 'When he found out that the raincoat he was to wear was missing, what did Miyata-*san* say?'

'He said "What shall I do?" He asked me to find something quickly. He kept saying, "I know it was here last night." '

'Wait a minute. Was Miyata-*san* on stage until the last scene of that play?'

'Yes, he wore that raincoat in the last scene.'

Imanishi crossed his arms. The memory of Miyata Kunio's death returned forcefully. 'I'd like to ask you something else. There was a staff member named Naruse Rieko here, wasn't there? The girl who committed suicide.'

'Yes, I knew her well.'

'It might be impolite of me to ask this, but were Miyata-*san* and Naruse-*san* on close terms?' Imanishi asked the wardrobe mistress.

'I don't think they were especially close, but Miyata-*san* seemed to like Naruse-*san*.'

Imanishi had heard this before. He himself had seen Miyata standing under Rieko's apartment window trying to draw her attention.

'That night, did Miyata-*san* go straight home after the performance?'

'I wouldn't know about that.' The wardrobe mistress smiled. 'Usually he seemed to go home alone after performances. He didn't drink much and didn't seem to have many friends.'

'What about Naruse-*san*?'

'I don't know about her either. Probably the other office people would know.' She turned to look at the clerk standing beside them.

'I can't be sure,' the clerk cocked his head in doubt. 'I don't remember if she went home right away on that particular day. Naruse-*san* was a very hard worker. She never left the office early.'

'Do you have a time card system here?'

'No, we don't.'

Imanishi wanted to find out whether Naruse Rieko had left the theater during work hours on May 11. 'Was Naruse-*san*'s work the kind where she could have left for a while during her work hours?'

'Well, if she had wanted to, she could have. Her responsibility was to make sure everything was orderly after the performance was over. During the performance, she wouldn't have been that busy.' The clerk added, 'But she never left the theater during a performance.'

'You said on that occasion the theater was the Toyoko Hall. So naturally, Naruse-*san* was at Toyoko Hall as well?'

'Yes. There's no doubt about that.'

'Sorry for asking such troublesome questions.' Imanishi bowed to the two theater employees.

If the murderer had put the raincoat on over his bloodstained clothes, no one would have noticed. He could even have taken a taxi without difficulty. That raincoat was the one Miyata wore on stage. And Miyata had shown a special liking for Naruse Rieko. Rieko, in turn, was passionately in love with another man. A thread connected these figures.

Imanishi recalled a passage from Rieko's journal.

Must love be a lonely thing?

Our love has lasted for three years. Yet nothing has been built from this love . . . At night, despair haunts my dreams. And yet I must be strong. I must believe in him . . . This love always demands sacrifices of me. I must feel the joy of a martyr as I make sacrifices. Forever, he says. As long as I live, he will continue to demand that I sacrifice.

The passage spoke of three years. Rieko had started to work at the Avant-Garde Theater four years ago. Her first move was one year later. That meant that for three years she had lived at an address she had kept secret from the theater.

'This love always demands sacrifices of me,' she had written. And she had actually sacrificed for her love. She had stolen a costume from the theater for her lover and had taken it to him. It was also she who had cut up her lover's shirt into tiny fragments. She had had no regrets about these acts that were against the law. 'I must feel the joy of a martyr as I make sacrifices.'

Imanishi had been wrong. Not only had he mistaken the identity of her lover; he had also made a great error in his surmise that her apartment had been used as a hideout. No wonder no hideout could be discovered even after so much investigation around Kamata Station.

Imanishi ruminated, putting his thoughts in order.

A certain man decided to commit a murder. He realized that his clothes would become bloodstained. He could not hail a taxi in such a state. Before committing his crime, he called the Avant-Garde Theater at Toyoko Hall from a public phone booth. It was late at night, but Rieko was still there. He ordered her to bring him something to wear over his clothes. He also told her where to meet him. On the spur of the moment, she stole the raincoat, which was a stage costume worn by Miyata Kunio. Perhaps she had asked Miyata to sneak the raincoat out. That's it, that must have been it. Otherwise, even if it were just one raincoat, her conscience would have prevented her from stealing something from the theater troupe. By taxi, it was a short ride from Shibuya to the scene of the crime. If she had taken the train, she could easily have changed at Gotanda or Meguro to reach the site. She met her lover, who was standing in the shadows, and handed him the raincoat.

Imanishi felt that what had puzzled him for so long had finally been made clear. There were still many things he did not know, but he told Yoshimura what he had concluded.

'I agree with you completely,' Yoshimura said in response. 'I'm impressed, Imanishi-*san*.'

'Don't flatter me,' Imanishi said, embarrassed. 'If I had figured this out right off, I might be able to accept your praise, but this is the result of having gone around in so many circles.'

Three people related to the Nouveau group in some way had died since the Kamata murder was committed. Miyata, Miura, and Rieko. Imanishi now believed the Kamata railroad yard murder case was linked with these three deaths.

At about three o'clock the next day, Imanishi realized he was hungry. Finding a break point in his work, he headed for the fifth-floor coffee shop. Many others were already there. He ordered coffee and a piece of cake and took a seat.

At the table next to him were some men from the crime prevention section. He knew them by face, but not well enough to strike up a conversation. Among them were two men who were not in the police department, members of a crime prevention association. They were engaged in a lively discussion.

'These days many houses are equipped with burglar alarms,' one of the men from the crime prevention association was saying. 'I think public relations by the police have had quite an effect in that area.'

Imanishi alternately ate a bite of cake and drank a sip of coffee.

'Alarms might be enough to dissuade burglars, but what hasn't declined is the number of door-to-door peddlers,' a detective in the crime prevention section put in. 'This is a real problem for us. You may avoid trouble by buying something for a hundred yen, but it is ridiculous to buy something knowing that it's worthless.

'Some housewives become frightened and hand over money to the peddler right away. Then the peddler becomes more obnoxious and pushes more items onto the poor victims. If they were to go ask for help from a neighbor, the peddler might steal something while they're gone, and if the neighbors hear that it's a gangster-peddler, they're not likely to come to help out. It's really a serious problem.'

'These days, though,' one of the crime prevention association members said with a chuckle, 'there's a miracle cure to get rid of pushy peddlers.'

'Really? What is that?'

'You have to install a special device.'

Imanishi overheard this comment and turned to look at the speaker. His ears had perked up when he had heard the word 'peddler' in their conversation. Now that the talk was about equipment to repel peddlers, his attention was drawn even more.

'It's like this . . .' the man from the association explained. 'First I'll tell you the effect. The peddler starts to feel sick and scurries away.'

'Really? Is that true?'

'It's true,' the speaker nodded.

'Well, that really is a miracle cure. It's funny to think that those pushy gangster-peddlers would run away feeling sick. What sort of equipment is it?'

Imanishi became even more curious. Drinking his coffee, Imanishi concentrated on listening.

'The machine is called an ultrasonic peddler repellent,' the man said.

'Ultrasonic . . . ? Oh, yes, it must be a piece of electrical equipment.'

'No, it's not electricity that causes this effect. A high sound can make the person feel sick.'

'If it's a high sound, then wouldn't the neighbors hear it?'

'No, it's not that kind of high sound. I don't understand the theory myself, but instead of causing a noise, it echoes in your body directly, making you feel strange.'

Imanishi remembered the fragment of a boring newspaper article. He had put it aside. The word 'ultrasonic' had appeared in it. It was a strong force. It could drill metal, he recalled. He was intrigued. He waited until the group stood up, then he grabbed one of the detectives he knew by sight and whispered to him, 'Who is that person who was talking about the peddler repellent machine just now?'

The detective told him, 'That's Yasuhiro-*san* of the crime prevention association. He runs a bicycle shop.'

'Could you introduce me to him? I'd like to ask him something.'

'Sure, glad to.'

'This is my name.' Imanishi gave Yasuhiro his card. 'Thank you so much for your cooperation.' He bowed.

'Please don't mention it.' The man named Yasuhiro also gave Imanishi his card, and the information he sought.

Imanishi left headquarters just after four o'clock. He had not felt so impatient about reaching a destination for a long time. Normally, he would have taken trains and buses, but today he made the extravagant choice of taking a taxi.

The communications research center was located in an empty lot surrounded by a flimsy wire fence. On the roof of the white, two-story, Western-style building were a parabola antenna shaped like a bowl and some steel towers for wireless transmission.

Hamanaka, the researcher Imanishi had come to see, had given instructions for a security guard to escort him to the sitting room. Soon the door opened and a man of about thirty-five with thinning hair above a broad forehead appeared.

'My name is Hamanaka.'

They exchanged name cards. On Hamanaka's card was the designation 'Post and Telecommunications Specialist.'

'I'm with the government, on temporary loan to this research center,' Hamanaka explained.

'As I mentioned to you over the telephone, I heard about the electronic peddler repellent device from a member of the crime prevention association. I hear that you invented it?'

'No, it's not really my invention.' Specialist Hamanaka squinted his large eyes and chuckled. 'The theory is very simple. But I may have been the first one to assemble it into something for practical use.'

'Could you please explain that theory to me in a way that a layman can understand?' Imanishi asked.

Hamanaka continued to smile. 'It's actually a sound.'

'A sound?'

'Yes. If I can explain a bit. We live every day among many sounds.' Hamanaka spoke, searching for simple words. 'These sounds can be like notes of music, or they can be just noise. Among those sounds, there are some that are very unpleasant. For example, the sound of a saw screeching as it goes through wood, or the kind that makes you grind your teeth, like fingernails on a glass window. Those are unpleasant sounds, aren't they?'

'They certainly are.'

'The difference in tone causes them to sound unpleasant. These tones come to us as waves through the air, so we call them sound waves. If these sound waves are sent in cycles at certain frequencies they can be very unpleasant for human beings. The peddler repellent device utilizes this acoustic effect.'

'I see.' Realizing that the theoretical discussion would become complicated from here on, Imanishi waited for the next words.

'If I can give you an example,' Hamanaka continued, smiling, 'let's say that you were made to listen to a low-frequency sound of ten cycles for several minutes. In this case, the sound is not what we normally call sound, but might be better described as vibrations. So it might be considered that you are not listening to the sound but are feeling the sound.'

Imanishi looked confused, so Hamanaka's explanation became even more basic.

'You would feel uncomfortable after hearing that vibration for a while. Your head would start aching, and your body might start shaking. It's a strange phenomenon.'

'Does one really react that way?' Imanishi asked, leaning forward.

'Yes, most definitely. What I just explained was a low sound that may just barely be heard or not heard at all. The same can be said about high sounds.'

'High sounds?'

'Yes. High sounds over ten thousand cycles in frequency. If one is exposed to twenty-thousand- to thirty-thousand-cycle sounds, rather than hearing them, one starts to feel strange. Both high-frequency and low-frequency sound waves are felt as very unpleasant sensations.'

He continued, 'Please look at this. This diagram plots the average range of auditory senses of a number of people in terms of frequency and volume. The numbers along the bottom are the frequencies, and the numbers on the left side are the levels of volume. On the right side is sound pressure. The range of audible frequencies is usually said to be from ten thousand to twenty thousand cycles. As this diagram shows, the range narrows at lower volumes. We call the curve at the bottom the minimum auditory value, or the auditory limit. This means that we cannot hear sounds below this point. The curve at the top of this diagram is called the maximum auditory value, or the sensory limit. If we hear a sound higher than this, we feel discomfort or pain, or some other sensation.'

'So,' Imanishi said, 'between twenty thousand and thirty thousand cycles, sound can make you sick?'

Hamanaka nodded.

'Very, very sick?' Imanishi asked.

'It would depend on individual susceptibility, of course. Those who are especially vulnerable could even die – if the cycle of sound waves went on and on.'

'I see,' Imanishi said. And he did.

16. A Certain Family Register

A letter addressed to Imanishi arrived from the town office, Nita Town, Shimane Prefecture.

Imanishi Eitaro, Police Inspector
Tokyo Metropolitan Police
   Your previous request for information about Motoura Chiyokichi has taken some time to investigate. The following is a report of the information we have been able to obtain so far.
   Reviewing our old records, we have found that Motoura Chiyokichi entered Jikoen Sanatorium in xx Village, Kojima County, Okayama Prefecture, on June 22, 1938. As so much time has passed, we have not been able to obtain all the details, but we have finally uncovered the record books from that time, enabling us to report the exact date. However, this record book makes no reference to Motoura's son, Hideo, who was said to have accompanied him. It is likely that Miki Ken'ichi, the police officer stationed in Kamedake who made the arrangements, dealt with the matter.
   That information would have been in the daily records of the police substation. However, the records for 1938 have already been disposed of.
   It can be surmised from the situation surrounding the event that officer Miki arranged for only the patient Motoura to enter Jikoen Sanatorium, separating him from the apparently healthy boy, Hideo.

We are most interested in what Hideo decided to do after he was taken into protection, but, regrettably, that is unknown. Judging from officer Miki's character, we think that he must have arranged for Hideo to stay with a family. Our investigation turned up no information about this. We conclude that Hideo ran away from that family of his own volition. This is a common occurrence when a child has led a life of wandering.

I submit this as our final report on this matter.

General Affairs Section Head,
Town Office, Nita Town

Imanishi remained deep in thought for a long while. He could see the Kamedake road in early summer. On a hot day, a father and son, wandering beggars, walked along this road. The father's body was covered with pus-filled infections. Seeing this unfortunate pair, police officer Miki persuaded the father to enter Jikoen Sanatorium and took the seven-year-old son under his wing. But the boy, used to a traveling life with his father, was unable to respond to the care he received. One day he ran away without warning. Covered with dirt, the boy crossed the ridge of the Chugoku mountain range to the south. There, he took one of two possible roads. One road led to Hiba County at the northern edge of Hiroshima Prefecture, the other to Okayama. Which road had the boy taken?

No, he could have retraced his steps alone in the direction from which he and his father had come. That would lead to Shinji and on to Yasugi and Yonago. He might have continued walking to Tottori. These three were the routes that the waif could have taken. Whichever road he had walked, he had finally reached Osaka.

In Osaka, the waif was taken in by someone and possibly adopted into a family.

Imanishi could not waste time on a letter of inquiry asking for an investigation. He boarded the night express train to Osaka. Imanishi closed his eyes as he sat on the uncomfortable seats and sipped whiskey from a pocket flask that he had bought for the journey. The sound of the night train followed a simple rhythm. It was not an unpleasant sound. In some ways it was as gentle as a lullaby.

Sounds. Sounds.

'Both high-frequency and low-frequency sound waves are felt as very unpleasant sensations.' Hamanaka's voice echoed in his mind.

Imanishi arrived at Osaka Station at eight-thirty the next morning. At the police box he asked for directions to Ebisu-cho in Naniwa Ward. The policeman turned around to look at a large map on the wall.

'That's west of Tennoji Park, mister,' he said in a thick Osaka accent.

'Is the ward office near there as well?'

'It's about five hundred yards to the north.'

Imanishi hailed a taxi that drove south through Osaka's morning air.

'Driver, where is the Naniwa Ward Office?' Imanishi asked as they started up Tennoji hill.

'The Naniwa Ward Office is that building you can see over there.' The taxi driver had a thick Osaka accent as well.

Imanishi looked at his watch. It was ten minutes before nine. The ward office would not be open.

'Mister, do you want to stop at the ward office?'

'No, I'll do that later.'

Imanishi gave an address to the driver. They turned onto a street lined with shops, none of which had opened yet.

'The stores in this area look very nice,' Imanishi said.

'Yes, it was totally rebuilt after the war.'

'Does that mean that this whole area was burned in an air raid?'

'Yes, mister, it was totally destroyed.'

'Which air raid was that?'

'It was near the end of the war, on March 14, 1945. A large contingent of B-29s rained fire bombs on this area.'

'I suppose many people died?'

'Yes, several thousand.'

The date was the one Imanishi had etched in his mind from Tokyo.

'Mister, we're here.'

Imanishi looked to find that they had stopped in front of a clothing wholesaler. 'Is this the number I gave you?'

'Yes, sir.'

Imanishi paid the fare. In this neighborhood all the houses were new. Not one old, prewar building survived. The clothing wholesaler's sign read 'Tangoya Shop.' Imanishi stood in the doorway of the shop, which was fitted with shelves crammed with bolts of cloth. He was made to wait a while to see the shop owner.

'Welcome,' an old man over sixty said in the Osaka merchant's dialect, as he came from a back room wearing a kimono with a navy blue traditional apron. He had been told who Imanishi was. 'Thank you for coming. Is there something I can help you with?' The old man kneeled down.

Imanishi heard what the Tangoya shop owner had to say. The old man, who was as thin as a withered tree, said that his family had lived in this spot for generations. Therefore, he was very familiar with the area's history.

After listening to the old man for some thirty minutes, Imanishi left the shop and walked up a gentle slope to the ward office. He assumed there was a school nearby, since he could hear the clamor of children's voices. Again he was reminded of the nature of sounds. Annoyingly loud noises. Unpleasant sounds.

Imanishi remembered the words the dying Emiko had uttered. 'Stop it, please. Oh, no, no. I'm afraid something will happen to me. Stop it, please, stop, stop . . .' He continued to think as he walked, his shoulders hunched over. A streetcar passed by. The tracks were curved, and the wheels produced a screeching, metallic sound. Abrasive sounds, unpleasant sounds. A flock of pigeons flew up in the sky. The bright sunlight glanced off their wings.

Arriving at the ward office, Imanishi showed his police identification to a young woman clerk at the window of the family register section.

'I'd like to ask some questions.'

'Yes?'

'Is this the family registered at Number 120, 2 Ebisu-cho, Naniwa Ward?' He showed her the address in his notebook.

After peering closely at Imanishi's handwriting, which was difficult to read, the woman said, 'Please wait a moment.' She stood up and took a book from the shelf where the originals of the family registers were stored. Imanishi waited two or three long minutes. The clerk returned to the window.

'We do have that name registered.'

'You do?'

'Yes. We definitely have that family register's original record.'

'Is that the authentic record?' Imanishi's question slipped out.

'Of course it is,' the clerk said, sounding annoyed. 'The original register at the ward office would not be a forgery.'

'I'm sure that's the case, but . . .' Imanishi was thinking that, although there might be no doubt that it was the original register, it might have been created intentionally. 'I'm sorry to trouble you, but could you please let me see the original register?' Imanishi requested.

'Go ahead.' She passed the thick volume through the window.

Imanishi had imagined that an original family register record would be on old, brown-tinged paper with its edges crumbling away. But this original record was still new. He looked at the entry in question. 'Original domicile: Number 120, 2 Ebisu-cho, Naniwa Ward, Osaka City . . .' Imanishi compared the entry to the notation in his book, but each character was the same.

'Both the head of household, Eizo, and his wife, Kimiko, have the same date of death, March 14, 1945. Does that mean that they died in the air raid?' Imanishi asked for confirmation.

The clerk peered at the entry and said, 'Yes, it does. That day there was a large air raid on the whole of Naniwa Ward. Practically all the houses were burned down. It looks like these two people died in the bombing at that time.'

Imanishi's attention went back to the newness of the original family register record book. 'It looks like the paper in this volume of original family registers is very new.'

'Yes. The previous record book was burned in that same air raid, so this was created later to take its place.'

'Were these records copied from the ones at the Bureau of Justice?'

'The Bureau of Justice was also completely burned down in that day's air raid, and their originals were also destroyed.'

'What?' Imanishi's eyes glinted. 'Then what was this record based on?'

'This one was recorded from the information provided by the person himself.'

'The person himself?'

'Yes. In cases where the original record was destroyed during the war, the law provides for the resubmission of the family register. Please take a look at this.'

The clerk showed Imanishi the statute printed on the first page of the original family register record book:

In those census registration areas where the ward offices and prefectural government offices were destroyed by wartime disasters,
notifications of resubmission of family registers are to be presented
between 1946 and 1947.

Imanishi raised his eyes. 'Then, does this mean that the
resubmission for this family register entry was presented
between 1946 and 1947?'

'No, not necessarily. There are cases when it was made later.'

'I'm sorry to keep bothering you, but could you check when
the notification of resubmission was filed in this case?'

'I can find that out right away.' The clerk took the original
record book and leafed through it. 'In this person's case, notification was given on March 2, 1949.'

'Nineteen forty-nine?' Imanishi thought about this. 'Is it
necessary to have someone like a guarantor to prove that the
claims of the person are correct?'

'We prefer to have someone like that vouch for the information, but in special circumstances such as war damage, there
may not have been anyone to offer such proof. In such cases, we
are forced to rewrite the register based on the information the
person concerned provides.'

'Then, in this case, you did a resubmission of the family
register according to what the person himself gave as
information?'

'Please wait. I'll check on that for you.' She left her chair.

Watching from where he stood, Imanishi could see that
the family register section contained several archival shelves.
Crouching down to reach under a stack of shelves, the clerk
searched for something. It took nearly ten minutes. She
seemed to be having trouble finding what she was looking for.
At the window, the line grew longer. Imanishi started to feel
apologetic. Finally, she returned to the window.

'I just checked the files, but that request form is one that we only keep for five years, so it has already been disposed of.'

'I see.' Bowing his head, Imanishi said, 'I'm sorry to have taken up so much of your time.'

'That's quite all right.'

'I'd like to ask you something in addition about that request for resubmission. Do you fill in the information just as the person himself designates?'

'Yes.'

'For example, if someone had registered a domicile falsely, there would be no way to check that?'

'No, there wouldn't. Since all the original records have been destroyed, we have no way to tell if a false record is registered.'

Imanishi thought for a bit. 'Is there no way that such a forgery could be found out? Is there some way to uncover it?'

'There is a way,' the clerk answered, as Imanishi had expected. 'For example, if this head of household Eizo's place of birth was recorded, then we could confirm it with that location's city hall or town office. It would be the same for his wife.'

'And in this case, did this office go through that procedure?'

'We must have done it. Otherwise, we wouldn't have accepted the record.'

Imanishi asked her to verify that this procedure had been followed. The clerk once again asked him to wait. She went to the shelves and searched through a thick, bound volume. It was a long time before she returned.

'I searched the transaction records for that time, but the clerk who accepted the record no longer works here. According to the transaction records, we accepted the registration with the stipulation that the head of household Eizo's and his wife Kimiko's places of origin were for subsequent completion.'

'Subsequent completion?' Imanishi had no idea what that meant.

Anticipating his reaction, the clerk explained to him, 'It's my guess that the person who came to record this registration had forgotten the exact locations of the family domiciles of the head of household Eizo, and his wife, Kimiko.'

'Had forgotten the locations?'

'That's what I think. After all, the person who submitted the registration was sixteen at the time. His parents had passed away suddenly in a war disaster, and he may not have known the exact location of his parents' places of origin. There was no way that he could fill in those sections, so the registration was probably submitted as is. I would suppose that we accommodated him by having him promise that if he found the places of origin of his parents, he would report that to us. That procedure is what we call "subsequent completion."'

So that was it. Imanishi thought that a bright boy could easily have submitted such a registration.

'Thank you so much for all you've done.'

Imanishi headed for the high school. He had thought that it would be close to the city of Kyoto, but it was near the Osaka prefectural border. The high school stood on a hillside in the outskirts of the city. Imanishi took a taxi to just below the school and walked up the lengthy stone steps, perspiring.

The school principal, a thin, short man in his mid-fifties who seemed kindly, received him. Imanishi stated the purpose of his visit.

'Hmm. What class was this student in?'

'He didn't actually graduate,' Imanishi responded.

'He left partway through? Then what grade was he when he left?'

'I'm afraid that's not clear.'

'Do you know what year he left the school?'

Imanishi scratched his head. 'Actually, that isn't clear either.'

The principal looked perplexed. 'That's a problem. Then we'll have to go by his age. What year was he born?'

Imanishi told him the date of birth.

'That means he attended this school under the prewar system of education, when it was a middle school. That *is* a problem,' the principal said, with a grimace. 'Our school was destroyed during the war, and all the records of the prewar middle school were burned.'

'What, here, too?' Imanishi felt dejected. 'Was it the March fourteenth, nineteen forty-five, air raid?'

'No, this city was bombed earlier. A munitions factory was located here, so we were an earlier target. There was a massive air raid on February nineteenth, nineteen forty-five. It was then that the major part of the city was reduced to ashes. Our school was then located in the center of the city, so it was destroyed as well.'

'Then the directories of graduates and students during the middle school era were . . .'

'Yes, they were all lost. We are in the process of trying to reconstruct the records, but the older the record, the harder it is.'

'That's a shame.' It was unfortunate for Imanishi as well.

'Yes, it is a shame. The school was founded around nineteen twenty, so it is a blow to us to have lost those records.'

'Is there any way that I might find out? I mean, regarding the person I'm inquiring about?'

'Let me see. You gave me his birth date, so one way might be to figure out when he entered the school.'

'What do you mean?'

'We have a fairly good idea of where the graduates from that time are now. There might be some classmates around who remember him.'

That sounded hopeful.

'Would there be someone like that in this neighborhood?'

'Yes, there is. He's a sake brewer now. I think he was a student at just about that time.'

Imanishi retraced his steps to the city. The downtown area was made up of newer buildings. The outlying areas, however, retained the older houses. There was a clear demarcation as to which areas of the town were razed and which had remained standing. Following the high school principal's suggestion, the destination Imanishi headed for was a sake brewery called Flower of Kyoto. He could see the sake warehouses from outside the wall. The front entrance was decorated with latticework common to traditional Kansai-style shops. A large 'Flower of Kyoto' sign topped the roof.

Entering the shop, Imanishi asked to see the owner. Imanishi explained that he had been referred here by the high school regarding a possible classmate of his, one who had left partway through.

'Wait a moment,' the young brew-master said, crossing his arms and looking up at the ceiling. He made an earnest effort to recall. 'I've got it.'

'Do you remember? Was there such a person?' Imanishi looked intently at the young man's face.

'Yes, I'm sure there was. Yes, yes, he quit partway through. I think it was during the second year,' he said.

'Do you know where this student lived?'

'Let me see . . . I think he was boarding somewhere in town.'

'Boarding?'

'Yes. He said that his family lived in Osaka, so he was boarding here.'

'Do you know where he boarded?'

'It's not there anymore. That area was completely burned down, so there's no trace of it.'

'Do you know the name of the family he boarded with?'

'No, I don't. He quit school soon after the second year started, so I don't think any of the other classmates would know either.'

Here, too, the effects of the war proved a stumbling block in the investigation. At this point, Imanishi asked if he knew that a person with the same name had become well known in Tokyo.

'No, I didn't know that.' The young master shook his head.

Imanishi took from his notebook a clipping of a newspaper article that was accompanied by a photograph.

'He looks like this now. Does this face look familiar to you?'

The young master took the clipping in his hand and gazed at it for some time.

'He was at school just for a short time, so all I can remember is that his face looked vaguely like that. So the fellow has become that prominent in Tokyo?' He expressed his surprise.

'Is the teacher who was in charge of your class still around?' Imanishi asked, putting the clipping back in his notebook.

'Our teacher unfortunately died in the air raid.'

That evening Imanishi went to Kyoto Station. There was still some time before the 8:30 limited express to Tokyo. He entered a diner across from the train station and ate some curry and rice.

It had been worth his while to come here. He had surmised what had happened; now he had confirmation. The seven-year-old boy who had traveled on foot in the mountain depths of Shimane Prefecture with his father, who had an incurable, loathsome disease, had run away from Kamedake and gone to Osaka. He was taken in by someone there. He spent several years growing up. He was probably not adopted. He might have been a live-in errand boy. That shop and the owner seemed to have been destroyed during the war. At any rate, there was no trace of them now. Following this, the boy went to Kyoto. He left in the second year of middle school and went to Tokyo.

The names Eizo and Kimiko had been made up by the boy

when he had submitted the registration. Proof of that lay in the fact that the place of origin of this couple was not given. It had been very clever of him to establish his supposed parents at Number 120, 2 Ebisu-cho, Naniwa Ward, in Osaka. This was an area where all the original family registers had been destroyed in an air raid. His school and the city had also been largely destroyed during the war. There were traces of his past, but nowhere was there concrete proof to establish his personal history, a history he had taken such pains to hide. Naturally.

As Imanishi finished his spicy curry and rice and drank his tea, he noticed an evening paper left by another customer. He reached for it. Skimming through it casually, his eyes stopped at an article in the cultural section.

Excursions Abroad Set for Messrs Waga and Sekigawa.

Mr Waga Eiryo announced that he would be departing for his trip to the United States from Haneda Airport at 10:00 P.M., November 30, on a Pan American flight. He plans to visit various locations in the US, starting with New York, and to head for Europe afterward.

Mr Sekigawa Shigeo will leave for Paris on an Air France flight on December 25. Following his stay in France, he plans to tour West Germany, England, Spain, and Italy, before his return in late February. His trip to Europe is to attend an international symposium of intellectuals as Japan's representative.

Reaching Tokyo in the morning, Imanishi returned home.

'It must have been tiring for you. It would be good if you could take a bath at a time like this, but the public bath doesn't open until ten o'clock,' Yoshiko said, concerned.

In order to accommodate a bathtub, the Imanishis would need to add on to their house. It was hard for them to save up enough money to pay for it.

'It's all right. I don't have much time. I'm going to sleep for an hour.'

Imanishi gave his wife some Kyoto specialty pickles as a present.

'Oh, you said you were going to Osaka. But did you go to Kyoto, too?'

'Yes. It's impossible to predict where we may end up in our line of work.'

'They say Kyoto is a beautiful city. I'd love to spend some time there,' Yoshiko said as she gazed at the label on the package of pickles.

'I know. When I retire, let's take a leisurely trip there with my retirement pay.'

Imanishi lay down on the tatami.

'You'll catch cold. I'll lay out the futon right away. Why don't you change your clothes?'

'No, I don't have that much time.'

His wife pulled out a comforter from the closet and placed it over him. His complexion was sallow with fatigue. She awakened him shortly after he had fallen asleep.

'It's ten o'clock already.' Yoshiko sat beside him, looking at him in sympathy.

'Is it?' Imanishi flung off the comforter and got up.

'Aren't you still sleepy?'

'No, sleeping even that little bit helped a lot.'

Imanishi washed his face with cold water. He felt much better.

'You'll be home early tonight, I hope?' his wife asked as they ate breakfast.

'Yes, I'll come home early tonight.'

'Please do. Otherwise, you'll come down with something.'

'You're right. I used to be able to spend two nights in a row without sleep on a stakeout without feeling tired.' He was getting on, there was no denying it.

He reached headquarters after eleven and reported to the section chief.

Imanishi next went to the Kamata police station to see Yoshimura and bring him up to date on his findings. Yoshimura listened intently, eager to catch every word.

'That ends the part about Kyoto,' Imanishi said. 'Now it's time for Tokyo. Since we last met I've learned something about acoustics.'

'Acoustics?'

'The study of sound.' Imanishi described what he had learned.

'Oh, I see.'

'Next, it's this,' Imanishi said, leafing through his notebook. 'Look at this.'

Yoshimura looked at the piece of paper he had picked up near the spot where Miyata had died.

'Do you think this has anything to do with Miyata's death?'

'I thought at the time that someone must have dropped it there by accident, but now I think it was dropped intentionally.'

'What do you mean, intentionally?'

'It can be viewed as a challenge by the person who put it there.'

'A challenge?'

'When people become arrogant, they feel like sneering at others, certain that they won't catch on. That's what I think this represents.'

'But this is a listing of distributed insurance amounts.'

'Yes, it is. There's no mistaking that. I suspected these figures, so I had them checked out. I didn't think there was any reason to write down patently false figures, but I had it checked out just to be sure. These are the actual figures.'

'What's the relationship between these numbers and Miyata's death, then?'

'Look at it carefully. There are parts where no monetary amounts are filled in. See, under nineteen fifty-three, nineteen fifty-four, and nineteen fifty-five. From nineteen forty-nine on none of the years have figures, while there are two lines between nineteen fifty-three and nineteen fifty-four. Even if the years before nineteen fifty-two were omitted, why are there two lines between nineteen fifty-three and nineteen fifty-four?'

'I can't figure it out.'

'I thought initially that there was some statistical reason for this. But when I thought carefully about it, it seemed odd. There's no reason to leave blank spaces like this.'

'Do you think there's a particular meaning to the blank spaces, as well?' Yoshimura asked.

'I think so. The blanks between nineteen fifty-three and nineteen fifty-four make it look as though there were no further disbursements during that time, that there wasn't a second, or a third, payment during that year. But just the opposite occurred. These lines were placed without any meaning when you look at this as a statistical table.'

'I don't think I'm following you,' Yoshimura said, resting his chin in his hand.

'The amounts of unemployment insurance disbursed are noted as 25,404 and 35,522. If you read these numbers in the normal way, you would read them as twenty-five thousand four hundred and four and thirty-five thousand five hundred and twenty-two. I just told you what I heard about acoustics, right?'

'Yes.'

'In simple terms, the human ear can't hear sounds that are too low or too high. In ordinary cases, sounds over twenty thousand cycles can't be taken in as sounds by people . . .'

'Oh, I get it. These numbers of 25,000, 30,000, 24,000, 27,000, and 28,000 could signify high-frequency cycles,' Yoshimura said.

'Exactly. They're ultrasonic waves. This table of insurance distribution is also a table of suggested distribution of ultrasonic frequencies.'

'Then do the blank spaces signify rests, the kind they often have in music? I think they call them pauses.'

Imanishi was totally ignorant about music. 'I think that must be it.'

'So the high-frequency sounds were not to be emitted continuously, but there were to be pauses in between. If you followed the table that's what would happen,' Yoshimura said.

'That's how I interpret it. The high-frequency sound wasn't continuously transmitted. By putting the pauses in, the frequency would change as noted in the table.'

Yoshimura's expression showed his admiration for Imanishi's deductions.

'It would probably have a greater effect on someone to have slight frequency changes rather than a continuous emission of the same frequency sound wave.' This was not Imanishi's own opinion, but based on information that he had heard from Hamanaka. 'I think that these pauses weren't complete rests and that there was some kind of sound during these pauses as well.'

'So it wasn't a complete blank during the pause?'

'No, it wasn't. The sound continued, but it became a pleasant sound.'

'Pleasant sound? You mean music?'

'Yes, exactly. Between the different ultrasonic waves, music was played.'

Imanishi went on, 'Assume that Miyata and Emiko were murdered using these ultrasonic waves. This is a new method of committing murder, one that we haven't seen before. But we have to consider something here. Just suppose . . . this is just a supposition . . . if the person who killed Miyata and Emiko is the same as the one who killed Miki at the Kamata railroad yard, you notice a big difference in the style of the murders.'

Yoshimura nodded. 'There's a huge difference. That murder was by strangulation, and then the victim's face was battered with a stone. You can't get much more violent.'

'That's right. That method of murder was simple and brutal. We could also say that it was spontaneous. In other words, it was not planned. If Miyata's and Emiko's deaths were murders, however, the murderer used his cunning and killed them after intricate planning. Isn't there a contradiction in this? If these crimes were committed by the same murderer, how do we explain this?'

'Let me see.' After some thought, Yoshimura said, 'Could it be because Miki arrived in Tokyo unexpectedly?'

'That's exactly what I think. Miki arrived in Tokyo early on the morning of May eleventh,' Imanishi said. 'He was killed between midnight and one A.M. the night of the very same day he arrived in Tokyo.'

'Yes, that's true.'

'Miki had a reason for coming to Tokyo. And his movements from the morning until the night of the eleventh are what caused him to be killed.'

The two men were silent for a while, each thinking his own thoughts.

'At any rate,' Yoshimura said, breaking the silence first, 'the murderer wasn't yet prepared to kill Miki ultrasonically.'

'That's what I think. That's why we need to find out if the murderer procured the needed equipment between May 11 and August 31, when Miyata was killed. I think that will be one of the conclusive pieces of evidence.'

'But wouldn't the procurement of equipment have been carried out in strict secrecy?'

'That may be so, but he seems to be convinced that no one

can figure it out, that he is too clever to be caught. Even if he made his preparations in secret, I think there must be some place he was careless. That's why we must look.'

Yoshimura's gaze fastened on Imanishi's face.

'Imanishi-*san*, those words Emiko uttered just as she was about to die – "Stop it, please. Oh, no, no. I'm afraid something will happen to me. Stop it, please, stop, stop" – were they about these ultrasonic waves?'

'She wouldn't have been able to hear the ultrasonic waves.'

17. The Loudspeaker Announcement

For two days, Yoshimura had interviewed people connected with the Broadcast Technology Research Center. He asked a lot of questions and received many answers. He had also gone to a number of stores dealing in wireless equipment.

Although the investigation into the case had been for all practical purposes closed months earlier, the station chief now placed great hope in the 'voluntary investigation' based on the new evidence Yoshimura had obtained from talking to Imanishi and from his own inquiries.

Imanishi went to the Avant-Garde Theater. The usual clerk came out to meet him.

'Sorry to have bothered you the last time I was here.' Imanishi smiled. 'I've come to ask you for a little more help.'

'What is it this time?'

'I'd like to meet once again with the wardrobe mistress.'

'That's no problem at all. She's here right now.' The clerk called in the wardrobe mistress.

'Thanks for the other day,' Imanishi said. 'What you told me that day was very helpful.'

Imanishi was taken to an empty sitting room by the wardrobe mistress, who had perceived that Imanishi's business needed privacy.

'You said that a costume had disappeared. I suppose it hasn't been returned since then?'

'No, it hasn't. Since you asked me about it, I thought I would reconfirm, so I checked through the numbers again. It hasn't been returned.'

'I have a favor to ask of you,' Imanishi said, bowing his head. 'Could you please let me borrow the replacement costume, that raincoat, for a few days?'

'You mean lend it to you?' The woman's expression indicated a problem.

'I'll take complete responsibility for it. Of course, I'll write an official receipt for the loan.'

'Our policy is not to allow theater belongings off the premises.' But this was a request from the police. 'I guess it's all right. If you'll take responsibility for it.'

Imanishi and Yoshimura met that evening at a diner in Shibuya. They both ordered curry and rice and began to eat.

Imanishi heard Yoshimura's report on his inquiries at the Broadcast Technology Research Center and the shops specializing in wireless materials. Yoshimura explained that a parabola was shaped like a bowl. In transmitting a certain sound wave, if a parabola is used, the waves become condensed and stronger. Imanishi wrote in his notebook the word 'parabola.'

Yoshimura continued, 'You know, those big saucers stuck on towers on top of tall buildings? That's what it is. That's a parabola. Those are very large. When I checked, just as you thought, he had been secretly buying equipment like that from July on. Of course, it's not just a parabola that he bought. The device used against the peddlers combines a parabola and a tweeter, one of those small speakers for high sounds. I've written down the details . . .'

'Miki was killed in May, and Miyata's death was August thirty-first, so July is just at the midpoint between the two,' Imanishi noted.

'Yes, it is, just as you surmised, Imanishi-*san*; so there was plenty of time for preparations.'

'It seems so.' Imanishi nodded, but he did not look pleased. 'We've got the main outline. The problem is how do we get evidence? Otherwise, it just remains our inference.'

'You're right about that.'

'It's a real problem. There must be some way we can get the evidence,' Imanishi said.

'The closer it is to a perfect crime, the less clues there are.'

'It can't be helped; if we can't get evidence, we'll have to resort to tricks.'

'Tricks?'

Imanishi handed Yoshimura a bundle wrapped in newspaper that he had been holding under his arm. 'This is a costume I borrowed from the Avant-Garde Theater. It's the raincoat they bought to replace the one that disappeared. The color and shape are exactly like the one that was stolen, and it was lengthened to fit Miyata.'

'What am I supposed to do with this?' Yoshimura was bewildered.

'You're going to wear this raincoat.'

'Where to?'

'To that house, of course. You and I won't be the only ones going there. We'll be accompanying the officials in charge of prosecuting violations of broadcast laws.'

'When do you plan to do this?'

'Tomorrow morning about eight o'clock. Your station chief should have been notified, so when you return to your office, you will get instructions.'

'Imanishi-*san*, will we make it in time?'

'We'll have to manage somehow.' But Imanishi's uneasiness showed. 'While the scientists and doctors are doing their experiments, you and I have something else to do,' Imanishi said.

'What is that?' Yoshimura asked.

'Let's think about the circumstances of Miura Emiko's death. She had a fall, and died after a miscarriage because of the shock from the fall. We thought that she might have miscarried as the result of this fall, but what if we place it earlier?'

'You mean, the miscarriage was preceded by the killing of the fetus by ultrasonic waves?'

'She was subjected to a type of "surgery." '

'Why didn't she go to a legitimate physician?'

'I think the reason she had such an unusual "operation" was because she didn't want to go to a regular doctor. In other words, Emiko wanted to have the child.'

'Then she was tricked into it?'

'Probably. Sekigawa must have asked for this favor.'

'And she died from it?'

'Yes, she did. I don't think they intended to kill her. She died because the "operation" failed.'

'Does that mean Sekigawa knew of this device?'

'I think he did. I can't say when he first found out about it. He may have figured it out because he had doubts about Miyata's death. If there hadn't been the problem of Emiko's pregnancy, his knowledge about this would have given him a permanent advantage over his good friend. You must have noticed that Sekigawa's reviews of Waga's music suddenly turned favorable. Sekigawa's position of advantage was reversed when he asked Waga to "operate" on Emiko.'

At eight o'clock the following morning, five men visited the home of composer Waga Eiryo. It was quiet in the residential area. On the streets, only the commuters walked with quick steps. It was a cold morning, so several of the men wore overcoats. One had on a dirty gray raincoat. A middle-aged woman opened the door as she wiped her hands on her apron.

'Good morning,' a tall, young man said to her. 'Is the master of the house in?'

'Could I ask who you are?' The woman seemed to be the housekeeper.

'This is who I am.' He gave her his name card. 'We would like to see him.'

'The master doesn't seem to be awake yet . . .'

'Please excuse me, but could you let him know that we are here to see him?'

Facing five men at once, the housekeeper seemed over-whelmed. She retreated into the house.

Imanishi stood in the entryway and looked around. Directly above the raised step into the house was fixed a small golf ball-sized metallic sphere, a tweeter. Some of the others in the group saw this and nodded to each other.

The housekeeper returned. 'Please come in. The master was resting, but he will be able to see you shortly.'

'Excuse us.'

The five men were shown to the Western-style living room. The furnishings were simple but elegant. Sheets of musical scores were piled on the mantelpiece. Some photographs of Westerners were displayed. They did not recognize them.

The others took their coats off, but Yoshimura kept his rain-coat on. The five men sat, smoking silently. They heard the distant sound of a door close. Perhaps the master of the house had gone to wash his face after rising. It was so quiet a neigh-bor's radio could be heard. They were kept waiting for a full twenty minutes. The sound of slippers was heard, and the door opened. Waga Eiryo appeared wearing a kimono. He had just combed his hair.

'Welcome.' He held the name card the housekeeper had given him.

The five men stood up from their chairs.

'Good morning,' one of them said. 'We're sorry to have come like this so early in the morning.'

'No matter.'

Waga looked around at all of them, as if to clarify their positions. When his eyes came to Yoshimura, they opened wide for an instant.

His glance had not been directed at Yoshimura's face. Waga's gaze was fixed intently on the raincoat. For an instant, his eyes betrayed alarm and doubt. Imanishi, sitting unobtrusively amongst the others, watched Waga's face. Waga's expression of alarm lasted for a mere few seconds. Imanishi let out a sigh.

Waga sat down facing the five men. He took a cigarette out of the case on the table, his hands shaking slightly. The young composer struck a match and leaned forward to light his cigarette. Smoke rose from the corner of his mouth. This fraction of a moment gave him the time needed to regain his composure.

'Could I ask what you have come here for?' Waga raised his eyebrows and turned his eyes toward the officer who had greeted him.

The man took out a piece of paper folded in thirds from his pocket. 'We are most regretful, but I must ask you please to take a look at this.'

Waga opened it and read it without showing any reaction. Then a faint smile appeared on Waga's face. 'You're saying I have violated broadcast laws?'

'Yes. Recently there have been many cases of violations regarding VHF transmissions. We're charged with overseeing these cases. So we've been using radar to find the source of these transmissions. We have found that your house seems to be the source of some high-frequency electronic waves ... Waga-*san*, do you have such equipment?'

'Well, yes,' Waga responded, with a tight smile. 'You may know that my music is what is called electronic music. So I use electronic equipment for experiment and practice. But I haven't done anything that would violate the broadcast laws.'

'Is that so? But if you have such equipment we'd like to see it, if you don't mind.'

'Please, go ahead.' Waga seemed unconcerned. 'It's over here; I'll show you.'

'Thank you.'

All five men stood up. Once again, Waga glanced at Yoshimura.

They followed Waga across an outdoor hallway to a separate wing of the house and into an oval room. Its ceiling and walls were completely sound-proofed, like a broadcasting studio. At one side was a glassed-in area like a broadcasting booth. Half of the small studio was taken up by sound mixing equipment.

'This is quite a set up. Waga-*san*, we'd like to take a careful look at your equipment now,' said one of the officers. 'I am afraid it is necessary to ask you to accompany me to headquarters for further questioning about possible violations of Article four, Section one of the Wireless Telegraphy Act, which requires those intending to establish a broadcasting station to be licensed by the Ministry of Posts and Telecommunications.'

Sekigawa Shigeo was also subjected to a long session of detailed questioning by Imanishi and other detectives at his home.

A meeting of the Homicide Division was called. The chief asked Imanishi to summarize. Imanishi stood up to address the team.

'This case has taught us many lessons. The suspect was questioned today with respect to violations of the Wireless Telegraphy Act. We have allowed him to return home this evening, but I remain convinced he is guilty.

'Starting with motive, I cannot help feeling some sympathy for the suspect. Here is a man named Motoura Hideo. His father, Motoura Chiyokichi, contracted leprosy and was divorced by his wife. At this time, he took charge of his only child, Hideo.

'Motoura Chiyokichi led a life of wandering after he became ill, probably trying to find a cure for his disease. In nineteen thirty-eight, Motoura, along with his son, Hideo, who was seven years old at the time, arrived in the vicinity of Kamedake, Nita Town, Shimane Prefecture. At that time there was a kindly policeman named Miki Ken'ichi stationed at the Kamedake branch office. Seeing that Motoura was in the terminal stages of his disease, Officer Miki, following the law, arranged for Motoura to enter Jikoen, a sanatorium for leprosy patients. At this time, and according to the regulations, the son, Hideo, was separated from his father, and I assume that Officer Miki arranged for his care at the child-care facility he himself had founded.

'I would like to comment on Officer Miki's character. He was a very upright policeman. Even now, his good deeds are still talked about.'

Imanishi drank some tea.

'When I went to the location, I heard at great length many anecdotes about his good deeds. I imagine that Officer Miki intended to care for the young boy Hideo after he made arrangements for his disease-ridden father. Perhaps he would even have eventually adopted him, despite his background. Miki was an exceptionally saintly man.

'However, having become accustomed to a wandering way of life, Hideo ran away from Kamedake, despite Officer Miki's kindnesses, and went off on his own. This is the start of the tragic case that we are investigating.'

Pausing at this point, Imanishi looked around him. All of the men were waiting for his next words with bated breath.

'The whereabouts of Motoura Hideo since that time have

remained unknown,' Imanishi continued. 'It is thought that he went to the Osaka area. I will go into that later. Officer Miki was promoted to assistant inspector and voluntarily resigned in December nineteen thirty-eight. His conduct is something all police officers would do well to emulate.

'Thereafter, Miki-*san* opened up a general store in Emi-machi in Okayama Prefecture. He adopted his shop boy Shokichi, who married, and lived happily with them during his later years. Here, too, Miki was reputed to be as kind as Buddha.

'This past spring, Miki decided to take a trip to Ise Shrine, which he had long wanted to visit. He left Emi-machi on April fourth, and started a leisurely trip, going to Okayama City on the tenth, to Kotohira-cho on the twelfth, and to Kyoto on the eighteenth. We know his itinerary from the postcards he sent to his family from inns at these locations.

'Miki spent the night of May ninth at Futami Inn in Ise City. He happened to go to a nearby movie theater to see some movies. At that theater he saw something. He left the theater that night, but returned the next day to the same theater to confirm what he had seen. What had he seen?

'It was not a movie. It was a commemorative photograph displayed inside the theater. That photograph was of the family of a certain current cabinet minister whom the theater owner respects highly. The group in the photo happened to include a young man who was often at the minister's home. Reading the description attached to the photograph, Miki discovered that this young man was Waga Eiryo, a prominent young composer.

'This young man's face reminded Miki of Motoura Hideo, the son of the man with leprosy, whom he had cared for. Hideo was seven years old at the time, and Miki's recollection must have been hazy, but when he examined the enlarged photograph for a second time, Miki became convinced that this was the missing Hideo. Miki was overcome. He changed his plans for returning home and came to Tokyo.

'I think that Miki may have not quite believed it until he saw the person in the photograph with his own eyes, but there was no mistake. I do not know how their meeting was arranged. We have nothing to go on. It is certain, though, that the two of them did meet. They went to the Torys bar near Kamata Station on May eleventh after eleven P.M . . .

'Motoura Hideo, now Waga Eiryo, had achieved much and was on the brink of attaining even more. Just at that moment, there appeared this figure from the past. Of course, Miki had no ulterior motive. He had come to Tokyo to see the boy whom he had taken under his wing, for whom he felt responsible, the boy whom he'd lost. For Hideo, however, this was a moment of great panic. If he was discovered to have had a father who had suffered from an odious disease and to have falsified his personal history, his engagement would be broken off. No family – especially one like the Tadokoros – would permit a wedding between their daughter and the son of a leper. The alarm and anguish that he must have felt are no doubt in-expressible in words.

'I said that Hideo forged his personal history. When I looked into Waga Eiryo's personal history, it stated that he was born the oldest son of Waga Eizo and Kimiko, registered domicile, Number one hundred and twenty, two Ebisu-cho, Naniwa Ward, Osaka City. The deaths of Waga Eizo and Kimiko are recorded as March fourteenth, nineteen forty-five. This was the day of an extensive air raid that destroyed the entire area of Ebisu-cho, Naniwa Ward. The ward office where the original registers of domiciles were stored, as well as the Bureau of Justice, were reduced to ashes along with all official documents. In such cases, the law allows for the preparation of a family register upon the submission of a request by the person himself. This is what

Hideo did. In other words, there was no Waga Eiryo. The family register that was submitted in nineteen forty-nine was entirely the creation of Motoura Hideo. That an eighteen-year-old boy was able to do this shows that he was quite precocious and ingenious. When one thinks that his motivation was to extricate himself from his disease-ridden father's family register in order to pave the way for his own future, this boy deserves sympathy.'

The group was solemnly silent as they listened to Imanishi's words.

'What we know about Hideo's later life is that he went to a Kyoto Prefectural High School. He left during his second year. After this, he came to Tokyo. His natural talent for music was recognized by Professor Karasumaru of the Arts University, leading to the achievement of the position he has today. He must be considered a very unusual success. From his origins as a mere waif, he has become the new hope of our country's composing circles. He is a unique figure even among the so-called Nouveau group. Yet it seems clear that to protect his personal standing and to assure his own future, he decided to kill Miki.'

Imanishi continued his briefing.

'I think it more than likely that Waga already intended to kill Miki when he suggested that they go to the bar near Kamata Station. That was why he purposely dressed in casual, inconspicuous clothes. It was at this meeting that Miki was heard speaking with an accent. During his long years of service as a policeman in Nita County, Shimane Prefecture, he had picked up the local accent. This is what the witnesses mistook for a Tohoku accent from northeastern Japan. The investigation was led astray for a time because of this confusion, but we were finally able to discover the truth.

'Waga found out from the newspapers that our investigation was centering on the Tohoku dialect and the name "Kameda."

'It'll be soon now,' Imanishi said to Yoshimura as they waited outside.

Yoshimura stood shivering slightly, his hands in his pockets and his eyes watching the passageway.

'It's been a long investigation.' Imanishi let out a sigh. 'Hey,' he continued, 'you show him the arrest warrant. Grab his arm forcefully.'

'Imanishi-*san* . . .' Yoshimura protested.

'Don't mind me. From now on, it's the era of you young people.'

The passengers came walking down the passageway in a line. First came a large American couple. People were going through exit procedures: baggage check, passport control, and currency exchange. Those who were finished entered the waiting room.

The lounge was not large. The first passengers entered and sat down.

Imanishi pointed with his chin at a young Japanese man standing in the middle of the line.

A tense Yoshimura approached Waga. 'Waga-*san*.'

Turning to the man who had spoken to him, Waga gave a start when he saw his face. It was the detective in the raincoat who had been among those at his house the previous day.

'Excuse me.' Yoshimura called Waga aside. 'I'm sorry to disturb you. Please pardon me.' He led Waga over to where Imanishi stood.

Taking an envelope from his pocket, Yoshimura pulled out the document inside and handed it to the composer. With trembling hands, Waga took the piece of paper and ran his eyes over its contents. It was a warrant for his arrest on suspicion of murder. The blood drained from Waga's face. His eyes stared vacantly off into space.

'We won't handcuff you. There's a police car waiting out

front. You are to come with us.' Yoshimura put his arm around Waga as though he were a close friend.

Imanishi stepped to Waga's other side. He did not say a word. His expression did not change, but his eyes watered slightly.

The other passengers watched with puzzled looks as the three men retraced their steps along the passageway.

On the observation deck, those who had come to send Waga off stood looking down at the large airliner. Lights illuminated the walkway with the intensity of high noon.

The first passenger left the building. The well-wishers all turned toward that person. It was a tall American military officer. Next followed the large American couple, then a short Japanese, a foreign woman with a child, a young Japanese woman in a kimono with a young man, and another foreigner.

Waga was nowhere in sight. One of the first passengers reached the top of the steps and turned around to wave at his friends. The boarding continued. The last person left the building, a fat, elderly foreigner. Sachiko's face clouded with puzzlement.

Everyone looked bewildered. The Tadokoro family's expressions became anxious.

At this moment, an announcement was broadcast.

'This announcement is for those seeing off Waga Eiryo who was scheduled to depart on the ten P.M. Pan American flight to San Francisco. Waga-*san* has been detained by urgent business and will not be boarding this flight. Waga-*san* will not be boarding this flight . . .'

The voice was modulated, the cadence of the words was slow. It sounded as lovely as music.

several bouquets under his arm. Beside him stood his fiancée, Tadokoro Sachiko, in a cobalt blue suit. She smiled more than anyone else.

It almost seemed as though they were about to leave on their honeymoon. Tadokoro Shigeyoshi stood next to them, his ruddy face all smiles. Because he was a cabinet minister and a leading politician, other politicians with no connection to the music world were also in attendance. Members of the Nouveau group stood directly in front of Waga. Takebe, Katazawa, and Yodogawa were joined by some others. For some reason, Sekigawa had not come.

They were saying that he must have had some unexpected business to attend to.

Surrounded by many people, Waga gave a speech. His expression was bright. The large flower in his lapel seemed to symbolize his happiness.

The boarding announcement began. 'The ten o'clock flight for San Francisco via Honolulu is ready for boarding. Passengers on this flight, please proceed to the departure area.'

A cheer went up. A multitude of arms were raised in waves. Those who were seeing off others stared at the crowd around Waga.

The enormous foreign airliner was already positioned on the apron. The crowd flowed from the lobby to the observation deck. They prepared to wave to Waga as he entered the airliner. The boarding ramp was moved slowly up to the body of the plane.

Waga walked down the hallway reserved for passengers only. On either side of the corridor were sections for customs, visa inspection, currency exchange, and other procedures. Beyond this area was a passenger departure lounge. Here the passengers waited until the stewardess made the boarding announcement.

'One of Waga's friends is the critic Sekigawa Shigeo. When Sekigawa found out that his lover, a bar hostess named Miura Emiko, was pregnant but refused to have an abortion, he asked Waga's help in dealing with the situation. From here on, we have Sekigawa's testimony. He asked for Waga's help because he had heard Waga say that it was possible to induce abnormal physical conditions through exposure to electronic music. Emiko was brought to Waga's studio. She ended up like Miyata. I think that, in this case, there was no intent to kill on Waga's part. He used this method hoping only to cause an abortion. Emiko fell because of a dizzy spell as she left the studio. When she fainted, she fell off the raised outdoor hallway onto the hard concrete underneath.

'It was not only Waga, but also Sekigawa, who was shocked at Emiko's death. This had to be kept a secret. Sekigawa was placed in Waga's power. And suddenly, this envious friend and formerly severe critic began to praise Waga's work.

'This is a brief summary of the evidence gathered so far. The suspect is scheduled to leave Japan from Haneda Airport tomorrow night. I will answer your questions now. Depending on your conclusions, I would like to request a warrant for Waga Eiryo's arrest.'

There was still almost an hour until the departure of the 10 P.M. Pan American flight to San Francisco. The international lobby at Haneda Airport was always filled with cheerful people seeing others off. Tonight, long-haired youths and young girls dressed in colorful clothes stood out among the others. It was an elegant crowd of well-wishers. These people were seeing off the prominent young composer Waga Eiryo.

The clock pointed to 9:20. Those who had been chatting in the lobby gathered around Waga. This evening, Waga was wearing a new outfit. He had a large rose in his lapel and carried

Realizing that we would eventually investigate Kameda in the Tohoku region, he sent the actor Miyata Kunio there after instructing him to behave suspiciously. Miyata went and did as he was asked without knowing why. This is my conjecture, but I think that Naruse Rieko, a clerk in the Avant-Garde Theater whom Miyata was drawn to, asked him to take on this task.

'Next, Waga invited some of the Nouveau group members to observe a rocket research center in the town of Iwaki. In fact, Waga had urged his friends to go along with him. I think that he went to find out what the effect of Miyata's actions had been.

'Rieko was Waga's secret lover. After his crime, she delivered to him a raincoat that Miyata was using as a costume in a play. She also disposed of Waga's bloodstained shirt.

'In mid-June, Waga was hurt in a traffic accident near Sugamo Station. Even his friends wondered why he was riding in a taxi when he usually drove his own car and what he was doing in that section of Tokyo. My supposition is that this accident occurred on his way home from visiting his lover Naruse Rieko in Taki-gawa. That happened to be the day that Rieko moved there.

'However, after this, she despaired of her lover who was guilty of such a terrible crime, and who had made her an accessory to it. She committed suicide. After Rieko's death, Miyata began to suspect what his role had been and he confronted Waga.

'Miyata was supposed to meet me in Ginza the evening he died. He went to Waga's house after he left the theater. I assume that he was shut up in that oval shaped studio and subjected to weird electronic music, which caused psychological confusion. Then, when he started to feel sick, he was given intermittent barrages of ultrasonic waves. I think that Waga knew that Miyata had a weak heart. In order to seal Miyata's lips, Waga killed him by utilizing electronic music and ultrasonic waves to cause a heart attack. I would like to stress that this is a method of murder that has not existed before.